ALSO BY MICHAEL LAVIGNE

Not Me

The Wanting

The Wanting

Michael Lavigne

Schocken Books · NEW YORK

Copyright © 2013 by Michael Lavigne

All rights reserved. Published in the United States by Schocken Books, a division of Random House, Inc., New York, and in Canada by Random House of Canada Limited, Toronto.

Schocken Books and colophon are registered
trademarks of Random House, Inc.

Grateful acknowledgment is made to the following for permission to reprint previously published material:

The Permissions Company, Inc.: Excerpt from "Requiem" from *The Complete Poems of Anna Akhmatova,* translated by Judith Hemschemeyer, edited and introduced by Roberta Reeder. Copyright © 1989, 1992, 1997 by Judith Hemschemeyer. Reprinted with the permission of The Permissions Company, Inc., on behalf of Zephyr Press, www.zephyrpress.org.

University of California Press: Excerpt from "God Has Pity on Kindergarten Children" from *The Selected Poetry of Yehuda Amichai* by Yehuda Amichai, translated by Chana Bloch and Stephen Mitchell. Translation copyright © 1996 by Chana Bloch and Stephen Mitchell. Reprinted by permission of the University of California Press.

Library of Congress Cataloging-in-Publication Data
Lavigne, Michael.
The wanting / Michael Lavigne.
p. cm.
ISBN 978-0-8052-1255-6 (alk. paper)
1. Israelis—Fiction. 2. Fathers and daughters—Fiction.
3. Suicide bombings—Israel—Fiction. 4. Life change events—Fiction.
5. Extremists—Fiction. 6. Arab-Israeli conflict—1993—Fiction.
I. Title.
PS3612.A94425W36 2012   813'.6—dc23   2012020642

www.Schocken.com
Drawings by Annie Blackman
Jacket photograph © Mark Owen/Trevillion Images
Jacket design by Linda Huang

Printed in the United States of America
First Edition

2   4   6   8   9   7   5   3   1

For my Russian family, Nuka, Anyula, Sasha, Masha, Dasha, and Vitya Ortenberg and Olya, Seryogja, and Liza Ratchetnikov—for the love they showered upon me when I was a stranger in Moscow. And for my beloved Gayle, forever the source of home.

God has pity on kindergarten children.
He has less pity on school children.
And on grownups he has no pity at all.

—Yehudah Amichai

Like birds in flight
He sends them on their way
To what shore or branch
Or outstretched arm
I cannot say
Only that, once gone,
They may never return

—Pierre Chernoff, "The Children,"
from *The Winter Notebook,*
discovered at the former
Gulag Kolyma, 2003

The Third Temple movement is dedicated to the creation of a new Jewish Temple on the Temple Mount in Jerusalem. "Finding a red heifer is one precondition to building the Temple. Another, it is generally assumed, is removing the Dome of the Rock from the Temple Mount."

—From Gershom Gorenberg,
The End of Days

The Wanting

Chapter One

✡

I DON'T KNOW WHAT IT WAS. It might have been a head, or perhaps a hand or foot, it went by so fast, but following it, as if pulling a wire, came the explosion, and instantaneously the window I was sitting beside shattered. I can remember distinctly the feeling of glass slicing my skin—it was remarkably painless. At the same time, I fell sideways off my chair and landed at the foot of the drafting table, which I suppose is what saved me, for the entire window, the window I loved, the window that gave my studio an enchanting hint of antiquity in this otherwise modern neighborhood and suffused the entire room with light all the seasons of the year, crashed down in a thunder of tinker-bells, but not upon me. The drafting table was my umbrella. When it was finally quiet—and it was a quiet I had never heard before, a quiet that was a chasm between the breath before and the breath after   I looked up and saw a huge spur of glass hanging over the edge of the table, teetering just above my face. In that second, I thought of two things. I thought of God, and I thought of *Kristallnacht*. Then everything was noise—I couldn't tell what—screaming? sirens? cries for help?—and an incredible ringing in my ears that I thought might be angels crying, or laughing, or perhaps it was the ringing you hear when you are actually deaf.

Looking up at the overhang of glass, I almost thought I was standing behind a waterfall, and the thunder I was feeling was the water careening down the cliff face. But I understood this was an illusion. I was on the floor and a bomb had just gone off. And the object flying past my window? It probably had been the head of the bomber, winking at me. But I was also aware that Amoz and Tsipa were speaking to me. Their desks were situated far from the window, all the way on the other side of the office, where I had put them. Now they were bending over me, breaking the curtain of water. I could see they were moving their mouths, but I could not hear them, so I smiled up at them and said shalom. But they did not seem to hear me either, and they did not smile back. And that is all I remember of that moment.

I woke up in the ambulance. The paramedic was ultra-orthodox, like the guys who come around afterward and pick up body parts. His name tag read MOISHE. He had a greenish piece of salami stuck between his teeth and a beard that would be hanging down to his navel except that it was stuffed in a paper bonnet. He was wearing a Day-Glo orange security vest, a black scull cap, and eyeglasses that had slipped down onto the tip of his nose. But he seemed to know what he was doing.

"Keep calm," he said.

"Where am I?"

He looked out the back window. "On Yehudah Street."

Literalness, I had learned, was often a consequence of study-ing Talmud. "I mean, what happened?"

He patted my hand. "You were in a terrorist attack. I'm guess-ing it's Hamas, but it could be Fatah or Islamic Jihad. I don't think it was Hezbollah. Yes, most likely Hamas."

"How do you know?"

He shrugged. "You get a feeling for these things."

"Am I going to die?"

"It's possible." He felt my torso. "But highly unlikely. It looks like you have some superficial cuts."

I tried getting a glimpse out the window.

"Don't move! One move and you could push that piece of glass right into your brain. Then you definitely would die."

"There's glass sticking out of my head?"

"A very big piece. If it was a mirror, I could do my makeup in it. And frankly I wouldn't talk so much, there's also glass jutting out of your cheek. You don't want to cut your tongue off. But don't worry. I'm here to save you. That's my job."

"You're a religious man, right?"

"Of course."

"What does God say about all this?"

"About what?"

"About bombs going off in cafés and architectural offices and innocent people having their heads blown off and me with so much glass in me I could pass for a Tiffany lamp?"

"Not a café. It was the bus stop at the corner under your building. But you knew that from the trajectory of the head I sent as a warning."

"Yes, I saw it. I ducked."

"You didn't duck, you moved five centimeters to the left and raised your right arm ten centimeters from its position above your drafting table, which caused the flying glass to be deflected from your carotid artery and instead cut the nerve in your triceps brachii, which will cause you only minor annoyance for the rest of the year, instead of having killed you instantly."

"What about the glass in my forehead and my cheek?"

"Incidental. It will give you scars of which you will be justly proud. It will possibly end in several highly successful sexual encounters, if you play your cards right."

"So you saved my life?"

"I did."

"But why?"

"But why?" he asked back.

"Yes, but why?"

"Hold on, I have to check your fluids."

Being in the hands of someone so experienced seemed to calm me down, and I passed out again. When I next awoke I was still in the ambulance, but there was a beautiful Sephardic woman leaning over me, green eyes and coffee skin.

"Where's the other guy?" I said.

"What other guy?"

I attempted to search the ambulance, but my neck was in a brace and I couldn't move.

"It's just me," she said. "You'll have to settle for me."

"I don't understand."

"You were in a terrorist attack," she explained.

"How . . . ?"

"I don't know. A bus stop, I think."

"But how did you get here?"

She took my hand. "We're almost there."

"Where's that Moishe guy?"

"Stay calm."

"But he knew what he was doing!"

When I opened my eyes again, I was in the hospital, and Anyusha was sitting next to the bed reading a comic book. "Hi, Pa*poo*la!" she said. She called me Dad using the Russian diminutive because I hated when she did that.

"What are you doing here?" I said.

"Duh," she replied.

Anna, whom I call Anyusha—a name I made up one day, although sometimes I call her Anya, Anyula, Anechka, Anyuta, or Anka depending on my mood—was only thirteen at the time. She set her comic book on the chair and moved closer to me. She was staring at my face with what I thought was morbid curiosity.

"Is it bad?" I asked her.

"Well, it's gross, but it's not bad in medical terms. You have two black eyes and lots of little cuts all over, and then there is a big thing on your forehead where they gave you stitches and one long one going down this side of your face"—she traced a line on her cheek—"and your face is all bandaged except where the stitches are, well actually a lot of you is all bandaged—arms, legs—and your right ear is kind of messed up and also your right arm. That's going to hurt most, they said. You have some glass in your other arm that they still have to pull out, and your hands are cut up, but the doctor said you are really, really lucky, because nothing got in your eyes and no nerves in your face were severed."

"Where did you learn to talk like this?"

"I'm smart."

"Get me some water," I said.

"I have to get the doctor. They told me to tell them when you woke up." She skipped out of the room.

A moment later she came back, her brilliant white arms shining like silver candlesticks. "I told the nurse." She spit out her chewing gum and sat down in the chair. "They said you were hallucinating when you came in," she said matter-of-factly. "You were talking in Russian so they got a Russian doctor. What were you hallucinating?"

"I don't know."

"Something weird about your ambulance. I'll ask the doctor what you were saying."

"Why?"

"Because it's important," she said.

"I was in shock," I said. "I was just yammering."

"That's when the truth comes out," she explained.

"What's that comic book you're reading?" I asked her.

"It's not a comic book. It's manga. A graphic novel."

"Ah."

"*Fushigi Yûgi.*"

"What?"

"*Fushigi Yûgi.* It's about Yui and Miaka. They go to see the oracle Tai Yi-Jun, and Miaka is trapped inside a magic mirror while her reflection—who is very, very evil—takes her place in the real world, so Yui has to save her. It's very complicated, Papoola. You see, they find this book (they find it in the first chapter, because this is chapter eight), and they can be *in* the book, and whatever they read happens to them, although they can change things, too—anyway, they have to use the power of the Four Gods of Earth and Sky because Miaka is actually the Priestess of Suzaku, which is the God of Fire."

"You should be reading Pushkin," I said.

The doctor came in. He was Feldman, a Russian, and he spoke to me in Russian, even though he heard me speaking Hebrew with Anyusha.

"You're awake! That's good! Let's take a look!" He pried open my eyes, shining his little searchlight into the irises. "Looks good," he said. Then he evoked a serious tone. "You know why you're here?"

"I think so."

"Still fuzzy. That's normal. What's the date?"

"It's Wednesday, May 8, 1996."

"It's Thursday, actually."

"I lost a day?"

"You've been out for a while," he said, "but now you're back. And that's what matters."

"Listen," I said, "I want to thank the paramedic who brought me here. I think his name was Moishe."

"I'll check on it," said the doctor. "In the meantime your stitches look good. We're going to keep you bandaged up for a while, going to watch for infection."

"Pretty bad, huh?"

"You should see the other guy!" he quipped.

That's when I remembered the head, soaring past my window with a look, I now realized, of envy in its eyes.

Obviously, there was no Moishe. A mere hallucination. Why then could I never forget him? The event itself was lost in haze, a dream, but this imaginary medic was now part of my life. And as for the head? My nightmares.

I have always been a dreamy person. I think I may have inherited this disposition from my father. I am not saying that my mother is not also an imaginative person; it is just that I did not partake of her dreams. It was her fears I lived. Here is an example.

At a certain age, we lived in a strange apartment building on Veshnaya Street in the center of Moscow. It had been constructed in the thirties at the specific request of the NKVD boss, Yezhov, and it was still filled with party functionaries and a few midlevel KGB officers. How our family got there was an entirely different story—but suffice it to say every wall of every room was implanted with a secret microphone, every telephone in every foyer was connected to a single exchange for easy recording, and every day, twenty-four hours a day, stalwart teams of spooks with binoculars and photographic cameras watched the comings and goings of everyone in the building—or at least we thought so, because no one ever saw anything or heard so much as a peep or a chirp or a muffled cough or anything at all, for that matter, and their invisibility only gave us greater assurance of their immanence, their power, and the purpose they gave to our lives.

One day, my little sister Katya and I went out to play in the courtyard. Unlike the typical Moscow courtyard that could be entered from the street and from many doorways and passageways, our courtyard had but one entrance from the back of our building, cut off from the street. The yard itself was surrounded by three gateless, unpainted concrete walls, walls so high neither Katya nor I could see to the top. Even from our apartment, which was on the third floor, it was impossible to see over the wall. We were forbidden to set foot in that yard, but unknown to our parents, there was, in fact, a great treasure lurking there. It was a pile of debris we liked to call Chinese Mountain. We called it Chinese Mountain because of an old print that hung in our living room, an ink drawing of a strange mountain, a thin cloudlike waterfall cascading down its side, and a tiny monk leaning on his staff far below. Faded Chinese characters were stamped in one corner, and birds flew off another. Our backyard mountain looked just like that, especially when it rained or when the snow began to melt. For a long time we were content to watch it from our window, but eventually we could resist no longer. Why? The sheer joy of its mystery. From whence arose this magic pile of treasures? Lengths of wood, metal pipe, old shoes, rusty nails, empty tin cans—all precious materials—and all abandoned. After all, no one went back there, and even if they did, no one would ever throw anything away in that yard—because no one ever threw anything away, period. One afternoon, we secretly made our way down and, with huge effort, pushed open the old rusted door that led to the yard. It was the beginning of December, and the first snows had fallen—the best snows, really, clean and dry—and the ground was white milk against a clear blue sky, the snow shimmering like diamonds in the sunshine, just like the enchanted forests in our storybooks. Even the few, sadly bent birches in the far corner of the yard looked stately, and the mangy squirrel who had to forage even in winter took on the luster of the sly red fox.

Katya was five, I was six, and we stood before Chinese Mountain like two explorers on the moon, only she was wearing a knit cap of red wool that tied under her chin with a bow, and I a fur-lined hat, the earflaps hanging down like puppy dog tongues, bouncing whenever I moved.

"Look!" she said.

She stretched out her mittened finger. There was something decidedly shiny, decidedly pointy, sticking out of Chinese Mountain. Our eyes widened.

"What is it?" she asked.

"I think it's gold," I answered and grasped her hand.

I imagine that if you could look down from that cloudless sky, you would, even now, see Katya and me, two dots in a sea of snow, frozen for all eternity, the earflaps of my hat curling up like question marks, the red of her cap like a drop of blood on a white page, the hems of our coats flaring like the bottoms of Christmas trees, the breath coming out of us in ripe plumes, locking our gaze on that mountain of junk as if it were the lost ark of the Lord.

Katya dropped to a crouch and hugged her knees. "I'm freezing," she complained.

But I said to her, "I'm going to get it."

"Don't!"

"It's gold!" I told her.

I took a step forward and stopped. But what could I do? She was watching me carefully. All right! I said to myself. And just like that I marched up to Chinese Mountain. The very smell of it made me dizzy. It was all tangles and decoupage—everything pasted together in a jumble: devil's horns here, giant eyes there. Terrified, I reached out and grabbed the golden object. The feel of it in my hand, even in the cold of December, burned through my mitten. I turned around and faced Katya. Her eyes were as big as five-kopek coins. I held the treasure high above my head. In triumph I called, "It's a magic picture frame!"

From the vantage point of so many years, and remembering this as I did from a hospital bed in Jerusalem after almost being blown up by a decapitated Arab, it would seem a small and odd thing to remember. But when something explodes—a heavenly object, a star, a planet, or a person for that matter—all the parts of it that ever existed are blown out into space, where they persist forever.

What happened next was this. I ran from the Chinese Mountain as if I had just filched the pot of gold from under the dragon's nose; I cried out in victory, Hurrah! Hurrah!; waved my head of Goliath before Katya's awestruck gaze; and took my victory lap around the courtyard.

I could not wait to show it to my mother. It was so beautiful, and hardly broken at all. True, it had no glass, but the wood was turned quite delicately, and the gilding was largely intact. Plus, it was big enough to slip over my head and wear like a necklace.

We ran up the three flights of stairs and raced into the apartment. Mother was in the kitchen with Babushka peeling potatoes. Grandfather was asleep in the big chair, a copy of *Heroes of the Battle of Stalingrad* still in his hands. Father was not yet home, and neither was Uncle Maxim or Aunt Sopha; Julia and Danka were at the dining table doing their homework.

"Oh!" cried my grandmother with delight. "And what's this?"

But Mother took one look and said, "Where did you get it?"

"Roman got it off Chinese Mountain!" Katya blurted with pride.

"Oh, and what is Chinese Mountain?"

Katya fell silent.

"Well?" said my mother.

I had no choice but to tell her. The color drained from her face. "Show me."

So we all traipsed down the stairs and out into the yard. We stood some distance from the pile. Mother held the picture frame carefully in the palms of her hands, like an offering. It was already growing dark.

"Where exactly?" she asked.

I pointed to the right side.

"Where? How far up?"

I told her about a half a meter from the top: there, where the piece of concrete was jutting out.

"Was it on the concrete?" she asked.

I told her, no, it was just over there between the broken jar and the bit of metal tubing, where some emaciated weeds had tried to sprout before the winter cold had set in. But it was dark and I could barely see.

"You're certain?" she said.

My mountain seemed more like a hulking bear than a mountain, more like a shadow to itself, a darker black than the black all around us, more like a hole in space, and not at all like a treasure trove of precious objects.

"Well? Are you certain?"

"Yes," I said.

"Then take this," she handed me the frame, "and place it back exactly where it was when you found it. Exactly. Not a bit to the right or to the left or too much up or too much down. Put it back exactly where it was."

I ventured a few steps into the darkness. When I looked back, my mother and sister seemed to fade away, black holes in black space, having no mass, no substance. My hands were shaking violently, and my feet were two frozen bricks. The approaching night had crushed Chinese Mountain into a ball, and all its detail had merged into a strange, misshapen singularity. What could I do? I threw the frame onto the pile, not even looking where it landed.

Then I ran back to where my mother and sister were waiting. I took a breath only when I reached them.

"Very well," my mother said. "Now no one will ever know."

And with that she led us back to the house.

This was the fear my mother instilled in me, the fear I always sensed lurking in my heart. But Anyusha sat beside my bed with folded hands and the smile of an evangelist and explained to me how it was completely possible that a messenger of God had come down in the form of Moishe the medic in order to set me on a certain path. What this path was, she could not yet discern. And she said all this in the same tone she employed to describe the two Japanese cartoon girls who became characters in a book they were reading. I did not want her to fall into an existential confusion, and even more so I did not like her talking about messengers from God. I hate everything having to do with my religion except the food. When she said messenger of God, I thought only of the head flying by my window. The former brain in that head had received messages, too.

"It wasn't God," I finally said to her.

I got out of the hospital a few days later. My face would be scarred for the rest of my life, but as Moishe said, scars are good on a man. But the people at the bus stop were not so lucky. Nine died instantly, including the bomber, whose head I believe swept across my sky in the split second before my window shattered. One more died in the hospital. Forty-two others were wounded, quite a number of them Arabs. Some went blind; others lost limbs; several lost vital organs that had to be replaced. There were those who both went blind and also lost limbs; these I would say were the worst off. Worse even than the one who became a vegetable—count her among the dead. She was only sixteen and very beautiful, at least from the pictures they showed of her on television. Her name was Dasha. All of us lost our hearing for a while. Several will never get it back. I myself still have the ringing, and one of my eardrums did not heal quite right. They tell me I need an operation. Dasha, I knew, was really Darya. She was Soviet, like me, but she was probably too young to remember any of it. Still, I could see from her photo that she retained that Russian look—it had to do with her hair and the gold threads in the sweater she'd been wearing.

Before the hospital released me, they sent round a psychologist to see me. She introduced herself as Sepha Katsir, Ph.D. She said she was a grief and trauma counselor.

"I know you don't realize it now," Sepha Katsir said, "but you will have issues."

She gave me a pamphlet and told me she was available for counseling. "Unless you prefer someone in Russian," she added.

As soon as she left, the Minister of Blown-Up People came by. He was an underdeputy of some cabinet member who thought someone ought to say something reassuring to people who've been blown up by Arabs. He was a small man, in his late seventies, I guessed, still with the look of the old pioneers, even though he was in fact too young to have been one. But there it was: the open, flared collar, the suit jacket that looked like a potato sack, worn-out leather sandals over navy blue socks, his skin tan, chin smooth-shaven, hair—what there was of it—wild around the edges, sausagelike fingers on hands that once farmed and perhaps still gardened and whose owner spoke Hebrew with a touch of Polish. He had the whole shtick going for him, avuncular yet somehow also cold-blooded.

He stood at the foot of the bed with his hands behind his back, rocking on his heels, and assured me that, one, retribution would be enacted; two, I was a hero of the Jewish People; and, three, all my medical bills including rehabilitation, counseling by Ms. Katsir or the Russian speaker of my choice, and any necessary prosthetics would be taken care of courtesy of that same Jewish People for whom I had so recently become a hero. "And no copay!" he added. Finally he inched a little closer, patted the air above my hand, and asked me if there was anything else I needed. I could tell he was not much moved by my plight. I had only a torn-up face, busted eardrums, and a severed bicep. He was probably, and rightly, thinking of Dasha Cohen, the girl in the coma, only six-teen years old; or rather he was probably thinking he did not want to face her parents. Her picture had been in *Haaretz* and *Yedioth Ahronoth* that morning. And even though the doctors forbade me to read the papers, Anyusha brought in several anyway, because I asked her to, including *Vesti*, which I never read because I don't want my news in Russian, but, in this case, I did. This was on the second day of my internment, the first time I saw Dasha's face, but of course at the time I only vaguely understood her importance to me. In fact, I was more interested in finding out what had hap-pened to me. Natural enough. Where exactly did the bomb go off? When exactly? How strong was the explosion? Of what did the bomb consist? How much of my lovely street corner was in ruins?

In the meantime the Minister of Blown-Up People set a little Israeli flag in a tiny stand upon my night table, beside which he placed his card. And with that he said shalom and left the room.

Anyusha got up from her chair, made her way around my bed, and picked up the card.

"Cool," she declared.

"Why?"

"I don't know. I just think it's nice."

Suddenly I was frightened for her. Who was taking care of her?

"Where's Babushka?" I said.

"Don't worry about Babushka. I'm staying with Shana."

"Shana?"

"Don't you remember her mom came with me this morning? She already told you I was staying there."

"So you're okay?"

"Of course, I'm okay. I'm always okay. Or don't you know that by now?"

"So you're okay?" I repeated, or at least I think I did, but maybe I fell back asleep, because when I opened my eyes again, she was gone.

. . .

It had been Anyusha who first mentioned the name Amir Hamid. He had not yet made it into the papers, but his face was already on Channel 1, "At least once every five minutes," Anyusha exclaimed.

"Then it will be in *Maariv* this evening, for sure," I said. "Bring me a copy."

"No problem, Papoola," she smiled.

The newspaper photos Anyusha smuggled in were not very helpful, and the doctors wouldn't let me watch TV. "For God's sake, just rest," they'd ordered. But I needed to see, not sleep. I needed to gauge exactly how close I'd come to dying, by what measure the thread of my life was frayed. I needed this in order to appreciate my woundedness, to feel the gravity of my suffering, to let the pleasant shudder of horror sweep over me, to be afraid. And so I craved to see with my own eyes the headless torsos, the severed limbs, the twisted metal, the broken glass, the blood-soaked benches shredded into splinters. Otherwise, I was just in the hospital with a few stitches on my forehead. I might as well have slipped in the tub or walked through the patio door on my way to the barbecue. So I studied the newspaper photos with great, even exquisite care. But all they were were shots of emergency workers lifting gurneys into ambulances.

"Have you been to see it?" I asked my daughter.

"I'm sure it's already cleaned up. The only thing different is probably the bus shelter is gone."

"Well," I said, "don't go over there. You understand?"

She shrugged and returned to her comic book. "By tomorrow the shelter will be back, too."

Over time, I gleaned the facts. Young Amir Hamid from a town somewhere near Bethlehem in the Judean Hills, the son of Abdul-Latif Hamid, a shopkeeper specializing in auto repair, and Najya Hamid, the mother of four—Amir had three sisters—was given a vest into which were sewn eight small tubes of C-4, a high explosive popular in American action movies, which were activated by pressing the unlock button of a Mercedes-Benz ignition key. The

key had been wired to a simple detonator fitted into a small pocket
in the suicide vest and was powered by two double-A batteries
that had previously lived in the remote control of Amir Hamid's
father's television set. This was the small detail that finally ripped
the veil of lassitude from my eyes.

Did Hamas suicide vests come with a label that read BATTER-
IES NOT INCLUDED? There must have been a story, more than what
I learned when Najya, the mother, appeared on Al Jazeera and
Palestine TV triumphantly holding up the remote control with its
empty battery compartment and crying, "These are the batteries
of martyrdom! Victory is Allah's, mighty and benevolent, and to
his servant, Muhammad, may a prayer of peace be upon him!"
No. They'd done a little test, his Hamas babysitter and Amir, and
the original batteries were duds. "I have some at home," Amir
must have told him, probably thinking, Why spend money on
new batteries that are only going to be used once? I imagined the
frustration when Amir opened the back of his radio and found it
used C batteries. The camera, Walkman, and nose-hair clipper—
they all took triple-As. Finally, in desperation he popped open his
dad's beloved remote control. He must have known how pissed off
Abdul-Latif would be when he came home and tried to turn on
Who Wants to Win a Million? on Syria TV. But what could he do?
Mr. Hamas was waiting at the safe house with a vest full of C-4
and a video camera, so he muttered a prayer of regret, stuffed his
father's Copper Tops into his pocket, and placed the now-lifeless
remote on his father's pillow with a little note—"Sorry, but your
batteries are needed to liberate Palestine. Love, Amir." Maybe he
thought he should have left a few shekels for new ones but decided
he needed what little he had in his pockets for carfare. Perhaps then
he took one last look around his father's house, the house of his
childhood, his youth, his young adulthood now come to an end,
took in with a sigh the photos on the walls—the family portrait
taken when little Salah was only two, or the one of himself on his
twelfth birthday, or his parents' wedding photo, or his three sisters
in their school uniforms—perhaps he hesitated one moment more
to inhale the scent of tobacco, the musty carpet, last night's egg-

plant fatteh, and the peculiar residue of motor oil that permeated any room his father long inhabited; I can only hope his mother was then taking her midmorning nap, so he could, at last, having refocused his mind on the Koran and the blessings of Allah, quietly slip through the door and run back to the moldy basement where Mr. Hamas was waiting impatiently, perhaps worrying that Amir had changed his mind.

Hamas must have been using some crappy batteries from India, I thought.

But crappy batteries or not, Najya Hamid was a proud mom. Even some weeks later, after the IDF bulldozed her house, and she, Abdul-Latif, and the girls had to move in with Abdul-Latif's brother a few blocks away on Armenia Street, she said she wished Amir would come back to life so that he could blow himself up all over again. This was in a little film called *Mothers of Martyrs* that was broadcast repeatedly on PBC.

I was struck by this incident of the batteries. I wondered what Mr. Abdul-Latif Hamid felt when he learned that it was his own batteries that set off the explosion that blew his son to pieces and massacred eight other people, including Suliman bin-Sula and Mukhtar Raif, two Arab construction workers on the first leg of their long commute back to Ramalah. I remember thinking this weeks later, and in great agitation rising from my chair and walking across the living room to Anyusha who was doing homework at the kitchen table, and running my fingers through her thick, dark hair, which she had recently cut short and spiky to look like her Japanese comic book heroes, and thinking: What of mine will you steal to kill yourself with?

The bomb went off at exactly 4:23 p.m. on that Wednesday afternoon in 1996, in a bus shelter on the corner of the street my office is on. Even though the explosion was timed with the onset of rush hour, the authorities speculated that it ignited prematurely, perhaps even accidentally, as the C-4 would have caused significantly more damage had Amir actually stepped onto the bus before pressing the unlock button on the Mercedes key. As it was, the pressure wave shattered windows in a fifty-meter radius and sent debris flying in a more or less perfect circle at a velocity approaching the speed of sound. This short (less than one second) but quite lethal (nine dead, forty-two wounded) shock wave exceeded one thousand tons per square millimeter at the epicenter of the blast; by the time it reached my office, approximately twenty-four meters away, the pressure had decreased to a mere three hundred and twenty kilograms per square millimeter, enough to break glass and pop eardrums and throw a seventy-five-kilo man off his chair but not enough to rip apart my innards or soften the masonry in my three-hundred-year-old building significantly enough to bring the walls down around my head. However, the Egged bus that had, some seconds earlier, come to a halt in front of Amir was thrown three meters into the air and landed across the street, on its side, like a dead horse. The bus shelter was vaporized. There remained only a few stems of twisted aluminum poking up from the ground. On one of these, a life-size poster of Rita on the cover of her new album doggedly hung on, flapping in the wind, her face dripping with blood.

This particular detail I know because it was described to me by several bystanders, mostly people who were in the coffee shop across the square, a coffee shop I myself frequented most days of the week. Everyone knows me there, and everyone found it necessary to tell me the same story. I wondered if they had all seen it or if they had merely heard it from one another. It didn't really matter. I asked my friend Lonya—who now calls himself Ari—who happened to be coming to see me that day and had just turned the corner onto my street when the bomb exploded. He could not remember the poster.

"I just hit the ground," he said. "When I looked up there was blood everywhere." Which is also what everyone says.

Lonya, too, had the ringing in his ears. "It sounds like fleas," he complained. "Like a million fucking fleas, all day, all night. Sometimes I want to blow my own head off."

All this I found sad, fascinating, disturbing, and meaningless.

But back to the hospital. They finally let me go, and I arrived home at about two o'clock on Saturday afternoon, Shabbat. Shana's mother, Daphne, picked me up. Shana was Anyusha's best friend. They all came up to the room, the girls carrying balloons in the shape of hearts and Daphne with a basket of food cradled in her arms. We ate a little lunch, and then the two girls ran around tossing all my things in a bag. They found this highly amusing. I pulled the curtains around the bed so I could change into the clothes Daphne had picked out for me, and I emerged feeling much more myself—a man with a pair of pants. Then I went into the bathroom to brush my teeth and foolishly took a moment to actually examine myself in the mirror. What I saw was something more like the invisible man, a creature of science fiction, its face entombed in bandages. The question was, What lay beneath these bandages?

Daphne and her daughter lived only a few doors down from me. Our town was situated just north of Tel Aviv—not Herzliya, not Ra'anana, but nice. The apartments in our small complex surrounded a garden, so it was almost like we all lived in one great big house, although, come to think of it, I had no idea who most of my neighbors were. I might recognize their faces when I passed them, might say good morning or good evening, but I didn't know their names, their stories. I knew Daphne mostly because of Anyusha, and her story was this in a nutshell: Daphne was divorced. Her husband had remained in the army and over time had changed, at least according to her. "He became hard," she once told me. She repeated the word "hard" with a distant, almost mystical, look, as if she could see the heart inside him calcifying before her eyes. "He spent a lot of time in Gaza," she explained.

Daphne was an artist, but she made her living doing computer graphics. At night, though, she toiled over her watercolors. To describe her, I would say: average height, average build, just an average girl. Her bland, ocher hair was neat and short. Her lips were the color of mouse, always in need of lipstick. But the main trouble was her eyes. A very deep, almost tarry brown, that always, and quite improbably given her circumstances, radiated hope.

"Here," she said, as we gathered my things and made our way down the hospital corridor, "hold on to me. You probably can't even see with all that stuff on your face."

She led me to the car, guided me into the seat on the passenger side. I was actually surprised that I needed the help. More shaky than I'd thought. She reached over and fastened my seat belt.

When we were on the road, I couldn't help myself. "Can we pass by?" I asked.

"There's nothing to see," she said.

"Still."

"There's nothing there."

"Nothing for you, perhaps."

"It will upset the girls."

"Don't worry. It's already cleaned up," I insisted.

"Then why go?"

A muffled, disconsolate voice came from the backseat. "He won't stop until you do what he wants. Just do it."

She had to change directions altogether and head toward the center of town. As an architect, I had thought location important. A beautiful building, one of the oldest in town, white stone, low, exotic doors, unquestionably Ottoman; but I gutted the inside of our suite, installed brazilwood floors, stainless credenzas, a glass conference table surrounded by six Herman Miller chairs. I had a small Snaidero kitchenette with brightly enameled three-legged stools, a sitting area with Barcelona chairs and a genuine Børge Morgensen coffee table. And, of course, the floor-to-ceiling window that later came crashing down on top of me and was the reason my face was wrapped in gauze and a searing pain was shooting down my right arm and up across my shoulder.

Anyusha was right. You would never have known a bomb had exploded on my corner. Only instead of our bus shelter, there was a new cardboard sign on a pole. And my glorious window was boarded over with huge sheets of plywood. I gasped, I think, because Daphne took my hand. Bits of stone and plaster had been blasted from the façade of my building, revealing layers that had never before seen sunlight. These sad old blocks of stone! I could see directly into their broken hearts.

Anyusha suddenly leaned forward and threw her arms around me.

"Don't be sad, Pop," she said. "You can fix it up. You're good at that."

"Now can we go home?" Daphne asked.

I think it was on the way back that Daphne's daughter, Shana, asked me why I was an architect.

"What do you mean, why?"

"I mean, how does someone become one? Was it like, a calling?"

"No one has a calling," I said. "Because there's no one to call you."

"Oh boy," said Anyusha. "Here we go."

"We all just do what we decide to do," I said. But I knew that was not completely true.

I was about thirteen and had already been obsessing about university for some time. To get in, I had to be in the right high school. But in the past year, I had been turned down by the special school for mathematics, even though I'd passed all the tests, and also the special school for French, even though I was quite fluent, and also by the polytechnical preparatory school, even though my paper on electromagnetism won a prize and was published in *Junior Scientist*. I should not have been surprised. Even the most brilliant Jewish math students—far more formidable than I—often ended up studying nothing more than mechanical engineering, and the most promising Jewish science students became mere lab technicians. But something in me refused to accept this simple truth. Every day I would fill out another application or write a letter of protest to some ministry. My father encouraged me: "Keep trying! Keep working! Let them know you exist!"

"Why are you letting him draw so much attention to himself?" my mother complained.

As for my grandfather, he scratched his head. "What's all the *tummle*? Use our connections."

"Papa, everyone you know is dead," said my mother.

"Well, Lyopa has connections."

"Lyopa does not have connections. Lyopa cannot get a respectable job for himself. How is he going to get something for Roma?"

Lyopa was my father. "I have a respectable job," he said.

"Phhhh," my mother replied, and went back to her chopped onions. My father at that time adjusted hearing aids.

"I have a respectable job," he repeated. "And you," he said to me, "don't give up." He raised his voice and spoke directly to the walls, "A good Soviet boy always is an example to his peers!" Then he winked at me. "Come on. Let's go for a walk."

Outside it was a beautiful spring evening. Weather like this always meant school would soon be over, but I couldn't enjoy it. All I could think about was how little time was left to get accepted somewhere where I could further my academic ambitions.

"I'm the best kid in my class," I told my father.

"I know that, Romka."

"I want to be a great scientist. I want to study physics. Particle physics. Atomic physics."

"To make another H-bomb?"

"Well, yes," I admitted.

We walked along our little block until we came upon a small park hidden behind an old church that was still in use, the portico half falling down, held aloft by braces of raw lumber hastily hammered together. From behind its crooked doors, dark waves of incense issued a rich, tender note of strangeness. A few old ladies, their colorful scarves topping their heads like faded flowers, made their way up the uncertain stairs, and soon their voices could be heard sifting through the evening breeze, beautiful in their dissonance. A little farther along, there stood a few dilapidated benches and, beyond that, a little shack and, even farther along, quite unexpectedly, a little rivulet running through a maze of broken twigs and dead leaves. From whence it sprang no one could say—the Neglinnaya had been buried two centuries ago, but perhaps it had found a tiny outlet here, a few blocks from my house, or perhaps it was just spring runoff or, more likely, overflow from some pipe that had rusted out decades ago. But the water had a fresh, wild smell and the dancing sound of a mountain stream, and it glistened as it rolled over the pebbles, turning them into sparkling amethysts in the low, golden sun.

"A bomb is not the best use of your brain," my father said.

"There are lots of things physicists do. I could discover time travel."

"That would be good," he agreed.

"I could just work on subatomic particles. I could look back in time to the beginning of the universe."

"That also would be good." He bent down and picked up a stick, poked at the water, and then brought it up to my nose. "See? *Carabini calosoma.*"

A small beetle was desperately clutching the end of the stick. "See how it looks black and dull, but when you turn it just so . . . see? All the colors of the rainbow!"

"Don't you miss the university?" I asked him.

"Why should I? I have my laboratory all around me. So much going on right here in this little bit of grass. Right here in Moscow! Can you imagine?"

He set Mr. Carabini down upon the wet earth and with a little push of his forefinger nudged it on its way. "Yes, this is the best laboratory! No one to report to except myself. No one to look over my shoulder. Just the joy of doing."

"But for whom?" I said. "Who will see it? Who will learn from it?"

My father mussed my hair. "You," he said.

"What good will that do?"

"Well," he sighed. "I'll publish all my findings sooner or later. Don't worry about it."

But I wasn't worried. I was ashamed.

"Come," he said, "let's walk some more."

We emerged from the little park by way of an alley that led through a courtyard and finally found ourselves on a great boulevard. My father's hidden paradise had been only minutes from Prospekt Kalinina. There the traffic sped by in great, noisy waves, and the bright new buildings loomed over us: apartment blocks, offices, ministries, shops.

"What do you think of this?" he said.

"I don't know," I said. "It's modern, I guess."

"Not these awful monstrosities," he said. "Look more carefully."

We stood there, two logs impeding the flow of pedestrians. "Come on, Papa, let's get going."

"No, no, just look."

"But at what?"

"You're missing it!" he cried. "Come on!" He marched me forward a few paces until I was face-to-face with one of the hundreds of lampposts that stood guard over the magnificent boulevard. "Look up! Look straight up!"

So I looked up. But what was there to see?

"There," he pointed, "where the lamps curve toward the street."

And then I saw it. At the top of the pole, where one arm went to the right and the other to the left, there, in the hollow formed at their junction, was a bird's nest.

"I've been observing it for quite some time. It's a spotted nutcracker. Can you believe that? What is it doing on this busy street? Go out to the woods, you silly birds! It's already got chicks. For a long time the mother bird would sit and the father would forage. Now they both go hunting for their babies. What do you think of that? Right here on Prospekt Kalinina. Clever little things!"

He was already going on about how no matter how hard they

make it—always *they*—life finds a niche, you can survive, you can thrive, even here on Kalinina. Even where Soviet reality overwhelms the spirit, nature prevails.

But I really wasn't listening. I was up there in the elbow of the lamppost. It wasn't the force of nature that enthralled me. It was the nest. I was trying to figure out how so minuscule a birdbrain could have constructed such a sturdy little home. My heart stopped when I noticed the clever way it was attached to the aluminum pole and how it was woven tighter than any scarf my grandmother could knit and how, so exposed, the babies were nevertheless hidden and warm. It was the most miraculous thing I had ever seen. And in that moment, my love of architecture was born.

I looked in the rearview mirror. Shana was asleep. Anyusha was reading her manga.

"Don't worry," said Daphne. "They've heard it all before. They just wanted to get your mind off your troubles."

But as we pulled up to our complex, I found myself exploding, "Why can't they leave us in peace?"

"It's a war," she said simply.

"War? What kind of war? Are we blowing up their buses? They didn't want us back in Russia; they don't want us here. Why don't we just walk ourselves right back into the gas chambers and make everybody happy?"

"Roman," she said softly, "the children."

"Yes," I said, "yes, sorry." And I stepped out of the car, walked up the pretty pathway to my house, and waited for Anyusha to come along with the key.

Chapter Two

✡

WHEN I AWOKE THE NEXT MORNING, having fallen asleep almost immediately upon arriving home, I did not at first notice Daphne curled up on the floor. But there she was, her body snailed into the one vacant corner without even a blanket to cover her. She must have spent the night watching over me. Her stomach silently rose and fell with the tide of her breathing, and I realized it was rather like Anyusha's when she used to fall asleep on my lap. I slipped the quilt off my bed, gently laid it over her. There was an open book lying beside her; it was *Fathers and Sons* translated into Hebrew. I'd used it to practice my reading. In fact, I had a whole collection of Russian literature in Hebrew. Perhaps because of that my Hebrew has a slightly literary feel, or so my sabra friends tell me—but I doubt it is a compliment.

In the living room, the girls were already watching TV. They had large bowls of American cereal in their laps and were sitting Bedouin style on the carpet, mesmerized by *Beavis and Butt-Head*.

"Do you think I could watch the news?" I said.

"You're not allowed to," Anyusha quickly replied, her mouth full of Cocoa Puffs. "Ari called. He's coming over. And Babushka, too."

"What did she say?"

"She was all crazy that we didn't tell her you were coming home. Didn't I tell you we should call her?"

"*Chyort!*" I cried.

"I told her she can't be mad at you because you are a victim of a terrorist attack."

I sighed and padded into the kitchen. Arrayed before me were the gardens of Babylon—flowers of every denomination—vases of carnation, lily, and daisy, baskets of mixed colors, hyacinth erupting from glazed pots. Wherever I looked, there they were, sprouting on the kitchen counter, poking up between the blender and cappuccino maker, blanketing the kitchen table, the terrazzo windowsills, even on top of the microwave—flowers. For now I was a celebrity among my family and friends. People would want to know, was it in slow motion like in the movies? Did it sound like a mortar or was it more like a wave crashing over you? Did you go flying into the air or did you just collapse in a heap? The truth is, most Israelis have never actually witnessed a suicide bombing. As often as they occur, still they are rare enough, far apart enough, or perhaps close together enough, that you have to be quite unlucky to experience one firsthand. You don't even usually hear them, because they're not all that loud. A few blocks away, it's just a car backfiring. A few more, a door closing. A few more, perhaps a slight change in the rustle of the leaves, as if a bird had landed on a high branch and busied itself preening.

"For God's sake," I said surveying all the geraniums, "it's just a scratch!"

"There's vodka, too. Ari sent that," Anyusha added.

Ari was part of my old life, and so he is a part of this one, even though the rules have changed and we no longer have the same interests or desires. In Moscow he was a fixer. In Tel Aviv, where he lives, he is also a fixer, but of air conditioners and refrigerators. We called him Lonya in those days, and I still do, though it annoys him. He thinks he's Sharansky who has to change his name. In the old days, he was passionate about girls, football, and ice hockey and, when he got a little older, vodka, and that unfortunately describes him to this day. In one of his most famous escapades, Lonya rented a shack in the countryside—far away, in the Urals—and, with the help of a few of our friends who knew a thing or two about chemistry, decided to set up a still deep in the woods so that, in his own words, "We won't have to drink that utter shit they call vodka in this country! Better we should drink American vodka than that shit. They should piss on that shit! They should shit on that shit!" One cannot make up such language. One can only record it in one's memory as one does any great poetry. "No!" he declared, we would make a vodka so sublime it would taste "like cunt! A veritable elixir of pussy, pussy of the gods! You will drink it," he said, "and your dick will turn to platinum."

It took us a full week to build that still. Then it blew up and Lonya lost his left eye.

Whenever he tells it, he makes it sound very funny.

He was the first to show up that morning.

"I'm so pleased God was your ambulance driver!"

"I told you, Lonya, he wasn't the driver. He was the medic. And it wasn't God necessarily. It could have been an angel."

"Oh, well then. Not such a big deal after all."

Lonya was not quite the man he used to be. He reminded me of Ariel Sharon: in the old days all muscle, now all fat. He also wore short pants and a Ralph Lauren polo shirt. Add to this the glass eye and the cigarette always in his mouth, the eternal three-day-old stubble, and that is Lonya.

"Still, these things mean something," he insisted.

"It doesn't mean anything. It was a dream. Haven't you had a million dreams, and in your whole life has any of them come true?"

"They don't have to come true because they already are true."

"Let's talk about something else," I said. "I'm going to need help replacing my fucking window."

"Oh!" he cried.

"What?"

But I saw it, too. The Arab's head floating past my patio doors.

"How is that possible?" I said.

"What?" he said.

"That fellow's head."

"What head?"

And then I realized he hadn't seen the head at all. He'd cried "Oh!" because Daphne had entered the room.

"Aren't you going to introduce me?" he asked.

☪

At the last minute there was a face, a young girl looking out the window of the bus, and not even looking at me, just out the window, her eyes wide with the life that was so new to her. Perhaps she was thinking she had not done her homework, and the wide eyes were imagining the scene when she would be called upon to do her report, or maybe she was just watching the people pass by, I don't know. But her eyes were blue, like mine. I decided to press the button, but not on the bus. Just like that, things change. So the last thing I saw before I pushed the unlock on the key that Ra'id Mashriki had given me was the way this little girl blinked, so slowly, as if she could not bear to close those wide eyes to this beautiful world even for a fraction of a second.

I was not intending to kill anyone specifically, with the exception of course of myself, but I certainly had it in my mind to destroy as many of my enemies as I could. So in spite of the girl, I am proud of that. I am content.

But I am confused that I am not in Paradise with my dark-eyed maidens and rivers of wine, at peace with the pleasure of Allah and his angels. I am aware I have been following this man, Roman Guttman. I understand, though I don't know how, that he is an architect, famous for a certain style, which his admirers refer to as "Roman-esque." It is a style you will not see in the neighborhood in which my mother, Najya, is now secretly weeping uncontrollably and my father, Abdul-Latif, is sitting on the floor staring at his hands. The apartment Roman Guttman designed in Netanya with the swimming pool in the living room, or the house on Mount Carmel, which looks rather like a tarantula wearing a golden skull cap—these you will not find in Jabal or Hebron, in Qalqilia or my own Beit Ibrahim.

Shouldn't Roman Guttman be as dead as I am? Shouldn't he be suffering the torments of Hell? Apparently Allah had other plans, since He sent my head to warn him, why I cannot say. Who am I that Allah might confide in me? I would quote from the Holy Qur'an at this point, but that is the problem, that is the essence of the whole problem: I have never been able to memorize it. Not really any of it, save the seven tender verses, and not even those very well.

Perhaps I'm supposed to speak to him, but where are my vocal cords? It seems I am all thought and no sensation! Except for this feeling of mute giddiness, the kind one gets when dreaming of flying—weightless but always on the verge of falling, as if held aloft by an endless length of twine that at any moment could be cut and down you go.

It's not a bad feeling, really.

On a hillside above our town there was a ruin, some stones piled in a heap, white as lye, the bare outline of a foundation. Probably it was just an old Arab house, but perhaps it was a Roman villa, or a merchant's stables from the time of Saladin, or a Turkish outpost, or maybe it was the threshing floor of my great-great-uncle Kemal, or perhaps the French army stored sacks of their soft white flour there, or it was a remote British armory blown up by the Jews or ransacked by the Mufti; whatever it was then, it was peaceful now, the goats gracefully tiptoeing through the rubble, munching the bits of grass that shot up through the fissures in the stones, scenting the air green. I was munching something, too—cucumber, on the edge of a knife, and tomato, sliced into quarter moons, with salt and savlik—yes, that was me. I watched my feet hanging over the remains of the ancient wall, and alongside me I felt with all my senses, more than the jingling of goats' bells and the gentle bleating of the lambs—his laughter. I furrowed my brow. Was he laughing at me again?

"Oh, Amir," he said. "Look at that! A hawk. Coming right at us. No, stay put. It won't come that close."

"But it wants my cucumber!" I cried.

"It thinks you are a mouse. It wants you!"

I heard myself bleat just like the baby goats, "Go away, bird!"

"Hold up your cucumber!" he said. "Maybe he'll take that instead of you!"

Desperately I ducked down, holding the cucumber as high as I could, an offering to the wide-winged beast. But when I looked up, the hawk was gone, floating somewhere among the clouds.

Fadi laughed again but held me tight. "It's all right, little one," he said. "He's gone. And anyway, I was only joking. Come on, don't cry. I'll give you my mammoul." He took the mammoul from the basket and put it in front of my nose. I could smell the walnuts, the butter.

"I'm telling Ummi." I pouted.

"Don't be a baby. Take the mammoul, and we're even."

Who could resist mammoul? Even now, if someone were to offer it to me, I might feel regret for having given up life so easily; to smell that sticky scent again, to have the mammoul melt in my mouth, my tongue awash in honey and walnut paste.

Of course, Fadi had brought two mammoul and we both fell into a happy eating. Down below, our village was like a pop-up book against the open pages of hillsides and roads and, in the distance, the edge of Bethlehem and its teeming thousands. Between the two was the refugee camp—not a camp—this word confused me because there was no army and there were no tents—but, pressing upon one another, little huts and shacks and then big buildings, too, lots of them—it was more or less a city, wasn't it? I never went there to play. The boys were too rough, Umm always said. Everyone draws on the walls there, she said. Everywhere they were hanging illegal flags.

We finished our mammoul, Fadi wiped his mouth with the back of his hand, and then I very carefully did the same.

"See that?" he pointed. "That's your house."

"Which one?"

"That one."

"But which one?"

"Pretend you are that hawk, Amir. Pretend you are flying high above. Swoop down from the hills, and see—there is the minaret of the White Mosque, and there, the other one with the round roof, is the Jabir, see it?"

"I've never been in it."

"That doesn't matter. You're a hawk, remember? Now, fly from the White Mosque to the Mosque of Jabir, and you go one two three four five six seven eight, ah! And you see the little house with the brown roof, and you go over that roof, straight ahead—"

"Which way?"

"Away from where we were now, straight ahead. And you see one tall house—that is Mukhtar's house, yes, your friend Mukhtar—and so just beyond that one . . . you see that TV antenna? You see it? That is your house, Amir. That's where you live."

"Yes!" I exclaimed, even though I wasn't sure I actually saw it. It didn't matter. What I did see was a beautiful sky, a shining village, hillsides of goats and bright grasses, fields of soybean, orchards of pistachio and almond, olives and figs.

I looked over at Fadi. He was already standing up, brushing off his shorts.

Fadi. Like a brother but not a brother. Like a father but not a father. Fadi.

"Come on," he said. And he took my hand.

Roman Guttman walks in his gardens. Inside, the guests are arriving, wondering where he is. They hover in the kitchen, not knowing whether to eat something or not. Everything in this kitchen is icy steel, although at the moment it's covered with flowers, and that is beautiful. There are also three bedrooms in this house, one his, one his little girl's, and the third is empty. It is completely empty. It contains nothing. This room, this empty room, stops me, stops me colder than the stainless steel, and disturbs me more than the two bathrooms with their elaborate fixtures, more than the washer and dryer hidden behind folding doors, and more than the second bathroom with its marble tub, and more than the two TVs and the Nintendo with its maze of wires. I think of this empty room and my head goes spinning, literally, round and round, nobody to stop it, no gravity, no connection to anything but the disturbance going on inside it.

He loiters in his garden. He searches the sky once more, looking for me. Can he see me? For some reason, I have to be honest, I hope that he can't.

✡

The house was beginning to fill up. My mother had arrived, my old army buddies, some Russians, my employees. They all did the same thing when they opened the door. They gasped. My mother fanned herself with a magazine and wailed, "Bojha moi! Bojha moi! My God! My God!" But as soon as she realized Daphne had gone into the kitchen to cook something, she threw down the magazine. "My darling," she said to Daphne, "go. Sit. Let a mother do her work." She spoke in Russian, but I suppose the language of mothers requires no actual words, and Daphne slipped gracefully out of the way.

Lonya watched all this carefully. "Where did you find her?" he asked.

"She's a neighbor. Leave her alone."

"Not for me," he said. "For you!"

Lonya casually made his way over to Daphne, and I stepped out into the garden. What was it I had seen? It was not possible, of course. It was just a symptom. But I was absolutely certain it was there anyway, hovering just beyond my periphery. Whenever I turned, it was gone. Idiot, I told myself. What are you looking for?

· · ·

I tried to relax and breathe in the perfume of the garden. How different this was from the yard in Moscow, contained not by towering gray walls but by meandering garlands of morning glory and tea roses bursting from trellises Anyusha and I had built together. There was also a small square of velvet lawn and three happy banks of flowers: bulbs in spring; foxglove, delphinium, hydrangea, and scarlet in summer.

I checked the bird feeders. This was one of the first things Anyusha ordered me to do when I got home. "You might be half dead, Papoola, but that doesn't mean our little birds have to be. And after that," she chirped, "you can feed *me*."

It would be a while till I'd be able to cook for her; at least I could attend to the birds. But when I bent down to pick up the bag of seed, my head began to throb, my chest constricted, and great shining swords of electricity sparked at the corners of my eyes. The doves and swallows, the warblers, whitethroats, and finches that for so many years had come to my little garden for their evening meal would fly away hungry tonight, and my heart broke for them.

So I went in, saw my well-wishers, and after about half an hour, collapsed into my bed, even though it was only four in the afternoon.

Chapter Three

DEAR YOU,

> *Mysterious Gods of the Seven Winds*
> *Power of Seven Wonders and Seven Sins*
> *Seven times Seven times Seven again*
> *Open your Portal and Let Me In!*

MY FATHER IS A MESS, and that is why I am writing this incantation. I believe that if I write it correctly, my father's life will be more like the story I am writing and less like the life he is living. *My writing is magic. My writing is magic. My writing is magic.* I can write his story, and he can jump right into it. I can be in it, too. And Shana. And even Mom, if he wants. I know this kind of thing mostly happens only in manga and science fiction movies and graphic novels. But I am hoping this will work on my father. I ask forgiveness for stealing the idea from *Fushigi Yûgi,* but I don't know any other actual incantations. I am not stupid. I know that *Fushigi Yûgi* is just a made-up fantasy, and so it is not a real incantation. I have actually transformed it, though. Subtly, and you may not have noticed it. I have moved some words around and changed some, too. This way God will listen to me.

Pop doesn't know this, but I have been talking to a rabbi. He would kill me if he knew. He hates religious guys. He thinks they are to blame for everything. He told me once it was hard for him not to spit when he passed one of those "morons with side curls" (his exact words). That's how much he hates them. But my rabbi is not ultra ultra. He's just, I don't know, he talks to me. My friend Yohanan, he is from a religious home, not haredi, just kippah sruga, you know, regular. He goes to his own school, of course, but they live in our complex, and he hangs out with me and some of my friends. I like him. He's different from the other boys. Not that he can't be mean, but he thinks about things, he's more interested in what's inside, not just what's on the surface. Of course he does not read *Fushigi Yûgi,* no boys do, but he likes graphic novels, too, only he prefers things like *Vampire Hunter, Transmetropolitan,* and *Sin City,* all of which he has to hide from his parents. Recently he brought a copy of *Maus* home. His parents didn't know what to think about it, because it's about the concentration camps and anti-Semitism and things like that, but after a while they made him throw it away. He didn't, of course. He gave it to me. Actually, I keep all his graphic novels. My dad doesn't care about these things. He says I can read whatever I want. He believes in freedom. Anyway, I was talking to Yohanan about my problem, and he said I should talk to Rabbi Keren about it, so one day I did. He just sat me down and asked me what it was I was worried about. I told him. He said, Anna, the way you feel is exactly as you should feel. And then he said, Sometimes people imagine things. And sometimes what you see is really what you see.

We are not exactly studying Torah or anything like it, though he gives me quotations and stuff from Torah or the prophets or whatever. Then he has to tell me the story that it comes from and what the comments about it are, and finally I decided it's just easier to read it all for myself. So he gave me a Bible and some commentary, and I took it home. I mean, we study the Bible in my school but mostly for history, and everyone hates it. Pop came into my room once when I was reading it. What are you reading *that* for? he asked me. It's just crap. Throw it away.

I knew he wouldn't make me throw it away, but I decided not to read it at home anymore. It's the one book I keep at Yohanan's! Isn't that funny?

I began to write this journal for Pop not long ago, just yesterday actually. That's when I thought of it. I would do a *Fushigi*

Yûgi for Pop. At first I thought I would make him rich and famous, but then I thought probably not, because in a story you always have to take away what someone has, and they have to struggle to get it back, but when they get it back it's not what they thought it was. That is your basic story line. But I don't want Pop to struggle.

What I want is for him to SEE.

Also, since this is the first entry in my journal, I will confess it is not my idea to keep one. I got it from a book called *Finding the Good When Things Go Bad*. It's basically the stupidest book I ever read, but I liked the journal idea, so here you are. I didn't know what to call it until that last sentence, but as I wrote it, it just came to me. Here *you* are. Get it? I'm calling it "*YOU*." Which is all kind of circular, but so is algebra. And nobody seems to have a problem with *that*.

Chapter Four

✡

PERHAPS I DID NOT MENTION that I was on pretty heavy painkillers, Demerol, in fact, though at some point I believe I was taking OxyContin. I can't remember, which is the one happy outcome of opiates. But by now, my doctors were strict with me. They pulled me off the medication long before I wanted them to, and I ended up, basically, with a handful of aspirin. Probably that explains what happened.

I had bused into Tel Aviv to have my dressings changed at the clinic. I hadn't been out on my own in some time, and the idea of sharing some fresh air with the rest of humanity seemed especially pleasing, so I went for a walk. It was a busy time of day and the streets were crowded. I noticed immediately people were staring at me—it was the bandages, of course, and, I guess, the dragging lower lip and the purple neck. One could see in their faces the usual mixture of horror and pity. This was entirely normal, I told myself. I would have stared, too—anyone would.

At the crosswalk, the light changed. I took a step off the curb, and there right in front of me, stepping off the curb opposite, was a young Arab. Modern. Secular. Jeans. Striped polo. Running shoes. Shiny watch. He looked straight at me. He neither grimaced nor raised his eyebrows in sympathy, no acknowledgment at all; he just moved toward me, his gaze fixed. I found myself also staring at him, locking onto his eyes: dull eyes, lacking in all inquisitiveness. He was passing to my left, he in his flow of pedestrians, I in mine. So slowly did this unfold that I saw a bird flap its wings, one, two, three, as it passed just above us; I saw a woman pull at her ear, watched the skin stretch like taffy; in the middle of all this stood a policeman, and in his whistle I could clearly see the sounding ball bounce up and down, up and down, almost glacially, though I could not yet even hear the sound. Then the Arab blinked, and I smashed him in the face with my fist.

Suddenly there was a huge commotion. Someone grabbed me from behind, and some other fellow, I had no idea who, was on the ground in front of me, screaming, *Help, Help, Help!*

"Stop it!" someone shouted in my ear.

I looked over my shoulder. It was the cop.

The man on the ground was still screaming, "You maniac! You crazy person!"

"Calm down!" the policeman said to me.

"Me?"

I was confused, though, because the man on the ground was screaming in such excellent Hebrew.

Some hours later I was given the police report. According to Mordecai Kashani, a sabra of Iranian-Jewish descent, he had been crossing Ibn Gvirol Street thinking of what to get his son for his graduation from the third grade, which was happening in less than a week, so he was not paying attention to anyone, when out of the blue this "lunatic hit me on the chin and began to pummel me mercilessly and call me a stinking Arab, a goddamned murderer, a motherfucking Hezbollah rag-head baby killer, I'm going to shove a fucking pipe bomb up your ass, how would you like that, you Hamas piece-of-shit garbage?" Mr. Kashani went on to write, "This is word for word, exactly as I recall it. I never saw the man before. I never saw the man when I was crossing the street. In fact, I never noticed him until he hit me. But never will I forget him. Even when all those bandages come off, I will recognize him."

I laughed. "I never said any of that," I told the officer.

"No?"

"Of course not. I'm an educated person. As a matter of fact,

I belong to Peace Now. I would never say such things. Here. I'll show you my membership card."

"Why don't you tell me what happened?" he said.

My policeman was about fifty, with a full head of hair and tanned, well-furrowed skin. When he lit a cigarette I noticed he had the same thick, fat fingers as the Minister of Blown-Up People. His nails were dirty, too, probably also from gardening. Another ex-kibutznik. Could never quite tear themselves away from the soil. On the other hand he had a couple of tennis rackets tucked in the corner. He assumed a very casual pose with me, just two guys having a chat. It was being made clear to me that this was not an interrogation, which was why I knew that that was exactly what it was.

"I don't know," I said. "I was crossing the street and the next thing I knew this guy was . . . well, actually, I don't know. He did something. Came at me or something."

"But you hit him?"

"I think I did. But just once. I wasn't '*pummeling*' him, for God's sake. That's nuts. Why would I do that?"

"So you hit him the one time?"

"I think so."

"Do you think that was the right thing to do?"

"Of course not, no. I'm sorry I did it."

"Then why did you?"

"I—actually, I can't remember. He must have done something. Pushed me or something."

"That's it? He pushed you and you slugged him? Does that sound like something you would do? He must have done something worse."

"I suppose I must have thought he had a bomb."

"Any reason for that?"

"Don't be stupid," I said, suddenly tired of the game.

He stood up, came around, and placed his hand on my shoulder. "You've been through a lot."

"Not so much."

Immediately the face of Dasha Cohen, the girl in the coma, flashed before me.

"Guttman," he said, "you've had a trauma. You are a victim of terrorism. We all know that. We all appreciate your sacrifice."

"Except for Mr. Kashani," I said.

"Well," said the lieutenant, "perhaps he has his reasons." He placed two photos on the desk and slid them over to me. Two photos of the same guy, first from the front, then from the side. His face was a patchwork of black and blue, his left eye a swollen orange, his chin mottled with dried blood, his nose like a squashed soda can.

"Who is that?" I said.

The lieutenant held out several typed sheets. These were statements of witnesses, he told me. "Read a little," he suggested.

They described a gruesome scene. A madman in bloodstained bandages screaming obscenities and racial epithets and beating an innocent pedestrian. No provocation. No reason. Onlookers taken by surprise. Policeman and three others pull him off.

"He wants to press charges."

I looked up at the lieutenant. "I did this?"

He nodded.

"Maybe you should lock me up, then."

Instead he motioned to someone behind me. An older woman, a grandmother, really, in a simple floral dress. She looked vaguely familiar. But it wasn't possible. It could not have been Golda Meir. I thought she was dead—of course she was dead! But there she was. I knew I had been seeing things, heads, angels, but it was definitely Golda! And now she, Golda, beckoned to me, raising one formidable eyebrow. Even for such an old woman, she was overflowing with—what can I say?—erotic energy, the energy of the all-night dream that you'd rather not have had at all.

She led me to a small room down the corridor. I looked around. No one-way mirror, so I decided the interrogation was over. A long Formica table, a number of plastic chairs all orange and green, the lunchroom. Golda took a chair from the far side of the table and dragged it all the way around so she could sit down beside me. So I got up, moved my chair to the other side of the table, and sat down facing her. Above me I was certain a bloodstain was forming on the ceiling and emerging from it a pair of eyes and then, perhaps, the outline of a head—his head.

"Look," she said to me, "I'm here to help you."

"Why?"

"Perhaps you are having hallucinations," she began. "You've been looking at the ceiling and calling me Golda. Do you think I'm Golda Meir?"

"Of course not, " I said. "You're the shrink from the hospital."

"And you think I resemble Golda Meir?"

"I didn't say that."

"I don't think I resemble her."

"No," I said.

"Only insofar as all old Jewish women resemble her."

"Not at all," I said.

"So you are not hallucinating."

"No."

"What about the incident with—what was his name?"

"I can't remember."

"Kashani. His name is Kashani."

"It's hard to remember."

"You find it hard to remember his name?" she said.

"Yes, I do."

"So tell me, have you gone back to work?" She waited awhile for me to answer. "Have you asked what will happen when your bandages are removed? I understand that will be in just a few days. Maybe you wonder if you are disfigured?" She fiddled with her eyeglasses. "No doubt you want to forget the whole thing. But I'm guessing it's just about the only thing you ever think about."

"How could you possibly know what I'm thinking about?"

"I really don't. Why don't you tell me?"

"Of course I want to go back to work. You have no idea what I've lost."

"Lost in what sense?"

"Lost in the sense of money. I had several important projects. Now, I don't know."

"Your clients have abandoned you?"

"Well, no. Well, I don't know."

"You haven't called them?"

"It's all up in the air."

"Tell me about your employees."

I closed my eyes. "Just two. Both are architects. And also we have someone come in to do the books. But she wasn't there."

"Where?"

"There."

"Were they hurt?"

"Who?"

"Your employees."

I kept thinking I saw something on the ceiling. It definitely looked like a bloodstain. But flying heads don't come inside, do they? The next thing I heard her say was, "What wasn't?"

"What?"

"You said it wasn't your fault. We know that. That's why we're trying to help you."

"No, I didn't say that. You misunderstood."

"What were you saying then?"

"I thought you were asking about my employees."

"Are you concerned about them?"

"Who?"

"Your employees."

"No, not really. I don't know."

"You want to go back to work, but you haven't called anyone. You're desperate about your projects, but you haven't gone in. You don't even inquire about your staff. Are they working? Are they well?"

"What do you want of me?"

"I just want you to see for yourself that you are not at your best right now. You need help. I think I can help you."

"How?"

"Well, for one thing, I can probably get the charges against you dropped."

"But what if I don't want them dropped?"

Instead of replying, she took out her cigarettes. Carefully, as if she were contemplating a great philosophical question, she struck a match. From my little plastic chair, I watched her every move. In the old days, I had been invited to the Ministry of the Interior and also to the Committee for State Security—the KGB; I had undergone similar cross examinations at the Office of Visas and Registration, even at the local police station; I had been in a courtroom, too, and I had been in a prison—in the visitors section, I mean—where they stole all the food I had brought but strangely allowed me to deliver the book I'd thought would surely be confiscated. Of course that was a long time ago. Another universe, really. So there was no reason to distrust—I realized I couldn't remember her name; I'd been thinking of her as Golda. She peered at me over the smoke that slithered around her eyes.

"Why are you looking at me like that?" I demanded.

"Like what?"

"I don't know."

"You think I'm looking at you in some specific way?"

I sighed. "I hate the shrink thing, so please stop doing it," I said.

"It must be hard," she went on, "to come all this way from the Soviet Union only to have this happen to you. In Russia it wasn't so easy to be a Jew."

"Here it's suicide," I said.

She smiled. "Look, try telling me how it felt."

"How can I possibly explain it?"

"Why don't you start with how you are feeling right now?"

"You know," I said, "there was this lady in our building. Actually, our first building, when we still lived in the communal apartment. Do you know what that is?"

"I do."

"I don't think you really do," I said, "but anyway, there was this neighbor, Raya Cherbuka. I liked to go near her because she had this scent—it was dark and lush and I found it unnerving, exciting—I can still remember the shiver that went up my legs whenever I was near her, and when she spoke it was with a creamy Ukrainian accent that somehow reminded me of the caramel candies my grandfather kept in his vest pocket. I don't know, I was probably four years old, it's one of my earliest memories. She would be standing at the one stove—we all shared the stove, you know—and I would come up to her as close as I could, and she would bend down and pinch my cheek, or my thigh, or my tummy, and say, 'You play with your sausage, don't you? It's all right, you can't help it, you're a Jew. You love doing that, right? Almost as much as you love money, that's your fate, poor thing. You're a Jew. What can you do about it? You know how you will die? We'll hang you from a tree by your little penis until you bleed to death.' I swear to God, that's what she said. I never told anyone, especially since my mother forbade me to go near any of the neighbors, but I couldn't help myself, so I ran back to our two rooms and there was my grandmother who was always so kind and loving. 'Babushka! Babushka!' I cried. 'Am I a Jew? It's not true, is it?' I swear to God. And she said, 'Well, of course, my sunshine.' That's how she talked. And I said, 'But I don't want to be!' And she asked me, 'Why not?' And I screamed at her, 'Jews stink!' I don't know, maybe she saw the shadow of that neighbor, Raya Cherbuka, or just heard the slam of her door. Anyway she grabbed me up and hugged me. And she said to me, 'Didn't you know that I'm Jewish, too? Am I stinky? I hope not.' I remember her laughing. 'Papa is Jewish, did you know that? Mama is Jewish. Yes! Dyedushka is Jewish, too. And Uncle Max and Aunt Rita. Everyone!' 'What about the baby?' I asked, because my sister Katya was at that moment asleep in her stroller. 'Baby, too,' my grandmother said. And she even said, 'We're all very proud of being Jewish.' But it was just at that moment my mother sat up on the couch upon which she had been sleeping. She called me over. I went to her very slowly because it was so dark in that corner. And then she just laid it out for me as only my mother could do. One, keep away from the Cherbukas, and two, just don't tell anyone you're Jewish. I told her I didn't tell anyone. But she grabbed me and shook me, I mean really hard, and with this voice of stone said, 'What's the matter with you, Roman? Just don't tell *anyone.*' And then she turned around on her couch, presented me with her back, and closed her eyes and went back to sleep.

"I now understood being Jewish was a miserable fate. I thought about it constantly, day after day, months on end. I could no longer enjoy anything—a stroll in the park, an excursion to the toy store—what was the point? Everyone knew. You didn't have to tell them. Finally, some years later—I must have been in school by then—I was walking down the street by myself; it was an autumn day, and I was kicking the leaves, thinking how much, in spite of everything, I loved to kick leaves, how deeply satisfying it was to bury my foot deep in the muck and send a great cloud of color wafting into the air in all directions—and I said to myself, Well! Being a Jew, it's terrible, really terrible, a real disability. But it could be so much worse. I could lose my foot! I could lose my whole leg! I sent another pile of leaves flying. How much worse, I told myself, if I lost my leg! And that, Doc, is how I see being Jewish."

Golda took a drag on her cigarette and smiled. "Do you think this is such a unique experience?"

"I was so fucked up," I said. "I was on the side of the Arabs in the Six-Day War."

"Sorry?"

"I remember coming home from school, and the whole family was crowded around the radio trying to figure out what the news was, and my grandmother was crying and my father was white as a ghost, and I put my arms around them and said, 'Oh, don't worry. We'll beat the Zionists. They're just pawns of the Americans. America can't even beat a little country like Vietnam! Socialism is stronger! Don't worry!' "

"It was confusing for you," Golda said after a long pause.

"My grandmother gave me this crazy look, and I told her—I swear to God—'Don't be afraid, Babushka. We'll beat back the Jews!' You know what she said?"

"What did she say?" said my Golda.

"She said, 'What's the matter with this child?' "

After a moment, I took a deep breath and slid down in my chair and sighed. "I realize I didn't answer your question."

"What question was that?"

"How I'm feeling. You asked me to tell you how I am feeling. I don't know how I got into all of this. I don't know why all these memories are gushing out of me."

My eyes wandered to the posters on the wall—about safety, about watchfulness, about CPR.

"I know you're not Golda Meir," I said.

"Well, that's a start," she replied.

"Listen," I said, "there is something you can do for me."

She lowered the cigarette. "Okay."

"In your rounds of us victims—you probably met this person. Her name is Dasha Cohen. She's in a coma."

"Ah, yes."

"She's young. Not much older than my daughter."

"Okay."

"I don't know what she was doing on that corner or anything, but I was wondering if maybe you could tell me how to get in touch with her."

"You can't get in touch with her. She's in a coma."

"What I mean is, where is she? I want to visit her."

She waved off the smoke, rested her chin on one fist, took another drag, and blew it out of the side of her mouth. "All right," she said. She fetched her ballpoint and wrote something down. "On this side is me. This is my private number. I expect you to call and set up an appointment. And when the time is right, on the other side I'll write down the information on the Cohen girl. But you have to see me first, you understand?"

I nodded.

"I'm going to recommend they drop the charges against you."

"Even though I want them to charge me?"

"Even though."

I examined the card. Only now I saw her name was Sepha Katsir, not Golda Meir, just as it was when she'd introduced herself in the hospital. Katsir, Meir. Anyone could make that mistake.

"Don't you want to know why I want to see her?" I asked.

"Do you want to tell me why?"

"I don't know why."

"Then perhaps we should find out."

And with that, she crushed her cigarette in the ashtray and waved me out of the room.

☪

Is it me who has lost his head, Roman Guttman, or is it you? Is it my heart that has been blown into jelly, or are those bits of aorta that can still be found mashed into the pavement not far from your office, actually yours?

You look at me but don't see. That's what all you Jews do. Oh please, yes, come, take my land because, after all, I do not exist. That's your story, isn't it?

I also have a story, and if this blown-up brain can recall it, I will tell it. Allah, Creator of All Tales, give me the power to speak!

It was in the school yard—yes. The school yard with our teacher, Mr. Nashir.

We kicked the ball, always keeping him in our sights. He was standing to one side, watching us, ready to hit any boy with whom he was displeased, which was all of us. He rode up and down on his heels, his white vest and blue shirtsleeves pressed and shining, his tie rigidly knotted even on that hot day. "Uzair Nazari!" he shouted. "Tie your shoe! . . . Yahir Zayad! Straighten your shirt!"

Suddenly, though, he raised both his arms. "Boys! Boys!"

We all stopped and looked at him. He held his arms aloft, waiting.

And then we heard the sound. You can't mistake it. Even the young ones know it. The sound soldiers make as they walk, so laden with metal and leather they creak and rumble like rusty machines.

Four or five of them entered the playground. They spread out a little as if on reconnaissance, their weapons twitching in their hands. Their boots were as large as a boy's face.

"You!" one of them yelled. "You!"

Mr. Nashir stepped forward, his back bent in just the way we bent ours when he called us to his desk. "Yes, sir," he said to them. "You understand this is a school yard? This is a school."

"And what's that?" the tall one said, pointing with his white fingers to the third floor of our building. We all turned.

"Oh!" gasped Mr. Nashir. "Oh no!"

Someone had hung a flag from the window of the science room. Not a real flag exactly, just something someone painted on a small piece of burlap. We hadn't even noticed it.

"That flag is illegal," the smallest soldier barked in his perfect Arabic. He was an Arab Jew. They were always the worst. "You," he said to the fat kid, Mu'ad Shafri, "take it down."

Mu'ad was two years older than I, but he froze into some kind of rock, a rock of fat flesh, shivering like an olive branch. His eyes flew about like two crazy mosquitoes, but his feet would not move.

Mr. Nashir said to him, "Go ahead, Mu'ad. It's in room 305. Yes, yes, go ahead. Just lean out the window and pull it in. Go, my child."

"Run!" cried the soldier.

And Mu'ad ran. He ran so hard it seemed to us we could hear him clanking up the staircases with his heavy feet, his breath coming in shorter and shorter gasps. You could almost feel the sweat running down his sides into his underpants, and you had to resist the urge to tug at your own.

Then the little soldier said in Arabic—it wasn't so perfect after all, maybe it was Iraqi, maybe Moroccan—"How is it you have a PLO flag? Are you hiding terrorists here? What are you teach-

ing them, you son of a bitch? We'll have to search the whole goddamned building."

"It's just boys," Mr. Nashir said. "Just boys. You know boys.
They do pranks."

"Pranks?"

"They like flags," he said.

Mu'ad Shafri's head appeared at the window.

Beneath him, the flag was but a speck of green and black, red
and white, held in place by two nails, which Mu'ad now tried to
yank out with his fat fingers.

"What's the matter with you? Pull it out!" yelled the soldiers.
"Are you so weak you can't pull out a fucking tack?"

"Goddamn it!" they screamed.

"Forget the nails. Just rip the goddamned thing out."

"Do it!"

But anyone could see that Mu'ad was shaking like a leaf and
could no longer understand what they were saying to him. Half
of it was in Hebrew anyway, half in that foreign Arabic, and some
even in English because when they thought you couldn't understand them, for some reason they talked to you in English. Mu'ad
tugged at the flag with all his might.

One of the soldiers started to laugh, and then another.

Mu'ad called down, "I'm trying! I'm trying!"

But he could barely get the words out because of all the tears
he was trying to choke back into his throat.

And then the Arab Jew soldier looked around at all of us,
deciding. He pointed to Isa Muhammad, even though he was only
in the first year and couldn't even read yet. "Should we send this
little baby up there to help you, you stupid little prick?" he shouted.

Mr. Nashir, his head still bent, took another step forward.
"He's only five."

The Arab soldier shrugged. "All right. Then let's find someone
else to help him."

He scanned our little group. He pointed here, pointed there.
Then he pointed directly to me.

I felt a hot, horrible, wet spreading in my pants. O Allah, I prayed, no!

Mr. Nashir came as close to the soldier as he dared. "Please," he said, "please. They're just boys."

Suddenly, one of the other soldiers snapped, "For God's sake, Shimi." He threw his weapon over his shoulder and ran inside the school. This time we really did hear the clanking up the stairs.

Mu'ad's head disappeared, and the soldier leaned out the window. He waved to the others below, and in less than a second our precious banner fluttered to the ground like a fallen angel, its wings sheared from its body. It lay there in the school yard, just a piece of burlap.

I slipped to the back of the group of boys and stood, bent over at the waist, hands covering my groin, fighting now my own tears, tears that had nothing to do with flags and soldiers and Mu'ad.

Mr. Nashir reached down and picked up the flag, folded it in two, and handed it to the soldiers.

When they were gone, Mr. Nashir sat down on the edge of the fountain and waved us back to our games. Upon his face was the look of a person asleep in his own head, and when the boys came near, he smiled at them exactly as I had seen my parents smile at a sick person or a beggar, without blinking, without looking, without speaking.

As for me, I ran from the yard, rolled in the dirt to cover my shame, and made my way through alleys and back ways, through bushes and under eaves, until I was safely at home.

"Umma!" I burst out. But she merely held out her hand to me, and I gave her my pants. All I could think to do was go to the sink to bathe.

Now the face of Mu'ad Shafri fills my mind—and the tears he refused to shed cut through my heart like razors through time. They find their way to my own eyes where they have long ago thickened into the black blood of martyrdom. Now, do not ask me, *Shahid, why do you kill the innocent?* There are no innocent.

Chapter Five

Dear You,

I wasn't going to even write about what happened the other day, but it happened, and therefore it's history, and you don't hide history or try to change it, unless you're Stalin or something. I know that history is supposed to be written by the winners, but it seems to me that is not a good approach. Take the Bible. It's the first history, but it's actually told by the losers, since in the end the Israelites are expelled from their own land and they have to go to Babylon, as in, by the rivers of Babylon we sat down and wept (psalm whatever), and I think it's because they're so weepy that the writing is so good. Take the story of David. The way poor King Saul gets written about, it's like he's an idiot and a maniac, because you think, well, it was written by David's guys. But by the end, David looks more like the idiot and maniac, even though he's supposed to be the hero. Point: there comes a time in everyone's life when only the truth will do, and you have to look reality square in the eyes. This is one of those times. Also, when you look into the past, you see the future. This is physics.

So this is what happened. As per usual, Pop was lying on the couch with a bowl of prostokvasha on his lap (translation: disgusting homemade clabbered milk that Babushka still makes), and his sweat suit stunk like the Carmel fish market, and his socks were absolutely despicable on the bottom because he insists on walking into the garden with them on, and here it was two in the afternoon, and I was already back from school because it was Friday, and I said to him, Pop come on, let's DO something, even though to be honest, I don't usually want to do that much stuff with him. I'm fine, he said, go have fun, I'm working. But of course he wasn't working. He acts like he's working, but he hasn't done anything for weeks. So I said, Let's go see Ramat Ginsberg. Ramat Ginsberg is the new neighborhood where he is supposed to be building this amazing house for the guy who invented Kree, the moronic video game, and I know he was very focused on it before the bombing, but of course he hasn't mentioned it since. So I said, I bet it's already built by now, and wouldn't it be great to see it? He said, They built it? What the fuck? Who told them to? Bladt! Bladt! Bladt! (Sorry, but I'm going for historical accuracy.) And I said, I don't know, maybe we should check it out? But Pop's driving the car is not a great idea, at least not yet, as you will see when I finish telling everything. So I told him I was going to call Yehudah. Yehudah is our driver. Not like our driver like we're rich, but just when Pop is away, Yehudah is the one who drives me, and also he takes Pop to the airport or whatever. (Basically, Yehudah owns his own cab.) I also suggested Pop take a shower or at least wash off the *effluvium* from the corners of his mouth—it's Latin, I explained. However, about fifteen minutes later he emerged in actual clothing. He had on his khakis and a pressed hunter-green short-sleeved shirt, the kind of thing he wears only when he wants to look very official, and his hair was combed, and his teeth appeared to be brushed. Then he pointed to his pants and shirt and said, Is this OK? I couldn't answer, and he said, That bad? But it wasn't bad. It was beautiful. The way flowers that open up suddenly are beautiful. I thought it would be best if I just went ahead and called Yehudah.

When he showed up at the door, Pop naturally said, "I don't know why you're here. I can drive myself."

"I don't know either," Yehudah said, "but I'm here, so get in."

And off we went. Ramat Ginsberg is north of us, not exactly on the coast, but it's ritzy, or at least it's going to be. It's not skyscrapers; it's mansions, which is the new thing. They named it after the poet Allen Ginsberg, which is quite ironic if you ask me, because (a) he was a Buddhist, and (b) mansions? But he once visited the moshav that used to be there, and so when the moshavniks decided to become developers instead of farmers they insisted on Ramat Ginsberg. That is Israel in a nutshell.

Anyway, it used to be orange groves, but now it's just dirt and junk in various states of construction.

"I thought you said they finished it," Pop said.

"I guess I was wrong," I replied.

In fact, all they'd done was put in the foundation and then left it, and it was like a dried-up riverbed down there, cracked earth and broken concrete.

Pop began his walk around the property—the architect walk, I call it—and as usual I went with him. We strolled to where the back of the house will be, and Pop knelt down and I knelt down with him, and he touched the earth with his fingers and I touched the earth with mine. Pool goes here, he said. Gazebo there. I saved some of the orange trees, he said, and we'll replant them here. The client likes his juice.

He actually smiled at the thought of this rich Jew and his fresh orange juice, and I thought . . . but then he stood up and said, OK, let's go home. Suddenly I got the idea that I was incredibly hungry, so I cried, Let's get ice cream! To which, of course, he replied, No. OK, I said, but what if Yehudah drops us at the movies? We can always take a cab home. Pop said he was tired, and there was nothing good playing anyway. But I'm so bored, I said, aren't you just bored to death? No, he said. I'm not bored. I'm tired.

But then something happened. Something I cannot explain to this day. He yelled, "What was that?"

"What was what?" I said.

"In the sky."

"Where?"

"There—what the fucking hell was that?"

"What?" I said.

"Don't you see it?"

"It's clouds," I explained.

"It's not clouds! For God's sake, it's not clouds—he won't stop looking at me!"

And then—wham!—he fell down. He just slipped off the edge

of the concrete and fell into the open foundation. I didn't know what to do. It was like my voice got lost somewhere in my throat. He was lying there in that hole, and I wanted to say something, but I just couldn't. I should have said something. I should have done something. But. I don't know, all I could think was: He *fell*. And he was so, I don't know, *fallen*.

I think I started to sweat because I was a little dizzy, but then just like that he stood up, brushed himself off, and reached his hand up to me. He was shaking, I think, and his eyes were red, and there was mud on his face. Come on, he said, help me up and let's get the hell out of here. Finally I could do something. I put my arm around him, and I think I was actually holding him up, because he was so *heavy*, but my own legs were shaking like crazy, too.

Finally I said to him, "Abba, what were you looking at? What were you yelling about?"

"I wasn't looking at anything," he said.

But he *was* looking at something. And he fell.

That's how it happened. That is history. And it is not so easy to write this kind of thing.

✡

It is highly unlikely that I believe in God, and not only because I grew up in a Communist country and loved Lenin more than I loved my own father until I was twelve years old: I simply don't have a feel for it. So, why then, lying in bed, my nerves ready to spring at the slightest creak from any dark corner, did I obsess about Moishe, my imaginary paramedic, whom, I had come to believe, was, yes, a messenger from God. Even though there is no God.

I jumped at the sound of every passing ambulance and sometimes even raced to the scene to get another glimpse of Moishe lifting some new victim onto his high-tech gurney. To be honest, there were no more bombings in the few months after mine—the intifada was over, peace reigned supreme!—but if I came upon a traffic accident, a heart attack, a beating, a suicide, I pushed my way past the yellow tape to grab the medic by the shoulders and cry, Moishe! It's me! only to be met by a confused and alarmed glare and the outstretched baton of a policeman. And each time I asked myself, why are all of these paramedics who so closely resemble Moishe with their beards flowering like bougainvillea and their side curls neatly twined over the tops of their ears not, in fact, Moishe? Yes, yes, I knew he was a hallucination. What else could he be? But one with divine powers. And I knew that at every moment of every day, somewhere in this country a siren was playing its heartrending song on its way to someone's wrecked body, and Moishe was on his way with it—to breathe his salami breath up some poor guy's smashed nose.

A few weeks after my run-in with the law, I called the shrink, Sepha, and made my appointment as promised. Her office was in a fairly upscale section of Ramat Aviv, which she shared with three or four other shrinks.

I asked her to okay it with the parents to let me visit Dasha Cohen.

"A deal is a deal," she said, "but now I do want to know, why do you want to see her?"

"I think she has some sort of answer for me."

"Because she's Russian?"

"I don't know."

"Because you are ashamed of your survival?"

"I said I don't know."

"And I don't know if it's such a good idea," she said.

"But a deal is a deal," I reminded her.

"Not yet," she said.

I kept returning to see her, but the only reason was my desire to connect with Dasha Cohen. I had become obsessed with the idea of seeing her. Maybe I could help her. Maybe I could—who knew what I could do?

So I sat on Sepha's couch, and she sat on a large rattan fan-back chair that made her look like Buddha with a cigarette stuck in his mouth, and it always went more or less the same way:

Dr. Sepha: So?
    Me: So what?
        Silence.
    Me: Okay. I had a few negative thoughts today.
        Silence.
    Me: I got angry at the garbage guy. He left a mess around the trash bins.
Dr. Sepha: Did you say anything to him?
    Me: Who?
Dr. Sepha: The garbageman.
    Me: No.
Dr. Sepha: Why not?
    Me: Because he comes by at five o'clock in the morning. He was already in Hebron by the time I got up.
Dr. Sepha: And this makes you angry.
    Me: What?
Dr. Sepha: That he was in Hebron.
    Me: He wasn't really in Hebron. How the hell do I know where he was?
Dr. Sepha: But you said Hebron.
    Me: It was a joke.
Dr. Sepha: Ah. Should I laugh?
    Me: Yes, you should laugh.
        Silence. I sigh. She adjusts her skirt. More silence.
Dr. Sepha Tell me about Anna.
    Me: Anna's great.
Dr. Sepha: By which you mean?
    Me: She's terrific. She's wonderful. She's been a real soldier.
Dr. Sepha: So you don't think this whole thing has affected her?
    Me: Of course it's affected her.
Dr. Sepha So you've spoken to her about it.
    Me: Spoken? Not really.
Dr. Sepha: Why? Is she also in Hebron?

Dr. Sepha was driven by the belief that I should confront the event. But what could that possibly mean? How can you confront the purely physical? It's like saying I'm going to come to terms with that mountain in front of me. I'm going to understand why it's standing in my way. I'm going to dig deep into the fact of that mountain, and then somehow it is going to melt into the air or just flatten itself out like a mud pie. That if I just got to know the mountain, I would never again be in its shadow no matter how the sun happened to fall upon it, and as for all the life on it—the goats, the trees, the snakes, the gazelles, the insects—well, to hell with them, they don't need to exist either. I ask you, who was the trauma victim, me or Sepha? She was the one who wanted to vaporize the facts and process them into extinction. She was the one who spoke of assimilation and absorption. It was the alimentary school of psychotherapy. But you cannot eat your life. That's what I told her. And this, she actually found funny. That's when she finally gave me the details on Dasha Cohen.

It turned out she had been moved to a facility south of Be'er Sheva called Ganei Z'rikha—Sunrise Gardens, I guess you would say—to be nearer her family. It wasn't a hospital, of course, just a holding tank. There was nothing more they could do for her. From now on it was all machines and IVs.

I plotted my move.

Anyusha was already up that morning, hogging the bathroom. In the old days, the bathroom door was always open; now it was bolted like a Mossad safe house. What did she think I would see? Not that I wanted to see, God knows. I could not have put into words the horror I felt at the very idea of her—even now I can't quite say it—but the truth was, she already had two tiny Katyushas shooting out of her blouse, aimed at—I didn't want to know whom, either. I realized I was supposed to have had a talk with her, but somehow I could never bring myself to do it. Instead, I purchased three or four varieties of sanitary products and left them in the cupboard. "Oh, for heaven's sake, Papoola," she said, "you didn't even get my brand."

Anyway, the door was finally unlocked and out she came, all dressed except for the Elvis Presley slippers, which flopped on the floor like lazy, long-haired castanets.

"Hey, Pop," she said, "don't worry about breakfast. I'll pick up something."

"I can make you breakfast," I replied.

"Not hungry."

"I'll drive you to school," I said.

"It's okay, I'll take the bus."

"I don't want you taking the bus. I told you that."

"Then I'll get a ride with Shana. Or walk even. What a concept!"

"Why don't you let me take you?"

"You're not dressed."

"I can get dressed."

"Don't get all crazy, Pop. It's fine." She packed her book bag, glanced inside the refrigerator, let out a sad little sigh, and went to put on her shoes. Then she came back, took me by both hands, and sat me down at the kitchen table. "Okay," she said, "tonight for the thing at school, what time?"

"Seven o'clock."

"Five thirty!"

"Right. I know that."

"I put it on the refrigerator, see?"

"Okay," I said, "I got it."

"So five thirty we have to actually be there."

"Enough, Anka."

She finally let go of my hands, hefted her bag, smiled that milky smile of hers, and called out in English, "See you later, alligator!"

"Just don't take the bus," I said. And she was out the door.

I sat there for a minute listening to her footsteps clack down the front path and disappear beyond the gate. In the sad, empty well she'd left behind her, I could almost taste her sweetness and thought how lucky I was to have such a daughter.

Then I looked at my watch. I could drive down to Be'er Sheva and be back by five thirty, easy.

I packed a lunch—nothing much: a banana, a bottle of kefir, some halvah, a half loaf of stale black bread, a bottle of water. I don't know why, but I grabbed my old army knife, probably because it was sitting in the basket with the keys. I slipped behind the wheel of the Fiat. Nothing felt right. I fiddled with the seat, adjusted the mirror, pressed the key into the ignition, went back to adjusting the mirror, caught sight of myself: blue eyes, like in the severed head of Amir Hamid. Indeed, I half expected to see him staring back at me. Finally, I kicked the starter, threw it into gear, and there I was, on the road again. I got on the 4 and swung over to Highway 40 at Ashdod. From there, I simply pointed the car in the direction of the Negev. Back in those days, the Negev was still mostly empty space, 40 was still a two-laner, and though it was only a two-hour drive at most, even if you stopped for a nice lunch, which I didn't, I felt I was on an adventure. As I passed Rahat, I ate my banana. Then I had to drive through Be'er Sheva itself. They say Abraham lived here. And here Sarah learned that her husband tried to murder their only son. Her broken heart still hovers over the city in a rainless cloud. Through the open window I heard a lot of Russian and whatever it is Ethiopians speak. I finished my halvah and kefir.

I arrived at the convalescent home just at noon. The sky was cloudless and ethereally blue; the sun, of course, was scorching, and a fiery wind swirled through the parking lot tossing up eddies of dust. As I stepped from the car, sand and pebble swirled around my feet and pelted my face. They'd put Dasha in the middle of nowhere. Jesus, I thought, there's Soroka Hospital in Be'er Sheva—why hadn't they taken her there? Through the vortex of flying sand, I could make out the security guy already lumbering toward me.

"Hey," I said.

"Hey," he replied, looking me over. "What happened to you?"

"A terrorist incident," I said.

He stepped over to my car. "You mind opening the trunk?"

"Not at all."

He sniffed more than looked, circled the car, came back to where I was standing.

"What's your business here?" he asked.

"I'm visiting someone."

"Name?"

"Dasha Cohen. It's probably written as Darya."

"No, your name."

I gave him my name.

He scanned his list. "I don't see you here."

"Do I have to be there?"

"Yeah, you do."

"Well, then, I'm there."

He looked again. "No. Not here."

"Here's my ID."

"It doesn't matter. You're not on the list. You can close the trunk," he said.

"I'm supposed to be there."

"But you're not."

"It's not an army base, for God's sake," I cried. "It's just a rehab center."

"Sorry. It's how it is."

"Shit. I'm going to call the doctor who was supposed to set this up."

"Suit yourself," he said. He walked back to his station in front of the clinic and sat himself down on his beach chair. I got into the Fiat, dug up Sepha's card, and dialed her on my cell. Naturally, I got her voice mail.

I stared out the window. Except for the tiny clinic and its parking lot ringed with flower beds and a bit of lawn set up for croquet, all was wilderness. Ragged shrubs, piles of rock, and in the distance a few scraggly goats grubbing for a blade or two of Egyptian broom. I heard the beep at the end of her message.

"Okay, Sepha, it's me, Guttman, the one from the bombing who hit the Iranian guy. Well, I'm down here in Be'er Sheva where you said I could see Dasha Cohen, but guess what? My name's not on the list. So I'd appreciate if you called and straightened this out and then called me back." I recited my number and hung up.

There was nothing to do but sit there. The security guy seemed to have forgotten all about me and went back to reading an old copy of *Blazer*. But the car was stifling, so I stepped out onto the driveway. The goats had moved on toward the crest of a little hill, impervious to the heat. The only shade was under the overhang above the entrance, which was taken up by the guard and his beach chair plus a small table on which he had placed his radio and can of Coca-Cola, so I moved off in the direction of the goats without any real plan in mind. As always in the desert, the horizon seemed to flee before me. Blades of hot air, rising like serpents, resolved into amusing images: a hat, a man on a bicycle, a three-legged camel, a caravan of shoes. But what was that? Blacker than the stream of mirages, something quite solid. Ah! The tip of a Bedouin tent peeking over the edge of the hill. It flapped silently in the burning wind. I admired it for its forlorn shape, how it sagged bowlegged like an old beggar. And yet, you outlived the golden palaces of emirs and caliphs, I thought, and even the great temples of Pharaoh.

I stepped over the border of poppies they'd planted along the edge of the parking lot and felt the desert floor crunch beneath my sneakers. The wind picked up, and the tent bent with it willingly, and I thought of all the things I had ever built and wondered, what creature has ever built a nest better than this? I was determined to take a closer look, but as I approached, a young man came rushing toward me, cursing and waving me away. His brother was beside him, holding up a fist. "Private land! Private land!" they cried. "No pictures! Get out!" Maybe they thought I was a government agent trying to serve them orders to move. The thing everyone says about Bedouins is that since they stay in no place in particular, everywhere they are is home. But it's not true. They mark out their territory just like anyone else, and within their boundaries they are just as lost as the rest of us.

I turned around and made my way back to the guard. He looked up warily from his magazine.

"Nobody trusts anybody anymore," I said.

"What do you want?"

"Come on. I'm just here to see this girl."

"Sorry, I can't do that."

"I don't want you to do anything. I want you to not do anything."

He laughed. "You were really in a bombing?"

"It's nothing. Just a few bruises."

"Yeah, well, you're going to have some beautiful scars. You want a Coke?"

I squatted down beside him. He reached into his cooler and handed me a can. I opened it beneath my nose so I could feel the spritz.

"I could get you a chair," he said.

"No, I'm good."

"You're not on the list, my friend," he said.

"I understand that. Really, it was just some sort of miscommunication. Is this not how we do things in the Middle East?"

He laughed. "I can't place the accent."

"International."

He laughed again. "You're still not on the list."

"Actually, I'm closely related to your patient, Dasha Cohen."

"Really?"

"Absolutely. I'm not lying to you."

"How can you prove that?"

"I can take off the last of these bandages."

"She was in the same event?"

"Yes."

"And if you took off those bandages, I would see what that I haven't seen before?"

"Not a goddamned thing. What's your name?"

"Carmi."

"Nothing you've not seen before, Carmi."

He clicked his tongue. "You don't want to tell me the particulars."

"No."

"You want an ice cream? I've got some Eskimos."

"Take pity on me, Carmi."

"I do pity you," he said.

"Then be a friend."

We finished our Cokes in silence. Then he got up and said, "You have to avoid the nurses. If anyone is there, you have to come back."

"I promise," I said, and he unlocked the side door.

I felt like I had stumbled into one of those abandoned churches in Moscow, all cobwebs and echoes and ghosts, although without the cobwebs, since the floors were sparkling with wax and the walls had been freshly scrubbed with disinfectant, but the halls were empty and there was not even the hum of a water cooler. I made my way down the corridor, scanning the name tags on the doors. MEYER, BEN YONA, NAPHTALI, TARPIS, and, finally, COHEN. Below her name the inevitable notation, DO NOT RESUSCITATE. *Lamed. Hey.* Two letters, that would be the end of her. Each door had a little window, like in a prison. I pressed my face to the glass. Her room was all flowers, get-well cards, balloons. It looked like a little party was going on in there, but when I opened the door, it wasn't flowers I smelled but piss, stale breath, unwashed skin. I almost fell backward into the hall. Still, I let the door close behind me, swinging shut on its hydraulic arm with a great hiss, as if the air were being let out of a tin of coffee.

Dasha Cohen no longer looked like her photographs. Her mouth was slightly parted, revealing teeth that had been allowed to yellow, and here and there, in the cracks and joints and along the creases of her gums, the color of green tea. I bent over her. The scent of her breath pooled around me, thick, soupy, palpable, almost edible, like strong cheese. Her skin was white as chalk, leprous, yet blotchy, the blood having settled on the underside of her arms and neck. She looked like a two-tone Moskvitch, white and purple. They'd covered her in a thin sheet that did nothing to hide the contours of her rag-doll body—not fleshy and round as I knew she must have once been, but twiggy, skeletal, a girl of straw. Her two legs shot straight out from her hips, but her feet were skewed unnaturally, as if broken, which indeed they might have been. I felt I should have been able to read into them some intention, as though she were speaking through her limbs, drawing herself into a pictograph that, had I but the key, would reveal the meaning of all this, of her pain, her loss, her shattered life. Yet her hair, remarkably, was in perfect order; someone had brushed it. In her photo, it had been short, spiky, punkish, like Anyusha's. Now it was all soft ringlets upon her thin shoulders. Perhaps this made her mother happier.

But why, why couldn't they also brush her teeth?

I set my hand upon her forehead. It was neither cool nor hot. I checked my own just to see: we were the same. Then I let my fingers run along her cheek, her jaw, her lip. Her skin should have been smooth and fat, but it was dry and coarse, almost like salt, and the fine, golden hairs on her lip had become wiry, like an old woman's. I whispered, "Oh! Dasha!"

If I thought she would be moved by my tenderness I was wrong. She remained a stone beneath my hand. I leaned even closer. My lips grazed her earlobe, and the pores of her cheek were like moon pits in the corners of my eyes. She seemed to say to me, "Is this why we came here? All this long way? Is this the salvation we were promised?"

"I'm here to help you," I whispered.

"Who can help me now?" she seemed to say.

Her torpid breath plumed up my nostrils and reeled down my throat. "I have a daughter, she's only a little younger than you. You two would get along. You could teach each other."

But she said, "Look at me. Look at my young body. I'm snapped into pieces like dry crackers."

The sun cut through the jalousies and laid a swath of gold across Dasha's broken chest. "If you wake up right now, I'll take you home with me, I promise!" I said.

Overwhelmed, I took hold of her shoulders. I wanted her to know there was a bond between us that nothing could sever. "You've seen him, too, haven't you?" I cried. "That bastard!"

Just then the door opened.

"What are you doing here?" It was the nurse.

My hands went back into my pockets.

"I'm just visiting," I said.

"Poor thing," she sighed.

"I was in the same attack." I pointed to my wounds.

"Aha," she said.

"My doctor said I should come see her," I explained.

"But why?"

"She said it was part of my cure. I really don't know."

I felt the nurse's hand gently come to rest upon my forearm.

"Look!" I said.

"Yes?"

"She opened her eyes."

"No, love, she didn't."

"She did."

"It's an illusion. People often think that. But if it really happened the monitor would register it."

"You didn't see her open her eyes?"

"I'm sorry, no."

"It was just for a split second."

"Sometimes people in a coma do open their eyes, but it's just a reflex. But in this case, I was looking at her, too. It didn't happen. You wanted it to, that's all."

"There was writing on them."

"I'm sorry?"

"On her eyes. There was some kind of writing on them. I think she was trying to communicate."

"Sweetheart, maybe it's time for you to go home now," she said.

"Let me show you. Look, I'll just open her eyes."

She tightened her grip on my arm. "Don't touch her!"

"It's all right," I assured her, "really."

She must have pressed a button or screamed or something because the room was suddenly filled with people—men actually—and they swallowed me in choke holds and armlocks and dragged me outside. Vaguely I heard Carmi saying, "I don't know how the hell he got in. I thought he was still in his car."

When everything finally calmed down, I said, "You can call the police if you like."

"Look, *habibi*," someone said, "it's okay. We get it. You're suffering. But get some help, okay? Get help."

Someone else said, "There are places that specialize in that. In terrorist victims."

"In Jerusalem. At Herzog."

"Just go up there. Check yourself in."

"He doesn't have to check himself in. He just needs rest."

"He needs help. Are you seeing a shrink?"

"But that's who sent me here," I said.

I looked to Carmi for some sort of support, but instead he more or less shoved me all the way to the Fiat. He waited impatiently until I started the engine and only then felt it safe to go back to his Coca-Cola and magazine. I pulled out of the driveway.

Obviously she hadn't opened her eyes. Obviously there was no writing on them. Still, I said to myself, what had those letters meant?

I felt my head drop to the steering wheel and let out a cry of pain. I had landed on stitches that were still unhealed. I pulled the car to the side of the highway and sat there for a very long time.

☯

Dear You,

My father is a complete a-hole and I don't care if he reads this. Totally messed in the head. So I come home and he's not there and this afternoon is the presentation at school, so of course I waited and waited and it was already five fifteen and I was all dressed and I don't know, I called Shana, and her mother said we should go over together, I shouldn't wait, we could walk. So we all walked to school. She said don't worry, he'll be there. Tonight was awards night, and I won third for my Green Israel project, which he helped me design, by the way. It was so stupid—I saved a seat for him and everything, between me and Avi Issachar's father who kept making funny noises with his nose—and I couldn't concentrate because I kept looking at the door waiting for him, so I entirely missed them calling my name, and the principal said I guess she's not here, and Shana's mom yelled, "Yes, she is!" and had to nudge me. Oh God, I wanted to run out of there as fast as I could, but of course I didn't, I just went up to the stage—and the guy from the Technion shook my hand and said something I can't even remember although I bet it was really important, like you have a scholarship when you grow up, or here's a million shekels or something, your idea is absolutely brilliant! Who knows what he said! I didn't even notice the plaque in my hands until I sat down—next to an empty seat, of course. Everybody else's father was there. Most kids had *two* parents there, even the divorced ones. I don't care if he is a terrorist victim. I hate him.

Chapter Six

☪

ALLAH, Fashioner of Forms, Indulgent One, I pray, release me!

Was it because I didn't go inside that stupid bus? Is this the source of Your enmity toward me? If I could do it again, I swear before You I would step on that bus! I would show no mercy! I wouldn't care one bit about the girl with the beautiful eyes!

I have tried to talk to him, but he doesn't listen. No matter how much I shout at him: *Guttman, go home! Your daughter is waiting for you! You have a house! You have a job! You have a life!*—he merely sits by the side of the road and mutters to himself. His lips are moving, but whatever language he is speaking—it has no words, as if nothing can come from him but vapor and bad breath. It is true what is written. Jews are the offspring of pigs and monkeys.

Allah has ordained that I tarry with this Guttman, but thoughts still urge me home, as if there were some lesson to learn from the shadows of my life. But there isn't. There is only what happened.

We were making our way hurriedly through the souk, and I wondered with growing excitement, what will we buy? Candy? Shoes?

T-shirts? Cassettes? It was always hard to keep up with Fadi, because he walked too fast.

"Come on, little cousin," he said to me, "you're dragging us down. If you insist on coming along you have to keep up."

"I'm coming," I told him.

Partially it was because we weren't in our little village market but in the souk in Jabal. My eyes were everywhere, and I wanted to stop and look at everything—the brilliant piles of clothing, jewelry, knives; the array of vegetables, meats, fish.

All too soon, we met up with Rafi, Kouri, and Hilal.

Rafi looked me over and said, "Why is *he* here? How old is he anyway?"

"How old are you, cousin?" Fadi asked.

"I'm twelve."

"He's ten, maybe nine, maybe even eight," said Hilal.

"He's just small for his age," Fadi assured him.

"How old are you, really?" Hilal asked.

"Twelve," I said.

But I wasn't twelve. And everyone knew it.

Rafi spat on the ground. "Plus, he talks too much."

"Don't worry about it," Fadi said. "Let's just go."

A cruel smile appeared on Hilal's lips. "Fadi's shadow!" he said.

Kouri was the tallest one. He said to Hilal, "We're already late."

They finally decided there wasn't much they could do about me, so off we went, and it was fine with me. Then they began carousing through the stalls, knocking up against one another like wild bears, stealing an apple here or a date there, and falling into hysterical laugher. But as we walked on, their conversation became more subdued and serious, until they were talking in whispers and half sentences, like women in the back of the mosque.

"What are we talking about?" I finally asked Fadi.

"Don't worry about it," he answered.

We emerged from the markets and onto al-Nasser Street. From there we turned into Hassan al-Banna, which is only an alley running between Hussein and al-Kindi, and then everyone poured into the Faisal Café. I followed, pushing myself between Fadi and Rafi.

They each ordered a nargeela.

"I want to smoke one, too," I demanded.

"You can share mine," Fadi said, "like brothers."

But Rafi still wasn't happy. "He shouldn't be here, Fadi. It's not right. And he's got that big mouth."

"No, he doesn't, do you, Amir?"

I pressed my lips together and shook my head.

"See?"

"Fadi," Kouri said, "he can't come with us."

Fadi sighed. But then a smile appeared on his face, and his broad teeth were a kind of sunshine, and his dark eyes two iridescent birds. "Amir!" he declared. "I've got a great idea. Come with me, okay?"

Of course I will come with you, I thought. What a stupid question! This Rafi and Kouri and Hilal—I hate them.

We walked along, the two of us, up Hassan al-Banna Street, and I asked him, "Where're we going?"

"You'll see."

We made our way back to al-Nasser. And suddenly there before us—I couldn't believe my eyes—was Matti's Ice Cream Palace! This was the world-famous place I had only dreamed about, heard stories about, but never in my wildest dreams . . . since my mother would never let me go to the refugee camp, and my father always said places like that were a waste of money. But here it was, Matti's Ice Cream Palace, and Fadi was holding the door open for me.

I stepped over the threshold. The scent of sugar and strawberries, mint and chocolate carried me along the shimmering tile floor.

The waiter pointed to a table, and Fadi motioned me to a chair as if I were some sort of emir. I sat down, and Fadi sat down right next to me, not even across the table. Without a word, he wrapped his arm around me, and I felt through my shirt the weight of his arm and the warmth of his dark skin.

"Happy?" he asked.

My tongue couldn't find my mouth, so I only nodded.

"Maybe later we'll go to the arcade in Beit Ibrahim," he said. Still no way to speak.

"You don't want to go?"

"I don't have that much money," I finally said.

"Don't worry about it," he cried in his biggest voice, the voice he used at parties and with girls. He threw a big wad of bills and a lot of coins on the table. "Here," he said. "When the waiter comes, order yourself whatever you want."

"I already know what I want," I said.

"What's that?"

"Ice cream!" I said.

"Good for you!" he laughed. "But if I were you I'd try the banana split. It's their specialty. Everybody knows Matti's banana split!"

"I don't know what that is," I said.

"It's the best ice cream in the world," he said.

"Is that what *you* want?" I asked him.

He smiled and put down the menu. "Listen, Amir," he said, "I have to go back to the Faisal Café for a few minutes, okay? I have some business there. You stay here and have whatever you want." He bent his head close to mine, almost touching foreheads. "Enjoy yourself for once!"

"What business?" I demanded.

"Have as much ice cream as you want. Eat the whole store up."

But there was a terrible lump in my throat. "I don't want ice cream," I heard myself say.

"Come on, Amir, don't be that way."

"I don't want ice cream!" I repeated.

"Then have baklava. Whatever you want."

"I don't want anything! Why do you have to go?"

"Don't be a pest, Amir. Just stay put and I'll be back in five minutes."

Fadi was already on his feet, patting my head the way he always did when he was about to leave me. With his other hand he grabbed up some of the money because when you looked at it, anyone could see it was way too much.

"You're too young for business," I shouted at him.

"Have fun!" he cried, and even before he finished his sentence, he was out the door and gone.

I sat at the table by myself, insulted by all the happy faces around me. The din of silverware and coffee cups, laughter and conversation, and in the background Amr Diab singing about love.

I noticed my right leg fluttering up and down like a hummingbird's wing and my fingers drumming on the table and the money just sitting there, abandoned and looking worthless, even though it was worth everything.

All of a sudden the waiter was standing beside me.

"What would you like?" he said.

"What?" I said.

"What would you like?"

I looked at the money on the table, at the door through which Fadi had just gone and through which I already knew he would not return, and at the waiter whose eyes were riddled with the disappointment of his life and the impatience of one whose every second was counted in shekels and agorot; and I jumped up from my seat, and all Fadi's money went flying everywhere, and I said, "To hell with you all!" and ran from that place as from Satan's mouth.

Some blocks away, I stopped. I fell against a wall, and all I could think of was what an idiot I was, how I had missed my chance to try, for once in my life, the famous Matti's Ice Cream Palace banana split. And I thought about that thing, that banana split, whose taste I could not even imagine, and no matter how hard I tried, I could not imagine it. Fadi's shadow! Who cared about Fadi or his shadow! Not me! Not Amir! And if something burned in my eyes, believe me, they weren't tears. And if something pounded in my chest, it was only because I'd been running too fast. I took a deep breath, and then another, and thought to myself, well, if

I just wait here a few more minutes, maybe Fadi will come back after all.

I cannot say how long I leaned upon that wall, or if, indeed, I am leaning there still, being the baby that Fadi knew I was. I only know that here, in the gateway to their Jewish Negev, where the Jew Roman Guttman seems to have fallen asleep in the front seat of his car with his motor running and the air-conditioning blasting, I am certain that what I felt that day, I also feel today: a wanting. A wanting for something I have never tasted, but without which life cannot be said to have been properly lived.

Chapter Seven

✡

I DO NOT BELIEVE I HAVE MENTIONED the name of Anyusha's mother, have I?

Somehow I had fallen asleep by the side of the road, and when I awoke I realized it had grown dark. I looked at my watch and cursed. Even if I could fly I wouldn't get to Anyusha's school before the awards were given out. I sighed the sigh of the father who is a total fuckup. Surely I was not always this way. Surely until this moment there had been nothing more important to me than my Anyusha. But I didn't rush off. The Negev stars had burst forth from the wide sky like shimmering schools of minnows, and the deep silence of the desert wrapped itself around me.

I had been dreaming of my friend Marik, who lived somewhere in this part of Israel, and that led me naturally to thinking about Bracha, his wife, and the fact that she was his second wife, his religious wife, and this, of course, made me think about Irina, his Russian wife—really Russian, not Jewish. She was insufferably beautiful, tall, slender, hair the color of sunflowers, elegant features, and lovely, remarkably weightless breasts the size of Jaffa oranges; she never wore a bra, her nipples were always taut, and there was not a man alive who could keep his eyes off them. Her mind was as sharp as her nipples, ruthlessly witty even though she had read hardly anything. I fell in love with her from the first, when Marik brought her back from the Urals, already his wife. In most of the years we knew each other, she was blithely unaware I went to sleep each night thinking of her. In the meantime, Marik was fucking anything that moved. I once tried to tell her what he was up to. She blew little rings of smoke toward the ceiling and spit in her palms. "What is it? Do you want to get in my pants?" she said. "Why else would you say such a thing?"

When Marik decided to emigrate, she refused to emigrate with him and refused to let their son, Alex, leave either. "If I knew anything about anything," she said, "I'm sure I would want to leave this place. But I am an uncultured Russian peasant. Where else in the world could I live so happily in such ignorance?" As it happens, she never remarried.

But that night, stepping out of my car and standing under that ancient sky, I saw her once more as she was all those years ago. And then, naturally, my thoughts turned to Collette.

It was my last year at the Architectural Institute. On Fridays I always still met with my old crew, Fima, Lonya, Marik, Pavlik. I would walk down Zdanova to Dzerzhinsky Square and meet up with them at a little coffee bar not far from the famous toy store Children's World, where we could look out upon the Lubyanka. It was October, and the weather had already turned bitter, early even for Moscow; the first, feathery snows had already spilled from our murky clouds, and the gray of winter had begun to settle in our souls. Steam obscured the windows of the little café and burst from the door each time it was opened. As always, I approached with my heart racing, in the hope Irina would be joining us. I knew I ought to hate myself for coveting my friend's wife, but the fact is, I didn't. If I'd had the chance, I would have stolen her.

I yanked the door open, felt the hot air rush over me pungent with coffee, cigarettes, and smoked fish—the specialty here was paper-thin slices of sturgeon on meager wafers of stale white bread; that, and tiny cups of coffee, which required many cubes of sugar to overcome the fact that they tasted like beets. Irina wasn't there. Lonya, on the other hand, had brought someone with him. "My cousin," he announced, "Chernova, Collette Petrovna. As kids we always knew her as Galya, but now she bravely employs her very foreign first name. Collette, this is my friend, Guttman, Roman Leopoldovich. He is in need of a good woman. You could be it. Look! He blushes! A good sign."

"Please," I said.

She smiled in a friendly enough way.

As usual someone said, "We should have gone to the Green Beast. The coffee's better there."

As usual, everyone agreed. Then the talk began about the weekend, and it was decided, also as usual, that we would drink. Collette melted effortlessly into our little group, as if by a sort of coffeehouse osmosis; we knew that she was a distant cousin of Lonya's, and that they had only recently reconnected. Aside from that, no one asked her anything about herself; in return, she showed no interest in anyone. We passed around cigarettes, had a few more coffees, more sturgeon, another round of pastries—exactly as we always did. Later we went together to some party, I can't even remember where—maybe at Volodya Menchkin's—we ate from whomever's table it was, we got drunk, the same as always. Fima passed out. Lonya wandered off with some girl. Marik headed home, or maybe decided to stop by Alla Friedman's, which he often did—she was always glad to see him. I don't know what happened to Pavlik.

It was about two in the morning. Most of the guests had gone home or fallen asleep on one of the couches or were curled up on the carpets in a heap. I had gotten into several raucous political discussions—the kind that only happened in the kitchen after several bottles of vodka—and I felt riled up, strangely excited. Naturally, someone produced a guitar at this point and began playing "Kalinka Kalinka," and then someone else, Tolya Lucharsky, cursed at him, grabbed the guitar out of his hands, and started in with the chastushki: *My sweetheart has great sex appeal / Gives me a blow job every day / And by the way we are all outraged by the actions of General Pinochet.* And then there was: *Uncle Saveli had a trick / Broke three boards with one stroke of his dick / Just another confirmation / Of the growing might of the Soviet nation!* But soon no one could think of any more verses, and Tolya's fingers were so benumbed by alcohol, the guitar kept falling to the floor. I wanted to escape before they decided to make breakfast and start all over again. That's when I noticed Collette standing on the balcony smoking a cigarette and spitting bits of tobacco onto her fingertips. The sound of the door surprised her, and she turned to face me, revealing a remarkably pale skin in the glow of the apartment lights, a skin so white and flawless it was almost like a geisha's mask, troubling, erotic, necromantic. Against this skin, cascades of profoundly black hair glistened even in the dark of night, and beneath this sea of hair blazed bloodred lips. When she smiled, however, I saw that her teeth were slightly crooked and widely spaced, a sign of good luck. She brought her cigarette to her mouth and released a languid cloud of smoke. Once again she spit out the few shreds of tobacco that had clung to her teeth.

She was utterly unlike Irina. Where Irina was slender and tan with short blond hair, upturned nose, a sharp tongue, and a straight-forward, rather hard intelligence, Collette was rounded, with a full bosom and voluptuous thighs, and when she spoke, as she did to me that night, it was more in circles than straight lines. Perhaps it was because she was so unlike Irina that I hadn't really noticed her. I'd only gone out to talk because I couldn't take another round of songs.

I tore my eyes from her and took in the view, which was noth-ing but the haggard apartment house across the street. "Aren't you cold?" I asked.

"I'm fine," she said. "I don't mind it at all."

"I guess it's better than the music."

"I don't mind that, either." She took a long, luxurious drag on her cigarette, let it drop from her fingers, crushed it under her high-heeled shoe, then bent down and picked it up.

"Here," I said. I took the cigarette butt from her, slipped it into my jacket pocket.

"Let's go for a walk," she suggested. "I'm bored."

She grabbed her coat, put on a pair of leather gloves, a fuzzy pink scarf, a little woolen beret. We rode the elevator down and stepped out into the black Moscow night. All the apartment win-dows were dark except for our hosts', and most of the lights in the courtyard had long ago burned out, though here and there a putrid glow spilled from a lamppost onto the broken pavement. We made our way through the underpass and out onto the street.

"Let's go down to Razina. I like to look at the churches," she said. From where we were we could easily walk, and we strolled along like any couple, me with my hands in my pockets, she with her arms folded in front of her to ward off the cold. Across the way, a drunk was falling against a telephone pole; down the block, another lay collapsed in a doorway. There were almost no cars on the streets, of course, and the buses and trams had already been garaged for the night. Every so often a taxi would swing by, slow down, then move on, or a traffic cop in his Lada would speed by—sometimes these would slow down, too, but in the end, they just waved us along.

"So," she said at some point, "you are the great Roman Guttman."

"I have a reputation?"

"But that's a good thing, isn't it? No one wants to be anonymous."

"In our country," I said, "everyone wants to be anonymous." She laughed.

We walked down Chernyshevsky, and I pointed out some of the old houses—the Apraksin Palace, the Botkin House—and explained how they were constructed, some of their history.

"I know all this," she said. "Talk about something else."

"Well, that's where the old Church of the Ascension used to stand, but then Stalin tore it down. You may not have known that the decorative element around the bell tower was the Star of David atop a seven-branched menorah."

"I did not know that," she admitted.

"Well, there you are."

"Isn't there anything else you like to talk about?" she asked. "Other than palaces and houses?"

"I like constructivist architecture as well," I replied.

"Ah."

"I'm joking," I said.

I looked to see if she was smiling, but her scarf covered her lips, and her eyelids were closed. When she looked up again she said suddenly, "I've applied for Israel twice already. That makes me a refusenik. Does that bother you?"

"No."

"I think it does. Your crew isn't political, I know that."

"Why should it bother me?" I said.

She slipped her arm through mine. "Never mind. Look at the sky. See how peaceful it is! It's almost morning, isn't it? The dawn has crept up on us, like a thief."

"I think we still have a few hours yet till dawn," I said.

"Even so . . ."

Razina is a tiny street, very famous for tourists and architects, that runs more or less easterly from the southern tip of Red Square toward Nogina Square and Kitay Gorod. It lies somewhat lower than the modern street level, as if you were walking through a little gully of antiquity. The old houses are preserved, as are a series of small, beautiful churches. I wanted to tell her about these churches in some detail, but I resisted, and in the quiet that followed she said, "I used to come here as a child." And then, out of the blue, she told me her story.

But a bright greenish light interrupted my memories, the headlights of a truck, which I could hear rolling toward me across the long miles of desert road. It was soon upon me; its great brakes squealed under the weight of its huge tires. The driver leaned out his window and shouted, "Everything okay?"

"Everything's fine," I said. "Just taking a leak."

"All right then. Good night."

"Good night."

"Be careful out here."

"I will."

He set the truck in gear and continued his way south. I also started up my engine. I would be home in an hour and a half. Anyusha would be angry, of course, disappointed in me, which was hard to bear, but it would pass quickly because—well, she was Anyusha. It was so easy to visualize her face—the crazy haircut, the onyx eyes that always blazed with troublemaking, the goofy smile with teeth still too big for her face, the white, doll-like skin—but then, down by the horizon, rising like a second moon in an alien sky, I saw it, blotting out every pixel of Anyusha's face, its Cheshire fangs grinning, the gore of its torn neck forming a crescent of blood, a smirk, a wink, a suggestion, a dare—and just like that I turned the car about and headed toward Bethlehem.

☯

I lied to Shana's mother and told her Babushka was coming to stay with me. I still call her Babushka, the Russian way, I can't stop myself. But I just wanted to wait for Dad by myself, and also I was already bored with them, well not bored, because Shana's not boring, but they don't really talk about anything. I'm not saying they're not fun or they're not nice, because they are and I love them, but I have been thinking about things lately. I have been thinking about what's going on and why things seem so difficult for me. I have been thinking about my problem a lot, which I have never actually written about in my diary. So I came home to the empty house. Everyone is very worried about Pop, but Daphne, Shana's mom, keeps saying he's just dealing, by which she means he's basically psycho right now. I feel that sometimes I am, too, but I always have been. I'm just psycho. So what?

I like our house, I do, but it's not like normal houses. It's sort of bare. Actually barren would be the word. Everyone else has all these photos of their family on their refrigerator, or they put up all the drawings of their kids from the time they were two, stuff like that. But this is against Dad's aesthetic. He's a postmodernist or a neomodernist, I'm not sure which, only I know he's not a modernist, because everything modernist is so straight lines and he doesn't believe in straight lines. He is what he calls a minimalist. One picture all by itself on the wall. One chair all alone in the middle of the room. And *nothing* on the refrigerator! On the other hand, the place currently is a total complete gross-out. Dad threw out all the flowers people sent, but aside from that he just stopped picking up, and crap is piling up everywhere. Dishes, clothes, newspapers, everything. This is called *entropy*. (Greek.) You can't blame me, because I've barely been home.

Anyway, I decided to call Yohanan. I've been spending a lot of time with him lately, but it's not what you might think. We're not *doing* anything. It's completely platonic, totally intellectual. Plato of course was a homosexual, so it's not clear to me what "platonic" really means. I have not yet read too much Plato, but he is on the list. Yohanan and I discuss our graphic novels and manga, and then we study things Rabbi Keren has given us. We do the graphic novels at my house and the Rabbi Keren stuff at his house. I can't tell Pop, and I also can't stop the reading and the talks with the rabbi because if I did, well, I think I truly would go psycho. So maybe I am a liar. But I don't think it's so awful that I don't tell my father everything I do. It was too late for Yohanan to come over anyway. I could hear his mother screaming at him to put the phone down, who would call at such an hour? It was only nine, but they're religious.

Actually I've hidden some of my religious stuff in my room. I made this secret compartment in my dresser. A little box attached with Velcro under the bottom drawers. When I want what's in it, I reach my arm underneath and pull it off. That's what I did this evening. I started reading, taking notes, which is what I like to do, because otherwise nothing makes sense. But I didn't get very far. In the middle of it Yohanan shows up at my window. I thought you couldn't come out, I said. I can't, he answered. In that case, I told him, come in.

I made him sneak in through the window, I don't know why. Yohanan is a little chubby, to say the least, and I knew it wouldn't be easy for him to squeeze in. His kippah fell off his head. He had to go back outside to get it. I had calculated this would happen. Now I had to decide whether to make him go back out through the window again.

Yohanan

Yohanan going through my window

Of course when he found out my dad wasn't even home, he got pissed off. But then I asked him how come he came over when he wasn't supposed to. Were you worried about me? I asked. No, why should I be worried? he said. Because my dad didn't show up tonight. For what? he asked. (I'd forgotten that Yohanan wasn't even in my school, so when would I have told him?) Where is he now? he asked. I don't know, I told him. He just went off in the car and isn't back yet, he probably has some business, and just got stuck. Probably, he said. Then he said, There's a special class tonight, wanna come? Right now? Yeah. At the rabbi's? Yeah, it's supposed to be great. You have to sit with the girls, though. Sure, I said, let's go.

Rabbi Keren is different because he teaches boys and girls together, but not exactly together. The boys are in front and the girls are all in the back. He's American, maybe that's how they do it. Anyway, I stuffed my pillows under the covers so Pop would think I was asleep when he got home.

"But we have to go back out the window," I said to Yohanan. "I don't want anyone to see us."

When I got home it was very late. This time I knew I really

would have to sneak in the window. But there was something wrong from the first moment. I could feel it. The house was telling me. Pop wasn't home. He'd never been home. He wasn't coming home. I picked up the phone because there was a message from him. It was kind of garbled. He said he was on his way to some business thing. I knew it was bull. He never went anywhere on business or anything else without tons of planning and having Yehudah drive me everywhere and Babushka moving in. Even when he had a hot date, he never stayed out all night, not once, never, ever. But tonight, obviously, something was fishy in Denmark.

Which is funny because I usually know things already. I don't see the future or anything like that, but I do see things around me. I mean, I hear it, sort of. That's the problem I wanted to tell you about. For instance, Daphne is not healthy. I don't know what she is sick with, but I know that she is. She just isn't aware of it yet. Or when I look into a tree, I can see all the birds and insects hidden in the leaves. I can see them talking to each other. I can tell that they are frightened all the time. Or I can look into a car and know if the people inside it are happy or not. I can be on a bus, and I can pass a grocery store, and I can know if there is a mother in that store who hates her children even though she's smiling at them. I can see a soldier, and I can know if he has killed someone. I can look at a rock, and I can know whether it is willing to shelter a snake or a family of worms, or if it prefers only dead things, like other stones. I have been this way for a while now. It just suddenly started, I'm not sure exactly when. And then everything was speaking to me, telling me secrets.

I told Yohanan about it. He said maybe I should go see Rabbi Keren. This was, like, a year ago at least.

I don't know why, but I told Rabbi Keren much more than I told Yohanan, and he said, Don't worry, the world is not as it appears. The truth is not really visible to any of us. Sometimes we get little glimpses of reality, little tidbits like your bug. As long as you don't forget to live in the world as it is given to us, it's OK. He asked me if I heard voices, and I said no, and he looked relieved. So no one is telling you to do things in your head? he said. I guess he was worried I was schizo. And honestly, I had to ask him, Am I crazy? He said, You think you're crazy? I said, No. He said, I don't think you're crazy, either. I just think you are a highly sensitive person. Sensitive? I said. Yes, very sensitive. It's a blessing. It's a good thing. It is? It is. Then he laughed. If you think *you're* nuts, he said, you should read Ezekiel! And then we both laughed, but I had no idea why I was laughing. (Now I do, because I've read Ezekiel, and believe me, he *is* a nut.) One time Rabbi said to me, All these words in the Bible, these words are for you, just for you. What about you? I said. For me, too, he said, but the way you read them, the way you understand them, the things you see and you hear, this is a message meant just for you. It was written that way from the beginning. From the beginning of time. Before Moses. Before Abraham. Before Adam. Moses didn't write the Torah. He just wrote it down. Same for crazy Ezekiel and the Psalms and all of it. It was written before time began. It has a million, million hidden meanings, and what you are seeing was written just for you. And since the world was created through Torah, what you read in the world is also a message just for you. Put there from eternity for your eyes. *Your eyes.* You merely had to choose to see it, he said. But I didn't choose, I said. Then it was chosen for you. Those were his exact words.

I don't know. He's a little weird, and maybe I don't like him so much, but I decided it was something I wanted to do, studying the religious stuff. I asked him once about not telling my father. I asked him, What about the truth? Doesn't God want us to tell the truth? I don't know, he told me, what about when it will hurt someone? He then described this thing from the Talmud, where there is a story of the ugly bride. Is it better to tell the husband, oh, you have an ugly bride, or to look through the husband's eyes and say, oh you have a lovely bride? He told me to think about that. I said, I think you shouldn't say anything at all. I asked him, Am I right? He answered, Are you right? That's how they teach this religious stuff.

I just wish Pop would come home. I checked all the doors and windows about twelve times. I was a little cry-y before, and I almost called Babushka, but now I'm totally fine.

Chapter Eight

✡

SINCE THE INTIFADA they had begun to set up roadblocks. Generally cars with Israeli plates had little trouble, but when I saw the soldiers and the lineup of cars, I found myself driving past the exit to Bethlehem and instead headed straight into Jerusalem. It was late anyway. I took a room, called Anyusha, who still wasn't home from her awards, and climbed into bed.

I lay there staring at the ceiling. Sepha said I would have days like this, manic, confused. She also said we would work it out. So why hadn't she set up the appointment as she promised? In the end you have to come up with your own answers. But the answer is never actually available to you. It's like the conscious mind asking itself what consciousness is.

Still, I said to myself, it must be possible that I was saved for some reason. That surely is why Moishe was in my life, and why Dasha Cohen spoke to me with her cuneiform legs and lettered eyes, and why that head followed me wherever I went, even though it would not speak. It was also why the story of my days unwound itself upon the map of my crazy wanderings, even though I didn't want to remember any of it.

And there I was again, back in Moscow, Collette pressing her shoulder against mine as we walked that first night through Razina Street, her voice singing in my ear like a woodlark, a wondrous bird. I stole glances at her skin, white as a loon's between the folds of her scarf and the brim of her beret, and wondered at this remarkable woman. We barely knew each other, but the brightly colored churches of Razina melted away before her, and all that was left was the alabaster of her skin and the silk of her voice.

Her mother, she told me, had died in childbirth, and her father had disappeared when she was only a few months old.

Oh, I said, my father left us, too, when I was about fourteen.

No, she snapped, he *disappeared*. They came for him, I'm certain.

It was in the fifties, just exactly the time of the Doctors' Plot when Stalin was going after the Jews. Her father was suddenly overcome by a passion to write, and he wrote about everything: he wrote love poems to his dead wife, and poems about hope and freedom, he wrote an entire story that took place while the characters were waiting in line for sour cream; he mocked the new Soviet Man; he mocked the little people who ran the local council; finally he mocked Stalin himself, but he called him something else, Omar Omarsky, who ruled the land of Omarka, the place where only Good prevails. Her father, she said, was afraid of nothing. She had found his journals hidden in a false drawer of an old armoire—found them seventeen years later.

All of it could have been avoided. Her whole life, she said, was a kind of mistake. Her grandfather had been "the great Sergey Abramovich Chernoff. What? Never heard of him?" she laughed. The family—her family—was very rich before the revolution. They even had an estate—"the only Jewish estate in all of Russia," her grandfather boasted, "except for the Ginzburgs' and Rosenheims'." Her grandfather had become a Communist and had to flee abroad with all the great Bolsheviks—Lenin, Trotsky, Zinovyev, Bukharin. Even so he still lived in high style in a grand apartment on the rue de la Varenne in the Seventh Arrondissement not far from the Invalides. The Communists didn't mind: they loved him because he knew how to raise money, and after the revolution they even made him an economic attaché to the embassy in Paris. But when Lenin had his stroke in '22, he was promptly recalled to Moscow. Her grandmother was pregnant with a child, Collette's father, Pierre, and naturally wanted to stay in Paris, but Sergey Abramovich smiled at her, stroked her cheek, assured her the very best doctors in the world were now in Moscow, and instructed the valet to pack their bags. Thus the child, her father, Pierre Sergeyevich, was born in a communal flat in Moscow, and so was Collette.

"I don't belong here," she said. "I never belonged here. It's all a terrible miscarriage of fate."

"I feel that, too, sometimes," I said rather lamely.

By this time we'd crossed the river and were walking past the reconfigured mansions that served as embassies for the French and British. Traffic had awakened the boulevards: the swarms of taxis and official cars, a few private Zhigulis and Moskvitchs, an ancient Pobyeda held together by nothing but wire and electrical tape, the occasional Zil with its police escort. In this particular neighborhood, foreign cars were also a fairly common sight: gleaming Volvos and Mercedes, as if from another planet rather than just across the national border.

"It was his writing, then, that got him arrested?"

"I don't see how. They would have confiscated his papers, but I found them in the armoire."

"Maybe there were other copies."

"Maybe. But also he never went back to his work in the factory after I was born. That's what my grandfather said. He spent all his time on me. They accused him of being a shirker, a malingerer. And you know where it goes from there."

"You cannot think it's your fault," I said.

"I don't."

"You were an infant."

"Of course."

"Collette, you were an infant."

"Oh look!" she said. "It's morning!" The sun had finally risen over the eastern skyline casting a bright winter gold upon the river. Collette unknotted her fuzzy pink scarf and gulped in the foul city air as if she were standing in a field of sunflowers. "I have to go."

"But we could have breakfast," I said.

"Not today," she replied.

We found the nearest metro. Once inside, she threw open her coat and slipped off her gloves. I had not until this moment noticed her scent. It was not of perfume at all, but of hay and earth.

Without thinking, I bent down and kissed her. For the first time she looked directly at me, and her eyes were little bees in full swarm.

Night had fallen so profoundly upon Jerusalem that nothing stirred, not even a breeze, as if God had stopped breathing. Tomorrow I would rouse myself and seek out Abdul-Latif Hamid and his wife, Najya.

It's not that I wanted an explanation. There was none. Nor did I want an apology. What I think I wanted was a way in. I kept thinking, how could they be impervious to the tearing of their son's flesh? Wasn't it Amir himself who led me here?

And yet in the room in which I had placed myself, under the thin covers and upon the hard bed, I felt nothing present but my own body. The spirit that had been assailing me—the head of dripping blood—had apparently abandoned me to myself and my useless memories. I thought this absence would give me some peace, but in fact, it only left me more sleepless than before. And I asked the walls and demanded of the ceiling that was a firmament between us: Why will he not speak to me? Why is there between us only silence and pain?

☾

I look down upon the beautiful and mostly dead Dasha Cohen. Strangely, I have not been able to leave her to her feeding tubes and catheters but hang here in the lovely desert sky of my most precious homeland, looking through the skylight, it seems, but that cannot be, since there isn't one. Somehow I see her, yet remain outside, shut out. Why do you not cry out, Dasha Cohen? Why do you not curse the world that brought you to this end? Because you are nothing. Less than nothing. Less even than a ghost or a vapor. You are simply what is left over when everyone else is done with you. A melody with no words, a story with no end . . . and what good is a story, Dasha, that has no end?

They always said I was a liar.

Where were you?

I had to help Mr. Nashir in school. He asked me to help grade papers.

Why would he do that?

He has an eye infection and can't read. I read the papers aloud to him.

Is this the truth?

I can bring home a note tomorrow if you don't believe me.

Amir, where did you get that watch? You know we don't have money to spend on watches.

Oh, I didn't buy it. It was a gift from Farid bin-Barzi. He gave all the boys watches.

What?

In honor of his son becoming something in America.

What do you mean?

His son is the main judge in America now. It's huge. Didn't you see it in the news?

I didn't see a thing.

Oh. Then let me tell you all about it.

I didn't know why I did it, only that I couldn't help myself. Other things, too. Sometimes I would walk through town, sit down in some empty lot, and imagine what life was like for the insects there. I could imagine the rise of their civilization, its downfall every time the grass was cut. I would sit near the fountain and watch people go by, and I would dress abu-Gazen in rich robes, and Nadiah Khamal would be a famous pop singer, and Mukhtar Astof was an alien from another planet.

One day I said to my father, "I just want to get out of this fucking town."

He didn't say anything. He just slapped me with the back of his fist. I took the slap and went back to work. I thought, at least he can be proud that I took it like a man.

It was afternoon, dinnertime.

I had just come home from somewhere—from school, of course, although I may have stopped at the library, because I often went there to be alone. I read whatever they had, which was usually all the same things, so I often read the same book over and over. When I entered the courtyard, my uncle was sitting on the back stoop waiting for the midday cooking to be done, smoking his pipe and talking to himself. His lips were continuously moving, his long fingers never stopped gesturing, his eyes looking off into nowhere through the thick cataracts that clouded his sight. My father said he had the palsy, but to me it always looked like he was talking to someone no one else could see.

"Uncle Ahmad!"

"Is that you, Amir?"

"Yes, it's me!"

"Well then, come sit by me if you have a minute."

He squeezed over to make room, and I sat down beside him on the concrete step, taking in the dark smell of unwashed clothes and tobacco that was Uncle Ahmad. He was much poorer than we, and every day he appeared at a different house for his meals. I always regretted our family was so big—it meant he came to us only every few months.

"Will you stay for lunch?" I said, knowing full well he had already been invited by everyone else in the house.

"Allah willing," he replied.

My uncle Ahmad was the storyteller in our family. He knew all the classical tales and new ones, too, ones he created out of his mind. He also knew the history of everyone's father and mother going back many generations, and whenever there was a wedding or anniversary Uncle Ahmad would weave wonderful stories about the bride and groom's ancestors, all the way down to the very moment these two were betrothed. Sometimes he played the oud, sometimes not. Even when we used to gather to welcome some guest at the madhafah, which still existed when I was very little, where everyone was allowed to tell stories, his were always the best.

"What's that in your hand?" he asked me.

"Books," I told him.

"Which books?"

"This is algebra. This is history. This is Arabic."

"That's all? That's all they teach you?"

"No, there's more."

"Good!" he said, much relieved. "But I don't know if they teach you this." He reached into his satchel and brought forth a small volume. The cover was worn to tatters and all the pages were dog-eared and it had the smell of sour rags.

"What is it?" I asked him.

"You can read, can't you?"

"Of course I can read!"

"Then see for yourself."

I took it in my hands. It was remarkably light but also a little sticky. I could make out the title only by rubbing off the dirt and squeezing my eyes almost shut to focus on the faded letters. *A Book of Tales.*

"Open it," said Uncle Ahmad.

If I expected jinns and ghouls and princesses and caliphs to jump from the pages and into my yard, I was not that far wrong, because the names did jump out and dance before my eyes: Antar and Abla, King Azadbekht, Kalilah and Dimna, and, best of all, a whole section on Joha and Mulla Nasruddin.

One day Joha declared, "I have become a Sufi Sheik! These are my acolytes—I am helping them reach enlightenment!" "How do you know when they reach enlightenment?" asked his friend, the merchant. "Nothing to it! Every morning I count them. The ones who have left have reached enlightenment!"

"But that's not how it goes," I said.

"Everyone has the right to tell a story the way he sees fit," replied Uncle Ahmad. "I tell it my way. This book, another. Someday you'll tell the story your own way, too."

"Oh no, I don't tell stories."

"That's not what I hear." Uncle Ahmad scratched his chin with his shaky fingers. Whenever he scratched, I knew he was about to tell me what he was thinking about. "I've been thinking about you, Amir," he said. "I see how you watch everything, and I realize stories are always happening before your eyes. You can't help yourself, can you? The world is too boring for you. So it was for me at your age. The world must not be allowed to be an ordinary place—am I right?—where things happen and that's that. It has to be filled with characters you want to understand, with plots and subplots, with beautiful pictures and unforgettable melodies."

"That's crazy," I said to him.

"As Allah wills," he nodded. "But maybe being crazy is not such a bad thing."

"Still, I can't take your book," I said.

"Oh, I can't read anymore anyway. These eyes—they are already peeking into the other world."

My mother called us to the table. I slipped *A Book of Tales* between my schoolbooks, took Uncle Ahmad's hand, and led him into the house.

My father joined us from the bedroom where he had been napping, went to the sink to wash, sat down, readied himself, and nodded at Uncle Ahmad without really welcoming him. My sisters brought out the meal, and then my mother also sat down. In our house, we all ate together. This was one of the mysteries of my father. He had once been a Communist.

"In the Name of Allah," said my father, and we all repeated, "In the Name of Allah." It was just about the only prayer you would ever hear from his lips. Why he prayed before eating when he never did salah even once a day, let alone five times, or fast on Ramadan or ever set foot in a mosque is something only he could explain but never did. I didn't pray either then, not salah and not at meals. As he uttered the prayer, my lips moved, but no sound emerged. I looked over at Uncle Ahmad. He was like a Sufi, dizzy with God.

My father reached for the bread and only because of the glaring eyes of my mother handed the first piece to Uncle Ahmad before putting the rest directly into his own mouth. Then the ordeal of the chewing began. It was a simple meal—lentils, kibbe, squash, yogurt—but the noise of my father chewing, and the noise of my sisters, and the noise, yes, even of Uncle Ahmad chewing filled me with a disgust that had no name. It was worse than sitting down with goats, who at least do not talk with their mouths full. I fought the urge to run from the table; I closed my eyes and sang a song in my head, anything to drown out their eating.

"So," my father said between bites, his mouth dripping kibbe drenched in yogurt, "Ahmad, are you well?"

"Thanks be to God."

"You look well," he said.

"Eat more," my mother said, pushing the dishes toward him.

"Oh no, thank you, may Allah's grace be upon you," Uncle Ahmad replied.

"You don't like it?" my mother asked.

"It's delicious," he said. "Wonderful!"

"Then eat."

So Uncle Ahmad scooped a little more into his bread, but he was only nibbling. Almost nothing went down his throat.

"You look well!" my father repeated.

After Uncle Ahmad was gone, my mother said, "He's so thin."

My father picked his teeth with a match. "He's going to die soon, anyone can see that."

"Poor man."

"Why? He's had a decent life."

"What kind of life?" my mother cried. "No wife, no children. No money, no land. What has he got? A bunch of old stories? He never even wrote any of them down. Who will remember him when he's gone?"

My father let out some gas. "The lentils," he said. "Too much salt." And then he went out by way of the courtyard, calling over his shoulder, "Amir, when you come to work after school today, try for once to be on time."

In my corner of the room, I took *A Book of Tales* from its hiding place between algebra and history and let its moldy pages fill the space around me with a delicious gloom—yes, that is what I called it, because that was how it felt: a gloom that gives pleasure, a fog of dark magic that transforms toadstools into pretty flowers, a golden sarcophagus holding curses and blessings. I turned one page over and then the next, catching a bit of story here, a bit of story there: *Once there was a merchant with three daughters . . . a ghouleh hid under the bridge . . . and he said, By Allah, whose bowl is this?*

"Amir! What's the matter with you?" It was my mother standing over me. "You have to go back to school!" She tapped her watch angrily. "You're late!"

A Book of Tales became my Qur'an, and in its pages I began to sense what happiness was. As always, I went to my father's shop every day after school for another evening of changing oil and repairing fuel pumps. But now my father's mechanics, Ghassan, whom everyone called George, and Ibrahim Farsoun, nodded happily when I came in. I'd been telling them stories from *A Book of Tales*—at least mostly from *A Book of Tales* because I found myself making half of it up out of my head. I would simply watch the words come out of my mouth, and if I got stuck, I would paste some other story I'd read onto the one I was telling, changing the hero's name or inventing some new country; I might turn a magic stove into a magic pen or a talking tree into a talking donkey, but it never seemed to matter. George and Ibrahim Farsoun laughed or grew angry, shook their heads in despair or clucked their tongues in appreciation at the cleverness of my maidens and princes, my beggars and enchanted birds. Their hands were black with sludge, their faces smeared with oil, but their eyes were fixed upon the landscapes I drew with my tongue. They never asked for a story, of course. But when they turned down the radio, they were letting me know it was time to begin.

That evening, I decided to tell them the story of "The Prince Who Married His Mother." It was a long one, and I remembered only a little of it, but so what? It was a story worth telling! Ibrahim Farsoun turned down the music, and the two of them fell back into the lazy rhythm of their work, waiting for me to start.

"*Oh beloveds,*" I sang, "*long ago, in a remote time, in the city of Bagdad, there lived a prince so handsome no woman could look upon him without swooning and falling desperately in love . . .*"

"Ah, yes . . . ," whispered George.

"*But he was proud, was our prince, and not one of the women of his kingdom pleased him. Then, one evening, walking upon the rooftop of his palace, he spied across the courtyards a maiden who glistened beneath her veils like the moon itself—*"

"Amir, can you come into the office?"

I looked up. My father stood in the doorway with his arms folded. George and Ibrahim Farsoun continued working as if nothing had happened.

I followed my father into the little alcove he called an office, nothing but a chair, an old table, a cash register, and an old television that was always on without the sound.

"You have to stop this now," he said.

"Why?"

"It bothers the men. They can't do their work."

"No, it doesn't. It makes them happy."

"And you. You do half the work you're supposed to. Since you started with this business, all you do is sit around and tell stories. How can you work and tell stories at the same time? It can't be done."

"I do my work."

"Amir, I'm not telling you again. No more stories. Do you want to end up like that Ahmad of yours, begging from house to house? A man of no respect? A man of no qualities?"

"*I* respect him."

"You don't know what to respect. Sometimes I think you have no brains at all. You're twelve years old—why can't you be more like Fadi? Look at him. A success in business, a good friend, a blessing to everyone. What are you, Amir? You can't even fix a carburetor."

"I can fix a carburetor."

"Then go out there and fix one! Mr. Ephron's Opel has been waiting for two days!"

"I'm working on the Opel," I muttered.

"Speak up! Talk like a man! Why do you always mumble?"

"I don't know," I said.

He shook his head in despair. "What am I raising? A little girl?" And with that he waved me away.

When I came back, George and Ibrahim Farsoun didn't look up. I went over to the Opel, Mr. Ephron's Opel. Its hood was gaping open like the mouth of a baby bird. I stared into that mouth of an engine, with its tongue of steel and rubber hose. It was waiting for me to feed it. But then something came up my own throat, something bitter that I tried with all my might to keep down but couldn't. It wasn't vomit. It was a scream.

☯

Dear You,

After I got back from Rabbi Keren's, and Pop still wasn't home, I found myself walking around the house from room to room, like I was buying the place or something. Without Pop in it, the house was so empty, and I had this strong desire to just memorize everything about it, probably because of what happened at Rabbi's tonight and how I agreed to everything and said yes and how—well, I'll have to tell you about that later.

Believe me, our house was NOT a pretty sight. First of all, the kitchen. I opened the refrigerator. There was no milk, no eggs, just an open thing of kefir and a couple of apples. There were a few other things—stuff that had been there for a long time—some pickles, for instance, some feta, mustard, a crusted-over can of tahini. I was hungry, but God knows I wasn't going to eat any of that. I grabbed an open bag of Bamba and stood in the kitchen listening to myself munching, noticing how messy everything was, dishes in the sink, all kinds of pots piled up, garbage not taken out, cups of cold tea, and yet there was nothing there you could say belonged to a family. Nothing to say we lived here. Only that some slobs had eaten here. There was a basket hanging from a hook in the ceiling with onions in it, only the onions were not even there—just a few dried-up skins lying on the bottom of the basket. They reminded me of the ash that's left after someone is cremated. The floor, I don't even want to mention. It sort of stuck to my sandals, squeenchy squeenchy squeenchy. I can't remember the last time it got washed. OK, enough with the kitchen. So I strolled past the dining table, which was covered head to toe with magazines, files, mail, binders, blueprints, napkins, books, and wine bottles. Jackets were piled up on the backs of the chairs till they looked like humpback whales. I turned on the TV for a minute, which is something I'm never allowed to do that late at night, so that's why I did. Guess what again? Nothing on. It didn't matter. I had no intention of watching TV. Anyway it was making too much noise, and I was trying to listen, because as usual everything was talking to me, but actually it was almost impossible to hear. So many dirty clothes piled everywhere it was like in the Negev where you find the ruins of twenty civilizations all right on top of each other—you could excavate our lives, week by week. But I didn't feel like cleaning anything up. You'd have to have a tractor for that.

Just at that moment, I realized I had to go into Pop's room, I don't know why.

Pop's room basically has just one piece of furniture, his bed. But that doesn't matter because you can't take one step in there. All you can do is jump from the door to the bed, or else you'd have to slosh through the clothes and debris on the floor. Not to mention the sheets are pulled away from the corners of the bed, so you get a nice view of his mattress. Three or four—no, wait—six—water glasses are squeezed onto the tiny reading table attached to his headboard. Every single one of those glasses still has water in it. I was kind of shocked at how many pill bottles there were, and mostly not the same kind of pill. For pain, I guess. There were a lot of books on the bed, all opened with their spines up, spread out on the white sheets, whining because they felt abandoned. From a distance I bet you would think they were birds flying through the clouds. Pop has a few pictures on his wall, though—the big wall on the right side of the bed, but it's so dark you can barely see them. I don't know why, but I felt l would like to look at them, so I squeezed myself into the space between the wall and Pop's bed. So here are the photographs: A lot of me. Of me and him. Of me and my school. Of him and his friends. Of Babushka. Of Dyedushka, whom I never met. Of my aunt Katya, whom I also never met. Of a bunch of other people I haven't the slightest idea of who they are. And there, in the corner, very small, stuck between lots of bigger photos is my mother. Well, no. Actually it's just an empty space, because my father took it down a million years ago and put it in my room. But I took it out of my room and gave it back to him. I said, I don't want her picture in my room, and he said, Well, I'll keep it for you then, and I said, It's not mine, it's yours, and he said, I'll keep it for you anyway, but as you can see, he never put it back up. Maybe he tossed it, after all. So there's this empty place on the wall, just a picture hook. Isn't it weird he only had that one picture of her? Like, where are their wedding pictures? How about at the beach? Hiking? Honeymoon? I looked for a long time into this little space where the picture wasn't. It was silent. In fact, I could actually hear my own heart beating. But you can't look at an empty space forever. I fell back onto Pop's bed. Don't tell him, but it smelled. On top of that, I landed on one of his upside-down books, and it hurt. I got mad and I shoved them all onto the floor. There was so much crap on the floor they barely made a sound. I lay back down, and my head sank into Pop's pillow, I *love* his pillow, it's so soft, not like mine. Now I could smell his hair. I like the stuff he uses. Honestly, I think I could smell Daphne, too, because she has a very peculiar scent, I don't know what it is. That sort of wacked me out. But really, it didn't upset me. Actually, I like the idea. But the wild part is, I haven't a clue when she could have been in that bedroom, because she never was in there when I was home, that's for sure. Well, except for the time we brought him home from the hospital, but she slept on the floor. Do you think they come here when I'm at school? *Yaalah!* Anyway, I was lying here in his bed, and I spread out my arms, like an angel, all of my four sets of wings, my four sets of feet, too, like that drawing by Leonardo da Vinci that's so famous, and my four faces, too, so I could see in every direction, even down through the bed. I wanted more than anything to hear my pop's voice, to know where he was, what he was doing, but of course I had to settle for what the bed was telling me, which wasn't much except for the Daphne business, which I guess is a lot. One thing, though, the pillowcase was stained with whatever the stuff is he puts on his cuts and scars, and there were even some bloodstains. You'd think I'd be grossed out and all, but I just lay there, trying to hear, trying to hear. One thing was really nice—looking straight up, the ceiling was very clean, very flat, very perfect. It was, I don't know how to express it, filled with echoes. Hello, hello, hello . . . So I turned on my side, and guess what? There was something hard underneath my head. I slipped my hand under the pillow. It was a metal picture frame. It had glass on it. It was a photo for sure. I know, I know, I should have taken it out and looked at it. But then, I don't know why, I just couldn't. Maybe it was the photo of my mother, but maybe it was Daphne. I don't know. I just felt I better not. There are some things you really shouldn't touch.

᷂᷂᷂᷂᷂᷂᷂᷂᷂

Wow, I must have fallen asleep. I was lying in Pop's bed writing in my notebook all the things that just came before this, but then— well, I don't know, I opened my eyes and the notebook was right there in my hand, and my pen, too, but I wasn't writing. Light was actually peeking through the slats of the Venetian blinds. I looked at my watch. Yikes! It's already morning!! Yikes! But it's OK. I'm not going to school today. You know what? I'm going to put the words on paper: FUCK IT. Fuck it all! Yeah. Fuck fuck fuck fuck fuck fuck. ☺☺!!! Why should I go to school? Who's going to care anyway?

I have to say it was weird sleeping on Pop's bed. I haven't done that since I was a kid.

~~~~~~~~~

I just took a shower and changed my clothes. But the thing is, I got thinking about, of all people, my mother. Who knows why? I don't like to think about her. I don't like her, period. You will probably think that's strange, and even sick. I can't help it. It's how I feel.

Anyway, I have to admit I reached under the pillow again, and there it was, that picture of my mother, the one I told you about. I think I was relieved it wasn't Daphne, but why he would keep a picture of my mother under his pillow I have zero idea. I took my time looking at it, and at first I just got mad, because I always get mad when I think about her. But she was, I don't know—all in her winter clothes, with the gorgeous fur collar and the silvery shapka (which is what Babushka calls every hat including a yarmulke!), a shapka made of extravagant and beautiful gray fox (because in Russia they don't care about animal rights and ecology), and her face beneath the fur was tilted just a little to one side, and she had the slightest of slightest smiles, which I believe you would call coquettish, or impish maybe, a smile I hated the last time I saw this picture, but this time it seemed, I don't know, like she was asking me something, or inviting me to come into her photograph, or there was a secret just between the two of us that both of us already knew. Of course, that was impossible—I wasn't even born when this picture was taken. But still. Her lips were very thick and lush, and even in black and white you could tell she had on wads of red lipstick, kind of like that model, Angelina Jolie—I used to think fat lips were gross, and I couldn't *imagine* my father kissing them, but now I saw: wow. And that's when I turned and looked in the mirror on the closet door, because my own lips—And in the photo her lips were parted just a teeny little bit, and you could just make out the space between her two front teeth—which is exactly the same as mine—we're total teeth twins!—and even though I always hated that space between my teeth, for some reason right now, it was kind of, I don't know.

The one and only photo of my mom

Anyway, that's when I just had to see if my father kept anything else about her hidden in his room.

And so, OK, yes, I started snooping inside his drawers. I know, I know, I'd kill him if he did that to me. But that's what I did.

And what did I find?

Nothing!

Pop is so boring! Underwear? Check. Socks? Check. Checks? Check. But secret journal? No way. Love letters? Forget it. Hidden reserves of cash? Well, yes, but I didn't take any. (Honest.) I did find some notebooks, but they were only filled with architectural ideas and algebra and phone numbers of clients. So I plopped down on the bed to consider what to do next.

I mean, it was like both my parents were secret agents or something.

Chapter Nine

✡

IT WAS THE MAID KNOCKING at the door that woke me. It was already nine thirty, which meant if I called home again Anyusha would be in school, but I called anyway and told her I'd be back by dinner. I had to use the hotel phone, because my cell was already dead. In those days they lasted only a few hours, and you had to take extra batteries with you. But of course I hadn't. "We'll go out," I crooned into the phone. "In fact, we can go into Tel Aviv and do something special like Orna and Ella or Café Noir. We'll get some sweet potato pancakes or schnitzel, okay? Big kisses, and don't worry. Just be ready to go out and have a good time."

I showered, went down for coffee, and found a shakshuka place. I hadn't had shakshuka in a long time, and it made me feel very Israeli. It was so late hardly anyone was there, so I took my time, smoked my cigarette, read a newspaper. By the time I was done it was close to eleven thirty, and the place was filling up again.

I knew that Amir Hasan's village was near Bethlehem, one of several villages that found themselves squeezed between the overflowing refugee camps, the burgeoning Jewish settlements, and the old Christian city. I pulled the Fiat out of the car park, took out my map, and placed my finger upon the words BEIT IBRAHIM. And I even remembered a street: Armenia. They'd moved there after their own house was ripped down.

I felt in my pocket for my knife, put the car in first, and went on my way. I got onto Route 60 and then turned at the sign for Beit Ibrahim and within minutes found myself on the edge of the village. It sat in a small valley surrounded by olive groves and rough hillsides. Once it might have been a beautiful town, but now it had grown out of its old clothes and become a kind of anemic sprawl dwarfed by the refugee cities to the north and the dark clouds that seemed to emanate from them. To the south and west were the first inklings of desert, but atop the hills the bright circles of Jewish homes with their red-tiled roofs and golden stucco walls preened like peacocks.

A few meters up, the soldiers waved me over.

"What's your business here?"

"I'm going to see an old friend."

"A friend."

"From the days before."

They clucked in understanding. Who had not had Arab friends? Who had not done their shopping in Arab towns? Had their tailoring done there, their furniture made, their shoes mended? Who had not found time to sit and drink coffee, sit and play chess?

"You should be careful," one of them said to me. "It's dangerous."

"I'm not afraid."

"What happened to you?"

"Oh, the face? Car accident. Not this car. I wasn't driving. It was a bus actually."

"You okay?"

"Yeah, yeah, yeah. It's nothing."

"Most people travel this road by caravan. It's not good to drive alone anymore. Are you sure you want to proceed?"

"They're expecting me. Nothing will happen, I'm their guest."

"All right, then. Be safe."

"I will. Thanks."

They saluted me, and I drove off toward the village as if I knew where I was going.

Of course I didn't, so I just wandered around a bit looking for street signs, but there weren't any that I could make out. There were two or three main arteries; I went up one and down the other. The houses were a mix of old stone and new concrete, a few apartment buildings, a slew of shops and a market that was mostly empty, a mosque or two. Wherever I went, eyes followed, and I began to lose my nerve. Finally I stopped and asked a kid where Armenia Street was, and he said I was on it, and I asked him where Abdul-Latif Hamid was, and he said in his few words of Hebrew, "Oh, for car!" and pointed down a side road.

"Down there?" I said.

"Yeah, yeah. Down. Down."

"Straight ahead?"

"Straight, straight."

And to the other kids around him he said something in Arabic, and I understood him to be explaining that I needed my car repaired, and then I drove off in the direction toward which he had pointed. The road curved away from the center of town down a winding, ever-more-narrow and broken pathway, till the pavement gave out completely and turned to dirt and scree. Down below I could see a kind of stone shack with a corrugated roof and a wide driveway in which several pickups and old, worthless cars were abandoned helter-skelter among the weeds and trash. I pulled up to the open garage and shut off my engine. Inside, all work had stopped, and three men were staring out at me.

A wiry fellow emerged, wiping his hands upon a filthy rag. He spoke a very good Hebrew, and he said, "Shalom aleichem," and I responded, "Alaikum salaam." I looked about and saw the gang of boys watching from the top of the hill and inside the garage two men hesitating before returning to their labors. One of them was very large and bearded. The other was thin and wore a stupid expression.

But the man in front of me could not have been other than Abdul-Latif. He said, "What's the trouble with the Fiat?"

"Tune-up," I said.

"You came all the way out here for a tune-up?"

"I got your name from someone. He said to come to you."

He put the oil rag into his back pocket. "We don't get Jewish cars anymore."

"You won't work on a Jewish car?"

"I didn't say that. I said we don't get them anymore. Who sent you here?"

"I don't know, I don't remember. It's just I had your name written down as the best mechanic. Maybe it was years ago someone told me."

"I used to work on a lot of Jewish cars. Now I don't. But I have a lot of Palestinian cars, which I didn't use to have. They honor me with their cars, whether they need work or not."

"That's nice," I said.

He studied me for a moment and seemed to make up his mind. "Okay, I'll take a look." He motioned me to open the hood and start the engine. He listened for a minute, stuck his head into the engine compartment, then motioned me to shut it off.

"What happened to you?" he said, pointing at my face.

I didn't answer him, and he didn't press me.

"Your timing is off, and you need new plugs. I'll change the oil and filter, take a look at the brakes, transmission fluid. Anything else?"

"No, that's good."

"It will cost you a hundred twenty, plus parts."

"Okay."

"It will take an hour or so. You don't have a ride, so you can wait here or take a walk, I guess."

I glanced up the road and saw that the boys had vanished. "I'll be safe walking around?"

"Who's safe in this world?" he answered. "George!" he called. "Bring the clipboard."

The big man lumbered out with the clipboard, and Abdul-Latif filled in the estimate and had me write down my name and phone number.

"Mr. Guttman," he said, more to himself than to me. I handed him the keys, and he said, "Come back in an hour. It will all be done."

.   .   .

I immediately regretted writing down my real name but was happy to escape, because I suddenly had no idea why I had come to Beit Ibrahim. Why hadn't I just said who I was and what I wanted? Now that I had created this charade, how could I extricate myself? I would never be able to confront the parents of Amir Hamid, not with any dignity, anyway. I began walking back up the hill toward the center of town but then turned around and walked toward the edge of the village, where the houses petered out among some hardscrabble hills dotted with a few twisted olive trees and acacias. The earth there was covered in dry sheep pellets, and I supposed that in winter there must have been a bit of grass there. On the next hill I could see the ruins of an old Arab building surrounded by a largely fallen stone wall and, beyond that, past the Jewish villages of Nokdim and Teko'a, a cruel, rocky desert descended to the Dead Sea. I walked along the goat path toward the ruins, suffering a little under the hot wind that came up from Jordan. I descended into a gully, wandered through a dry little wadi, and then began my ascent. But as I rounded a little outcropping of rock, I realized I had made a mistake. I was nowhere near that old building. And then six or seven boys jumped out and surrounded me.

One of them stepped forward and said something in Arabic. I said to him in Hebrew that I didn't understand. He said something else in Arabic, and by his tone it was clear he meant to humiliate or goad me.

I said, "Doesn't anyone understand Hebrew?" No one answered, but I didn't believe them. "I don't want trouble. I'm only here to fix my car."

One of them spat at my feet. Then two or three of them began hissing at me, taunting me with words I could not understand. Their voices grew louder, more threatening. I put my hand in my pocket for my knife, but it must have fallen out in the car.

"Okay, okay," I said, "take it easy. I'm going." In Arabic I said, "Salaam, salaam!" But as I backed away, they inched ever toward me, step for step. My army training kicked in and I reached out and grabbed the biggest kid, twisted his arm behind him, and started screaming at the top of my lungs anything that came into my head. They were only boys, after all, and they were stunned, and then I pushed the kid away from me as hard as I could, right into the pack of them, and ran like hell.

When I turned around I must have been two hundred meters from them, and they were still crouched around their friend, whose arm must have hurt pretty badly, because he was crying.

"Jesus," I said to myself.

And then I swung around and ran as fast as my legs could carry me.

When I finally stopped, mostly because my lungs were exploding, I realized I had continued to run in the wrong direction, directly into the desert. I decided I wasn't exactly lost, but I also had no idea where I'd ended up. It was hot. I didn't have any water. But for the moment, at least, I was safe.

I tried to get my bearings—perhaps I might make out some famous rock formation, but frankly they all looked the same. I briefly considered hiding under a ledge to catch some shade, but there wasn't one close by, and anyway it seemed easiest just to close my eyes and relax, if only for a moment. So I sat myself down upon the ground. The heat from the earth seared through my trousers, but in a pleasant way, and my fingers found solace wandering through the arid soil and smooth, glassine pebbles. Above me, the ball of the sun was shooting great swaths of orange fire into the sky, and below me, insects had huddled in their burrows, and snakes and lizards had curled themselves into crevices or found shade beneath the sand. I needed a minute to think things through. First, my situation. I knew I wasn't that far from the village, though when I checked my watch I realized I had been traveling away from it for more than an hour. This was not a good thing, because it's not such an easy matter getting out of a desert, even one as small as this. All those canyons, meandering riverbeds, caverns, ridges. When you are absolutely certain you are headed west, you could actually be going east and end up right back where you started. Or you just get deeper and deeper in. These wadis, you think they're going somewhere, and then they just spill out into more wilderness. But really, I told myself, I was minutes from help from one of the Jewish settlements. I couldn't call, because my phone was out of power, and anyway, I'd left it in the glove compartment, but, hell, I could just walk all the way to Jerusalem if I wanted to. So why not enjoy the quiet? I had been born in the largest country on earth, the greatest landmass the world has ever known, and here I was lost in the smallest, with nothing around me as far as the eye could see—just barren cliffs, patches of sand, dried-up wadis, and endless stretches of empty sky. What an amazing life! I thought.

So much had transpired in the last few days. The truncated visit to Dasha Cohen—why? What was I trying to unravel? The decision (who can say why—because a decapitated Arab challenged me to?) to come to Beit Ibrahim. Crazy.

My eyes suddenly felt as if they had been scourged with steel wool. I blinked over and over, but no tears, no moisture, just the grinding of my eyelids that only made it worse.

And what about Anyusha?

Mother no doubt was already at the house, taking care of her. Naturally, she would be furious with me. And Anyusha—well, who knew what she was thinking? She was always so cool about everything, nothing ever seemed to faze her. She was a remarkable kid, a good kid, a great kid, I never had to worry about her.

I brushed the sand from between my fingers and wondered briefly where these grains had begun their lives. I tried to conceive the eons of time they had endured only to end up here, on me. Time. The one incalculable, moving in all directions, coming to rest where you least expect it.

A few days after our late-night walk, Collette called from a pay phone near the Tretyakov and asked if I wanted to meet her. We met outside the museum entrance on Lavrushinsky. It had already gotten cooler, and she was bundled in her woolen coat, but this time she wore no cap and her raven hair sparkled in the few brave rays of sunshine that had forced their way through the gathering winter clouds. Shreds of light sparkled on her moist lips, bright red as always, set off like rubies against her pale skin. She put out her hand in a friendly way, and I took it.

"You like museums?" she asked.

"Of course."

"Too bad," she said. "I want you to meet my friends. I just didn't want to say so on the phone."

She was so beautiful standing there, and I had only tasted her lips. "Fine," I said. "Let's go."

We hurried down the block and jumped on a trolleybus, got off some blocks from Pushkinskaya, and turned into Little Gnezdnikovsky Lane. She led me to an older apartment building, red-brick, turrets, cupolas, probably 1860s. We were quickly buzzed in, and I followed her up several flights of stairs. She knocked on a door; a woman in a purple beret stuck her head out, studied us for a moment, then motioned us into the tiny flat. Like the tram, it was overflowing with people; and, almost as one, they looked up and smiled at Collette. They were Jews and foreigners, not that I had actually met a foreigner before. Still, you had to be blind not to pick them out: the smooth, soft haircuts, the fine leather of the shoes, the perfect fit of the jeans. These people had an easy, confident manner, and the Americans especially affected a natural, lazy posture, hands in pockets, heads cocked to one side. But it was their smiles—open, almost stupid—that mesmerized me; when they laughed it was like just-popped champagne. One of them held court beside the bookcases, his audience of hungry Soviets hanging on every word as if the syllables coming from his mouth were droplets of honey. The whole room was enveloped in a golden light.

Collette said, "Come. I'm sweltering. Help me out of my coat."

I placed my hands upon her shoulders and lifted the coat. As she pulled her arms through the sleeves, her neck was revealed to me, and, beneath the opening of her blouse, the white cup of her bra.

"Just throw it in the bedroom," she said. "And introduce your-self if you want. Or leave if you're afraid."

"Why would I be afraid?" I said.

I took her coat, but when I came back, I couldn't seem to find her. I strolled over to the window, instinctively pulled aside the curtains. Two white Zhigulis were parked near the back. I made out two more around the side. Someone came up beside me. "You seem worried. Don't be. They won't do anything." He spoke well but had an accent—sort of like an old Jewish man from Odessa, but he wasn't old and I doubted he was Jewish. In fact, he was the American I had been watching mesmerize the Russians with his speech.

"I'm not worried," I said to him.

"All these Americans and Brits—we're your safety net." He gulped some wine and patted me on the back. "I'm Charlie."

He wore gray corduroy jeans and under his jacket a thick, ropey sweater that hung loosely on his lanky frame. His feet were encased in a pair of massive square-toe boots. "One good thing about America, we don't care what anyone does. You ever hear of Berkeley, California? You can walk down Telegraph Avenue with your dick hanging out and no one will even bat an eye. Here, you put on a pair of Levi's and you're immediately under suspicion."

"It's not true about the jeans, but your Russian is very good," I said.

Collette now appeared out of nowhere.

"Charlie!" she called.

"There you are, my girl!" he said.

They linked arms. "Let's talk," she suggested. "Roma, you come, too."

We stepped out to the vestibule and pressed ourselves onto the landing beneath a grimy blacked-out window. Charlie and Col-lette talked in whispers, and it took me a moment to realize they had switched to French. Maybe they thought the KGB didn't know French. It seemed silly. After a while, she wrote something down on a slip of paper, the names of some scientific books and jour-nals, and asked Charlie if he might be able to get them for her.

He said he would try. Then he reached into a jacket pocket and brought out a small jar of instant coffee. She dropped this into her purse. At the same moment, she slipped him a little bundle. He put it into his pocket the same way a train conductor collects a ticket: without so much as looking at it.

I stood there in the half dark wondering again what I was doing there yet feeling strangely elated. Collette moved quite close to me. I was aware of the pressure of her hips. Her hand came around the small of my back and settled there.

"Let's go in," she said. "It's cold."

We hung around the apartment for a while. I believe I was a success. With the foreigners I tried my English, and with the Jews I found myself more and more at ease as the afternoon wore on, even though they were Zionists and dissidents and academics and artists, most of them refuseniks and quite a few of them what we used to call "names"—they were in the upper reaches of some alternative social order, celebrities of oppression. As for Charlie, he came up to me when he was ready to leave.

"Roman!" he said. "You're a most interesting guy. I'd like to speak with you again sometime. Maybe see a concert or a play. I can easily get tickets. Maybe you'll come to Spaso House for a movie? That's the ambassador's residence. Everybody comes for the movies. Food's great. What do you think?"

"Oh," Collette interjected, "we'll have Charlie over for dinner, how about that?"

I did not know how to understand this remark, and in any case I didn't think I'd really be going to the American ambassador's house, so I soon forgot about the whole thing. I continued my waltz around the room, stopping to chat with this little group of three and that little group of four, but every few seconds I found myself checking for Collette. I did not have to search hard: she was a neon sign, ALL GLORY TO THE SOVIETS, CHAMPIONS OF THE REVOLUTION! Her mouth was the crimson star over the Kremlin. With the blinking of her eyelids, flecks of amethyst floated into the room. I was now completely and brilliantly aware that my life had changed. I stood in the ranks of a whole new company, on the shores of a whole new world, a more beautiful world, possibly, even hopefully, a more dangerous world.

I brought Collette her coat and followed her out the door and into the metro. We boarded the train, sat in silence as the stations came into view, vomited up their passengers, and disappeared again as the train raced off into darkness. It did not seem to matter that, in fact, she had not asked me to join her on her way home. I had this new knowledge, and it included the realization that, no matter how impossible it seemed only a few hours before, we were together.

Her place was located on the northern edge of the city, in what, not all that long ago, had been the village of Medvedkovo and was now the last stop on the orange line, an ugly little station, brand-new, the walls hammered to look like serpent's teeth waiting to devour the poor commuters who, like hordes of fat, sluggish potato bugs, ventured forth onto its narrow platforms. We rode the escalator up to Shirokaya Street. Whatever might have charmed the eye in bucolic Medvedkovo had been pitilessly obliterated by the new apartment blocks, massive bulwarks sprouting from the soil like Spartoi—only what were they guarding? The metro station? At the feet of these giant buildings cowered, muddy and dwarflike, an astounding array of identical kiosks—ice cream, kvass, cigarettes . . . ice cream, kvass, cigarettes—and, interspersed among them, glass message boards on which were posted the latest from *Pravda* and *Izvestia*. A few old men stood before them, reading, as if the revolution might yet produce some good news. The bread shop was emptied of all but a few stale loaves, all black; a line of shoppers snaked halfway around the block from the milk store; the shoe emporium proudly displayed its one model of oxfords, three pairs in every window, and the restaurant sat empty, awaiting its first customer of the day, or perhaps the week.

Collette pointed to a group of women in cheap coats and homemade hats.

"Disgusting, aren't they?" she said.

We found the entrance to Collette's building, one of the maze of apartment blocks in forlorn shades of pink and yellow. They reminded me of the girls at a party who never get asked to dance.

We pressed for the elevator. It groaned open, and a fetor stretched out toward us, followed by a large woman in a fur coat pulling a frightened little dog.

"Collette Petrovna!" she bellowed. "Hello! And who's this nice young fellow?" She bent down and petted her dog. "Say hello, Vova!"

Collette did not reply. Instead, she edged me quickly into the elevator and pressed her floor.

"Who was that?" I asked.

"Plotkina," she replied. "She's just a pest. Don't worry about her."

Collette's apartment was at the end of a long, narrow hall, its floors sodden by an endless parade of wet boots. She set the key in the lock and turned the bolt. We stepped inside, she flipped on the light, and I gasped.

The door had opened onto a room suffused in color and light. In the center was a kind of velvet throne with baroque finials and arms in the shape of lion's paws; beside it, a floor lamp carved to resemble one of the undulating pillars of Saint Peter's in Rome, topped with a shade of colored glass; the drapes were burnished taffeta, made dazzling with tassels of gold; and her rug—a riot of color, stitched, woven, glued, I could not say how, into a magic carpet. Her walls were hand-painted with tea roses, and in her tiny bedroom, a lace canopy was strung with silk flowers.

"This must be what France looks like," I marveled.

"How would I know?" she answered sadly. "It's all just junk I found."

I followed her into the tiny kitchen, watched as she put on the kettle. Her hands were not delicate like Irina's but rounded, like the rest of her body, fleshy and full, though the long red nails made them elegant and European. She brought one of these hands up to her face and languidly brushed a few untamed strands of hair from her eyes. By this time, her lipstick was mostly worn off, but her lips picked up moisture from the steaming kettle and seemed, if anything, more luminous than ever.

"Can I help with the tea?" I said.

"Wait a minute," she replied.

Collette lifted the telephone, rotated the dial a few notches, and shoved a pencil between the finger hole and the stop bar, transfixing it in the no-man's-land between on and off.

"That's the way they listen," she said. "When you break the connection, they go deaf."

"Okay," I said.

"You didn't know that? Everyone knows that."

"Of course I knew that."

She frowned. "I don't want them to listen to me. I'm sick of them listening to me." Just as suddenly she broke into a smile. "But I want you to listen to me."

"I love to listen to you, Collette."

She poured the tea. Her china was English or maybe Japanese, and I was afraid the teacup would shatter between my fingers.

"You have your own problems," she said. "Why do you want to hear mine?"

"I don't really have any problems," I told her.

"Then you live in a different world than I do." Suddenly she looked up at me. "Roman, do you know what love is?"

"Of course I do," I said.

"No. You cannot. How could you? You're the lucky one."

She put down her cup. "I met him because there is a God in heaven after all."

"Whom?"

"Do you want to hear or not?"

"Yes," I said. "Yes, I do."

"He appeared in the early afternoon," she began. "I remember this specifically, because I had been looking out the window, and only the youngest children were playing—school was not yet out. It was spring, I had thrown the windows open and the air was full of life—you know, children laughing in the courtyard, birds singing, bees buzzing—spring! When out of the blue, there was a knock on my door. I was afraid, of course. No one ever comes unannounced unless it's trouble. And then through the door I hear *Je cherche Collette, Collette Pierrovna Chernova.* Can you imagine? French coming through my door? I had not heard French since my grandfather . . ." She sighed as if Grandfather had only yesterday passed away. "And so beautiful. I peeked through the glazok. The face on the other side . . . the eyes so blue, so pure . . . *Mademoiselle Chernoff? J'espère que je ne suis pas venu à un temps incommode.* But Roman, you don't understand French, do you?"

"Well, yes. Some," I told her.

"Don't worry, I'll tell it in Russian." She glanced at her hands, then out the window. "He was so tall! He wore a tweed jacket. Do you even know what tweed is? And his name was Pascal. Pascal!" She was smiling happily now. "The first thing he said to me was 'I have a letter for you.' He was so nervous! He kept looking around for the police to come jumping through the windows!

"He seemed like a boy to me, the way he smiled, the way it was impossible to take offense at anything he said. I made him tea."

"Like for me."

"Yes, like for you. Only he didn't drink it like we Russians do, slurping and dripping and loading our cups with spoonfuls of sugar, but elegantly, unaffected. He seemed to enjoy it so much."

"Collette," I said, "what is the point of all this?"

"The point? There is no point. Just my life. If you're not interested, you're not interested."

"No, no," I said.

She sipped her tea very slowly, pouting. But at last she began again. "Finally, he reached into his pocket and handed me a big white envelope. Inside this envelope was . . . but let me get it for you."

"That's not necessary," I said to her.

"No, I'll get it. I want you to see it. To see I'm not making this up."

She disappeared into her bedroom and then reappeared with a white envelope, just as she said, only now it was somewhat darkened, dog-eared at the corners. She withdrew from it a smaller envelope and held it up to me. It was addressed simply to "Collette," and from that she withdrew a few sheets of onionskin. She held these to my face also, and I could make out, in a fine but shaking hand, tightly spaced lines in muted green ink.

"I'll translate as I read," she went on, "so you will forgive me if sometimes I make a mistake."

"Collette," I said again, "it's not necessary."

"You don't want to hear?"

"You don't have to translate. I know French."

But she translated anyway.

My dearest Collette *(she held the pages as delicately as one would a manuscript of great antiquity)*:

I am your great aunt Lorrette, the wife of your uncle Guy, whom you will have known by the name of Gennady, the brother of your grandfather Serges. I have known of your existence for some years, but only now have felt it safe to communicate with you, especially as I am getting quite old and do not know how long I may have on this earth. When your grandfather left, we wrote and wrote, but all our letters were returned. We guessed Serges was dead, caught up in that awful whirlwind, or in prison, and his family probably in exile, though we dared to hope we were wrong and it was simply that the mail was being intercepted by the authorities. Then came the war. Guy and I had the good fortune to escape to Spain, where we remained in hiding until 1945. Unlike most of the others, we returned to Paris and began life again. Guy went back to work, first as a restorer of fine textiles, and later as a curator and an author of many beautiful books, while I worked as a journalist. Again we tried to find Serges's family but, just as before, nothing. Still, in our hearts, we could not let go. Then, miraculously, in 1979, we met a man who was involved in what is called the Soviet Jewry Movement, of which perhaps you know more than we do, and of course we told him all about Serges and we asked him, can you find out about him? He took everything down in his little notebook, every little detail. Weeks passed, and then months, and then years, another hope dashed for us. But then one day—it was, I think, a full three years later—the telephone rang, and it was this very gentleman. Without any explanation at all, he declared not only that he had found Serges but that Serges had a granddaughter—you! We also learned that your father, Pierre, went missing, and that you are now alone, an orphan. From that moment, I was determined that you, my darling Collette, must come to France. I thought about this night and day, but because Guy was certain that you would be safest if we left you alone, I did nothing.

But now the days have passed. How long will be left to us to help you? I have always respected Guy's opinion in all matters, and this was no exception, but now we are both full of regret. All we want is to see you safe, here in France. Believe me when I say we welcome you with open arms. My dear Collette! Let us help you! We will do whatever we can to make your life more bearable and pleasant until they let you come to us at last.

We know this letter will come as a surprise to you. No doubt you felt we had abandoned you. We beg you to forgive us, and accept our hand in love.

We have asked this dear young man, M. Pascal de Gramont d'Hozier Dubé, to carry this letter to you. He is a dear and sweet person. He has graciously offered to make it possible for you to reply to us, which we so dearly hope you will do.

With great affection,
Your loving aunt and uncle,
Lorrette & Guy Chernoff

"I couldn't believe what I was reading," Collette went on. "Curator? Journalist? 'They're both retired now,' Pascal told me. 'But I don't understand,' I said. 'Oh, they're very old now,' he explained. And I said, 'Curator of *what?*' 'At the Louvre, of course. Didn't you know?' Didn't I know? Didn't I know?

"How could I know? Did I even have the slightest idea my grandfather had a brother? There were the thousand and one tales of riches long gone, of the house in Saint Petersburg, the estate in Tver'—my grandfather's voice came back to me, *Ah, if you could only have seen Basyinka! There was no place on earth like Basyinka!* On and on, day in, day out. But did he ever mention a brother? And then he would begin about the years in Paris, the house on the rue de la Varenne, believe me, I could describe every room to you in the smallest possible detail—but did he mention that a brother had come with him to Paris? Lived in the same house? Was clever enough to remain in Paris when my idiot grandfather was all too happy to fall into Stalin's net, that this brother married, studied, became an important curator of textiles at the Louvre while his wife, Lorrette, wrote articles for *Le Monde?* Of course not. Not a hint, not a slip of the tongue, nothing. And then one day, years after Grandfather died, voilà! An uncle! An aunt!

"I said to Pascal, 'How is this possible?' And he said, 'Everything is possible.' He took my two hands in his and said, 'Everything is possible.' "

Tears welled up in her eyes. "It's crazy," she said. "I thought I had to tell him my whole life right then and there, from the beginning up to that very moment. When I finished he was weeping. 'It's just my life,' I said to him. 'Things like that should never happen,' he said. 'I won't let this happen to you anymore!' Not like a big declaration, but in a very small voice, almost a whisper, like a breeze. And throughout all of it he never let go of my hands."

Collette went to the sink, rinsed out the cups, and laid them in the drainer.

"So just like that you were in love?" I blurted. "In one day."

"You think such a thing is impossible?"

I didn't answer her.

"You needn't worry," Collette said. "It's over."

"Why? Why is it over?"

"It's over. Leave it at that. Anyway, it's not what you think. He could stay in Moscow only a few days at a time, and they only gave him a visa once every few months. They watched us constantly. We never had a single night. How can you be lovers if they refuse to let you love? He wanted to marry me. But of course it was impossible."

"Why was it so impossible?"

"What difference does it make? I told you, it's over."

She had the habit—I might have mentioned it already—of pushing back the lock of hair that always fell over her eye. But this time she tugged all of her hair back with both hands, as if she were gathering it into a ponytail. She held it there for what seemed like several minutes, deciding, and then suddenly released it. The hair exploded from her hands like a flock of birds alighting upon the ripe branches of her shoulders.

"Don't misunderstand!" she cried. "He never hid it from me. I don't want you to think that he did. He hid nothing! But his wife would never divorce him. It was as simple as that. She vowed to him, never. He told me this in tears. On top of everything she was a true Catholic. He tried everything to convince her. He begged her. Offered her whatever she wanted. Money, the house. Whatever she wanted. But time and again she said no. I suppose she loved him. Naturally, he would never take her to court. How could he? Was he supposed to accuse her of something horrible? They had two boys! Pascal could not bear even to see them scrape their knees, so how could he do such a terrible thing to them? Legally, he could live separately from her for six years, then take her to court. But how could I ask him to do that? How could I separate him from his children, when who knows if they would ever let me leave? He said he would come and live here. 'Now I know you love me,' I told him, 'now I understand love.' But I loved him, too. So I told him no. I made him go home. I made him promise never to return, never to write to me, never even to think about me. So that is how I love, Roman. That is how it is."

"But you said it was they who wouldn't let him back in."

"Yes," she said absently.

. . .

We sat there for a while not speaking. Then she said, "I have some beautiful things he brought me from Paris. Would you like to see them?"

She led me into the living room and opened the doors of a small china closet she'd cobbled together with old windows she had scavenged and painted with glitter. But before she could lay hold of the cloisonné bowl or the alabaster elephant with the sapphire eyes, I took her arm, spun her around, pulled her to me, and kissed her with the full force of my mouth. She pulled away, regarded me coolly, and began to unbutton her blouse.

Chapter Ten

☾

O Merciful One, why do I tarry? Who is this Dasha Cohen to me, after all? What glues my eyes to the long silken tresses of her golden hair? In her bitter silence she is a lamp unto me. Her breasts, hidden beneath the veil of her garment thin as a bedsheet, are two fawns dancing over the gates of my heart. Her closed eyes are two curtains of silk, her lips are two figs split open, her cheeks are two ripe pomegranates. Wait. I know these lines from somewhere. Possibly some poetry I memorized, I don't know. Nothing is really clear anymore.

I can't seem to get close to her; I can only imagine her scent, which is most likely rosewater and cinnamon, and I can only guess at the color of her eyes, which must be amber. Amber. Have I not seen such eyes? O Allah, Store of Hope! Let me see those eyes once more!

It was in the house of my uncle Bahir, which was much larger than my father's house. Someone they called the Great Man sat in the place of honor in the corner, and Uncle Bahir himself placed a large platter before him. My aunt Ahd was so flushed she was already pressing sweets upon him, and Uncle Bahir had to wave her off.

Fadi, dressed in his best white shirt and gray slacks, his head respectfully bowed, was seated next to this man. My father and I were seated on the other side of the table, waiting. The others also sat and waited. Men from our family, men from their family.

Suddenly I felt dizzy.

My father shook his head at me. "Go outside and get some air," he said. "Just go quietly, and don't disturb anyone, for the sake of Heaven."

"Always for the sake of Heaven!" I snapped at him.

I left them all sitting there, laughing and nodding at everything the Great Man said. I passed by the women watching from behind the door, coming and going from the kitchen. Obviously, the Great Man was very rich. Anyone could see this. And he must have been somewhat traditional, for Uncle Bahir would never have dared hide Aunt Ahd behind a door; Aunt Ahd sat and ate with him all the time. In his house, like my father's, it was all one family. My sisters wore jeans and T-shirts, so did all their friends. But when I glanced over I saw my mother in the hallway with a hijab pulled up over her nose. I didn't even know she owned one.

I pushed open the door and felt the air cool my face. I took a deep breath, but it only made me dizzier. In the yard, amid the flat tires and discarded toys, I found a canvas chair resting under a tree. I thought I might sit in the breeze and let the waves of nausea subside. I sat there for a minute or two, my head in my hands.

"Hey."

I looked up. She was standing some feet away, framed in the olive tree, the sparkle of its leaves like a halo of precious stones above her head.

"You okay?" she asked.

I didn't want to answer, so I said, "Why aren't you all dressed up, too?"

"Oh please," she said. "*You* wear a hijab."

She was in Levi's, a pair of cowboy boots, a shirt that said COCA-COLA on it. Her hands were on her hips, and her hips were slung forward like the bow of a ship. "I don't wear hijabs. I don't wear chadors. I don't wear burkas. I wear DKNY. My father can go to hell. Do you have a cigarette?"

"No," I said. "I'm out."

She laughed. "You're out?"

"Yes. I don't know."

"It's all right," she said. "I'm sick of cigarettes. Isn't there any-place to sit down? I don't squat, either."

All they had were some old boxes and crates. That's what they used for chairs around there. "Take my chair," I told her. "I'm happy to squat."

"Don't be stupid. Sit on one of those boxes. Bring it over here."

I gave her my chair, fetched one of the old crates, and slid it along with my foot. When I sat down beside her, I could see how much taller than I she really was.

"You're Amir, right? So tell me."

"Tell you what?"

"About Fadi, stupid."

"Fadi? What about him?"

"Everything, of course."

"Everybody knows Fadi."

"Sure, sure, I know everything already. Do you think I'm stu-pid or something?" she said.

"I don't know anything about you."

"Well, that wasn't very polite. Hasn't your mother taught you anything about being polite? Oh, don't worry, I'm just kidding. I don't care what you think."

"Fadi is a great person. He knows everything. What do you want me to tell you?"

"Does he like girls?"

"Of course he likes girls. He's got lots of girls."

I could see her stiffen, but only for a second, because then she smiled at me. "Let's be friends," she said.

She grabbed a cigarette from her purse and lit it by striking a match with her thumbnail. She allowed the smoke to rise from her open mouth and fold into her nostrils, inhaling through her nose. "These Israeli cigarettes suck. What does Fadi smoke?"

"Marlboro," I instantly replied.

"Good. I like Marlboro. Does he drink alcohol? I do. I drink at the Highball in Bethlehem. Have you been there? Of course not, you're too young."

"What's high ball?"

"It's English," she said. "What kind of cologne does he wear?"

"I don't know."

"Paco Rabanne? Aramis? British Sterling?"

"I don't know."

"But something?"

"Yeah, sure."

"Good. I like a man who cares about himself."

But I was still thinking about the Marlboros. I had no idea what Fadi smoked. I couldn't remember if he smoked at all. I supposed he did. Of course he did. I was the one who didn't smoke. Too young, Fadi told me, you'll look stupid with a cigarette in your mouth. I wasn't happy that I lied about the Marlboros; this after all was going to be Fadi's wife; but when I thought about it, I couldn't be 100 percent sure I was lying. Maybe he did smoke Marlboro. Or maybe it was Time or Golf, I had no idea. Certainly he'd smoked Marlboro sometime or other.

"So?" she was saying.

"So what?"

"Does he really have many girlfriends?"

There was a fig tree in the yard and it was heavy with fruit. Already the ground beneath it was purple with seed and skin. When she spoke I found myself looking at it.

"Well, that's all right if he did. In fact, I prefer it. If girls like him, that's good." She took another drag on her cigarette and held it out to me. "Want some?" She waved her hand up and down impatiently. "Well?"

Without another word, she pressed her face to mine, closer than any girl ever did before, and blew smoke directly into my mouth.

"Bitch!" I screamed.

She burst into laughter. When I started coughing, she laughed even harder.

Without thinking, I brought my finger to my mouth to curse her. But she drew near again, the cigarette now tossed somewhere out of sight, burning itself out among the ants and beetles in the dust of the yard, and my lips suddenly froze. Inside the house, her fate was being sealed by the Great Man (who of course was just her father) and my uncle Bahir, who controlled the life of Fadi; money would pass hands, property, Fadi would then be brought into the business. I was only twelve, but at that moment I seemed to sense the misery of this beautiful woman in blue jeans whose body sang a song I had never before heard, a song whose words I longed to understand.

"Sorry," she said. "It was just a joke. You don't have to smoke cigarettes."

She bent forward and kissed me on the corner of my neck, as one might on the Hajj, chastely, even though her hair brushed across my cheek, and her arm, which was bare below the elbow, skimmed across my bicep as a pebble skims across the tips of the waves, and I looked for the first time into her eyes. They were glowing large as pumpkins, amber flecked with leafy green, shimmering, honeyed, hardened, and the wide, black pupils were like tunnels.

It was in that moment that I cursed their marriage.

Yet it was not from hate that I cursed her but from a surfeit of love, as the Prophet, may peace and blessings be upon Him, says, when a man loves his brother he should tell him he loves him, and if one of you sees something bad, you should change it with your own hand, and if you are not capable of changing it with your hand, then with your tongue. And I see the girl in her Levi's jeans and her Coca-Cola shirt and her amber eyes—the amber eyes that cannot hear the curse that had been lain upon them.

And now floating here in the night sky above the Garden of the Rising Sun in which the young Dasha Cohen lies dormant as desert lupine before the rains, what comes to me is a name. Nadirah. Most precious, most rare. Nadirah. May Allah be pleased with her!

Dear You,

I broke down and called Lonya. He's so lame he didn't even ask me why I wasn't in school, but I knew he wouldn't. He has no idea what year it is, let alone what day of the week it is. I didn't tell him about Pop disappearing either, I just said I wondered if I could come over because I had a question for him. He said, Why don't you just ask the question, and I said, Because, and he said, Because why, and I said, *Because,* and finally he said, OK, let's meet for coffee, and I said, Café Milano, because that's my favorite, and he said, When, and I said, Now, and he said, Is it really that important, and I said, Yes it is, and he whined and then agreed, OK in an hour.

So I'm sitting now in Café Milano, having a choco-latte and shakshuka with three eggs and also a brioche, and I'm sitting outside, and when I'm not writing this I'm just looking at people, and at this time of day there is every kind of person passing by, there are kids, there are hot guys, like in their twenties, and lots of women, some of them dressed cool and some are so not, mostly going shopping, and there are old kibbutzniks—I think you can always tell them, and it's not just how they dress, but how they always look a little lost, like *what happened?*—and there are a lot of people who work in offices and tons of Russians, they're like every third person. It's almost embarrassing.

But really, it's most excellent to sit here when everyone else is in school. And now I see, here comes Lonya, you can spot him a mile away—he's the one with the T-shirt that always says something like HELLO, I'M AWESOME or YES, I'M A MALE MODEL, or it has a photo of Marilyn Monroe's cleavage made to look like it's his, and of course the glass eye (unless he's wearing his patch, because he likes to lift it up and gross everyone out with the hole).

So here's what happened, which I am recording exactly as it happened. He came over, kissed me, sat down, ordered his coffee and toast, and said,

"OK. What?"

"I have a question," I replied.

"I know that. What?"

"Well, more than one question."

"Fine. What?"

"It's more like a discussion."

"Anka, please."

"OK, OK. It's just that—"

"What?"

"It's delicate."

"What, already?"

"My mother."

"Ah."

Silence.

"Suddenly you want to know something?" he said.

"Maybe."

"Well then, I suggest you ask your father."

"He won't talk about her."

"No, *you* won't talk about her."

"He, too. He doesn't talk about anything, actually."

"You have a point. But, even so, this is his territory."

"Uncle Lonya, I need to know some things."

"Since when is it 'uncle'?" His coffee came and then the toast. He spread so much butter on it, there was more butter than toast. "Look," he said, "why don't we call him, and he can come down and join us. I'll help you ask whatever you want. You know, he a buffer."

"He's off working," I said. "And he's never going to answer me anyway."

"Working? Really? That's wonderful. I'm glad to hear it." He pretended to spit into the palms of his hands and rub them together. He does this whenever anyone says something hopeful. To ward off the demons, I think.

"But I need to know about her now," I said.

"Why suddenly?"

I think he could see I was too agitated. He put his hand on my shoulder.

"OK," he said. "OK. I can tell you this, sweetheart. Your mother was a brave, brave woman, and she was a hero of the Jewish movement in Soviet Days, right up there with Sharansky."

But I'd heard that a million times! And before I could stop myself, I screamed at him, "If she was such a big hero, why did she give me away?"

"She didn't *give* you away."

"Yes, she did."

"Only in a certain sense."

"Yeah. In the sense that she gave me away."

"Don't be so hard on her. When you're older you'll understand these things."

"I am older."

"Look, she took the whole world on her shoulders. She sacrificed for all of us. That's the way it was, you had to either make a stand or—"

"Or what? What about you?"

"Me? I'm a bum."

"What about Abba? Was he a bum?"

"Your father was not a bum. How can you say such a thing? Look what he's done for you! Jesus, Anyusha, you have no idea—you're exactly like her! Impossible! An impossible person. Who can reason with you? It's like talking to a hole in the ground."

"I just want to know, that's all!"

"Then you'll just have to talk to your father!"

I wanted to say to him, how can I talk to my father? I don't even know where he is! But I kept my trap shut, and he stood up, put some money on the table, enough for my breakfast, too, bent down and kissed me, and walked away.

Just like my mother? Please!

How can I be just like my mother? I never even met my mother. My mother is a bitch and an egotist and what did she ever do but make people unhappy?

Of course grown-ups say things like that to kids just to get them to think about things differently. I know that trick. Pop does it all the time, and I do that to him, too, only he is unaware of it. But there was a reason I wanted to know about her, and it had to do with everything that had happened up till then, which I still haven't written about because, well, I doubt if I'm supposed to, and also it's very long and complicated. But I guess if I'm going to have this journal or diary or whatever it is, I have an obligation to tell everything. So here goes.

It began back there with Rabbi Keren and Yohanan and all that. And then Rabbi introduced me to Shlomo and Shlomo introduced me to Miriam, because it was Miriam who said to me, Come with me and let me show you.

You have to just know Miriam! I can't decide how old she is—but old. Probably thirty or twenty-five, and very pretty if you ask me, even with the scarf on, but she wears it in that way they do when they still show their hair, you know, kind of weaving her long ponytail through the scarf so it becomes almost a living thing, so elegant. And she always puts her arms around me, and she always laughs when I say something funny, because she gets me, and almost nobody else in the whole world does, and she smells like gardenias. Anyway, I was telling her, or I was *trying* to tell her, about my doubt, and she said, Come and let me show you.

When I think back, I can't remember exactly how it started. Suddenly I was just reading all this new stuff. It's not like I didn't know all the stories in the Bible, because everyone knows all the stories, but I felt I couldn't analyze, say, that crazy Ezekiel if I didn't go back and reread Genesis first, and then I just kept reading, because before I knew it I had gone through Leviticus and Numbers and then Deuteronomy, and I thought, this stuff is just totally stupid, but it's so *beautiful*. How can something be stupid and beautiful at the same time? I didn't really believe one single word of it, and the more I read the less I believed. But the more I read, the more I couldn't stop reading. Even all the gross stuff in Leviticus—you know, like what happens if you have pus coming out of your skin or how you have to burn the entrails with all the fat on it. It was disgusting, but it was also *terminal*. However, it didn't take away any of my doubt. In fact, it made it worse. And that's when I understood that doubt was my problem. That doubt was my weakness. That I'd never become anything in this world or in any other world if I didn't overcome it. You have to overcome your weaknesses, or what are you?

For instance, I am thinking right now about Kishuko So, also known as Tamahome, which means the fighter (let me tell you about this and then I'll get back to the whole Miriam thing). Tamahome is very powerful because he knows martial arts and he wears the symbol of the demon on his forehead. His mother died when he was twelve, which is just a year younger than me, and his father recently became ill, I guess just like mine. But in the Universe of the Four Gods, he has a purpose—to protect Suzako-no Miko, who of course in real life is Miaka. He also has a weakness. He loves money. This is probably because his family is so poor, so he steals money to feed his brothers and sisters. Of course, it leads him down very bad paths. His love for Miaka helps him overcome his weakness. He becomes a hero even in the real world.

Well, as I said, my weakness is *doubt*. I don't believe what anyone tells me. I don't believe my teachers. I don't believe the older kids. I don't believe adults like Daphne. I don't even believe Rabbi Keren. I suppose that means I don't believe God. Why should God tell me the truth? We're just like weeds on this planet, overrunning everything. You don't tell the truth to a weed. You pull it out. You spray weed killer on it and watch it die.

In the old days, I would say, so what? Just figure it out for yourself, you don't have to believe anyone. But that was before. Before I met Miriam and before I really got to know Yohanan. Now I see that the whole thing was put in front of me so that I could overcome this weakness, so that I could challenge myself like Tamahome with his love for Miaka. Even the thing with Pop. I was checking out the Bible etc. way before he was blown up by that suicide bomber, and when it happened, I didn't say anything to him because why should I upset him? But it scared me, it upset me a lot, I saw how at any moment anything could happen and then what? I wanted to hold on to him, but Pop, you can't just hold on to him, he'll go like, come on, what's the matter with you? That's because he never wants to think anything *is* wrong. That's what I realized. It's like, hey Pop, you just got blown up! So I made a journal for him. I went to my favorite store, Rafi's, where they have art supplies and all kinds of pens and notebooks and rice paper and metallic papers where the whole sheet looks like gold and papers with leaves and flowers pressed into them. They even have real papyrus. It's kind of woven, like fabric, only finer, in a muted tone; I think they call it ecru. So I bought some papyrus, and I bought some felt for the cover and some twine and a heavy needle and some glue—altogether it was kind of expensive, forty-five shekels—but I didn't mind spending it because I thought Pop should write down what he was thinking and feeling, maybe describe what happened to him, maybe even second by second, maybe ponder the meaning of life. I don't know. But that's what I would do if I were he. So I constructed this beautiful writing book for my father, hand-sewn and glued with this special glue they have, and a beautiful felt cover, and I made the title page with watercolors and markers and colored pencils, and I entitled it:

My Thoughts on Coming Face-to-Face with Death
by Roman Guttman
Spring 1996

I decorated it with flowers, birds, animals, leaves, stars, hearts, and I can't remember what else. And in the corner, down on the right, I signed my name. I did the title page in Hebrew, but I did think maybe I should have written it in Russian, because I believe he uses Russian to think his most personal thoughts. Even though he talks Hebrew to me and to his friends, something tells me his heart is still Russian. If I had done it in Russian, it would have looked like this:

Мой Впечатления от Встречи Личом к Личу со Смертю
Роман Леополдович Гутман

I wrapped it with ribbon and put it where I knew he would *have* to find it. But I have a feeling he never did, because he never said anything to me, and my dad is a very attentive parent. For instance, he would always take me to the site he was working on, and I'd see it from beginning to end. I especially like going when there is nothing built yet, just land, lots of rock, usually, or sand, and then we can imagine it together, what it will look like. But also I like it when it's finished, because when a new house is all done, I'm the first person he lets inside. That's our tradition. He opens the door, and I walk in, and I can hear my shoes echoing on the floor, and then he comes in after me and says, Well, Anyusha? And I say, This is your best one! Because, guess what? It always is.

People think it sucks to have just a dad. But they're wrong. I think it's better. I lied to Lonya. Pop is always trying to get me to ask about my mom. But what for? I think it's his way of saying he's not good enough, like he isn't doing a good enough job. I know, if I told people he was gone all night and then didn't come home this morning and probably will be gone at least till tonight, they'd probably say he was a horrible miserable rotten father and they would take me to court and I'd have to live with Babushka and he'd go to jail or something. But I know he's just doing his thinking. That's what I would do, too. And anyway, it's good luck he chose today not to be home so there are no prying questions. But the fact that he didn't get my notebook means it will be much harder for him to work out his thoughts, because it is always so much easier when you write them in a book, as I am doing now. It would have been easier for you, Pop, if you had the notebook. That's all. My feelings aren't hurt, so don't worry about it.

Chapter Eleven

✡

IT WAS ALMOST THREE IN THE AFTERNOON, and the heat was unbearable. I'd been sitting on this little patch of desert for more than two and a half hours, getting up only to pee. How could that be? I never sat around doing nothing. Daphne, Lonya, Anyusha, were always telling me, slow down, take a break, you'll have a heart attack. Only my mother thought I was lazy—"Why do you waste your time making these fancy houses? Why don't you build something great, like the Jewish Taj Mahal or something? Something we can actually be proud of." But now time seemed to have crawled to a standstill, or maybe the opposite, it was flying by without my noticing, while I was stuck somewhere in my own past, eating the same meal over and over, dreaming the same dream, kissing the same kiss, and all that time my real body was quickly withering away under the sun.

I found myself softly humming a little tune, an old Russian tune, actually, "Vecherni Zvon." *Evening bells, evening bells / How many thoughts do they tell! / O youthful days where I used to roam, / Where I loved, my father's home. / And how I, leaving these familiar climes, / Heard the bells for one last time—ding dong ding dong!*

I sang to the bright sky as to a child, as I used to do to Anyusha, every night in fact; long after she had fallen asleep, I would steal into her room, lean over her bed, place my lips beside her ear, and—not sing, because I can't sing—but whisper my incantation, *Papa will always take care of you. Papa is your best friend. Papa will never leave you. Anyusha will never be alone again.* I guess I was making promises I had no way of keeping. Perhaps it was even dangerous to her psyche. But I believed with all my heart if she heard these words over and over, night after night, she would grow up secure and self-assured, in true possession of herself. What more could a father want for his daughter?

I placed my hand on my wounds. The explosion had happened weeks before, and by now I'd removed most of the bandages, but what was revealed felt alien under my fingers. I could not quite believe that this was my face, my skin. I thought of my friend Lonya who now calls himself Ari and who missed dying by only a few seconds because he always dawdles to check out the girls, and of all the echoes of that frightful blast that so quickly faded into the white noise of our troubled city. And to be honest, I did not know if I wanted to go out and kill something myself or endlessly talk it through as Dr. Sepha wanted me to or translate it into a bright new apartment building as my assistant, Amoz, suggested or simply forget about the whole thing and go sunbathing in Crete as Daphne wanted to do or somehow, as I wished with all my heart I could do for Anyusha's sake, transform it into some sort of act of love, whatever that might be.

Lost in these thoughts, I was awakened by the sound of . . . well, I couldn't tell—a bird, maybe, or the high-pitched buzzing of a bee. Looking toward the sound, I noticed a small bluff, just a big rock, really, about half a kilometer to the southwest. I didn't recall seeing it there earlier, so I thought I'd go over and investigate. I shouldn't have, of course. I should have been making my way back to my car—without being seen if at all possible—and getting myself home. Or hiking to the nearest checkpoint or even working up the courage to face Abdul-Latif with the truth, although why I would do that I could no longer fathom. But the sound called to me, and I stood up quite stiffly—I had been sitting for such a very long time—and made my way toward a bootless little wadi that meandered vaguely toward the bluff. It was among the longest days of the year, and at this hour the sun was directly above me, so I cast no shadow, almost as if I weren't there. If the sun cannot find you, if the earth does not recognize you, what have you become?

A phantom? Of course nothing else cast a shadow either, not the scrubby little bushes with their desiccated needles and dead buds, not the beetle I spotted scurrying along the baked mud, not the arid eddies of rock and moraine left behind by the wild, improbable torrents of winter. If I were to come upon a snake or a scorpion, I wouldn't see him until he struck, but I trampled over the rocks anyway. The bluff was only a short walk, but in this heat it seemed an endless march. Still, I turned aside to listen for the little song I'd been hearing. It seemed somehow familiar, heartening. I followed the wadi as it wound between two rock faces—an easy path up to the top of the bluff. But I noticed that as it rose the pathway began to narrow and finally peter out, and I would have to climb between two sheer walls for the last few meters to the top. Once in this crevice, I inched along, thrusting my arm upward for a handhold and squeezing my torso around the jutting shale and ragged pinions of stone. As I climbed, the cleft narrowed, and the two walls closed in upon me. The rock was cool and pleasant against my skin, but I knew if I climbed any farther I'd get stuck. I figured I'd just back down, but then my arm got jammed between two jagged extrusions. The more I twisted, the worse it got. I tried to move forward again, but now I couldn't do that either. So I hung there, pinned on four sides, no way forward, no way back, sun above, nothing at all below.

"Whores full of shit! Stinking cock!" I cried in Russian.

The sun burned down upon my skull—I had stupidly forgotten to take a hat—but in spite of the heat, I shivered: could this be my grave, hanging upright, my body pinned like a butterfly's, my head a mass of blistering pus? I mentally thumbed through my IDF training manual. Radio for help, select one of your platoon to go for help, go for help yourself, create a signal by the use of flags, fire, flashlight, make yourself known using coded whistles, animal sounds, or specific phrases prearranged with your commanders.

"Fucking commanders," I said. *"Pizda! Pizdyulina zloebuchaya!"*

Then I felt something sharp, like a stiletto boring into my head. And there was that buzz again, too. I could feel small bits of flesh shear off from my forehead, and the stinging burn of the dentist's drill. With a great heave, I managed to crane my neck upward. First the sun, utter white. And then something placed itself between the sun and my eyes. On the ledge just above me, preening its green and red feathers, was a tiny iridescent Palestinian sunbird. He picked some lice from under his wing. Then he turned his beak on me.

I'm so far from home, I thought.

Sometimes, I guess, but very rarely, sunbirds do live in acacia trees in the wilds of the Judean Desert, but usually you find them in parks getting drunk on wildflowers or hanging around garden fences in Jerusalem or Tel Aviv or having their fill of insects and nectar on their favorite kibbutz. But here he was, in the middle of summer, in the driest of months, in the heat of the day, in the hottest spot on the entire globe, pecking my forehead into Swiss cheese. He hadn't so much as a branch to hang upon, not a flower, not even a telephone wire. He stretched out his long, slender beak and jabbed at my head again.

I've always hated the Palestinian sunbird. In the wild, they like to suspend their nests from a sheltered branch or under the eaves of a barn, but in Israel, these birds are just happy to hang a nest from a lampshade, a houseplant, or the edge of a bookcase. In other words, they'd just as soon live in your house as theirs. Everybody here seems to love them. Except me. I can't stand the sunbird. Too glamorous. Too self-assured. You can sense its sangfroid in the way it plumps its feathers on your dining room table. And this in a bird the size of my fucking forefinger. But now, at least, I knew the source of that unpleasant sound. These little Palestinian sunbirds can't carry a tune. It's sad, but true.

Suddenly, the bird looked me straight in the eye, as if to say, What the fuck are you doing here? You expect me to help you? I admit I hang around with Jews, I'll even set up house with Jews, but that puts me under no obligation to help any of you bastards.

"Well, just don't start singing," I said.

He cocked his head and smiled. "What are *you*?" he said. "Frank

Sinatra? Hassan Ammar? Nancy Ajram?" He stuck his beak in my ear and opened his clacky little mouth. His song went through me like an ice pick.

"Get away from me!" I yelled up at him.

"Why should I? I live here. Where the hell do you live?"

"You don't live here. You live on some kibbutz, or you came from Bethlehem or someplace. Get out of here."

"Why? I was here first."

"No, I was here first."

"No, you got stuck here. But I was always here."

"Lie!" I said. "Lie!"

"True! True! Plus I could poke your eyes out if I felt like it."

"All I have to do is turn my head back down and not look at you."

"Then I'll poke at the top of your head. Make you bleed."

"You're a fucking insect eater. Go eat an insect. I'm a man. You can't eat me."

"I can try."

I thought about this a minute. "Okay," I told him, "here's the truth. You weren't here first. We were here first. You little Palestine birds are always so full of shit. You think I don't know ornithology? In 1900, maybe twenty of you in the whole goddamned country; now you're the most common little rat bird in Israel. No problem. Live and be well. Just stop singing the same old song."

"Let's face it," he squeaked, "you're not subtle enough to appreciate the song of the Palestine sunbird, never have been and never will be. And by the way, you were born in Moscow. So who's the latecomer?"

With this, he began chomping at my hairline in earnest.

"Stop! You son of a bitch! Stop!" I cried.

But he kept on pecking, harder and harder, deeper and deeper, like he was churning a corkscrew through my skull.

"God in heaven!" I screamed at him. "I don't want to die like this!"

And then all of a sudden I was grabbing at that little bastard with my fingers. I felt his gummy little feathers in my palm and then a crazy flurry of wings and his wildly thumping heart, and then . . .

"Hey, mister. What are you doing there? Let me help you."

I felt a hand upon my leg.

"You're stuck pretty good. I'll go around the other way to get to the top."

Blood trickled over my eyebrows and down onto my lip, and I couldn't move my head enough to see who it was. But a moment later I realized my hand was free.

"There, now pull up!"

I stretched my arm as far as I could in the direction of the sky, grabbed at the ledge above me, sucked in my torso, and, like a rat squeezing under a door, I pulled myself free. And there I was, standing atop the rock, with the whole desert spread before me all the way to the sea. And next to me was Abdul-Latif.

He squatted, like Arabs do, with his arms around his knees, and watched me. "I heard about the boys and I feared for you. Been looking for two hours at least. Here." He handed me an old soda bottle filled with water. "I am full of regret for them."

I watched him carefully. I did not trust his water and set it aside.

Meanwhile, the bird had taken up a station on the far edge of the bluff. I noticed there was a small stream percolating up at the base of the rock, which until now had been hidden from my view. It was really just a puddle beneath a swarm of bulrush, but for those few meters the soil was moist and dark, giving life to a garden of thick plants and bushes. Well, so much for the mystery of my sunbird. I gulped down the wild perfumes of the date and hollyhock but felt no need for the water. There was a rustle among the leaves, and suddenly, miraculously, a beautiful ibex emerged from the brush and gracefully bent to drink from the spring. A male, it had vast curved horns, a feathery black beard, and silver hooves.

Abdul-Latif did not move. The sunbird hopped over and sat beside me.

"Idyllic, isn't it?" he said.

"Shhh," I said to the bird, "you'll scare him away."

Now the ibex raised his head, sniffed the air, became still as the rock we were sitting upon, and searched the horizon with its soft brown eyes.

"It's a stupid weak animal," the bird said.

"No, it's beautiful," I replied.

He whistled.

The ibex bolted, charged from the water's edge, and dashed across the stand of date palms.

"I told you to be quiet!" I said.

"Not me," he replied, and pointed with his glassy wing.

Now I saw it. A small leopard had sprung from a furrow in the rock and leapt at the ibex, corralling him with his powerful legs into smaller and smaller circles—the ibex, its eyes melting with fear, darted back and forth as the trap closed upon him—but they were both so glorious, and I did not know whom to love better, whom to hope for, root for: the leopard, nearly extinct, with his snowy body and deadly eyes, desperate for anything to eat, or the ibex, with his startling grace and resplendent horns, not in the least rare, yet all the more fragile.

"To the death," the little bird said.

And then the ibex made a run for open desert, suddenly, crazily, brilliantly, but too late. The leopard had him in his teeth, and they went down together.

In despair, I said to the bird, "Why did he save me?"

"I don't know," replied the bird. "For the hell of it." He winked at me, rose into the air, hovered there a moment as sunbirds can do, purposely annoyed me with his miserable little song, and then flew off toward Ein Gedi like a stone flung from a sling. I followed him until he was well out of sight, which was less than a second, so swift was he, and so small.

"Mister! Mister! We have to get you home. You are talking crazy. You have to drink that water."

"I drank."

"No, mister. You haven't drunk anything. Drink!"

But I don't believe I drank the water, because the next thing I knew I was in a bed, and the smell of fried kibbe was in my nose.

Lying there, I recalled the sunbird's song. It occurred to me, maybe it hadn't been singing at all. Maybe it was just the ringing in my ears. It never stops. I just ignore it. I forget about it. But of course it's always there, and maybe it fooled me, because how could any of that have happened? I held my hands out in front of me. My skin was coated with what looked like white powder. I must have been in the sun even longer than I thought. This country was out to kill me one way or another.

In Moscow, my father had once told me the only safe place for Jews was the Land of Israel. Here they say: Go to America.

Oh, we all had the same ridiculous ideas. How surprised we were to come here and find that half of Israelis were from Iraq or Syria, the other half acting as though they were still living in a Polish village in the seventeenth century, and the third half considered us Russians too loud, too garish, too aggressive, and altogether too dishonest. There was no crime in Israel until the Russians! Maybe so. They say we brought the Mafia to Israel; well, in Moscow, everything was Mafia, from top to bottom. If you didn't game the system, you were an idiot. The truth is, it's not so different here. The worst sin in this country is to be called a sucker, and as always, you wish you were someone else living somewhere else.

But for me it was not like that. For me, it was like entering a magical kingdom and finding the mystical house of Baba Yaga in the middle of the dark forest where all my wishes were granted.

I arrived at Ben Gurion with Anyusha in my arms. She already had a cowl of shocking black hair and those daring blue eyes. On the flight she ate continually and never cried. But that was Anyusha. She took in everything with her eager eyes and apparently found it good. Only when we stepped from the plane onto the Jetway did the howling begin. Perhaps it was the sudden change in temperature—we were met with a blast of hot air—but I think more likely she was frightened by the soldier with the Uzi resting on his hip. The poor guy reached out to soothe her. "Shoo, shoo," he said. But I said to him, "Let her cry. It means she's finally alive." He didn't speak Russian, so I tried it in Hebrew, "She shalom!" He laughed and said something I didn't understand, either.

But I must say, not understanding and not being understood— for the first time, I loved the Russian language. I now spoke a language that carried with it no consequences. My words flew out into space and never came back. As for Hebrew, it made no impression on me at all. It bounced off my head as if it had been varnished with clear coat. I experienced a miraculous and unex- pected feeling of peace.

Of course, it didn't last. They sent us to an absorption cen- ter in Dimona. I was delighted to be there, even though the huge apartment complexes reminded me too much of home. The one difference was I could go outside and it was never cold. The air was remarkably clear, and when you took a deep breath, notwith- standing the fact that you were killing yourself with radiation from the nearby reactor, it seemed like you were taking in 100 per- cent oxygen with none of the pollutants, the fumes of sadness, regret, frustration. Maybe that's why I have always felt solace in the desert.

They provided child care for Anyusha, and I went to Ulpan, where I was quite literally bathed in the Hebrew language. I was astonished by what happened. Hebrew came to me as if I were merely excavating some forgotten stratum of my existence. Almost without trying, I was speaking, reading, writing. There emerged almost instantly a naturalness to my Hebrew that belied my ori- gins. The distinctive grammatical errors and mispronunciations of the Russian immigrant are largely invisible in my speech. It is not exactly native Hebrew the way sabras speak it, but someone once said to me it was like how Hebrew must have sounded three thousand years ago, in the time of David. I think she meant a bar- barous Hebrew, a violent and poetic Hebrew, a literary Hebrew that refuses to look over its own shoulder or search for new words, a Hebrew without history. As you can imagine, my teachers mar- veled at my progress. I went straight to the head of the class.

The next obstacle was the army. In those days, a person of my age—I was only twenty-six—would normally be inducted rather quickly, become assimilated, master the nuances of slang and the general military culture that permeates the social fabric of Israel. Of course, I wanted to get my architect's license, but I wanted to be in the military even more, which strikes me as odd, since I'd spent so much time and trouble getting out of the Soviet draft. But with Anyusha, how could I? There was no wife, no sister, no cousin, no aunt, no grandmother to care for her. Plus she had been crying more or less continually since our arrival. I began to think the place was disagreeable to her. On top of this, I didn't know what to do with her, how to feel about her. She was just a baby, I hardly knew her. Then, miraculously, my mother was given her visa, and, two months later, I left Anyusha in her care and went off to basic training. I knew these months in the army would be the best, the most precious I would ever have in my life. And I must say, I was deliriously happy.

But now all these years later, as I studied the dead skin on my arms with a decidedly benign detachment, it was clear to me that that happiness had been an illusion. It was not without a jolt of nausea that I realized that whispered Arabic was seeping through the walls. I could not understand what they were saying any more than I understood the head hovering in my demented sky or the soldier greeting us in the Jetway, but I had the feeling they were not talking about my health.

I now took a moment to look around the room. On the walls, a few photos, a rug, some prints of sayings, I guessed, from the Koran. I grimaced when I saw the photographs and thought back to the head. I hadn't seen it since I'd left Ganei Z'rikha, but right now I really wanted to talk to him. I wanted to tell him to go fuck himself for what he did. I wanted to ask him if he was satisfied with himself, flying around with no body all over Israel. But we never did seem to connect. The asshole.

And here I was in his bed.

Chapter Twelve

Dear You,

I never finished telling about Miriam. That's because I had to go. I have to meet Yohanan, and I'm waiting for him right now at the bus stop.

But I think before I go any further with all this telling of everything, I absolutely *must* describe myself on this day, everything about me. OK. My hair, as everyone knows, looks exactly like Billy Idol's, only it's black, and I don't put anything in it, no goo or spray or any of that crap. I would describe my hair as a mop with a few sharpened points, like tongues of fire. Frequently, almost always, I have magenta streaks in it, ergo the fire, but today I rinsed it out because I wanted the world to see my hair in its pure state, what I would call my hair as a thing in itself. I used to have long, beautiful princess hair, and Babushka literally cried like a baby when I cut it; well, actually she cried *before* I cut it, and pleaded, yelled, offered me some of her famous "smile cake," threatened to shoot herself, all the classic Babushka tricks, but I was determined 100%, and when I make up my mind—SNIP!—short hair. Pop didn't say anything. He just shook his head and said, "It starts." Very annoying. But where was I? Yes, no magenta today. Now my hair is pure, absolute, and cosmically black, absorbing the entire spectrum of sunlight into its huge and terrifying blackness, a black hole in the middle of Ha'atzmayut Street, get out of its path, that's my hair. My skin, however, is (as always) very, very white, also unlike every other Israeli I know. I like it white. If it wasn't so white naturally, I'd put talcum on just to make it white. But all I have to do is use

Lady Lot SPF 40 sunscreen on every single inch of me, even on the parts that never show, because you never know when you will have to take off some piece of clothing that you never took off before, and though this has yet to happen to me, it could, it could maybe happen today. That could be quite a spectacular thing. Naturally, I did put on a little lipstick and eyeliner. I use Jade. I like the candy gloss for the lips, and the deep black eyeliner. Also today, blue iris eye shadow. As for clothes, I'm wearing my thigh-length black skirt over my pink-striped three-quarter leggings. I have on my red high-top sneakers and black-and-white polka-dot socks. You can only see about five centimeters of skin on my leg, but they are an amazing and mind-boggling five centimeters. I am also wearing a sleeveless black camisole that has a row of lace running along the top that I got on Neve Tzedek when Pop took me to Tel Aviv. I have on three bracelets, one yellow, one pink, and one the color of tropical seas. I have my three rings on my fingers, and just my black dot earrings, because today is not a day for dangles.

That's it. That is me today.

Why do I tell you my brand of lipstick and where I bought my camisole? Because every detail of today is of utmost importance. And now is the time for me to tell it all, everything, all my secrets. Of course, God probably knows how I am dressed today, but my father doesn't. Perhaps my mother knows, but I guess I don't believe that. Maybe God doesn't know either. Why should he? This is not his world, that's for sure. But I do hope someday my father will read this. I hope when he does, he will be able to see me exactly, precisely, as I am today, because when this day is over, the person who I am right now will be gone forever. You may think that is just a truism. But I hope he will read this and say Anna's outfit really kicked! Anna's eyeliner was absolutely fabulous! Anna's lips were glowing and shimmery with the perfect color. I hope he will see me just as I am and think, Anna was beautiful today. That's all I want.

So, Miriam.

First of all, it was really Yohanan who started teaching me all this stuff. He knows an amazing amount. He can read Talmud in

Aramaic, and he studies midrash. But after a while he said to me,
I can't teach you anymore. You're too smart for me. That's when I
started going to see Rabbi Keren. I think this was about a year ago.

You think girls don't study, but the modern Orthodox are
not Haredi, and you'd be surprised how many girls study. Usually they have a woman teacher, but not me! But I didn't want
to be in a class, so for a long time it was just Rabbi and me, or
just Rabbi, me, and Yohanan, because I felt better when Yohanan
was there, and Rabbi didn't care. If I said something stupid and
Rabbi's eyes went blank, Yohanan would say, "I think what Anna
meant was . . ." Some people wouldn't like that, but I did, even
when it wasn't exactly what I meant. Yohanan always said I would
outgrow him because I'm smarter than he is, but that's ridiculous.

So I started studying. You can always tell when you're special, and I could see I was special to Rabbi Keren. It wasn't like
school—I always wanted to go and I rushed there after class. But
Shabbat was my big problem. Women don't have to go to shul,
but I loved being there, and Pop would have killed me, but sometimes when he decided to go to work I did go. And also on Shabbat
night I could say I was going over to one of my friends, and then
I could stop by and do Havdalah with Yohanan's family. But then
after the bombing, Rabbi Keren introduced us to Shlomo, and as I
said, Shlomo introduced us to Miriam. And right away, you know,
I liked her.

It was when Shlomo explained about Kach and the martyred
Rabbi Kahane and the twentieth mitzvah and the Institute for
Redemption.

Now don't go saying, oh my God, *Kach!* Right-wing crazies
and all that. First of all, it's not true. They're not terrible people
at all. After all, a person has to defend himself (or herself in my
case). A whole people has a right to exist and to defend their right
to exist and to exist in their true homeland, even if you don't necessarily completely believe that God gave it to you. Still, it's been
your home for like four thousand years, way before anyone else
who's around today. Because let me give you the idea, OK? The
whole history of Jews is weakness. Being pushed around. Being

everybody's slave. You know the song—Calves are easily bound and slaughtered never knowing the reason why. That was about us. Israelis are different, for sure. But what do we do? When we finally win the Six-Day War and we finally get back Jerusalem, what do we do? We give the Temple right back to the Arabs. They don't even let us go there to pray. We want to do a little archaeology to find the remains of the Temple, they riot. They store weapons there, too. And they destroy all the evidence down in the tunnels and the cisterns where you can see the remains of the real Temple. Is that fair? Why don't we do something about that? And when Jews want to bomb someone, our police stop them. But when they want to bomb us, their police help them. They have so many children, just more and more and they all want to move back here and push us into the sea. Why should we let them? Why shouldn't we be able to pray at the Temple Mount? Why should we be so afraid of them? That's more or less how they explained it to us.

But I couldn't help myself. I raised my hand (even though it was just the four of us) and said, You want to rebuild the Temple and have animal sacrifices? With, like, the blood and all? I tried to explain to them that, based on what I read in the Bible and what little I knew of Talmud, God probably has moved on from that. For instance, I said, when Abraham went to sacrifice Isaac, God was saying, "Don't need no more human sacrifice! Not my thing anymore." And it also seemed to me that if God destroyed the Temple (because he *is* in charge of history, after all), then he's probably saying, "That's it for me with the animals! Let's sing some songs, read some prayers, and eat bagels." Because if God wanted animal sacrifice, we'd still have a Temple—*obviously!*

You could see Shlomo was very upset and about to say something terrible, when Miriam stopped him with a little wave of her hand. Actually, she couldn't stop laughing, and she said to me, Anna, come with me, and let me show you.

The first thing we did was go for coffee—well, she had coffee. I had a Coke. That's when she told me she liked my brain.

"You're always thinking," she said. "God wants us to think."

"I guess," I said.

"But he also wants us to see."

"See what?"

"That's what I'm going to show you."

After the Coke we went outside for a walk. We were walking very close to each other, and I didn't mind, and I also didn't mind the way she looked, with the long skirt and the long-sleeved blouse, because it was actually a pretty blouse and because, I don't know.

Then she asked me, Why do you think your father got bombed? I told her I didn't know. Think about it, she said. Why did he lose everything he worked for? Why do you think he hit that guy on the street?

I said, "What guy on the street?"

She kept saying, "Don't you think there's a reason?"

"Well, I guess they hate us," I said.

"Of course," she said, "but why you?"

"Me?"

"Exactly," she said. "You."

"It wasn't me. It was my father."

"It's funny with fathers," she said. "My own father didn't understand me when I became religious."

"Really?"

"Yeah, he went crazy. He even cried. He thought this was the end of everything. That he'd lost me forever."

"Did he?"

"Of course not. Yes, he has to become kosher for me to go to the house, and he has to observe Shabbat and some other things—then we can definitely be together again. But, no, it's not that he lost me. It's that *he's* lost. Know what I mean?"

"Yes," I said.

"But no matter what, Anna, when they strike the father, don't you think they are also striking the daughter?"

That felt like the truth to me. And I told her so. And then she took hold of my hands and said, "Everything has a divine purpose, doesn't it Anna?"

I had to be honest with her. I said I didn't know. That was my problem.

"Yes, tell me exactly what your problem is," she said.

"I don't know if I believe things have a purpose," I told her. "I just know they exist."

"But you don't have to believe," she said. "You just have to act. There is this old Jewish expression, *Do first, believe later.* You don't have to believe anything. You just have to *do*. When the Torah was given on Mount Sinai and Moses presented it to Israel, they replied in one voice, 'We shall do and we shall hear.' You don't have to hear anything, you just have to do."

I wanted to tell her, But I do hear. That's my other problem. I hear everything.

She said it's from Exodus. And then she explained what Sfat Emet says about it, which is that the commands that were already revealed, we promised to do, but that which isn't yet revealed we promise to be *ready* to hear.

"And how do we become ready to hear?" she asked me.

"By doing?"

"Yes!" she laughed. "When you fulfill the commandments, any commandments, you will automatically be ready to hear. It's easy."

"And then you believe?" I asked her.

Now she stopped laughing and leaned in very close and whispered into my ear. "God will be present through your *actions*," she said. "That's all you need to know." Then she ran her fingers through my hair and said, "I love your hair!"

"I cut it myself," I told her.

"Wow," she said.

We walked a little more, and I asked her, "Is that what you wanted to show me?"

"No," she said. "We're not there yet."

"Where are we going?" I asked.

"A long way, sweetie," she answered. "We've only just gotten started."

And that's when I really started on my journey. Only it's not a journey at all, because actually you are standing still, and everything else is traveling toward you. People don't think about this, but when you are reading, the words are coming at you at the speed of light. When you are learning and changing, it feels like you are moving, but you're not. This is Einstein's Theory of Relativity.

～～～～～～～～

I had just finished writing down those thoughts when Yohanan appeared at the corner schlepping his huge briefcase full of Talmuds and whatnot, and even though he was still a block away I could see he was sweating because there were these big wet stains under his arms, which were sticking out of his short sleeves like two uncooked kolbasi, pale and mushy, and of course the big glasses and everything. I guess that's why I love Yohanan. He has no sense of style.

A second later he was at the bus stop, throwing down his briefcase and plopping himself onto the bench next to me. Hot! he said. Beautiful, I replied, because everything really was beautiful at that moment. He said he needed a drink, that's why he was late. He repeated for the fifteen thousandth time how much he likes Prigat mandarin. But they didn't have it! he complained. So I had to get lemon. And I'm thinking to myself, why is life so mundane that even at the very, very most important moments, such as this exactly is, or could be anyway, all people can think about is juice. I really didn't care that he was late, but I said, I've been waiting half an hour and look at the time. He said to calm down, Shlomo had already called him, and we didn't have to be anywhere for another hour and a half at least, and it only takes forty-five minutes. You're always so antsy, he said, plus I'm only fifteen minutes late. Whatever, I said. And he opened his carton of juice and started sucking away. It's not even juice anyway. I don't think there's any real fruit in it. So why do they call it juice? I get all fidgety, I said. Just *try*, he said. And I said, You shouldn't drink that Prigat stuff because it's filled with deadly chemicals. It's *juice*, he said. It's the slurp of death, I said. Why do you have to be so nervous all the time? he said. I was not nervous, I want to make that perfectly clear, only a little excited, but now the next bus seemed to take forever to come, and I guess I was pacing or yammering or something, because all of a sudden Yohanan took my hand. I was like—what? I turned to him, but he wasn't even looking at me. He just stood there, rocking back and forth on his heels like he always does. But the feel of his hand on mine was, I don't know, I don't know. It was soft. I mean, yes, his skin was soft, because he's a little pudgy, but that's not what I mean when I say it was soft. I can't say what I mean. I don't know how to describe what I mean, which is completely odd for me because I can describe anything. As soon as he took my hand, everything got quiet. The voices of the trees and the insects and the cars and the people in them and the buildings and the pavement and the bullets wanting to be loaded into the gun that soldier standing near us was carrying on his shoulder and all the conversations going on in his head and in the heads of all the people at the bus stop, all of the stuff I was hearing that always makes me so crazy, that makes me want to shout at everyone, that lots of times makes me want to cry, it was gone. It was like coming up from underwater when you're holding your breath and you don't think you're going to make it, but you do, you get to the end of the pool and you burst through the water. I looked down at our hands. Mine seemed to have disappeared into Yohanan's, because my hand is so tiny and his is so big. He was still craning his neck, watching for the bus. Finally he looked at me. He said, There it is! I was confused. I wanted to say, Yeah, here it is, but I didn't know what *it* was. And then I realized, the bus. The doors opened and he stepped up and he pulled me along with him. He said, Show him your pass, and then I didn't know what to do, because if I went to get my pass I'd have to let go of his hand.

"Jerusalem," he said, and the driver waved us on.

When we got to the central station in Jerusalem, we had to take another bus to the neighborhood called Geula and then find this little street near Eliezar and Auerbach. It's so small it doesn't even have a name, but Shlomo told us we would see a sign for the Source of Righteousness Yeshiva in the Name of the Saintly Rebbe of Amdur of Blessed Memory and then another sign that says

DANGER, HIGH VOLTAGE, and then there would be a gate painted dark green where we should turn and then pass a flowering bougainvillea that hangs, as he said, like a waterfall of crimson, and at the garbage can turn onto the path that leads into the courtyard and then look for the stairs that go down, down, down, well, not that far down, to a cellar door, don't bother knocking, just come in, sit, wait, don't forget to drink water. He naturally reminded us to say our prayers when we got on the bus, say our prayers when we arrived safely, and maybe bring a deck of cards.

Me

This is my life, it's so weird. You would not believe it if I weren't telling you, would you?

Right now, where I am writing these things in my journal, I've never been here before and I guess I'll never be here again. It's kind of creepy, it's very creepy actually, and I don't like it and I am very anxious to get out of here, yet at the same time I don't want to leave. But I don't want to tell yet about that, because I've decided to try to tell things in order.

Chapter Thirteen

☪

DASHA'S TOES MOVE FROM TIME TO TIME, so slightly it is not possible for anyone to see. But I can see. Her breath rises from her lips in a rosy light, illuminating the melancholy room with a hint of the life that throbs within her.

In my village there was a secret place. At first it was Fadi's brother Halim's, but then it was Fadi's, and then he shared it with me. Nadirah never came there. Now that she was married to Fadi, she was supposed to be like a sister to me. But she was not like other women. Even though her father was so strict he might as well have been a mullah, when she and Fadi ate with her parents, she insisted on sitting with the men. Her father indulged her in this, as in everything. But the secret place was secret even from her.

What was that place to which she could not go? Just an old chicken coop no one used anymore. Halim had taken it over and set it up between some trees and covered it with branches and dried leaves, old cardboard and tires so that it looked like a pile of junk. But if you knew where the door was, you could enter the jeweled world. In its small space with the light of the kerosene lamp, magic. Over the years they had hung many things upon the two strings that stretched from corner to corner, crisscrossing in the middle. Photographs, bent spoons, shiny rocks, bits of writing, pieces of beaded cloth, a pair of broken eyeglasses. In the glow of the lamps they sparkled. If you brushed them with your hand, they sang like camel bells.

"Come on," he said to me, "let's go to the Glass Palace."

"Now? I have to work. Ab will be angry."

He took my hand, pulling me along. "More important," he said.

"We're rebuilding some guy's engine."

"How many times can you rebuild an engine?"

"A thousand times, obviously," I said.

By now we were already passing Abdul-Rahim's house and the new block of apartments, and soon we were passing Mahmood's falafel stand—Fadi always walked fast, and he dragged me along like a kite he was trying to get airborne. We passed the empty lot with the boys from Jabal playing football and screaming curses at one another and then the abandoned post office, all broken down, and the ruins of the old Jordanian army post. Hens were roosting there. You could smell them all the way to Bethlehem. Here the village thinned out, and only a few houses, separated by scruffy yards, stood between us and the fields. But this was precisely where we suddenly disappeared into a small grove of eucalyptus. This was where our secret place was hidden.

Fadi, as always, looked both ways to make sure no one was watching. Then he pushed his way through the rubble and found the latch of the door that was painted in camouflage like an Israeli soldier. He cracked it open a few centimeters, pushed me through, and followed me inside, letting the door smack shut behind us. When the door closed on its springs, it made us feel secure, like two foxes in their burrow.

Usually when we were in the Glass Palace, Fadi brought something to eat, a pastry, some fruit, sometimes a chocolate bar; or I might bring something my mother had baked or perhaps some cashews or olives that I kept in a jar just for this purpose. For a while we even had a little stove, and using dried twigs or little pieces of coal, we would cook khubz or pitas and melt labneh on them, but the smoke drew the attention of old abu-Kaseem who lived in the shack just beyond the trees and still herded goats with his son and grandson, and he started beating our roof with a carpet not knowing we had a house under there, so we had to dowse the stove and capture the smoke in my hat, and then old abu-Kaseem was happy because he thought he had put out a fire. But my hat was ruined forever, and that's how it ended up cut into pieces and hanging on the string with everything else. But on this day, Fadi had brought nothing to eat, even though it had been a long day at school. Fadi didn't go to school anymore, so he didn't seem to remember what hunger was. He was supposed to be working in the import business with Nadirah's father, but he hardly ever did that either.

Instead of food, he handed me a cigarette. In fact, he gave me the whole pack. "Here, take this shit. I don't want their goddamned Israeli cigarettes anymore."

"Why not?"

"Where are your eyes? How long can we go on this way? How long can we put up with this shit? First they take our land, then they take all we have left, rule us like we were nothing but donkeys. As if we were pigs. They're the pigs, not us!"

"I hate them, too," I said.

"No, you don't. But you should. And you think anyone cares about us? You think abu-Amar cares about us?"

"He does, too." I saw in my mind his posters: ARAFAT! LEADER! ONE PEOPLE! ONE LAND! They popped up everywhere and just as quickly were torn down by the soldiers. "Who else cares for us?"

"All right, he does, but what good is it doing? What has he done? Where is he? Tunis? Algeria? I don't know. Who knows? Who cares? Look at reality, Amir. What are we, huddled here in this garbage pile like two rats!"

"But we love this place."

"We do, we do. But I'm too old for it anymore, Amir."

My eyes filled with tears.

"Amir, listen to me. We have to stop all this crying. We have to stop being little boys. You see what they did in Lebanon, don't you? You've heard of the massacres there, haven't you? You see them in our streets, don't you? Look up on the hill, just above us. Nobody ever was on that hill! What kind of place is that hill? And there they are. They build their big houses with their red roofs and their pretty gardens and all around their village they cultivate their fields, or they have their little factories. Do we have money to build houses? Do we have water to cultivate new fields? Where are our factories? Didn't you hear how they murdered little Fatma Sahour? Just walking to school! Just like you! Walking, walking, walking, boom! That's all. Who is to pay for that? Who is to help little Fatma Sahour? Amir, we used to sit up on that hill. Remember the time with the cucumber and the falcon? Come on, come with me."

He took me by the arm and urged me toward the door.

"But we just got here. And anyway, I have to work in the garage today."

"Work in the garage? Work in the garage? What a baby you are! Come on, Amir. I'm telling you the truth here. There is a mufti I want you to hear. He speaks the truth. It comes out of his mouth like nothing you have ever heard. Never has to pause, never has to think about the next sentence, because he knows what he is saying. He teaches the true meaning of Islam. Let's go. You'll learn something."

He thrust open the door. The light behind him was so bright I could no longer see his face.

"Come learn something," he said.

But in the shadow where Fadi's face should have been, I saw my father's twisted features.

As if he were reading my mind, Fadi lowered his voice and drew me closer to him. "At some point he'll stop hitting you, Amir. They all do. No one hits me anymore. The same will happen to you. Don't worry about it. Trust me."

"But in the meantime, he's still hitting me."

"It's time to stop thinking about your father and think about your people."

But it was not easy to stop thinking about my father. The hand going to the strap, and the veins in his forehead swelling with anger, the bitter grunts as he let forth the blows. As for the people, all that came to mind was the gang of kids I hung around with and the old men loitering wherever there was the slightest space for loitering and the women hovering around the market stalls arguing with the butcher.

"Fadi, I have to work," I said.

"So that's it?" he sighed. "That's all you have to say?"

He let his hand slip out of mine. With the door open behind him, his shape, which was really only a silhouette against the brightness of the sun, was suddenly gone. There came a brilliant, blinding moment and then the door swung shut on its spring and I was left alone in the darkness of the Glass Palace—only in my eyes everything went yellow, and I had to sit there quite a few minutes until I could see again.

Fadi had been trying to take me to these mullahs or Fatah or whatnot for ages now. He didn't get it. I wasn't interested. All I wanted was to go to school and have a business that was not a garage. Maybe write a book of stories, my own *Book of Tales*. The Israelis whom I knew were not so bad. Sure, the soldiers could be assholes, but the ones who came to the garage with their cars—what was so wrong with them, after all?

Finally I got up and went out. I actually had plenty of time before I had to be at the garage. I knew my village in every single one of its ins and outs, even as it had grown into a town spilling across the valley like a pool of milk toward Bethlehem, and I knew how to travel so as not to run into Fadi. I didn't know exactly where his mufti lectured, but I knew he wouldn't be in this direction, because it was probably in the camp or in the Dar al-Qur'an, and anyway, I was going along the eastern edge of town and I intended to keep to the alleys and the backs of houses. Of course people said hello to me, and I said hello back. Salaam! And to you, salaam! How are you? Thanks be to God! And you? Thanks be to God! Little Amir! Greetings to your father! And greetings to you, abu-Mahmed.

At last, I turned the corner and slipped into the yard and hid among the bushes near the windows, which had been opened to let in the afternoon breeze. She had turned up the radio and was sitting, drumming her fingers lazily on the table. She took a last drag on her cigarette and crushed it in the aluminum ashtray next to her Coca-Cola bottle. Immediately she lit another. Her hair was done up with a few pins, but everywhere skeins of it had slipped out, down the nape of her neck and along the front of her ears like the side curls of the Jewish boys. One feathery strand flopped in front of her nose, and she kept blowing it away with her lower lip. She sighed because there was no one to talk to. She was wearing a striped jersey, and it clung to her like honey clings to the lips. It had a scooped neck, which made her look like a swan. Even Nadirah would not dare wear this outside the house. She sighed again: the music was boring her. She blew away the wild hair with a puff of smoke, put the cigarette down, and rested her chin in her arms. I don't know if she was sad or just thinking of something, maybe she was thinking of Fadi, but suddenly she stood up, marched over to the radio, and fussed with the knob until she found something she liked. A slow song, in English or maybe Italian, I couldn't tell. Then she picked up her cigarette and put it in her mouth, and it just dangled there, the smoke rising toward her eyes, which she now closed, and then she began to sway, right and left, making lazy circles with her hips, like a hawk with nothing to do but hang all afternoon in the blue sky, her cigarette just dangling in her mouth, her hips just back and forth, her jersey just melting onto her body as she moved inside it, her eyes just closed and never opening, the smoke just rising, the music just singing, and the breeze just passing over my shoulders on its way into the house to cool her face and neck, and the smell of fried eggplant coming from somewhere across the yard.

By now my father would be looking at the clock on the wall above the rack of tires and guessing to himself whether I would be punctual or late as usual, and each time the minute hand dropped another notch, he would feel a slight tremor in his neck. If he was with a customer, he would be smiling and talking with good humor, because that's how you talk to customers, tell them whatever they want to hear, but even as he promised the carburetor could definitely be rebuilt in two days, with every intention that the carburetor indeed would be rebuilt in two days even though he had six other things to do first and he never fixed a carburetor in two days and never would, his eyes would dart, every few seconds, back to the clock, because what he was really thinking was how unreliable I was, and he would absorb into his bloodstream this insult to himself and to his fatherhood, where it would boil up like hot oil until the top of his head felt like it must explode; and there would be only one way he could think of to relieve this pressure, this insult. Already his hand would be shaking as it touched the buckle of his belt, even as he nodded to his customer and told him to come back in two days, it will be ready without fail. I knew all this, and yet I could not pull myself from Nadirah's window.

Why did Fadi leave her alone like this? Look at her—so vulnerable, so fragile. Women needed to be controlled, didn't they? My father had taught me this. You must discipline your wife, he had counseled me, you must keep her from the dark ways.

Nadirah changed the station yet again and now was listening to Egypt, to Ahmed Adaweya singing his sha'abi. She lazily opened her mouth, and his song came to me through her voice, dark, warm, thick with smoke:

> *My woman has lost her way, you good people.*
> *She is wearing a nylon blouse and a pleated skirt.*

As Nadirah sang, her voice grew bolder, her mouth wider, until at last she was dancing with happiness, her arms above her head, her eyes wide with some vision of herself dancing. She spun around, and I had to quickly duck under the windowsill.

And then, bent like a little old man, I ran out of the courtyard and all the way to my father's garage.

I hear Nadirah's song even now, and my heart breaks in my own throat. But when I open my eyes, it is still Dasha Cohen I see—and in my ears nothing but her tortured breath. Is this your song, Dasha Cohen? Is this your dancing? Around her bed are all kinds of shapes and chimeras, jinns and demons, strange sea creatures and spirits, dim and sickly, like blighted wheat. And the whole world seems to me cast in shades of ocher, as if I am looking through a window whose shade is drawn.

Chapter Fourteen

✡

"I want to get up, I want to go," I cried out, but perhaps I'd only exhaled, because I could not actually hear my own voice. I tried to sit up, but when I raised my head I was attacked by a terrible vertigo, and I collapsed back onto the bed. I heard scampering and realized that several young girls had been standing in a corner watching me, and now they ran out. Abdul-Latif came in and sat beside me.

"Are you comfortable?" he asked.

I nodded.

"We're not like Bedouins. We have real beds."

"Why . . . are you . . . helping me?" I asked in what voice I had.

When he made out my words, he laughed. "You're my only customer today."

"I . . . have . . . to go."

"I can barely hear you. I can't understand what you're saying. Don't move around so much."

"Let me call," I wheezed.

"We don't have a phone."

"Mobile phone? Do you know . . . anyone . . . mobile phone?"

"No." He stood up. "My friend, you will be well here, if only you drink some water. It was at least forty-five degrees out there. You did not drink then, and you do not drink now. I press water on you, and you spit it out. I made you drink a few drops when you were sleeping, but you need more, much more. What, do you want to die? Rest a few hours, then you will drink, and you will be on your way."

Did you call a doctor? I wanted to say.

"Rest, my friend. Rest."

Through the tiny window I could see only a bit of sky. Where the sunlight hit a table or a chair, or me for that matter, it cast long, moody shadows against the whitewashed walls of the small room. It seemed to me a kind of sign. With the passage of time, the shadows we carry take on a stronger reality, outlining us in the black chalk of our sins, until finally we and our shadows merge into a single, impenetrable, absolving mist.

And so, against the screen of my eyes, that sacred play, whose chorus was the Judean wind and the bleating muezzin, held me down upon that bed as if with pins of iron.

In that time, I came to Collette every day; if she was not yet at home, I waited for her outside her apartment. The neighbors came to know me, and though I suspected they pitied me, I didn't care. I would listen for the elevator, and each time it was called down, I was filled with hope. When finally she did arrive, she would say, "Oh, Roman, it's you. Have you been waiting?" I would answer, "No, not long." This is how it went for weeks on end.

Then, suddenly, an idea began percolating in me; one night, I lay awake in the apartment I shared with my mother on Tishinskaya, seeing shapes upon the ceiling while my mother snored away in the room she'd taken over after Katya left to live with her husband near Moscow University. It was the first time in her life that my mother had a room of her own.

So I began by thinking about mother and her bedroom. From this, I wandered back to the house on Veshnaya, where we moved when I was four and from which we were so painfully evicted. Why did I think of this? Because I had conceived the idea of building a house, a house for Collette—and myself, too, of course—and that led me to thinking about Uncle Max, who owned a dacha where I could build my new house, and thinking about Uncle Max led me to recall the sleeping arrangements at Veshnaya. Here's how it went: my parents slept in the living room, sharing it with Babushka and Dyedushka, giving Katya and me and my cousins Julia and Danka the one bedroom, and Uncle Maxim and Aunt Sophie the other. Why did Uncle Maxim and Aunt Sophie have their own room instead of my grandparents or my parents? Because it was Uncle Maxim's apartment. All of us were there because of him.

And why did he have this apartment? It was part of the family lore and its legacy of impossible accomplishments.

THE CHILD TAILOR OF PILNIK

My uncle Maxim was born in the town of Pilnik—well, who in their right mind would call it a town? It consisted of a small market square, a baker who mostly just rented his oven for the use of the village women, a shul, a threadbare Russian Orthodox church, a small Russian grammar school, an even-smaller Jewish school, a post office, a general store, a barbershop with a makeshift tavern in the back, a doctor who was also the veterinarian, and a tailor. Little Pilnik! Once upon a time, you would find it approximately one hundred kilometers southeast of Kharkov, in the part of Ukraine that, on maps, resembles the snout of a pig. It was nothing but a mud hole into which farmers dropped once a week to barter a few vegetables and sell their cheese and honey. Pilnik, however, did have one specialty: the traveling salesman, the wandering tinker, bookseller, ragman, haberdasher. From little Pilnik these pilgrims spread far and wide along the countryside—up as far as Kiev and down all the way to Odessa and to every town, village, and farm in between—to sharpen your knives or mend your plow, sell you the latest dress from Warsaw or the finest shoelaces from Saint Petersburg. Jews and Gentiles, tall and short, swarthy and fair, they all went forth from Pilnik as if their main occupation was to get as far away from it as possible. Each and every time, they left with the same high hopes, and each and every time returned empty-handed, having sold their goods too cheaply, spent too much along the way, or simply found themselves robbed, pickpocketed, or liberated of their meager profits by the police, whose time-honored custom of levying fines and extorting bribes was simply the price of breathing air. Such a life, such a town, cannot fail to leave its mark upon its children. And thus it was with my uncle, Maxim Guttman. His father was one of the few men who did not march out each season. He was the tailor, whose shop was next to the post office. In fact, for as long as anyone could remember, the tailor was always named Guttman. But, of course, all this was to end.

First came the Great War and, even before that was over, the revolution. Maxim was but seven years old when the Bolsheviks took control. His father, my grandfather, was a socialist, and so the new regime was his cup of tea, though I doubt he guessed what was in store for good Bolsheviks in the coming years. In fact, I'm not sure he ever quite understood. His dying wish was to be buried wearing his medals. In the meantime, though, little Uncle Maxim kept himself busy in the tailor shop. No one was surprised he had learned his craft at such an early age. What was surprising was how quickly he outstripped his father in the quality of his stitching and the beauty of his patterns. This was a good thing, because it did not take long before his father, my grandfather, made himself a heavy vest, a woolen cap, a decent pair of warm trousers, and went off to join the Reds, leaving Maxim in charge of the shop, his mother, and his baby brother, my father.

Ukraine was running with blood, but Pilnik was so far off the beaten track, and had so little to offer—no government building to commandeer, no storehouses to raid, no political activists to either enlist or shoot—that both sides left it in peace. Occasionally, soldiers did pass through for a drink at the barbershop or the hospitality of the three prostitutes who did business in a shack behind the post office; they would also sometimes stop at the tailor and have a sleeve mended or a button reattached. If little Maxim was afraid of them, he didn't show it, and both sides delighted in coddling him. "Stay and take care of your mama," a Cossack once told him. Another time, a young Bolshevik whose elbows needed patching declared, "Soon your poverty will end! And when you are old enough you will join the party." As soon as they left, everything returned to normal, and Pilnik remained as it had always been.

It was 1920. The leaves had long since turned amber and decayed into mulch, knee-deep on the forest paths. The annual chill had swung down from the northeast, and the quiet of winter descended on Pilnik, as it had every year since Maxim could remember. One morning, however, this repose was broken by the thunder of animals, men, and machines. Into town they roared, pulling up on their horses, beating the mules that lugged the heavy mortars, screaming orders, cursing anything that got in their way. At the end of this terrifying parade, a small armored car with a large red star nailed to its grille and two red flags frozen solid atop each fender rattled down the road and screeched to a halt in front of the shop. A driver, two officers, and a man dressed in the gray quilted jacket of a factory worker got out and lit their cigarettes.

The factory worker was squat, round, piggish, with a stout face and a nose like a turnip. His cap was pushed back high on his forehead, revealing sharp peasant eyes and broad cheeks. Instead of stopping for a drink at the barber's or taking his turn lecturing the prostitutes (as the Bolsheviks liked to do), he scurried across the ice directly into my uncle's shop. My uncle Maxim jumped from his perch near the window and rushed over to his table, quickly taking up a piece of old cloth. The truth was, there was not a scrap of material in that shop that hadn't been stitched and restitched a dozen times before. In fact, in the past year, only one customer had ordered anything at all—a White colonel who, in spite of being chased all over the countryside by Bolsheviks, ordered Maxim to make him a dress coat of white silk with golden epaulets and braided cuffs in the Cossack style, fitted in the waist and ballooning gracefully to just below the knees, with fourteen brass buttons and a green velvet collar. Maxim had managed to find some material—not at all what the colonel had ordered—and finished the coat in just a few days, which was all the time the colonel had before he was forced to flee again. Maxim was paid in tsarist notes.

Now the door swung open, and the fat little peasant strolled in. He smiled broadly, showing one golden tooth.

"Ah!" he cried. "At last!"

"Hello," Maxim replied softly, commanding his hands to keep steady.

"Hello! Hello!" bellowed the other. He inspected a pair of dusty trousers hanging in the corner. "So! You are the tailor of Pilnik! Our dear Lenin would be proud to wear these! You see this coat?" he said, holding out his ragged cotton jacket. "It's finished. It's done. And," he confided, "it's a piece of shit anyway. I froze to death last year."

The man seemed to be about twenty years old, but he already wore the red armband of a high-ranking political officer.

"You would like a new jacket?" Maxim asked him.

"Would I like a new jacket? Hah! That's good! And why, young tailor of Pilnik, do you think I've come all this way? I'll tell you why. May I sit? Do you have any tea?"

Maxim made his way to the samovar, which was lit with a few tiny scraps of charcoal.

"But I've no sugar," he said.

"No sugar? Here!" The man reached into his pocket and brought out a large block wrapped in waxed paper. He pulled a massive knife from his belt and sawed off a thick slice of sugar. "This is for you," he said. "And this," he cut off a minuscule piece and stuck it between his teeth, "is for me." He drank a few loud sips of tea and then looked up and smiled, the golden tooth sparkling with moisture.

"So," he exclaimed. "Where were we? Well, I'll tell you. I ran into this fellow—he was wearing a coat. It was magnificent. White with green collar, gold braiding. Long. Elegant. You remember it?"

Maxim did not reply.

"This fellow had long mustaches and wore the Order of Saint Catherine on his chest—no? Don't remember him?"

"Yes, I remember."

"Well, to be honest, I killed him, I shot him in the head—but before I did I asked where he got his coat."

Maxim went back to his sewing.

"And he said"—the peasant in the quilted coat placed one stubby finger directly on Maxim's nose—"*you!*"

Maxim did not look up from his sewing. "My father is with Gavrilov," he remarked in his small voice.

"Ah! A good unit! An excellent unit! I know this unit." And suddenly he jumped up and down. "But who cares about politics at a time like this? You, my young friend, are not about politics! You are about pants! Jackets! Suits! You are a great talent stuck away in this little corner of the world that barely exists, this town with a name no one knows and no one will ever know. Vasily!" he suddenly called. The door opened a crack, and the driver poked his head in. "Get the package!"

Vasily disappeared and returned with a large bundle braided with twine. He set it upon the sewing table.

"Open it," the officer said to Maxim.

With great care, the boy tailor untied the knots and unfolded the burlap sack.

"Look at that!" the peasant cried. "Is that not the finest leather? And this—is this not a most beautiful wool? Don't even ask where it came from! I'll tell you—from the closet of a decadent capitalist in Kharkov, may he rest in peace! Believe me, he would have dressed himself like a king—if only he had a tailor as talented as you! So!" he concluded. "Can you make me a jacket, a leather jacket, lined . . . with felt or whatever you think—just plenty warm, all right? And from this, some woolen trousers and a pair of warm gloves? Can you do that for me?"

"I can," replied Maxim.

The man pinched his cheek. "I'll be back in a week. Have it done then."

"But I need to measure you."

"No time for that!" he cried, and out the door he flew, leaving the bundle of fabric, the block of sugar, and the half-empty glass of tea.

Now you may laugh. You may say these things do not happen. But they do happen, and everyone in Moscow has such a story. Of course, when these events are actually taking place, they don't seem so charming. For Maxim, there was no joy in this at all. He saw clearly that everything depended upon this next moment, that if he was not smart enough, that if he erred in the smallest way, that if in any degree he failed to fulfill the wishes of this crazy Russian, he would not survive. So he closed his eyes. He softened his mind into folds that hold the past and present in one pinch of space, and—there it was! The robust little peasant with the potato nose and the golden tooth: the slope of his shoulders, the thickness of his neck, the roundness of his chest—all this Maxim had taken in with his swift eyes as soon as the man had stepped into the room. Quickly he called to mind his height, the length of his leg, the measure of his sleeve; he fixed in his imagination the girth of his hips, the shape of his buttocks, and the size of his waist (which he could only estimate, since it was hidden under the old quilted jacket); and then opening his eyes at last, he took out his tailor's chalk and began to draw. When he was done, little Max slumped back in his chair and began to cry.

The officer did not return that week as he had promised, nor the next. But on the fourth day of the third week, the horses, the men, the cannon, all came roaring back, and the door to the shop swung open again.

"It's fucking Siberia out there! Where's my new coat?"

It was hanging behind the sewing table. Maxim reached up for it.

"Cease!" the man ordered. "Let me admire it first!"

And indeed, it was something to admire. The leather glistened in the late-afternoon light. It draped like sheets of molten silver flowing down from the simple wooden hanger. It had a wide, peaked collar that spread to the very edge of the shoulders, which themselves were square, bold, manly, confident, and the sleeves ended in folded cuffs drawn back with large black buttons that indicated, not style, but substance; authority, not rank. Even to Maxim, the coat seemed out of place in this humble room, like finding an icon of Andrei Rublev in a trash can.

"Now, bring it to me," commanded the officer.

Maxim slipped it off the hanger and held it out.

"Did you make the trousers and the gloves?"

Maxim presented these as well, and the fat little man put them on right there and then.

"Tailor of Pilnik!" he declared. "What is your name?"

"Maxim Yakovovich Guttman."

"Maxim Yakovovich Guttman! If I live through this, someday I will send for you! Do not forget me."

He made for the door, then turned to face his young tailor as if he had forgotten something. "Khrushchev! Nikita Sergeyevich!" he said. "Remember me!"

And then he was gone.

The man was true to his word, and one day, years later, my uncle Maxim was appointed tailor to the Kremlin. It was for that service he was awarded the apartment on Veshnaya, in the KGB building, with the yard no one dared to enter.

☭

I was thinking about these things in my room in Tishinskaya because of the house I had decided to build. Was it a true story? I don't know, but it was true for me, and it was true for him, and its telling was no different than the recitation of *The Iliad* or *The Lay of Igor*. As usual, I would begin my dreaming long before I fell asleep. The house: the elevations, the layout, the façade, the frame, the entry, the porch, the fence, and even the pictures I would hang on the walls. All these painted themselves in bright colors on the ceiling above me. How like my uncle I was! I perhaps did not realize it fully until that moment. I was also like my father, of course. And he had the greater vision, hadn't he? Though without my uncle, he would never have gone to the university, never have become the great scientist, the man of letters. And then, again, for what? Eventually, I did fall asleep, but only after listening for my mother padding down the hall on her final excursion to the toilet.

The next day, as usual, I went to see Collette.

I had this idea, I told her, to build a house. "Where on earth would you do that?" she asked me.

"My family has a dacha," I explained. "It's my uncle's, he was once a somebody."

"And where will you get materials? Are you the Ministry of Construction?"

"I know a few people," I said. "I can put together a little brigade. I didn't say it would be built in a week. Just—"

"Ahah! So Roman has his very own five-year plan." She laughed, and as always her laughter charged my body like a bolt of electricity. But she turned away and started washing the dishes.

I began my drawings.

The house, as all my houses (though I could not have known it at the time), emerged whole from my imagination like a cake coming out of the oven, almost as if it had been put in my brain by someone else. When I went to sleep that night thinking of Uncle Maxim, I had no idea that in the morning I would wake with the entire project clear in my mind—clear, except for how to construct it. My drawings were not about working out a design but trying to accommodate the fancies of my mind to the realities of gravity and the properties of materials like wood and glass. I had conceived beams that extended infinitely, eaves cantilevered to hang without any visible support, jalousies that undulated like the waves of the ocean, staircases that floated without any cables or spines; this was the curse of my training: to imagine everything, to build nothing. We worked for the eternity that was the Soviet tomorrow, our drawings rolled up and gathering dust in the corner beside our drafting tables. But this time, I was determined to build my house.

Collette, however, refused to take an interest in my project. Instead, she spent her time visiting her artist friends or going to the theater. And it wasn't just artists she hung upon: there were writers, musicians, academics, actors, dancers, even a few architects like me, and of course the foreigners, the Americans, the French, the Spanish, not to mention the Jews and Zionists who yearned for nothing but Israel or at least the good life in America. Very quickly I became accustomed to the political nature of these evenings and soon became adept at dissecting current events and critiquing Soviet society in a way quite unlike what I had done with my old friends or my colleagues at work. It was no different than learning to endure the stench of Collette's elevator or suffer the necessary chitchat with her neighbor Plotkina, who always seemed to be dragging her little dog, Vova, behind her. Charlie, the American, appeared frequently at these soirees. Like clockwork, he exchanged his little packets with Collette. By now, I understood these were letters from Pascal. She denied it, but I knew it was so. I began to hate Charlie, and no matter how many times he asked me, I never went to the American ambassador's house for film night, and when Collette had him over to her place, I always made an excuse not to show up.

I had questioned her about the letters more than once.

"To whom are you writing?" I asked her.

"To my aunt Lorrette."

"Why doesn't she come for a visit? It can't be that hard for her to get a visa. She could come with a tourist group."

"What difference does it make to you, Roman?"

"It just seems, all this writing . . . "

A few minutes later I would try again.

"Whom else are you writing?"

"What do you mean?"

"I just want to know."

"Why?"

"I just do."

"For heaven's sake, Roman. Nobody."

"No one at all?"

"What are you getting at?"

"I just want to know."

"What?"

"If you are writing . . . "

"To whom?"

"I don't know."

"To whom?"

"You know whom," I finally said.

"Say it then. Say the name."

But I didn't say the name.

I don't know why, but I found myself escaping into the shower, needing water and soap. I stood in the tub, feeling I could happily drown if I just swallowed enough water. I heard myself whisper brutally, "Roman, she belongs to Pascal, and to Pascal you will deliver her!" I wanted to be the person who could do that, who could sacrifice his own happiness for the happiness of his beloved. I was hoping the hot shower would somehow temper my spirit, and I would be reborn with a pure heart.

Even so, the day came when I stole the extra key that hung on the peg near the door. It was easy to do, because she would never have considered it possible I would stoop so low. Sometime later, when she had gone to work, I returned to her apartment.

I knew she kept her letters in a cardboard box tucked beneath her bed. She had decoupaged this treasure chest with flowers, crests, medieval angels, and small strips of colored foil. I set it upon the bed and carefully pried open the lid. Inside, it was also decorated with words clipped from magazines—"love," "soul mate," "honeymoon," "bliss." In the center of this maelstrom of sentiment she had scrawled in large roman script, *T T.* I did not know what this meant. I suppressed the urge to shred the cover to bits.

My attention was soon drawn to the neatly bound packets of letters stuffed inside like the stacks of rubles my grandmother used to keep in the suitcase in the front closet, in which she'd also packed a change of warm clothes, gloves, cigarettes, matches, a pencil and notebook "just in case." Sorting through the letters, I realized that the tightly written notes on pink tissue had come from her aunt Lorrette. I read a few of these. They were almost hallucinatory, filled with absurd hopes and silly chatter about this or that "crucial attempt to improve the situation" and continually inquiring if Collette had received the packages of food or clothing she sent through the normal post, which of course never arrived. Some of the other letters were from correspondents in the West whom I'd never heard of—mostly Jews in San Francisco, Dallas, and London. I read a few of these, too. They were all stuck in the same groove: *Remember we support you! We had a big demonstration! Don't give up hope!* They were sincere, hopeful, and laughable. But finally I had to turn to the stack of satiny, cream-colored stationery upon which a fountain pen had majestically inscribed itself in purple ink. These were lovingly bound with a luminous chiffon ribbon. The letters spilled out upon the bed as if freed from the bondage of a great and terrible secret. My hands shook as I opened the first one.

It was written in French, of course.

My darling Collette:
Each day begins in sunshine because I awake thinking of you, but then reality sets in and the day turns to cloud and rain.

My dearest Collette:
I want you to think of only two things: you and me. Keep this in front of your eyes even at the darkest hours.

My Sweet, My Perfect:
You must be careful now. Don't do anything foolish. We are working day and night to "resolve this situation." Right now is exactly *not* the time for any rash acts.

Darling Collette:
I implore you to be careful. None of this is worth anything if anything were to happen to you. My happiness is tied up so

completely with yours. I understand you must think of yourself first—of course you must! But how can I bear losing you?

My Heart:
This person, I won't name him, is he good for you? Is he trustworthy? I completely trust your judgment, but I worry that your desperation may lead you into the hands of someone who cannot understand your situation completely.

Collette, my beloved:
This thing with R. I know it cannot come between us, but you will forgive me if I feel jealous—not of him personally, but of the time he has with you. I know you are lonely, and I am hoping he can be of help to you, and so I do not begrudge you. I only want you to know how perfect is my love, and how I count the hours till we can be together again.

Dear C:
I'm working to get a visa to visit you, and I agree you should tell NO ONE. I don't know if it can happen, but I will let you know as soon as I have an answer. Our friend will come by and tell you. For now, I agree with you—best to keep it from R until it is absolutely necessary. I don't wish to hurt him at all. He is a blessed soul, and I love him.

Oh, My Love:
The visa was denied. I'm sure you already know. I have decided to go to the countryside for a while, to recover. I can't stand Paris today! We are already trying another way to get me a visa. As for your invitation, I understand it is ready and will come in the next mail.

My Little One:
Your letters are the precious jewels of my existence. Your passion is twice reciprocated—I, too, desire you in every possible way (and in every room of the house!). I, too, can see you naked in front of me, your hair wild and your nipples red from biting, I can still smell you, taste you. My mouth is still upon

you. Your mouth is still upon me. And more than that. I have fucked you in every way imaginable, and in every place—at the office, in the park, at the club, on the beach—wherever I am, that is where I have fucked you. I come thinking of you. I wake up in the morning hard and wet, dreaming of you. Never forget this, my love. No matter where you are or whom you are with, you are with me.

All were signed in the same obscure manner. *T T.* I puzzled over this a long time.

Eventually I realized it was getting late. I returned everything to its place and slipped from the apartment exactly as I entered it.

One Saturday afternoon, Collette collected me at our favorite café near the Lubyanka, and we got on the train to Fili. It was a lovely day in late spring; the trees were bright with soft, green shoots, and the first kingfishers and robins had already built their nests and were settled in for summer. We walked along Grozny Boulevard, taking in the fine spring air and chatting about some film or other, *The Irony of Fate,* or something by Daniela, when I turned to her and said, "I'm almost finished with the plans."

"What plans?"

"What do you mean, 'What plans'? The house."

"You mean this house that you are always dreaming of?"

"Yes, that house. What other house?"

"And so you finish these plans. What then?"

"I've told you. I'm going to tear down my uncle's dacha and build it there, in Zagoryanka."

"What about your cousins? Your sister? Your mother? Your aunt? Don't they love their dacha?"

"They'll be happy for us to live there."

I again described it to her.

"But Roma," she said.

"The entire rear wall looking out into the woods will be constructed of glass, or rather, it will appear to be a single sheet of glass, an illusion, of course, made possible by the use of aluminum framing, and the interior space, the living space all except for the bedrooms, will be one, flowing, continuous vista, again an illusion, because it's actually built on three different levels, one leading to the other . . ."

"But Roma," she said again.

"What, my love?"

"Are you crazy? This house can never be built, and even if it could, I don't want it. Why won't you understand that? I don't want anyone's house, I don't want anything here at all. Not a house, not a bigger apartment, not a car, not a better job, nothing. Do you know what I do want? I want to *leave.* Can't you get that into your head?"

"I swear to you, you'll love the house," I said.

"Let's go inside, Roman, for God's sake. We're here."

We entered an apartment building and climbed to the third floor. I knew she was angry at me, but I also knew she didn't understand what it meant to have a house and how that could change everything; a nest, a finely contained space with four walls that are your own, that were designed just for you, not a one-size-fits-all with its bathroom always next to the front door and the knife drawer always the first to the right of the sink, but a place that has your name on it, a place in which your soul might have a little rest.

"Roma, enough," she said. "I'm sick to death of your house. What kind of person would build a house in this country? Can you know me so little? And this from someone who says he loves me."

Styopa let us in. He seemed deliriously happy to see us. "Welcome! Welcome! I'm so glad you could come! Have some tea. Have some schnapps. You don't know what schnapps is? Sasha Fromish makes it." He whistled and wagged his hand to indicate how strong this schnapps was. "Everyone is here, you're the last," he observed. I saw Sasha Fromish standing over a large glass jug, pouring out his schnapps. It was dark as beer, and I could smell it all the way over here. His wife, Alla, was slicing a mushroom pirog. Someone had brought some gorilka from Kiev. Yuri Sochin, I think. Everyone said it was stronger than Russian vodka. "Not stronger than schnapps," Sasha Fromish said. There were a dozen people at least, the noise was huge, and everyone had brought something to eat.

"Listen, Collette," I begged her, "you're missing the point. It doesn't have to be a permanent place. Just something for now. Until you can leave."

"Me leave? What about you? Why don't you want to get out of this hell?"

"I do!" I said. But the truth was I didn't. And I didn't want her leaving either.

Collette tore away from me and presented her French potatoes, as she called them, to the assembly. They were bathed in milk and cheese, and there was the loud "Ooo." These were all Zionists, Jewish renewalists. There were children running around, also, and someone, maybe Volodya Rutman and also probably Maya Tsipkina, called them to order, and the kids piled into the living room and formed a circle on the floor. Volodya handed out skullcaps to the boys. They opened their carbon-copied Hebrew readers, and the lesson began. *Anakhnu lomdim lidaber Ivrit! Ekhat, shtayim, shalosh, arbah!* In the meantime, the parents were huddled in the other room, murmuring their delight.

Misha Abromovich stood up. "I want to welcome everyone, and say to you, Shabbat shalom!"

"Shabbat shalom!" everyone replied.

There was to be a lecture on Jewish history by Tamara Belkina, who had been doing research more or less openly for years and was considered by everyone a great scholar. I think she may have known what she was talking about, as far as any Soviet could know Jewish history, but as for me, I was already far away, in Zagoryanka, pouring the foundation for my house with the beautiful, protean concrete my friend Lonya would have managed in his Byzantine way to acquire with a case of export-quality vodka and a carton of American cigarettes.

The idea of it made me laugh out loud with pleasure. Belkina glanced up at me. "What?"

Collette did not even bother to look over.

Later she said, "I have to go home now. Charlie is coming over. Probably you won't want to be there."

Belkina. Charlie. Zagoryanka. What were these things to me anymore? Now there was only Anyusha, the Head, the Sunbird, Moishe, and the bedroom door, which Abdul-Latif had locked behind him when he went out.

Chapter Fifteen

STILL IN THIS BASEMENT IN JERUSALEM, waiting around for something to happen and naturally thinking about things, in this case, Pop.

The thing is, it isn't so easy being him. Take what happened to him when he was a kid. He grew up in a place where no one trusted anyone, not even your best friend or your mother or father or anyone. I mean, if I couldn't trust Yohanan or Miriam, I don't know what I'd do.

He used to tell me this story about some strange guy who lived in the basement of his house in Moscow—an old guy who had been in the Gulag and everything—and this is what he told my pop, word for word (I know because Pop told it to *me* so many times). In this story my dad is like six or seven years old. So imagine this old guy's voice, or rather Pop talking in this old guy's voice, with a thick Georgian accent and coughing up phlegm for effect, saying: "So, Roman, do you know what a traitor looks like? I will tell you! If he smiles at you too easily, he is an informer. If he doesn't smile at all, he's also an informer. If he wants to know what happened next, never tell him. If he makes a great show of not wanting to know, that is even worse. If he brings you real coffee, he will betray you. If he invites himself in, or if he never allows himself to come in, beware! If he says, 'I'll bring you something from the store; after all, I'm going out anyway,' then stay away from him! If he's very humorous, he will turn you in without any remorse. If he's strict as a commissar, then that's exactly what he is. If he showers you with kisses, if he gets you tickets to the Bolshoi, if he makes an effort to keep the hallway clean, if he complains about every aspect of his life, if he reads *Pravda* even once a week, if he always criticizes the leadership, if he's the nicest guy you ever met, it's all the same. You only have to do one thing, my Little Octobrist— look into his eyes! That's right. Look into his eyes. If they sparkle with joy and yet you feel the coldness of death, then he is the one. It's very simple. Even you can do it. Your parents taught you a lot, but they did not teach you everything. Oh! Somewhere in this world there is a county in which you can trust your neighbor and count on your friend, but not this one!"

When Pop tells me this story, I always ask him, But what was that guy doing in your basement? And he says, Oh, he had an important job! He sorted through the stuff coming out of our toilets. We flushed so many secrets down the bowl—they couldn't let all that information go down the drain. He was the last and the best of the Communists!

Then my father always laughed and kissed me good night.

But *I* think this story tells a lot about what Pop went through as a kid and how hard it was for him to be him. And that's what I want everyone to understand.

Luckily, Miriam and I spend tons of time together. Pop doesn't know anything about it. Miriam takes me everywhere. When we were talking about Noah (because there is this whole thing having to do with redemption in our time if everyone, even non-Jews, just follows the Seven Laws of Noah), she took me to the zoo to teach me.(!!) Then we went into Jerusalem and prayed at the wall—well, she prayed at the wall. I kind of watched and waited for something to happen, but nothing did. I thought she would be upset with me, but she just took me for falafel. Another time we went to visit the Temple Institute where they have this model of Solomon's Temple and all these crazy implements to use when they rebuild the temple again—you know, the menorah and the fire pans and the things to collect blood and everything, all of gold and silver and bronze. They even built an Ark of the Covenant, like Moses made. It was crazy, but it was also very exciting, to be so close to things that were exactly like they were in the Bible. Sometimes we didn't do anything religious at all and just talked about stuff, and I told her a lot about my life and also about Pop. She seemed to know a lot about him anyway. After all, he's an architect. Anyway, one day she said to me, Why don't you ever talk about your mother? And I said, I don't have a mother. She was quiet for a long time, and then she said, It must be hard, and I said, Not really, and she said, Yes, really, and then I didn't know what she wanted me to say. Once we went to her house with her husband, and she cooked, and that was the first time I wondered why she didn't have any kids, because Orthodox have kids when they're like thirteen or something, and I kind of let it slip, and she looked at her husband, and then she did that smile of hers and she said, HaShem—that's what she calls God—will deliver in his time. I wanted to tell her, I don't have a mother and you don't have a kid! But I didn't.

The question she really wanted me to focus on was what was the right way to live your life and what was the wrong way. As far as she was concerned, the Law is the right way, and protecting the Jewish People and the Land of Israel is the right way, and it's our duty, and nothing else is as important as that, because only that way will the Messiah arrive to heal the world.

But let's be honest. Forget the Messiah. He's not coming. Because something that's made up cannot actually appear. So I'm not interested in the Messiah, even for Miriam's sake. And as for leading a holy life, I'd really like to, but so far I can't. It just won't happen. I mean, I still eat shrimp.

But, when it comes to protecting the Jewish People? Well, after what happened to my father, things got a lot clearer for me.

You just can't let someone kick you out of your own land.

And also, if you don't stand for something, if you're just for yourself, what kind of person are you? Selfish, that's what. And that is exactly what I *don't* want to be.

So then this whole thing came up with the Temple Mount, and they kept asking me, like every day, and every day I couldn't say yes and I couldn't say no, and it was really horrible, plus I had no idea what they were actually asking me to do, they were kind of vague, and then when Pop didn't come home that night and when Yohanan came through the window, and when the house was so noisy and insane with laundry and everything, and I went to Rabbi's and they asked me one last time because it's all happening today, and it was Miriam herself who asked me and it was never Miriam who had asked before—I don't know—I just said yes.

And that was when everything seemed to happen. Yohanan and I and the others went off with Shlomo, and he told us where to be and when and how important it was, and asked us a million times if he could count on us, and made us repeat our oath like a thousand times, and grilled us on our quotations, and made us repeat our history, and talked to us for what seemed like hours and hours about Torah and Mishnah and Talmud and Akiba and Bar Kokhba and Israel and Zionism and how there needs to be a new Temple, a Third Temple, because without the Third Temple how could we ever make the korban, the four kinds of sacrifices: the sacrifice of peace, the sacrifice of guilt, the sacrifice of sin, and the burnt offering, because without sacrifice, my children, how can we come close to God etc. etc. etc. And I kept saying to myself, I don't have to exactly believe this, and that's OK. I don't have to be 100% sure, I just have to listen to what Miriam and Rabbi Keren tell me, and follow the commandments with an open heart. I just have to *do*.

Because, you see, during that whole time they were working with us, I couldn't tell them the truth. Not even Miriam. I was supposed to be ready to hear, but the noises around me got so loud that sometimes I could barely hear *myself*.

And then, this afternoon, when Yohanan took my hand, all the noise went away. That is worth thinking about.

Oh! I'll finish this later. They just brought us some McDonald's from the new kosher one at the mall in Mevaseret Zion—Shlomo thought he was bringing us gold and diamonds. All I really want to know is if Miriam is coming or not.

☾★

I saw Fadi less and less. The older I got, the more angry with me he seemed to be. His whole life was angry.

"How is it you're *not* angry?" he said to me.

"I don't know" was all I could think of to reply.

I knew that other boys my age were already trying to be in al-Shabiba so they could graduate into Fatah or even into the Fatah Hawks and go kill Israelis, or they hung around with the Popular Front or Islamic Jihad, but Fadi was Democratic Front. That's what he was always spouting about. And then he ran off every day to be with his new friends. He wore only black pants and a black shirt and a black band around his head. It was pretty obvious he created this uniform on his own—all his friends wore ordinary clothes, T-shirts, jeans, whatever they had; they were poor, but he had money now, so he bought American clothes and sunglasses. Once I mocked him for that, calling him a Paul Newman. He just laughed at me and said, "Go to your mother, little baby." Most of the time, though, he still tried to convince me. "Come on, Amir, come on. What's the matter with you? What are you still doing with playhouses and card games?" He looked at me sadly. "Don't you read the news? Don't you watch TV? Everything is happening right now! Are you deaf? Or maybe you're just an idiot."

But sometimes the old days returned to us, and Fadi was just Fadi again.

One evening we walked out by the Wadi Ibrahim, the small winter river that gave our town its name, or maybe it was the other way around, nobody really knew. The spring flowers were still in bloom, though the water was already down to a trickle running through the spine of the wadi, and the earth around it was already turning hard, like baked brick. This, oh this, was our time of the year! The smell of the drying earth, the fresh scent coming off the stream, the slight perfume of the flowers and shrubs, and the sound of our feet scratching along the rock and mud. How many scorpions had I killed here? And how many scarabs had I held in my palm for good luck? Each year we found a new stone upon which to carve our names. The first time, Fadi showed me how:

FADI

Amir
1980

And every year since, the same, 1981, 1982, 1983, 1984.

But then one year he didn't want to do it anymore. "We're not girls," he said.

So I went there by myself, found a decent rock, and carved,

FADI

Amir
1985

But now we were together again, strolling along the edge of the stream, looking for snails.

"Did you see what Djamel Zidane did?" cried Fadi in his old voice. "Three goals all by himself! Especially that one from at least twenty-five meters—pow!"

"And the one where Madjer was all over him, and then from nowhere . . . ," I answered.

"The kick! Ya-ala!" Fadi threw his arms in the air. "That is what you call real poetry!"

When his arm came down, it rested on my shoulder. Nothing would have been more natural than to reach up and take his hand, but I didn't. We walked along this way for a while, feeling like we used to feel, Fadi towering over me, his long, thin body embracing me in its shadow. In a year I'd probably be as tall as he. Then, I supposed, these moments would be over for good.

We spoke of nothing much—my school, his work, his problems with Nadirah, which I enjoyed talking about quite a bit, my parents, my sisters, more football, all the things that carry a person from one step to the next. Then he looked up and rubbed his eyes: the sun had begun to set.

"Let's get back," he said.

"Why don't we watch the sun go down together?" I suggested.

"What for?"

"I don't know. Just for the sake of it."

"You're getting crazy as you grow up, you know that, Amir?"

"Why? I just thought . . ."

"It's getting dark. What's the point of being out here in the dark?"

"Why not?" I demanded.

"I have to get home, Amir."

"Why? Because of Nadirah?"

"Of course because of Nadirah."

"Why is it always Nadirah? Nadirah, Nadirah, Nadirah! What about us?"

" 'Us'?"

"I mean . . ."

He crossed his arms. They might as well have been two scimitars. "It's time to get over it, Amir. For everyone's sake."

"Over what?"

"Oh, Amir!" he said.

"What?"

"I've been trying to be patient, but you just . . . I have to say something. I've been thinking about it for a while now. I think maybe you shouldn't spend so much time with Nadirah and me anymore. Maybe that would be best. Yes, I think it would definitely be best. You have to stay away from us, Amir. Nadirah and I, we need some privacy, you know? Can you understand that? Amir, you can't be with a person you don't like."

"But I do like you. I love you!" I cried.

"Not me, you idiot. Nadirah. You don't accept her. Everyone knows that."

"But you're my cousin," I replied miserably.

"She's also your cousin. And she's my wife. She will be the mother of my children."

"I know that."

"No, I don't think you do." He now took five steps back, and with each step receded deeper into the darkness of the approaching night. He held up his hand as if to wave good-bye, but actually it was just a shrug, as if there really were nothing more he could possibly say to me. He walked off in the direction of the village, and before I could say a word he was swallowed up in the misty blackness of that night, and I was left alone in our wadi with the water trickling over my shoes and the first flutter of bats swirling over my head.

You see? You see? This is exactly what the Prophet, Sayyidina Rasulullah, Allah's blessing upon him, warned: Beware of suspicion, do not find fault with each other, do not spy upon one another, do not compete with one another. But I was filled with envy! Strange feelings bit into my heart and strange thoughts interrupted my sleep. Even now, I feel the pangs of envy creep into my phantom groin. But what is it I covet? Even as I look down upon Dasha Cohen in her brilliant silence, in her magnificent stillness, I cannot say if it is she I desire, or my lost life, or simply the black freedom of death. Perhaps if she would speak my name, I would understand why I tarry. Perhaps if she cursed me, spit at me, if she blinked her eyes, one time for disgust, two times for vengeance, I might at least make sense of the connection between us. Shattered and pale, her hair a tangle of thorns, her nails clipped like a boy's, her legs slightly parted, her neck exposed to the collarbone, one ear protruding from her hair like a slice of ripe pear

Pear.

The months passed, the season turned to winter yet again, and I marched off, as I now did every day, in the direction of the garage and then, as always, detoured onto the Street of the Four Wells and then cut through the alley behind Nasser's vegetable stand, said hello as always to abu-Mahmed, who always seemed to be wherever I was, and bent under the banyan because I loved the smell, and anyway it was always raining this time of year, taking a minute to shake the water from my hair and pull my shirt from my back, and then I skirted the rear of the houses hiding myself under the eaves and pressing up against the walls because I wanted to remain as dry as possible. And then, at last, I reached the Tomb of Nadirah, which is what I now called the house in which she and Fadi lived, and there I placed myself beneath the window—that is, whichever window opened upon the room in which she happened to be, of which there were two, the kitchen where I had first seen her, which was also the main room with its one sofa and one chair upon which she sat to watch television, and the bedroom. In the last days, this was where I always found her, lying atop the half-made mattress of the wedding bed Fadi had given her as a bride price. She had one leg bent like a pyramid upon which she balanced her ashtray. As usual she was wearing her blue jeans with white stitching on the pockets and a heart of white sequins sewn upon the hem of her right leg, the leg which was now stretched to the edge of the mattress, her bare foot and bright orange toes dangling over the side. When she walked the streets in those jeans, old women and religious men yelled at her. Today she had been reading something, but the book was already lying open on her breast, an abandoned butterfly, rising up and down with each breath. I loved her blouses. Today she wore the T-shirt that said BON JOVI: BAD MEDICINE. I read enough English to see that. And anyway, everyone knew Bon Jovi. One sleeve was torn on purpose to reveal a slice more of her shoulder, the V where it came down into her arm like the mouth of a river. I knelt beneath the casement still as a rock.

How many times had I come here? After school, before school, in the early evening before Fadi returned, whole seasons had I come, four months, six months, eight. Spring had turned to summer, summer to fall, fall to winter. He thought I hated her. I did. Yet if I did not make my pilgrimage to the altar of her window each day, I was consumed with mourning for the day that was lost. What had she been wearing, what had she been reading, what had she cooked, what had she listened to, who among her boring girlfriends had visited her; and if she had not been home, where had she gone? And oh! if she was not home how my heart raced with anxiety. I would drop from her window, which then would seem just a stupid window on Fadi's house, and run first to Saliah's house, and if she was not there, then to the apartment building where I knew Adeela lived, where I would have to wait a block away and watch for the door to open and close, which it did almost constantly, but rarely with Nadirah coming through; and if not there, to Rima's or Monique's or Jala's; and if not there to the juice bar or the café or the bakery or the cultural center. One time I waited three hours near the movie theater, and when the film let out and she was not there, I was abject to the point of tears.

Today I was lucky. She lay with her eyes closed, the book splayed upon her chest, the ashtray upon her knee, the toes hanging over the edge of the bed, and I was happy. Then she stirred, placed the ashtray on the blanket, lay the open book beside it, let her feet come together on the floor, and pushed herself up. She stood with her back to me, yawned, extended her bare arms above her head, fingers spread out like dancing puppets. She disappeared behind the curtains that led to the toilet. I counted the seconds, stretched my ears to hear the slightest intimation of sound, any little crinkle, echo, swoosh, anything coming from her secret body, or even from her feet scraping along the floor, or, especially, the slap of her belt buckle as she reset it on her waist, or a sigh, or the gritty clang of the chain that would tell me what's what, that my wait was over and I missed the whole thing. The heart in my stomach cried out: to see you in every way possible! I would give anything. I would give anything. Instead, I heard someone come into the yard, a heavy, lethargic step. Abu-Mahmed! Again! He was like a shadow on the face of the sun, following me like the cat you once fed out of pity and now wouldn't let you alone. Why did I ever say hello to him, anyway? He was almost blind and practically retarded. Who else said hello to him? Only Amir. I decided I wouldn't even look at him. My eyes would be two stones aimed at the curtain behind which Nadirah was—

"What? You think I don't know you're there? Come out of there! You want to see me? Here I am!"

My ears went crazy, and I didn't know where to look.

"You think I can't see you? I can see you right through the bushes, you moron. Come out."

It was Nadirah, her arms folded like a locked gate.

"Well?" she said.

I climbed out of the mulberry bush. "What is it?" I answered. "What do you want? I'm busy."

"You're busy?" She held up her magazine to protect her hair from the rain, exposing the underside of her arm.

"I lost something. I lost Cat," I said.

"Cat?"

"Cat is the name of my cat, in case you don't remember."

She placed her other hand on her hip and leaned on one leg, the way she did when she scolded Fadi. "Do you lose this 'Cat' every day?"

"What do you mean?"

"You know what I mean."

"He runs away all the time," I explained.

"He must not like you very much. Maybe because you never bothered to give him a real name."

"Cat is a real name."

"So is Amir the Peeper."

"Who's peeping? Who cares about you? You're so conceited!"

"All right. Come in. You're wet all through. It's time to talk."

"I have to look for Cat."

"Come in anyway," she said.

"I'm too busy."

"Amir, enough." She reached out, and there was nothing in the world more beautiful or more frightening than this hand extended toward me, the tendrils of darkness in the folds of her knuckles, the sand-hued palm that was suddenly, impatiently, turned upward, the beckoning, rain-dappled, iridescent fingers with bright orange nails. The lids of her eyes were lowered ever so briefly. I was unsure of their meaning, only that I could not resist the pressure of that lowering, as if her lashes had slipped under my feet to scoop me up and set me down in her kitchen. Then, abruptly, she turned and walked back to the house. I followed her, chained to her eyelids, and also to her footprints in the soppy ground, which I copied step for step.

"Stand there," she said.

She had placed herself on her chair at the small green table they used to cut up vegetables. In a plate on the table was a half-eaten pear. The bite marks had left its flesh browned. She shifted her body sideways so that she was facing the window through which I had been gazing for what now seemed to me my entire life. Her eyes hardened upon me, and even in the chill of December, with my clothes soaked and my shoes leaking, my neck felt as hot as if the sun were bearing down on it.

She said, "What's the matter with you?"

At that moment, as far as I could tell, the whole world had gone to sleep except for what was happening in this room.

"Why are you just standing there," she said.

I took one step toward her, but then took it back.

"Take your hands out of your pockets," she commanded like a schoolmaster. "Are you deaf? Take your hands out of your pockets. I'm not going to bite you. You can come a little closer. That's enough. Now, this is no time for lies, Amir. If you lie, it is all over. Do you understand? I will know if you lie."

I glued my hands to my knees.

"You were looking in my window today, weren't you, Amir? Only the truth. No truth, we're done forever."

The nodding of my head felt strange to me. My head was an object I controlled only tenuously, as if with a rubber band.

"And this is not the first time, is it?"

By now my head felt more like a balloon, wanting to fly off.

"You have done it time and time again."

I nodded again.

"And what have you seen? Amir, tell me."

"You," I said.

"How?"

"Just you."

"No lies today, Amir."

"Drinking your Coca-Cola!" I blurted. "Dancing to ABBA. Eating hummus. Smoking cigarettes. Talking to Jala Idris. Making tea with tea bags. Tying your hair with ribbons and letting it out again. Kicking off your shoes. Losing your lighter over and over again. Writing in your notebook. Never finding your pen. Practicing balancing on one toe. Washing the clothes."

"You mean my underwear."

"Yes," I answered with pride. "Blabbing with Adeela. Reading your romantic books. Crying for no reason. Breaking eggs in the frying pan. Stacking things. Eating . . . your pear. Mopping the floor."

She looked at me a very long time and said, "I don't read romantic books. It's literature. Sahar Khalifa. Have you heard of this writer? You're not too young to read her anymore. You just act young. When I'm done with it, I'll give it to you."

"Thank you."

" 'Thank you,' " she repeated, rolling the words around in her mouth as if they were made of syrup. Then she said, "Amir, what do you want of me?"

And it just came out of my mouth: "I want to kiss you."

Suddenly she bit her lower lip and smiled.

She stood up, walked over to me, one step, then two, then three, until the space between us was so small that if you put an olive leaf between her breast and mine, it would not fall.

She placed her hands on my hips, locking her fingers upon them so I could not move one way or another. She looked straight at me, straight into my eyes. But then she looked down. A strange smile appeared on her lips. And with sudden horror I understood what she was looking at, even though I had been praying that she would not notice, or if she happened to glance, it would not show, but it was showing—a pole holding out my pants like a tent.

Why did I never have money for blue jeans like everyone else? Why did I have to always wear these stupid loose trousers? The tighter she held my hips, the worse it grew, but I couldn't help it. I almost didn't want to help it. But my knees were sand giving way beneath the weight of this enormity, and the whole of me was one massive, inexplicably pleasant humiliation.

"Why are you trembling?" She laughed. "Are you hungry? Do you need a bottle of milk?" She shook my hips. "Look at it bounce! No! Don't you dare pull back!" Her laughter was like a blade clenched between her teeth. "Amir! Amir! How will you ever dance with a girl if you do this with your thing all the time? Don't you know she'll be disgusted? You'll never even get to the dance floor. Everyone will laugh at you. Look, it still won't go away. You can't make it go away! Ha! Can't you see how disgusting it is? You're pathetic, Amir. You're . . . you're . . . so"—she searched her mind and finally exploded with delight—"*gauche*. Do you even know what that word means?" It was obvious I did not. She laughed again and said something else, but by now everything she said was all gibberish anyway. The whole world was gibberish, swirling, drunk. But I had never been so close to her, and the smell of her, the heat of her. . . .

She pushed me away and spit. "You want to dishonor me? In my own house? In the house of your brother? In the house my father made for me?"

She jabbed me with her sharp, hard fingers. "Who are you, you little pig, to speak to me at all? Look! Allah be praised! It's still there! Go sell it to Grandmother Fatma! She'll eat it up! Yum, yum, yum, yum!"

She jabbed me again, even harder.

I tumbled backward, slipping on the concrete floor.

She howled with delight. Ha ha ha ha ha!

She couldn't stop. She laughed louder and louder.

"I'm telling!" I cried.

"What?"

"I'm telling."

"Telling what, for God's sake?"

She narrowed her eyes, but there was no understanding in them. I myself did not quite know what was coming into my mind.

"I'm telling Fadi you kissed me. He has the right to know."

"Liar! No one kissed you. Who would kiss that mouth? Not me in a million years."

"I'm telling Fadi! You'll be punished! You know what happens to whores!"

I stood up, brushed the dust and bits of bread crumbs off my arms, ran my hand down my pant leg to smooth it out, tucked in my shirt, wiped something—her spit, I think—from my eye.

"Are you crazy?" she shouted, but I placed my right forefinger on the lower eyelid of my right eye, to say to her, You see? I've taken a solemn oath. It is upon my own head that I must do this.

"Are you crazy?" she shouted once more, but I was already out the door and into the yard and through the archway and into the alley and out onto the street.

Before I knew it, I was on Palestine Street. The rain had stopped, and the sun was trying to shine again. Have you seen Fadi? I asked. No, answered Ismail Sahlah, go look for him at Bouran's. I went down to Bouran's, and a couple of guys were there, drinking coffee and eating baklava, and Souri Hafez said, I think he's with his guys, try over at the cultural center, so I ran over to the cultural center, but Walid hadn't seen him all day. Maybe check the football field, they play rain or shine, he reminded me, and if no one's there, you know, everybody has gone into Jabal, I'm just staying here because Kouri would fire me if I left, not that he ever comes around until after dinner. I swung by the football field, it was a graveyard of broken nets and December mud, and, just in case, I went by the basketball court, and then the market, which was finished anyway, and the place where they usually stood around and smoked all day, and finally I gave up and headed toward Jabal. In Jabal, of course, you could get anything, because there were millions of people all crowded in there, but every big place is also just many small places put together, and it didn't take anything to find Fadi's pal Awad, who looked strangely perturbed when I asked him, but he waved me on, just down there, down there, he told me, straight, straight, and I followed the line of his finger, still running, not even out of breath, and a few blocks later I reached the corner he had mentioned, Hebron Street. Now, all the buildings in this part of Jabal were very big, six, eight, ten stories, and people were running back and forth all over the place, even more than usual, and even louder than usual. Sirens, cars, yelling. Honestly, I didn't want to be there. But in that moment of my life (they say Allah, Great and Loving, forgives everything, if only you submit!), finding Fadi was the entire purpose of my soul.

Several boys, flush-faced, rounded the corner and almost knocked me off my feet as if I were invisible. Crying to one another in excited voices, they gathered themselves into a circle, spewed out a barrage of fabulous obscenities, patted one another on the back, bent down, hands on knees, caught their breaths, and whispered commands to one another. Obviously, a football game was going on, but who had time for this? Fadi was just around that very corner. I wouldn't even wait for a break in the game; I'd just call him out and tell him about Nadirah. I imagined how Fadi would wave me off—Why are you bothering me? I'm playing! But I would insist and call him out again, and again if need be, until finally he would have to declare time out and trot over to me, irritated but also concerned—What happened? Did something happen? Nadirah? My father, my mother? My sister, Hafaz? I would force myself to speak. My voice, my eyes, my entire face overwhelmed with sadness, outrage, shock, empathy (for him!), grief, anger, compassion (for her!)—but even as I saw this playing out in my mind, instead of leaping onto Hebron Street, I found myself warily peering around the building's edge.

O Allah! Most Merciful! I am dead, what good can these visitations do?

There was no football. Instead, I saw a squadron of soldiers at the end of the block and, opposite them, a gang of shouting boys had formed a rough line, one, two, or three deep, not a line even, just an undulation of boys lurching forward a few steps, then falling tentatively back, then rushing forward again and letting go slings filled with stones or tossing bottles or pieces of rubber, whole sides of corrugated aluminum, a tire iron; whatever they could throw, they threw. The Jewish soldiers hid like babies behind their jeeps and armored cars and shot in the air, and everyone ran into some doorway or around some corner. But when they saw none of their comrades had fallen, the boys emerged from their holes, reloaded their slings, and surged forward again. I saw some kid running with nothing more than a cardboard box that landed at his feet when he finally unleashed it. Fires dotted the avenue where boys had doused tires with kerosene, while others were busy building barricades of junk, shouting, "Victory! Victory! Victory over Israel and America!" and "Remember Karameh! Revolution! Revolution until victory!" Music was blaring from portable players, *In Sabra a wound is bleeding! In Shattilla the rose is plucked! You will never live in my land! You will never fly in my sky!* and the announcer cried out, "Come, my brothers and sisters! To Hebron Street! To Amman Square! The revolution has begun!"

Through all the smoke and madness I could barely see, but one boy screamed, "Damn you bastard sons of whores! Lick my dick! A thousand dicks in your mother's cunt!"

"Fadi! Fadi!" I called to him. "Fadi!"

The soldiers fired in the air once again. I grabbed my ears, fell to my knees. But the boys laughed from their hiding places. Now they flowed once more from the doorways and alleys, their pockets heavy with stones and bottles. Yowling like young jackals, one by one they cast their missiles, shook their fists, shouted their slogans. Fadi—his black shirt, his black pants, his black shoes, his black headband, his face black with soot, flung his stones and howled with glee. A soldier fell! The other boys yelped in joy, ran up, flung more bottles; the soldiers buried their heads in their arms—another down! Screams of happiness!

"Fadi! Fadi!" I rose to my feet. "Fadi! Over here! Fadi!"

And now, pressing a stone into his sling, he turned.

He narrowed, studied, blinked, and then a smile of sunlight burst through the soot of his face—"Amir!"

Smiling, he dropped to one knee and then to the ground.

All the boys scattered again. But Fadi remained on the pavement, his legs crushed beneath him, his eyes facing Heaven, and his fingers tangled up in his sling. Only then did I hear the shots ring out.

. . .

Now the guns have gone quiet. The boys no longer rush forward. I have moved a little from my corner, not much, just a little, inching toward my beloved Fadi as if his open eyes are two great magnets. Unconsciously, unwittingly, I reach out my hand and, driven by the deep confusion in my heart, shove my head forward. Now I am standing on Hebron Street, looking down at Fadi. It is just Fadi and I, the burning tires, the overturned Opel; and at the end of the block, an Israeli soldier also stands and focuses the wrath of his rifle upon me. I look at him, this Jewish soldier, not in hate or anger, but in bewilderment, in wonder, in awe, and at the gun he has pointed at me. I look at him, and I see he is looking at me, also without anger, and with the same bewilderment, wonder, and awe. Yet in his eyes I see something else that I myself am not feeling, and that is hopelessness. He lowers his gun and waits for me to retreat behind the corner wall. Fadi is still breathing, but I know that this is my only chance, and the soldier has given it to me for a purpose neither of us can quite fathom, and so I do retreat, cover my eyes, and begin to weep.

And in this new silence, I hear a cry. I turn. It is Nadirah. Falling to her knees, she tears her precious blue jeans and curses the land to which she was born.

Chapter Sixteen

✡

"YOU WILL THINK IT STRANGE," ABDUL-LATIF SAID to me, "that we take care of a Jew."

"Yes."

"Lie still. Drink water. In the old days, I had Jewish customers."

"Yes."

"Someone you know was kind to remember me. Please, lie still."

I tried to tell him it was insane of me to come here, but all that came out was a kind of whimper.

"The boys in the town, they are angry. The intifada is over, nothing is accomplished, except that Arafat has returned, but what did he have to do with it? It was all the boys. And now . . . now . . . well. So you see, you are not welcome here anymore. Not like in the old days." He seemed to look around the room for something but couldn't find it. "The girls will bring you some food. It's not much. They don't know how to cook. My wife. She's not here."

"Where?"

"This is not even my house. My house no longer exists. She lives with my cousin and his son's widow. I rented this. She can go wherever she wants, but not the children. Two of them are gone anyway, and two are still unwed. They stay with the father."

"Four daughters?" I recalled he had only three.

"Yes. Why do you seem surprised?" He held the water in front of me, then put it down. "What happened to our house? Bulldozed."

I moaned.

"Yes. Is this not the most ironic? I care for you, and they bull-doze my house."

I tried not to look at him. It seemed to me his thin, hawkish face was on the verge of cracking open.

"My child is a martyr, all praise to Allah and his servant, *salla allahu 'alaihi wa sallam*. Only six weeks ago. Look how you shake. Must I pour water down your throat?" He shrugged and placed his hands on his chest and turned the palms toward me. "It had noth-ing to do with me. I knew nothing about it. I'm not sure about his mother. If she knew, she kept it to herself. To protect him." At this, he laughed quite bitterly.

"I'm so sorry," I tried to say. "I'm so sorry for you." But I doubt I actually said it.

"I don't believe in any of this shit," he went on. "But look what they've done to me anyway. Why do they destroy my house?"

I didn't know, really.

"You, you come here from where? I don't think you're a sabra. Somewhere far away. Russia, probably. South Africa. Who knows? Did they blow up your house? Did we?"

I shook my head.

"But mine they blow up." He took a deep breath, I think to try to calm himself. "And my wife? She's gone completely crazy, that's all. She is taken care of by the Fatah bullies, and she is now herself one of them. Probably I shall be, too." He stopped his ranting and studied me carefully. "It looks like they did blow you up, anyway. Oh wait, no, a traffic accident, right? A bus, yes?"

I nodded.

"A bus also killed my son."

We sat there together for some minutes. His thin arms hung by his sides like broken wings.

"You have not asked his name," he said. "Why is that? Don't you want to know his name? His name was Ami. That's what we called him when he was a baby. Ami. Later he took other names. I myself hadn't called him Ami since he was three or four. Since he was three or four we did not really speak as father and son anyway.

Not since he was six, probably. He hated me for what I am. He wanted something, I don't know what."

Perhaps he got what he wanted, I thought.

But maybe I said it aloud, because Abdul-Latif shrugged, sighed, coughed, brought up phlegm, spit into a little jar that he carried with him, and said, "If that is what he wanted, then praise be to God. Do you have a son, Mr. Guttman?"

I shook my head.

"But a daughter."

I nodded.

"And do you speak to your daughter?" He did not wait for me to answer him. "Then speak to her, Mr. Guttman. Excuse me, I don't mean to lecture, but my heart is broken, my heart is broken. Ah, here is your meal. Marya, do not be afraid, bring it here."

Marya was perhaps eighteen or nineteen, pretty enough beneath her headscarf. Her fingernails were painted pink, and I thought of Anyusha and all the crazy colors she liked to paint her nails when I let her. Thank God I would never have to worry about Anyusha the way he had to worry about Amir or his girls. I would only have to worry that one of *them* might do her harm. Marya did not like me; I could see that. If her father were not there, she would have stabbed me with her own hands or perhaps just called her brother's comrades, and they could do the job. She handed me a small tray upon which was a little lamb stew and yogurt.

"Is it all right, the meat with milk?" asked Abdul-Latif. "Very well," he said. "We shall leave you."

And with that they all quietly disappeared from the room, and I heard the key turn in the lock.

☯

Dear You,

I guess you could call this "Confessions of a Young Girl on the Brink." But I don't feel crazy, just impatient. Miriam didn't show up, and we're *still* sitting here in the basement with all the windows painted over. I know this sounds so crazy. Who is this Anyusha who does all this hiding in basements and studying Torah and everything? But Pop, it was God who led me here to this basement. Yes, I can see the look on your face when I say that, but it's true. OK, now I have to go backward in time, even though I said I wanted to tell you everything in order as it happened. Sorry, but I have to.

This was like six months ago. I was in one of my sessions with Rabbi Keren, and I was saying about how things talk to me, stones, bugs, trees, cartons of milk. And he said, OK, I want you to go someplace for me. I said, Why? And he said, I want to see if you hear anything. It made me nervous, but I said OK anyway, because, I don't know, and he said we'll drive together. I told Pop that I was doing something with Shana, and I jumped school early and met up with the rabbi, and holy smokes, we drove all the way to Nahariya, like over an hour, and that's where we picked up this new woman, Efra. And I said, Where's Miriam? and Rabbi said, She couldn't come, she was too busy. This Efra was religious, too, with her scarf and long skirt and no makeup at all. By now it's almost two o'clock and we haven't eaten a thing, and I'm starving, and it just comes out of me. *Where's the food? Where are we going?* And Rabbi Keren just smiles and says, Let's eat after. After what, already? And Efra suggested a place where we could stop, but Rabbi Keren said it was getting late and it wouldn't be long, but actually it was long, winding all through the Galilee past lots of little Arab villages and Ma'alot and Sasa, until, *finally*, where the road bends really sharply, he pulls into a parking lot. Food! I'm thinking, but Rabbi Keren shushed me and said, Anna, we're now in a very special place, a very special and mystical place, where a great rabbi, none other than the author of the Zohar, is buried. Do you remember what the Zohar is? You have to be an idiot not to know that, I said, Shimon Bar Yochai. He could burn people up with his eyes! (At least that's the story: he spent twenty years in a cave, buried up to his neck in sand, and when he got out he was so pure that anything he looked at that wasn't as pure as he—which was everything—burned up. So God made him go back in his cave for another twenty years! And this was where he was buried.) Aren't you excited? Efra asked. I tried to say yes, but I really was trying not to lie anymore (except to Pop, sorry), so she says, Well, you will be! You will be! and links arms with me, and down the stairs we go toward whatever was awaiting us. (Of course I now know what was awaiting us, but then I didn't, so I'm writing it as if I didn't, because that's how you tell a story.) And why is this Efra there in the first place? No mention of an Efra when Rabbi Keren laid out the plot for me. Because, she explained, women can't go where men go, and you need a chaperone. I wanted to ask her if she thought this was 1970. Anyway, we're in this little courtyard now, and Rabbi Keren disappears into one of the men-only chapels, and I'm standing in the courtyard, and some big fat Haredi rabbi with a big gap in his front teeth and a beard that splits in two like twin goat horns is exhorting the crowd, and then I don't know—all of a sudden, POW! *Voices.* From deep down below, from a hundred meters, a thousand meters, from the very core of the earth—not speaking, but murmuring, vibrating, pulsating, not actually saying anything at all, and they made me think of seaweed stuck to the bottom of the ocean, swaying with the flow of the water. They were stuck in the mud, these voices, but because of the tides and jet streams they let out sounds that resembled speech but weren't. Like when the wind resembles alley cats.

All I wanted was to escape those sad, gloomy voices stuck in the mud; they upset me so much because I couldn't make out a single word, nothing to separate one voice from another. I started getting dizzy, and I thought I was going to throw up. It seemed like it was getting dark even though the sun was shining bright, and it was too hot, and then—I don't know—honestly, I'm not making it up—I think I fainted, and when I opened my eyes I was looking straight up into the sky, and I saw a dot of pure white in that blue sky, a pinprick of white light so small you wouldn't see it unless you were looking directly at it, and even if you were looking directly at it you might miss it. And I could see right into it, and it was a tunnel, and then I understood: if you were to go into that tunnel you would hear complete and perfect silence. I didn't know where it went, I didn't even know what it was, but if you went into that tunnel of white, there would be only silence. And then Efra was leaning over me and saying, Anna, are you all right? Anna!

When Rabbi Keren came out from praying, he took one look at me and got really pale, and Efra said, I told you we should have stopped for food! She was very upset and didn't say a word the whole way back, though we did stop for hummus and kunafa in one of the Druze villages. Of course, neither Rabbi nor Efra would eat anything, because it wasn't glatt kosher, but I did. And maybe it all happened because I was too hungry and hypoglycemic, but even after I'd eaten I couldn't shake what had happened—the voices without voice that were so sad, the pinprick of white, the silence that lived only in that tunnel.

It was only after we dropped Efra off that Rabbi Keren asked me what happened to me at the grave of Shimon Bar Yochai. I thought about it. I turned it over in my mind: the noise from below and the white from above. And it made me think. Everybody in life is the seaweed stuck to the bottom of the sea, and we all look like we are moving, and we all look like we are dancing, and playing, and laughing. But it is only the sea that is moving us. And if it would suddenly stop flowing, we would all drop to the ground and lie there, and we would finally understand what we really are. That is why the voices were so unhappy. You would think, oh, she went to the grave of the famous rabbi who is the hero of the Kabbalah (and by the way, there are tons of big rabbis buried around there), so naturally she heard all the dead people coming up from the earth, and naturally that's why they were so sad. No. That is not what happened. It was the living I heard; it was all the people who came to that place for salvation or who came and didn't care about salvation. Who prayed or didn't pray. Who ate or didn't eat. Why were they so sad? Because inside they all know. They are stuck in the mud, and the movement of life is nothing but an illusion. That is what I thought, and what I still think. But that is not what I told Rabbi Keren. I told him I heard some voices, and I thought they were the voices of the saints. And he asked, What did they say? And I answered, They said they were happy. And he looked at me funny, and asked, Is that all? And I answered, They said God is everywhere, and the Messiah is coming. And then Rabbi Keren stopped asking.

So I lied. But I don't care because now I know. Dearest Pop, silence exists in only one place. Freedom from the mud, in only one place. Real life exists in only one place.

All these years since I started hearing this stuff, I kept trying to get there. It's not that I mind the voices. It's that I would prefer they speak to someone else. That's why I am here. That's what I understood when I saw the white dot at the grave of the great rabbi. And so I kept to this path.

But only when Yohanan took my hand at the bus stop and it really *was* quiet, did I understand completely that, yes, I am on the correct path. That is what I want you to understand. You can only hear if it's quiet. Please please please get it. God has led me here, to this basement. And God will lead me in all my steps to come.

Chapter Seventeen

✡

IN THE GENERAL SCOPE OF THINGS, I should have considered the appearance of Abdul-Latif a true miracle. Why would he search for me, and how had he found me? I had allowed the desert to overtake me, to embrace me, but he had decided otherwise. In life, odd things do happen: certainly one could accidentally come upon what the Bedouin call a camila, a spot, invisible to all but the Bedouin himself, where it is possible to scoop down into the sand until a black circle of water magically emerges; or you might search the horizon for an enclave of rushes or acacia and, lo and behold, some fifteen meters down, or, more likely, forty, you find a drop or two to drink—they say there is an ocean of fresh water beneath this desert. But Abdul-Latif, father of my enemy, was an oasis to me. How else could I describe it? And yet I could not bring myself to drink his water or tell him the truth. Instead I lay in that bed, drifting between the life in my hands and the one I had left behind so many years ago.

One Saturday evening, in the summer of 1981, I returned to the apartment I shared with my mother with my arms full of the drawings for the house I was designing for Zagoryanka. I kicked open the door and called, "It's done! I'm ready to build!" Mother did not answer immediately, which was unusual: she always pounced upon me the moment I arrived home, relieved I'd somehow survived the day. "Thank God! You could have fallen through the ice!" she once said when I was a few minutes late. Who could have an answer to this? Did she imagine I had sledded across the Moskva? So when she didn't rush to greet me, I grew a little alarmed.

I stalked the hall, checking our few rooms. Hers was at the end. It was frantically neat, as if one misplaced pin could endanger the entire household. I peeked in the bathroom, vaguely worried I'd find her unconscious in the bathtub, but she wasn't there. In the kitchen, two cups were set out as always, waiting for my return. In the entryway, the slippers were all in their places, but, as I scanned the row of shoes, there was a gap between the first and second pair. I dialed Katya to see if, finally, Mother had gone over there by herself, an idea that seemed absurd, since she rarely stepped out of the house without me. No one answered. I considered going out to look for her—who knows, maybe *she* fell in the Moskva—but really, she was a grown woman, what was there to worry about? I grabbed a beer, something I rarely did, flipped on the television, and sat myself down on the sofa, something I never did either except to watch football. *Goodnight Children* had just started. As usual, it ran short snippets of animated films—maybe Dr. Aybolit or something with the Hedgehog or Cheburashka. My favorites were the classics from the Stalinist days, *The Snow Maiden, Prince Vladimir*. But it didn't matter. I allowed the song of Krokodil and Genya and the grizzly voice of Carlson to wash over me, and also the pretty announcer, Auntie Valentina, with her wide-eyed smile and sugary lips. I took deep slugs off my bottle of beer, which was Estonian so it wasn't completely undrinkable. I threw my feet up on the couch, took another swig of beer. This was great. I'd never been alone in this apartment before. I'd never really been alone in Veshnaya either. I went to the refrigerator, pulled out my mother's jar of pickled mushrooms, found a half-open can of sprats, cut off a chunk of bread, and carried it all back to the sofa. Auntie Valentina was talking to the puppets now. I liked this part. They were just hand puppets, Stepashka, Karkusha, Khrusha, but who could not love them? I threw my feet back up on the couch and slurped down a sprat dripping in oil. I followed this with a slimy baby mushroom. Now they were singing a song. "Goluboy Vagon." I wondered if there was anything else I might want to eat. Maybe an apple or some cheese. My beer was sadly near its end, but there were a couple more in the refrigerator. I'd been saving them, I had no idea why. I put down my plate, skittled as quick as one of Dr. Aybolit's rabbits to the kitchen so as not to miss too much of *Goodnight Children*—and slumped back down on the sofa loaded up with new treats and more beer. I didn't even bother to take off my slippers. Don't think I'm coldhearted. *Goodnight Children* is not very long. I would look for Mother as soon as it was over. But this was what I had been longing for. This very moment. My moment. My beer. My show. This is what freedom meant to me at that point in my life.

The television glowed brighter and brighter in my eyes, the bold colors of childhood enveloping me almost like the embrace of my long-gone father; and in a richly detailed Russophile style, a style so realistic and sympathetically drawn I could almost believe it was actually happening, I saw a great prince raise a golden sword above the head of the fearsome witch as the narrator began: *In the time before time and the days before days, in a land beyond the mountains and past the far green sea, there lived a great prince in search of a wife. "Bring me the partner of my heart," he said, "a maiden true and fair, for I am lonely and wish to marry." He sent his minions far and wide to find the most beautiful and kindhearted maidens in the land, but search as they may, they found no one to suit him. So one day he donned the cloak of a peasant and the shoes of a stable boy, and went into the woods in search of the witch, Baba Yaga. . . .*

"What is this?"

"Huh?"

"What are you doing?"

I opened my eyes. It was Mother, her shoes still on her feet, her hands grasping the sides of her head, her mouth curled into astonishment.

"Uh, dreaming," I said. Indeed, the taste of sleep coated my mouth, and some story of witches and maidens—I don't know—some fairy tale that . . . I couldn't remember, exactly.

"You're drunk," she said. "And my mushrooms. You've eaten them all."

Ruefully I surveyed the mess of cans and empty beer bottles strewn about the sofa. "Where were you?" I demanded. "I was worried."

"With her," she said.

"With her what?"

"With her," she repeated. And then Collette sidled in from the entry hall and gave me a little wave of hello.

"Hi, sleepyhead!" she said.

The sight of Collette arm in arm with my mother was no less a fairy tale than the one that had been swirling in my head. Having fallen asleep watching *Goodnight Children*, I found myself not fully able to comprehend that the TV was no longer on and that Collette was standing in my living room. Smiling, she came forward, bent gaily at the waist, kissed my nose, and whispered, "Romochka. Idiot." Now she deftly cleared away the beer bottles, the emptied jar of pickled mushrooms, and the stinking can that once held my mother's delicious sprats. Mother offered me a look of disgust. "Clean yourself up if you can manage it," she said. But I lay there a few minutes more, wanting to taste not so much the minute particles of saliva Collette had deposited upon my nose as the syllables she had imparted to my ear: *Romochka. Durak!* She could have called me Roman or Roma. Guttman was how she usually referred to me at parties. She might have used Romka, Rommy, Romashka. But *Romochka*. As if I were a naughty boy. My little Romochka! How troublesome you are! What a little devil! *Durak!*

They'd gone to the Tishinksy rynok and brought home all manner of zakusky, fresh parsley, cucumbers, green onions, eggplant. My mother boiled some potatoes and found an ancient bottle of vodka, I think from the time of Khrushchev, from which she was able to eke three tiny glasses and which she doled out like nectar, drop by drop. In the meantime, Collette set down a tablecloth, and the two of them prattled away as if they'd known each other earlier in life, had met by chance at the bus stop on Kutuzovsky, and simply picked up where they'd left off, the years between only a comma in some ongoing conversation. I could not help myself—the glow, which even I had to admit had become tarnished through these months of rejection and jealousy, returned to Collette's person, filling the kitchen with golden happiness. Her smile, her hands, her hair, her neck, her eyes, the sound of her voice, the sway of her hips, the pleats of her skirt were all too beautiful, too wrenching, for me to hold a grudge.

"Stop fidgeting," my mother remarked.

They went on to analyze which stands in the rynok were the most reliable for green vegetables, where to buy the fattest chicken, the freshest fish, though in fact my mother almost never went to that rynok or any other. Then Mother began to bitterly complain about her neighbors.

"Oh!" Collette laughed. "I have this Plotkina with her little mutt, Vova. What a pair! I think the dog is smarter than she is. At least he knows where to pee!"

Then my mother did something I could never have expected. She cleared the dishes, sat back down, and said, "You know, my husband, Lyopa, left us."

"It is hard to be left," Collette replied.

"You're too young to say such a thing. Roma, do you remember when Papa left?"

Under the table, Collette placed her hand on mine, but her eyes remained altogether upon my mother.

"Lyopa was a brilliant man," she said, "maybe even a genius."

"Yes," replied Collette, "Roman has told me."

"And then gone."

"And then gone. I understand."

"Roma has already told you?"

"You tell me. I want to hear. I want to know everything."

"I didn't think so. He doesn't talk a lot."

Collette produced a smile that seemed to say: Yes, that's how he is. They were talking about me as if I were not in the room, and

I could not have been happier. Collette planted two elbows on the table, rested her chin on her two fists, and made it clear that my mother had her undivided and earnest attention.

My mother then told the story of how we lost my father and at the same time were evicted from the house on Veshnaya and how we came, the two of us, now that Katya was gone, to this apartment and the life we now were leading.

I was fourteen years old, the age at which I was eligible for Komsomol, and to which, in spite of everything, I yearned to be accepted as early as possible. Everyone of course was always accepted, but that did not ease my anxiety for one moment. I was desperate to be Russian and more than happy to become a devout Communist, if only it would help me to squeeze inside a pair of traditional felt boots. There was only one person who was in my way: Dima Chernapolsky. He was the most popular kid in school, a great basketball player, sang like an angel, his father was a colonel in the KGB, he lived in our building, and he hated me. He hated everything about me, and his main joy in life was to spread rumors about me that often reached the ears of our teachers. I was a thief, I was a homosexual, I was a Zionist, I cheated on tests. But I asked myself, in what way was he superior to me? Smarter? Wittier? Able to write a coherent sentence in history class? He was a party brat and belonged in a party school, and if he wasn't, there had to be something wrong with him. Probably he was retarded. Yet because of him my popularity had plummeted, and I was isolated and miserable.

One day, I came upon him laying claim to the hill of garbage that had grown like a Tower of Babel in the no-man's-land behind the row of garages that lined the alleys off of Bogataya Pereulok.

Look at him up there, I thought, king of the fucking hill. But it was my hill. I used to climb it many times; I used to reign over that stinky realm.

A string of curses erupted from my mouth. I would have to bring Dima to his knees. Crush him. Break him. It didn't matter to me that he towered over me, an athlete, a hero of the school. I wanted him to cry. Because even then I knew, once you cry, it's all over.

I stole around to the back of the trash heap and without any warning charged up the hill screaming my head off.

Amazing to me in that moment, and to this day, Dima Chernapolsky collapsed almost immediately and in no time at all was weeping. He begged me to stop hitting him. And finally I did, but not before I kicked him down the hill and watched, laughing, as he lifted himself up and limped away. Only when he was gone did I grow quiet and contemplate the magnitude of my victory. I could go to school again with my head held high. Dima was mine! I owned him. I took myself to an ice-cream stand to celebrate.

As soon as I got home, however, my parents accosted me. "Where have you been?" "We were worried to death!" "Look at you!" "What happened?" "Your clothes are filthy!" In the living room, the rest of the family was waiting, a single accusatory, disappointed look animating every face: Uncle Maxim, Aunt Sophie, Katya, my cousins Julia and Danka, and probably the ghosts of my grandparents and great-grandparents on every side. They all stood in the same forlorn posture, wringing their hands as if waiting to be shot.

Then my mother yelled at me, "What have you done to us, you stupid, silly boy?" She clutched my filthy shirt between her fingers. "Who made you this way?"

"All right," I heard my father say from somewhere that seemed very far away. "Enough."

But my mother shook me violently. "You!" she cried, "you!" And then, for the only time that I can remember, she slapped me, hard across the face, and I fell backward against the telephone table. "We did not raise such a child!" she screamed at me. "We don't know this child!" She spun around, addressing the walls, the ceiling, the windows, "Not our fault! Not our fault!"

Finally, my father emerged from the circle of family. He looked me in the eye—a look I shall never forget, a look that squeezed me into a ball and shot me into the most profound darkness—and then, without a word, he turned to my mother, held her firmly by the shoulders, and forced her to sit. "Calm down," he said to her.

Behind him, my illustrious uncle Max was about to speak, but my father lifted his hand. "Roman," he said evenly, "do not say a thing. We already know everything. Colonel Chernapolsky has already been down to see us. He gave us a letter. Shall I read it?"

I cannot recall his words exactly, but the charges were laid out like a denunciation in *Pravda*. Dmitry Valerivich (no longer Dima, but Dmitry Valerivich) had been brutally assaulted, to such an extent the police should be brought in to investigate. Such an instance of hooliganism must not be tolerated; the influence of a boy such as myself on the students of Moscow School Forty-two could only lead others into degeneracy and error, clearly the result of Western music and the Guttman habit of listening to the BBC, which, by the way, was well known. How, Colonel Valeri Chernapolsky asked himself, can a boy who has been given every possible chance, every possible advantage of our Soviet system, a free education, a universal education, and unequivocally the very best education in the world, a boy who is a Young Pioneer and a candidate for Komsomol, who in any other country would most likely be a pariah but here is treated 100 percent as an equal, even more than equal in the opinion of many, how could such a boy turn his back on those who nurtured and cared for him, those who taught him and tried to instill in him Soviet values and a clean, wholesome Soviet spirit—how could such a boy victimize the innocent and terrorize his schoolmates? Because he is an agent of terror! Because he is a reactionary bully! Because he is a Zionist hooligan!

"They're going to have us kicked out of the apartment," my mother bawled. "And you," she said to me, "you'll end up working in a factory."

"Don't be absurd," my father said. "It's just an argument between two boys. No one is getting kicked out of anywhere. Even Chernapolsky wouldn't go that far."

"Of course he would!" she cried. "You will go down and speak to Colonel Chernapolsky yourself. And you will speak to his wife, too. Because believe me, she's behind this. You will get down on your hands and knees and you will beg for mercy. You will say, Marta Gregoryevna, on behalf of my son, I beg mercy."

"Are you crazy? I'll do no such thing. I was once considered for membership in the Academy of Science, for heaven's sake. The highest honor!"

"I'm crazy? I'm crazy? Don't you see, you stupid Lyopa, what's happening here?"

"I'm telling you, calm down," he said.

"We'll be out on the street, all of us, and why? Because of your son. You and your academy. What academy? The Academy of Idiots? In your dreams there may have been an academy for you, but not in this life! Who made him like this? A fighter! A hooligan! A monster who refuses to listen to anyone! He thinks he knows everything! You know everything, don't you, Roman? I suppose I taught him this! It was you! You! You stupid, stupid Lyopa! Who walks away from the academy? Who turns his back on the university? No wonder he couldn't get into special school! No, Lyopa, you will go down there and you will beg. You will get down on your hands and knees. You will do whatever they ask. You will do whatever they want."

"My name is Leopold," he said. "You will call me Leopold."

"Go, Lyopa!" she cried.

"Tatyana," Uncle Max said.

My father was still standing in front of me, but suddenly he smiled and placed his hands on my head as if he were about to recite a blessing.

"Lyopa, go!" she commanded.

My father seemed not to hear her. Or perhaps he did not need to answer because he had already decided to go, for it seemed to me then that a yes had fallen upon his shoulders.

"Lyopa!" she demanded.

"Yes, all right," he muttered, still smiling at me. One could not call it a happy smile or even, as often happens between couples, a smile of familial contempt. Only now can I say with any certainty what that smile might have been—it was the smile of the ibex in the moment of flight. It was the smile of the leopard, unaccustomed to daylight but driven by starvation, that flashed through his eyes.

Then, so unexpectedly, he bent down and kissed my cheek. "Don't worry, Roma, my darling, everything will be all right. The morning shall come, just as always." He stood to his full height, looked around the room and into the eyes of his brother, Max, and walked out the door.

He did not return home that evening, and it was a very long time before I saw him again.

My mother was right, by the way. We were all to be removed from the apartment on Veshnaya. But Uncle Max being Uncle Max came to an accommodation with the colonel, and only my mother, sister, and I had to leave. At first we were compelled to live in a horrible place—with some distant cousins in Volgograd—but somehow Max, using what little pull he still possessed, and greasing the palms of those who knew someone who knew someone who *perhaps* could manipulate the waiting list for housing, in other words, *po blatu,* found us the apartment on Tishinskaya where my mother was now sitting at the kitchen table, lost in conversation with Collette Chernoff. Max spent a fortune on us, maybe everything he had, but never said a word about it. And as it turned out, my mother was much happier in this apartment than she ever was in Veshnaya. And why not? It was a small, cheerful building constructed with simple, decent lines, roomy balconies, and a friendly disposition: it seemed delighted to be sitting on its little tree-lined street. Plus there was considerably more room for the three of us, and it had all the modern conveniences, and the only complaints my mother had to suffer were her own.

My mother now concluded her tale to Collette, which, by the way, was completely different from the one I just told you—different in every detail. I believe my memory is more correct than hers—in hers, I am not even a part of the story; the loss of the apartment had nothing to do with me; my father had a mistress, maybe more than one; and he was an alcoholic, though he was clever and hid it very well; the entire family was against her because she declined to go along with his every whim; he did not beat her, but sometimes she was afraid he might; he called her night and day wanting to come back to her; when Max refused to change the locks, she packed our bags, stuffed Katya and me into a taxi, and left Veshnaya forever. In her memory there is only misery, injustice, and a final gesture of righteous vindication. In mine, a shield of bitter wisdom descended upon my father, and he, in turn, imparted to me a secret of life.

In any case, the table was finally cleared, the dishes were washed, and I at last could suggest it was time to take Collette home. They kissed good-bye, like mother and daughter. Collette and I sailed down the stairs in silence. As we passed through the door she quietly took my hand. Her hips had slid close to mine, and her head was slightly inclined, almost resting on my shoulder. This was the walk I had always dreamed of from the moment I'd laid eyes on her. At the corner, she faced me, cupped my hands in hers, rose on her toes, and kissed me. Her taste was almost like toasted bread. She leaned on her heels and studied my face. The glimmering hair was falling from her pins in long, fragrant rivers and her skin was a kind of living marble. Her mouth, thick red with cherry lipstick, was unbearable, and I began to kiss her again.

She pushed me away

"What is it?" I said.

"Don't take any of this to mean anything," she replied. "I just felt like kissing you. I only came to her because I wanted to see where you lived. Your mother is crazy, by the way. I don't know how you live with her. She's a monster." Collette's eyes turned hard. "Maybe that's what you think we have in common. Our fathers. Maybe that's why you hang on my apron like a little puppy. But it's a ridiculous comparison. My father never drank. He never had women. He was never cruel. My father was an angelic man. He was killed for his beliefs. He was a poet. Oh, don't look so stung, like the little boy who got a bad grade on his homework."

"But the way you kissed me."

"I'm in a strange mood today," she said. "None of it means a thing. Who knows why I do these things?"

She ran to the station, and I slouched back to my mother's house.

After this, Collette became frantic about leaving the Soviet Union. She applied again for permission to emigrate, was again rejected. Normally, one was not allowed to reapply before six months had passed, but she did anyway, and they accepted her papers. She saw this as a good sign, an excellent sign, a miracle, in fact.

"They're tired of me," she said. "They want me out."

But this was no different from every other time she applied, first securing an invitation from invented relatives in Israel and then collecting signatures from her place of work, her local committee, her building committee, all of whom were required to give their individual permission for her to emigrate. She had, as always, to prove she owed no obligations, no debts. At the end of all this, when she brought her dozens of documents to OVIR, they looked at her with great exasperation and explained as to a pet dog: "Haven't we told you before? You need to have your father's signature, too."

"He's dead," she reminded them, "you know that. You accepted my application the last time, and the time before that."

"Well, then, produce the death certificate," they said.

So she went to organize the death certificate, something her grandfather had failed to do and which she herself could not bear to do either, but now she had no choice. However, when she arrived at the Registrar of Vital Statistics, she was told it was not possible to execute her request at this time. Other documents were needed. She explained that her father had been arrested in 1953.

"And?" they said.

"And we haven't seen him since."

"How do you know he didn't just leave? Lots of men abandon their families. Maybe he knew what you would become."

"He was arrested," she repeated.

"You saw him arrested?"

"No, obviously. I was an infant."

"But you have witnesses?"

"No, of course not."

"Then we suggest you apply to the police or to the Bureau of Prisons."

"What are they going to tell me?"

"You have to ask them."

Of course there was no such thing as the Bureau of Prisons. And the local militia either had no records or was not willing to share them. She applied to her local Soviet and received a formal letter explaining that it was not the appropriate authority in such matters. She went several times to the reception room of the Main Directorate of Corrections at the Ministry of Justice, but there was never anyone there to meet with her, though she had arranged one appointment after another. Finally she declared she would go to the KGB itself. "Why not? They're the ones who killed him."

I told her, "Enough. No one will tell you anything. They were just playing with you. You should know by now, they have no intention of letting you go."

But there was no reasoning with her. She went with signs and posters to the Lubyanka. The guards threw her to the ground. She came again the next day. They pushed her, threatened her, kicked her. One of them began to arrest her but then, unaccountably, didn't. On the third day there appeared one or two reporters from Western magazines and a TV crew from Spain. She was briefly detained, then let go. After that, nothing more happened, but from that time on she was well known in the West, and prominent people began to visit her from America and England, bringing religious items for which she had no use, but also things she could sell, like miniature tape recorders and blue jeans. She was adopted by a large number of families in different towns in America, and people wore stainless-steel bracelets with her name on them, and the Council on Soviet Jewry opened a case file on her, and the State Department of the United States of America raised her name a bit closer to the top of their list, and Hadassah did an ad in the *New York Times* about refuseniks and one of the larger photos was of Collette. All of these things came to be known to us through emissaries or through her friend Charlie, who often brought people to see her. But none of this assuaged her. She feverishly wrote to American politicians. She made videos of herself appealing for help and smuggled them to Jewish organizations. And though she knew that her every move was watched, noted, recorded, and analyzed, she began to disappear for long stretches. She had new friends, of whom I knew nothing. She bought herself a chalkboard by which she could speak to people in silence, but she never used it with me. "Don't be silly," she would say, "what do you and I have to hide?" But she would return sometimes with notes in her pockets, which she would burn in the ashtray or tear into little pieces and flush down the toilet.

I was no longer invited along to her soirees or rendezvous. If Charlie came by, they would go for long walks, and though he was always polite, he no longer showed any interest in me. Sometimes they got into his car and drove as far as Peredelkino, got out, and walked in the woods where they might hear the crunch of leaves of anyone who might be tailing them. Once or twice I drove with them, seated in the back. It was clear I was to wait in the car while they walked, which I did, saying nothing on the long return home. But mostly I watched them drive off from the kitchen window.

So why did I stay? Who knows? But if I were not there when she arrived home, she would phone me angrily. She would not allow me to spend the night, but also would insist I stay until two or three in the morning. She cried frequently, and would vacillate between fits of temper and fits of laughter. "You must sleep," I said.

"How can anyone sleep in this country?" It went on this way for weeks.

From time to time I still saw my old friends, but it was not the same, especially with Irina, Marik's wife, whom I used to love. One day she telephoned me.

"Roman, you must listen to me for once."

"Why? What?"

"What are you doing with this woman? She's poison for you."

"How dare you!" I said.

"I dare," she replied.

"You don't understand. She's different. She understands things we don't. Her soul is—"

"What, better than yours?"

"Yes."

"What nonsense. She lives in her own world—anyone but you can see that. She makes things up. She has you wrapped around her finger. It's disgusting."

We fell into a weary silence.

Finally, I said, "Irina, why do you even care?"

"Idiot!" she said, and slammed down the phone.

Then, in the first terrible days of August when the air was thick as blood and the sun burned the sidewalks white, Collette telephoned me.

"All right, I'm coming right over," I said.

"No," she said, "I don't want you to. I don't want you to come here anymore."

"But why not?"

"I don't want to see you again," she said.

"But why not?"

"Don't be a baby, Roman. I don't need you anymore. Please stay away."

"You can't be serious."

"I'm perfectly serious."

"I don't understand."

Finally she said, "Pascal is back. He'll take care of me now."

"Pascal? You said that was over."

"How could it be over? If you knew me at all, you would know that. How can you love someone in the way we love each other and it be over? If you think that, you don't know what love is."

"You've been waiting for him all this time."

"Of course."

"You've been writing to him, haven't you?"

"Roman," she said, "what is there to discuss anymore?"

"You said it was over" was all I could think of to say.

I wanted to get drunk that night, but it was impossible for me to get out of bed. I couldn't lift an arm or move a foot.

Now that I had stopped seeing Collette, I quickly finished the engineering specs for my dream house, which I had to simplify almost out of existence because hardly any of the materials I wanted were available, and I went down to Zagoryanka, towing Fima Dragunsky along with me. Together, we tore down the old place. It came apart with a few blows of the sledgehammer and a few turns of the crowbar. When it was all in a huge heap, my uncle Max, who had acquired it for us in the fifties, unexpectedly showed up at the gate, having taken the train on some perverse impulse. He had been very happy to have the dacha torn down and a new one built. But now he sat on the upturned soil and wept.

After he left, we cleared the rubble and laid out the boundaries of the new foundation. We dug our corners, set the frame, leveled it, and waited for Lonya to arrive with the bags of concrete. I became impatient. A sort of desperation took hold of me. Fima reminded me that Lonya undoubtedly had to go through many steps to secure the concrete from his various sources, and on top of that he had to finagle a truck and scam some guys into loading it, and he probably had to find some extra vodka or cigarettes at the last minute to ease some complication or pay off some fifth wheel.

"Has Lonya ever failed you?" he reminded me.

But I hated Lonya at that moment. I yearned only for the icy scent of poured concrete gurgling over the lip of the wheelbarrow. From its smooth, ripe surface my house would blossom, and I could not wait another minute. But what could we do? We sat down on the tattered velvet couch that we'd set up near the overgrown vegetable garden and smoked our cigarettes. Fima produced two apples. He ate his very deliberately; I gobbled mine down. Then we smoked again, and when Lonya still hadn't arrived, Fima dug into his bag and came out with two bottles of Baikal. When this was consumed, and still no Lonya, Fima sang something from the Beatles.

"I think I do it well," he said.

At last, we heard the truck lurching up the road with the blood-curdling cry of rusty gears and the rattle of side rails hanging on for dear life. We charged up the path and went around to unload the cargo. But the truck bed was empty. I tore open the cab door where Lonya sat glumly, still clutching the steering wheel.

"What happened?" I said. "Where's my concrete?"

"Roma," he replied, "I have something to tell you."

"What? Those assholes want more vodka? I told you I'd pay for it. I know they have the fucking concrete, because I saw it myself."

"Let me out," he said.

"What is it they want? Just tell me. I'll get it. I don't care what it is."

"I didn't even go there," he said. "Let me out."

"You didn't go there? What did you do? You drank all my fucking vodka with your fucking Communist friends and their whores!"

"Jesus God!" He flung open the door, pushed me to the ground. He shook his fists at me. "Collette's been arrested."

"What?"

"Please don't tell me you didn't know."

"But I didn't know. I don't know anything."

Lonya leaned down ominously, his glass eye so close to my face I could see the scratches in it. "You swear to the God of this shit-fucked universe that you don't know anything. On Lenin's head!"

"I swear to you."

"Ah, Romka," he sighed. "For Christ's sake, it's all over Moscow. She tried to hijack a plane."

Chapter Eighteen

☪

I WOULD LIKE TO DISCUSS my confusion.

I'm here. I'm there. I'm nowhere at all.

And then suddenly I am in my father's house. And—impossible!

Is that Guttman? Guttman? In my own bed? Breathing the air of my very father and sisters as if he might suck the memory of my life from every corner of existence?

Can I describe this situation? Can I comprehend it? Have I descended not to earth but to Hell?

I have flown from the southern desert across the Judean Highlands; rising up from the Dead Sea, I have traversed the great cities of Dimona, Be'er Sheva, Arad, and circled the myriad towns and villages, the Bedouin encampments, the army bases without number, some so secret even the soldiers don't know where they are. I have encompassed in my vision all this ancient landscape stretching east to what they call Jordan and west to Sinai and the lip of the Mediterranean and south to the Gulf of Aqaba and north to the ripe Golan, but for what? To find Guttman in my bed? At the center of all my travails lies Guttman, dreaming?

Is he dying? I perceive, through the grace of Allah, that he is not willfully avoiding the water that lies a few inches from his right hand. He simply no longer comprehends that he is thirsty. Dehydration occurred in the first minutes he was exposed to the searing heat, and acute dehydration within, perhaps, two hours, some long moments before he became stuck in the crevice, argued with the sunbird, and witnessed the death of the ibex. He has by now cycled through the phases of headache, blurred vision, dislocation, and hydrophobia. He cannot recognize the very idea of thirst. Half a liter of water would save him, but he cannot abide the idea of it. He is confident in his body; indeed, he has a clarity of mind he has never before experienced. No longer exposed to the sun, he will survive much longer. But not ultimately, unless he himself takes hold of the water my father offers him. Do I pity Roman Guttman? I must ask him: Roman Guttman, did you think of the blistering sun when you foolishly turned your car toward Bethlehem instead of heading home to your little city in the Philistine plains? No. You did not consider the consequences of turning east instead of north, of ignoring the warnings of your own brother-soldiers, of trekking into the desert without your bottle of water, your hat, or your knife. And did you take into account the ramifications of your actions on others? For instance, on the ibex, for whom, had you not climbed that rock in search of birdsong, things might have gone differently, or for the white leopard who must now live with his murderous deed. And did you think of the young daughter, who even now must be weeping into the folds of her handkerchief, and did you think of, did you think at all of my father and my sisters and the pain of Beit Ibrahim?

He can't even see me, though here I am! How can I teach him anything? He opens his mouth to speak, but no sound emerges. Perhaps he thinks he is trying to explain his life. Roman Guttman—no one is around to hear! Even I cannot hear you! Only Allah can hear, only He, and He is far, far from this place.

In the outer room sits my father, his head in his hands, swaying under the melody of his sighs. My sister Marya and my sister Hanadi busy themselves with sidelong glances. Beyond the walls of the house a crowd is forming of my old friends and neighbors. A speech I discern coalesces in the minds of Issak Al-Daya and Abdullah Saad, the headmen of our local PLO. They are contemplating their tactics, a delicate matter, even for them. For they cannot intuit my father's wishes. Is it vengeance he seeks? Or is he an angel of mercy?

. . .

I, too, had days of doubt and foreboding.

In the hours before I donned the white robe of purity and posed with my Kalashnikov and Qur'an, again and again I demanded: Who is this God of such dark power that every calamity that befalls you is already inscribed by Him in the Book of Decrees? They told me the Prophet says, *Act, for each of you will find easy that for which he was made.* But I asked, is this what I was made for? What, do you think it is a light thing? The great weight of the belt even now pulls my soul earthward. Perhaps for others it was not so; they say most smile at that moment and the ascent to Heaven is swift; they say most have already ascended long before that day, and for them all is pleasure. They live not for this world, but for the next! Yet in the days and weeks of prayer and preparation I had nothing but feet and stomach, smell and touch. The hand of life had descended upon me, and I could not unburden myself of its desires. It hung on me with as great a weight as the belt, greater even, more oppressive, more terrifying. *Do not fear the unknown,* they told me, and we said the confession, *There is no God but Allah. . . .*

I did not go inside for the washing, though it was definitely my place to be there. They had wrapped Fadi in the kafan, and brought him out on a wooden board. I stood off to one side as they covered him with flags, black, red, green, the colors of Fatah and Palestine, a photo of Arafat at his head. Though in life Fadi spat on Arafat, in death the leader's smiling face was pasted to his shroud. Then there were prayers: *O Allah! Forgive those of us that are alive and those of us that are dead; those of us that are present and those of us who are absent; those of us who are young and those of us who are grown into adults, our males and our females. O Allah! Whomsoever of us You keep alive, let him live as a follower of Islam, and whomsoever You cause to die, let him die as a believer.* As always I began to feel sick. I looked around, and there, in the far corner, in her mother's arms, eyes closed, tearless, yet weeping all the same, Nadirah. The mullah folded his hands, and my Fadi was hefted like a refrigerator upon the shoulders of the men. I should have been among them, but I could not seem to get there; my feet simply wouldn't carry me. My father glared at me: Don't be so sad! Be proud! But he himself wept like some old Bedouin. "He was my pride and joy," he sobbed.

They gathered in a great crowd. Checkered headbands and kaffiahs, black masks, green scarves all paraded down Hebron Street. I was swept along, drowning. What did I see? The sky occluded with fists. The bier adorned with oaths. Fadi was to be buried here in Jabal, not in our village. "He died here," my father had said to me, "that is the law." Thousands came out for this funeral. Who were these people? Those of our khamulah seemed lost among them, retreating before the onslaught of strangers and famous sheiks. Finally, I tried to push through the ocean of screaming boys and men, but they refused to part for me. Who do you think you are? someone said. Stop pushing! And when we arrived at the burial place, I was still far back, just one of the numberless mourners.

I closed my eyes. Again, I saw Fadi setting the stone in his sling, turning toward me. . . .

"Amir!"

It was my father. He reached through the crowd with his willowy arm and grasped my childish hand in his oil-stained fingers. He slapped my face. "What are you doing back here? Come on!"

My father threw up his arms again, and the folds of people opened before him.

I was now in the circle of our family, our khamulah having congealed around the gravesite. The body in its white sheath was lowered into the grave, and Nadirah, in spite of all custom, in spite of the mullah's outraged objections, in spite even of the Prophet's proscription, had come to the grave site. Worse still, she now knelt over it, unafraid to watch as they laid the stones upon her husband. Brazenly she drizzled a handful of dirt upon him and then, without a word, floated back into the crowd, carried on the wings of her enormous, invisible sorrow.

I had never seen her dressed in the jilbab before. Gone were the jeans and polos and the sweaters that might have suggested to me the actual form of paradise in this or any other life. This new Nadirah I did not know; redesigned by grief, her hair and neck obscured by the hijab, her face a moon shining from a dark, remote, and heartless scarf, her eyes and lips as dry as the well that had always sat unused in the ruins above my village. The crowd bleated like a herd of goats desperate to be milked, and Nadirah was gathered up within it, swallowed and held tight. Now I understood. I would never see her again. I would never see either of them again.

The years after that passed in a kind of dream.

I sat with my father watching television. I no longer cared much about school. And as for stories? My throat was stopped up and nothing came out but a kind of bark. I went every day to my father's shop. I worked on whatever car was there, but in time there were no more cars. These were the days of intifada. Let's face it, I told my father, no Jews, no cars.

So the shop was closed, and my father and I watched television.

My mother hinted many times that I should be out there throwing stones. "What's the matter with you?" she said. I told her that everyone who throws stones ends up in jail. "Not everyone," she replied.

But I didn't want to be in jail. I didn't want to be anywhere. And I realized with a flash of terrible certainty that I didn't care about any of it. About Palestine, about Israel, about Nadirah, about my father, about my mother, or about my sisters. As soon as I had this thought, I closed my eyes and fell into a deep sleep.

How many more years passed until that day I was sitting near the Pool of Suleiman smoking a cigarette? I don't remember when I started to smoke, but by this time my cigarette had become my closest companion. Ab had stirred himself months before and reopened the garage. Everybody thought because of Oslo there would surely be a Palestinian state in two weeks' time, and tourists were pouring back into Bethlehem. My older sisters one by one were going off to Bethlehem University or getting married, and the others were still babies. My mother blithely forgot all the words she had said to me in the years of her insanity and went back to teaching school—and I was just sitting there near the Pool of Suleiman because it wasn't too far from our town and lately I often found myself there, not really thinking of anything, just sitting. I heard in the distance some children, and for some reason this brought to mind the storytelling of Uncle Ahmad. He was long dead, just as my father had predicted, of emphysema and Parkinson's, and his gift to me, his *Book of Tales,* was lost, I didn't know where because I'd never bothered looking for it, but then the image of Uncle Ahmad faded and I saw in my mind my father's garage. I'd begun working there again, mostly on Muslim cars now. Muslim cars! I laughed. And these broken-down cars reminded me for some reason of the prostitute I'd been visiting, Safa, and then the faces of one or two of the other girls, but the perfume of Safa wiped them away, and I was reminded by her perfume of the drinks I now consumed most every evening when I was done with her, and then I looked down and saw my legs dangling over the edge of the pool and this reminded me of something from so far in my past it could have been as ancient as this cistern, at least two thousand years old, and for some reason the sound of a hawk came into my ears, and the scent of cucumber filled my nostrils, and the song of goat bells filled the air, but I looked past my legs to the water, which in the light of approaching night was as dark as blood on pavement, and I thought of the water of the Nile that Mussa turned to blood and I understood that this water was not only blood; it was also flesh because I could make out the reflection of my own face and the bottom of my own feet, and the perspective made it seem that there was nothing between my feet and my face, and I thought, what is it that is between my feet and my face? And I answered, My heart.

I placed my hand upon my heart but could not feel it beating.

I listened to it in the pure vacuum of the coming night, but there was nothing to hear. And then I felt something salty and sweet sliding between my lips, and for the first time in many, many years, I recalled that I had tears.

"Amir, is it you?"

I looked up, wiping the edges of my eyes.

"It's me, Walid!"

"What are you doing here?" I said. I knew Walid from the old days. He worked at the cultural center. Now he wore a beard and a white cap.

"I was watching you."

"What do you mean?"

"I always admired you," he said. "You were our poet."

"Me?"

"Yes. A lot of us admired you. But you sort of disappeared. No one ever sees you anymore. When I noticed you here I couldn't believe it. So I just watched for a while."

In the distance the muezzin was calling the evening prayer. *God is most great! God is most great!*

"It's time for prayer," Walid said.

"I don't pray," I told him.

"Why not?"

I shrugged.

"It will do you good," he said. "God answers us and pulls us up."

"Not in my case," I said.

"How do you know that? Do you think that God can't do anything He wants? Do you think you are so big that He can't lift you up, too?"

"Leave it alone," I said.

The muezzin called through his loudspeaker, *I testify there is no God but God. I testify Muhammad is the messenger of God.*

"Well," Walid said, "I'll pray for both of us."

He laid out his rug.

Make haste to prayer! Make haste to prayer!

How often had I heard the adhan? I was nineteen years old, nineteen years equals six thousand nine hundred and thirty-five days, six thousand nine hundred and thirty-five days is thirty-four thousand, six hundred and seventy-five calls to prayer.

Walid was ready to begin. His face shone with some inner light, some inner conviction, some inner joy. He brought his hands up to begin his salah.

Suddenly I said to Walid, "Why should I pray if I don't believe?"

He smiled at me. "Brother," he said, "do first. Believe later."

That is when I began going to the mosque, wasn't it? Surely it was then I read of the punishments that awaited me because of the sin into which I had fallen, the torments of the grave, and so I began to perform the salah in its appointed time each day and study the Holy Qur'an in earnest and fervency and cleave to the words of Muhammad and try with all my might to glue these things to my heart so that it might start beating once again.

Oh my father! If I could sit with you in the kitchen where you now are preparing your own tea as if the girls did not know how. You never let anyone do it, except for Mother. You never let me do even the smallest thing for your comfort.

They told me there is a wall between Heaven and earth, but you can break that wall. They told me that each of us is already written for Hell or Heaven, but you can break that destiny. All you need is a single act of martyrdom—a single, final, perfect act of martyrdom. Become a shahid and you will ascend! Shatter the wall between earth and Heaven! Write your name for Eternal Paradise! And yet I cannot break even the air between my father and myself, between my sisters and me. I yearn to speak to you, with a greater yearning than I have for Paradise, with so great a yearning that even the dead whom I have killed feel my anguish.

Look up! Look up! Let me see your face!

Oh, the lies they tell you to blow yourself to pieces! But they needn't have lied. I would have done it anyway. I would have avenged Nadirah for less than a shekel. They said my mother, my father, my sisters, shall live in glory and my house will be a shrine for all Palestine and my name will be a beacon for all the youth of Palestine and the others that follow me shall speak my name in their final breaths. But my house no longer exists, and my father sits in his poverty like an old man who has forgotten how to wash himself. Outside, the crowd grows restless, and I can hear their whispers turn to shouts. Yet he sits there, like a willow flowing with the wind, unmoved. I swear I would have done it anyway, left my family to their poverty, allowed my name to disappear like the scent of apples carried off by the wind, been as nothing to no one, but when I see him sway like a broken twig in the cruel breeze of his sorrow, I regret. I do regret.

Father look up!

Chapter Nineteen

Dear You,

I don't know what happened to me, but I realized I had to call Babushka, I mean I HAD to. And there is no phone where we are in this basement, and no one had a cell phone—only people like Pop have cell phones, and his hardly works anywhere anyway. He's always complaining about it. But anyway, I suddenly had to call my grandmother because I had been thinking about Pop, and then I was thinking about the house, and then I was thinking about what I did in the house, and then I was thinking about—yes—my stupid mother. Why am I thinking about her? I NEVER think about her. But here I am thinking, thinking, thinking.

So I said to Shlomo, I have to use the telephone.

"There is no telephone," he said.

"Then I have to go out and find one, because I have to call my grandmother. It's critical."

"Why didn't you think of this before?" he said.

"I don't know, I just didn't."

"We're all supposed to stay in one place," he said. "So no. And what's so important anyway?"

"That's my business," I said.

"There's something wrong with you," he said.

I am beginning to dislike this guy, Shlomo. His shirt is always messed up. He's fat. His side curls are greasy. When he gets close you can see he has pimples under his beard. Just looking at him makes me furious. So I pushed my nose up to his and said, On my dick, *habibi*! It sort of just popped out. And then I said, because

I don't think he even knows what on my dick means, Yell all you want—I have to call Babushka! He turned completely red. All right, he said, what if I get her on the phone?

"What do you mean you?"

"I mean, give me the number, and I'll call her for you."

I said, "Why?"

And he said, "Why do you all the sudden need the telephone?"

And then it dawned on me. He thought I was going to tell on them.

So I said, "Where is Miriam?"

"I don't know where Miriam is. What difference does it make? Just sit there like a good girl and be quiet."

"I need Miriam," I said.

"Miriam isn't even in Jerusalem. It would take hours to get her here. We don't have hours. You have to get ready now. What do you think she is, the Messiah? She can't snap her fingers and be here."

"I'm sorry, Shlomo," I told him, "but no. She has to come."

And then he just threw up his hands and stormed off.

I'm writing all this down instead of telling you my deepest thoughts, and I know that I should be writing my deepest thoughts, but I feel I must tell everything that happened, because everybody thinks that if you write down the deepest meaning of things you understand something, but I think the meaning of things is in the things themselves, not in what we say about them. Every little detail is itself a whole universe—otherwise, why would everything speak to me? Facts are not things. They are more like animals. They breathe. They get annoyed. They laugh. For instance, the fact that I am writing in my notebook and more or less hiding what I'm doing from Shlomo, this action is a giggle, but also a salty tear rolling down the cheek of my notebook, because while it is funny, it is also sad. Have you heard of Wittgenstein? "The world is composed of all there is." That's Wittgenstein. He means the world is composed of facts, but not like the facts in the news—*Oh, Ariel Sharon invaded Lebanon today!* No. That is a statement, not a fact. A fact actually *tells* you something: what did the road feel when the tanks rolled over it, and what did the tank feel when it finally had to do what it was made to do but maybe thought it could get away with not doing, and when the bombs started falling, where did the birds actually go? And let's take the soldier. Fact, Private Roni Horowitz shot and killed two Hezbollah terrorists. Well, aren't you curious how his eyeballs felt when they got sight of these Hezbollah guys who one minute were shooting at him and the next were lying in a pool of their own blood? I admit these are extreme examples, but don't you think everything is extreme? I mean, what's the point of anything if it's not extreme? Look at me. I certainly am.

Here is a picture of the most important event in my life to date, minus the event of my birth.

So anyway, after Shlomo storms off, this other guy, Menachem, but everyone calls him Mutti, comes over, rubs Shlomo's shoulders, and says to him, Let's go for a smoke. Shlomo doesn't smoke, but that's OK, out they go, but when they opened the door and the scent of magnolia and jasmine came rushing in, I suddenly said to Yohanan, Should we go home?

"Why?" he asked. "Do you want to go home?"

"I don't know."

"Either you want to go home or not. Do you want to go home?"

I thought about it. Then I said, "No."

"You sure?"

"Yes."

"Totally sure?"

I looked up at him. "Why, aren't you?"

"Yes, I am."

"Well, so am I, so shut up."

This is how we talk to each other.

Anyway, then Yohanan went back to his book, mumbling to himself as usual. But a minute later he looks up at me. What's the big deal with Miriam anyway? I don't know, I told him, just. He crossed his eyes as if to say, *Women!*

And can I tell you the truth? I liked that very much. I did. My toes got itchy. I thought of asking him to scratch them, but I knew it would freak him out. He's very proper, naturally, but I just can't be. Why he likes me, I just don't know.

*Type of Girl He
Should Really
Be Thinking About*

Me

By the way, Miriam doesn't care how I dress. She says, *This is not the modesty I care about,* quoting Jeremiah. I repeated this to Yohanan just today. "It's Isaiah," he said.

One time Miriam told me something else from Isaiah. She was sitting very close to me, so I could smell the flowers that always seem to come off her skin, and also cardamom and sweet paprika. She closed her eyes and sang, *When you call, the Lord will answer. When you cry he will say, Here I am.* Then Miriam opened her eyes and looked directly into mine. Her eyes are bright blue, like jewelry. *Here I am,* she repeated. *Here I am.* You see, Anna? It's like picking up the phone, you dial and he answers. He answered you? I asked her. She smiled. Of course, silly, she said, and he will answer you, too.

That's the trouble. As far as I'm concerned, nobody's home. But at least I have the right number now. I know this because of everything that happened so far today, and especially with the way it got so quiet, and the way I can finally hear just the one thing that is in front of me. If you let in all the voices of all the world, how can you hear the one single voice of truth?

And then guess what? In comes Shlomo who announces, Here's a telephone, satisfied? He had a cell phone the whole time! What an asshole. In Russian, Shlomo is Solomon, and in both languages, he is the wisest man who ever lived. Just goes to show you how unimportant names are.

"And what about Miriam?" I said.

"Just make your call."

"Hi, Babushka!" I said.

"Where are you?" she said in Russian. "Why aren't you in school? What happened?"

So I answered her in Russian, "School was half a day today. I'm just at a phone booth and wanted to ask you something."

"So ask."

"What was my mother like?"

"What?"

"My mother." I spelled out the letters for her.

"What are you talking about?"

"What was she like?"

I could hear her thinking.

"All right, what's going on?" she asked.

"I'm just curious."

She stopped to think once more. "She was very smart and very pretty, like you."

"No, more than that."

"Like what more? What do you want me to tell you?"

"Was she a good person?"

This time the silence was much longer, and I could hear her wiggling in her chair. She sighed. "All right, what is this about?"

"Why won't anyone tell me?"

"Fine. She was a good person. She had strong ideas, that's all."

"What does that mean?"

"It means she did what she believed was right."

"Isn't everyone supposed to do what is right?"

"I suppose so, Sunshine. Yes, that's true."

"So what was it about her that was special?"

Babushka sighed again. "This is something to discuss with Papa."

"But it's too hard," I said.

"All right, then, come over and we'll talk."

"I can't right now."

"Why not?"

"I can't." Now it was my turn to sigh.

"Sunshine, what is it?" she said. "Tell Babushka."

"It's nothing. I'm just being crazy. You know me."

"All right, darling. But you can always tell Babushka anything."

"I know," I said.

But of course that was 100% opposite of true.

So I said to her, "Then you think it's a good thing to do what you believe is right?"

"Of course," she said.

"OK," I said. "Bye."

"Bye, darling."

And we hung up.

⁓⁓⁓⁓⁓⁓⁓

Here is the route I will take today. I want to write it down so as not to forget it because it's important I go exactly this way, though I don't know why, and, second, if anything bad happens, though I don't think it will, I want everyone to know where I was.

OK. We will leave Geula by car with Mutti. He will drive us up to the Ambassador Hotel on Mount Scopus. I've never been inside it, but I am sure it's horrible. Every time you go by it, it cries, "Demolish me! Demolish me!" (only in Arabic). But in my opinion, it should cheer itself up. It doesn't need to die. It just needs plastic surgery. Anyway, Mutti drops us near the Ambassador, and then we begin our walk down the hill. I have done this now two times in my life, and I remember it very, very well. You start down the Nablus Road, which the Israelis call Derech Shechem (I'll tell you why later). It's a winding thing so you have to be careful at the light at Derech Har HaZeitim, and then especially where it runs into St. George you have to be sure not to turn the wrong way, because it's not a straight line and you can get messed up, but anyway, we will go down the Nablus Road. We will pass the Al Ma'amunia School for Girls, and not long after that, the Good Luck Car Rental. We will continue down the hill, past the American Colony Hotel, which is actually Swedish, and also past the back of the Addar Hotel opposite it, which I think is Arab. It is quite ugly, but not because it's owned by Arabs. It's just a terrible building, that's all. We could take the number 18 at this point if we wanted to, but we're not going to because (a) it's a very short walk, and (b)—well, no b. Soon we will pass the Basilica of St. Étienne. It looks ancient, but I think it's only a hundred years old or so, though the inscription on the stone is in French. It used to be ancient, my father says, but the original was destroyed by the Persians, then rebuilt by the Crusaders, then destroyed by Saladin, and then I don't know who built it again. You can't tell how beautiful it is one way or another because from the outside all you can see is a wall. Soon after that, on the right, on the square, is the new police station, which we shall not avoid at all. In fact, we shall say shalom to any police officer we see. I always do that anyway. Next, the Nablus Road narrows. All the tour buses park here, and the street becomes one way going the wrong way, at least for us. Here the little market begins. It's a pretty sad market, if you ask me, only a few cruddy stalls selling rotten fruit and cheap sandals. It's not very busy. A few seconds later, we'll be in front of the Damascus Gate. We will stand on the sidewalk looking down upon the plaza. I will tell Yohanan to turn around and notice, across Sultan Suleiman Street, to our right, Schmidt's Girls College and, to our left, some other school, but it's in Arabic and I can't read it, so I don't really know what it is, and a dentist's office, Dr. Cozzen Aziz, Orthodontist. I will explain to Yohanan what a fine Ottoman structure it is, and I will point out the Palestinian restaurant on the ground floor. I will want us to take it all in, Yohanan and me. I will want us to see where we are, take notice of our location in the universe at that precise moment in time. I will want us to look up and see the sky, how it is framed by the buildings and the trees. I will want us to listen for the rumble of engines at the old bus station around the corner. I will want us to open our noses to the scent of chalk and saffron coming off the city walls. When we're done with this looking and smelling (because Yohanan will have had enough almost immediately) we will turn around and walk down the thirteen stairs, and then the eleven stairs, and then the ten stairs down to the plaza, and then we will cross the bridge over the dried-up moat that leads us into the mouth of the enormous and scary Damascus Gate, which we Israelis call Sha'ar Shechem because it leads to Shechem (real name), which the Palestinians call Nablus (fake name). This is our first moment of truth. Three soldiers will be standing in the enclosure of the gate amid all the tummle of shopkeepers and pedestrians, and they will be watching everything even though it seems they are not. I'm guessing they will be sitting on some empty crates cracking jokes or telling stories to the guy selling orange juice. They like to sit there because that's where the gate is darkest and the heat can't reach them, and the stone floor remains damp all year long. But the soldiers will not pay any attention to us anyway, and we in turn will ignore the beggars and the Arabs hawking crucifixes and postcards of the Virgin Mary and also the Arab kids pushing their heavy carts up the steep slope of El Wad Road. It is exactly nineteen of my steps from the time we enter the gate to the time the Old City jumps out at you with its hundred thousand aromas and the crush of so many human bodies. The shopkeepers bark at you as you pass, and wherever you go you hear the chatter of every language God has ever created to help people get along with each other or slice each other's throats, whichever they feel like doing. From that point, we'll walk along El Wad all the way to Suq el-Qattanin and squeeze our way through the suq (though usually it's not busy) till we reach the gate leading to the Temple Mount, the one that they call Bab al-Qattanin and where Jews used to go to pray but are not allowed to anymore. There I will say good-bye to Yohanan and make my way alone till I arrive at the Western Wall, about ten minutes later. I'll go through security, then cross the plaza and go up the ramp to the Morocco Gate and enter the mount near the garden of cypress trees, where I shall stand and admire al-Aqsa and then, when I'm ready, turn my attention to the Dome of the Rock.

The date today is August 14, 1996. I never put dates down because I don't believe in years. But today I will, because this is the most important day in the history of my world.

Chapter Twenty

✡

I COULD HEAR THE COMMOTION OUTSIDE THE house, but I still did not move. I lay there wondering if this was where my path would end, in the house of the father of the young man who already once tried to kill me—and for what? For some dream of a nation that never really existed? For a land that has since time immemorial been truly boundaryless?

Suddenly I deeply, deeply regretted that I had never taken Daphne to the movies or to a decent restaurant. Lonya would have taken her to the best places. I know he wanted to. Why did I stop him? Every time he saw me he asked about her.

"That girl, what's her name?"

"Daphne," I'd repeat for the hundredth time.

"You're lucky with that one! Good for you!"

Right now she was no doubt taking care of Anyusha, consoling her with well-intentioned fabrications: Be patient, don't worry; your father will be home soon, he just has a lot to think about, that's all. He's the victim of a terrorist attack, don't forget that. Was it simply Daphne's belief in goodness that repelled me?

She quoted the Noble Eightfold Path for me and tried to teach me yoga, but I found each position painful and laughable at the same time.

"It doesn't matter," she said to me.

"You don't care if I find this stupid?"

"No, why should I? You have another path."

One time I told her I didn't think I was really in love with her. She merely placed her fingers on my lips and said, "Love is everywhere."

The sounds outside grew louder, more restive.

I thought perhaps the head had made another appearance, because I had the sense that something was lurking in the corners of my vision. I wanted to tell him my story. I wanted him to know how terribly, terribly wrong he was.

And if I had wanted to, I bet I could have broken down that door with one blow.

After Lonya brought us the news of Collette's arrest, we piled in the truck and raced back to Moscow, leaving the foundation of my new dacha unpoured. I wanted to take a few minutes to cover the frame with a tarp, but Lonya threw me in the truck, and off we drove. All our lumber would be stolen by nightfall. Back in Moscow, we tried to unearth what happened to Collette. No one had anything new to tell us. The only official report was a small item in Moscow *Pravda:*

CURRENT EVENTS

On August 23, 1982, a leading Zionist terrorist was apprehended on the train leaving Moscow for Tallinn, Estonia. A criminal investigation has been initiated. More warrants may be issued.

In my panic, I decided to head over to Lefortovo. Perhaps I could bring her some decent food, some fresh clothes, paper, a pencil. What was I thinking? Paper? Pencil?

"We don't even know where she is," Fima argued. "We should try the police or the Ministry of Justice. They have to notify someone, it might as well be you."

But of course no one would receive us there either.

Lonya was the only one who could find even a scrap of information.

"She was arrested waiting for the trolley," he said.

"But I thought she was on a train?"

"I don't know. That's what I was told. Vera Lifkin was actually with her. They were waiting for the number twenty-two. These three cocksuckers came up and grabbed her. One of them was in uniform. She said they were very polite. 'I'm sorry to inconvenience you, Collette Petrovna . . . ,' and that was that."

"My God," I said.

"God should go take a piss in his own mouth," Lonya replied.

What we learned we learned mostly from the air around us, from rumors and "known facts," and from the *Chronicle of Current Events*. Our ears were glued to the Voice of America and the BBC. We mingled at the Choral Synagogue and milled around the compounds where the foreign reporters lived, hoping for scripture to float off their lips and make sense of all the contradictions in our lives.

Eventually the trial was announced. Collette alone was accused. No vast conspiracy, no Zionist plotters. We did not know if that was hopeful or ominous. Everyone had a theory. It was because Andropov was sick. It was because too many people were applying to leave. It was because George Shultz insulted Gromyko in a secret meeting in Brussels. It had everything to do with American troops in Lebanon. Fima said, "It's obviously because Andropov is actually a Jew. He has to cover it up or his enemies will destroy him."

The trial itself was short, and what actually happened will always remain shrouded under the cloak of state secrets. No friends of Collette's were allowed in. No reporters, other than those from Tass and *Pravda*, *Izvestia*, and *Novosti*. Citizens were bused in to fill the galleries. They were treated to lush buffets of caviar and sturgeon, white bread, and smoked meats. Not even family was allowed in, except for one unexpected and unexplainable exception. Collette's cousin, my best friend, the foulmouthed, one-eyed

Lonya Bruskin, was invited into the courtroom. They did not even object when he took notes, which I read years later—in fact, not until after the bombing. As for me, even though I was the closest person to Collette in all of Moscow, I was not permitted to enter. This, they explained, was because I was being called as a witness.

From the Transcript of the

TRIAL OF COLLETTE CHERNOFF
From the archives of the Union for Soviet Jewry,
as recorded by L. V. Bruskin
FEBRUARY 12, 1983

Presiding, Secretary of the Court Judge Kovalesky
Citizen Assessors, Minskaya and Grigorolev
For the People, Assistant Chief Procurator Ignatov
For the Defense, Advocate Fishman

The session began with Judge Kovalesky asking if Chernoff understood where she was and if her attorney was ready to present her case. Chernoff declared that she could not accept her court-appointed attorney and would defend herself. At this point, Fishman left the courtroom.

The judge then agreed to consider "two or three" of Chernoff's petitions, specifically the question of witnesses. "Though frankly," he added, "I can see no validity in your witness list. What could these people have to say pertaining to any of the charges? Not a thing, except more propaganda and incitement. As to your good character, the People shall be the judge of that, based on the evidence and nothing else."

Judge Kovalesky then read the charges. These included plotting to hijack an aircraft, revealing state secrets to the American CIA agent Charles ("Charlie") Spaulding, passing anti-Soviet information to Western correspondents, illegal demonstrations in front of government offices, and engaging in Zionist activities. Several of these were capital offenses under articles 64a and 72 of the penal code.

JUDGE KOVALESKY: Defendant Chernova, that is the death penalty. Do you understand?

CHERNOFF: I understand all too well.

The prosecutor then began his examination of Collette Chernoff.

PROCURATOR IGNATOV: Is it not true that you met repeatedly with a man attached to the American embassy, a Mr. Charles Spaulding?

CHERNOFF: Yes.

IGNATOV: Did it in no way occur to you that he might be working for the Americans?

CHERNOFF: Of course he was working for the Americans. He was attached to the American Trade Mission.

IGNATOV: And it did not occur to you that he is CIA?

CHERNOFF: I never asked him. Just as it would be pointless to ask you if you worked for the KGB.

IGNATOV: You passed letters to Spaulding.

CHERNOFF: I don't deny it.

IGNATOV: And he passed instructions to you.

CHERNOFF: What kind of instructions could he give me? He gave me personal letters.

IGNATOV: Letters from Israel. What relatives do you have in Israel?

CHERNOFF: I don't need relatives.

IGNATOV: You received invitations to reunite with a family that is not even your family. That is deception and fraud.

CHERNOFF: The fraud is demanding invitations from Israel. Everyone should have the right to freely emigrate, even you, comrade.

IGNATOV: Your Honor, note that the defendant admitted passing and receiving documents with the known spy Spaulding. The defendant admitted knowingly receiving false documents of invitation to defraud the orderly process of family reunification. This, I would argue, is typical of the entire Zionist conspiracy. By the way, Comrade Chernova, would it surprise you to know your friend Spaulding has fled the country?

CHERNOFF: It would not surprise me in the slightest.

IGNATOV: You should know the letters you passed between you have been presented to the court. They confirm completely your activities as a spy and provocateur.

CHERNOFF: I would like to see them, so that we can all read them aloud.

JUDGE KOVALESKY: You have already seen them. You wrote them.

IGNATOV: Is it not true that you wrote on July 15, "the only way out would be to steal a plane. Fly to Stockholm, like Dymshitz and that group."

CHERNOFF: I'm sure the next sentence explains it was only wishful thinking. In fact, Dymshitz and his group were arrested, and many innocent people were convicted on their account. Why would I want to repeat that?

IGNATOV: On August 12, you received a letter from the Frenchman Dubé in which he urged you to reconsider. "Think of Paris, not Stockholm!" But you were not to be deterred. More plans and more plans!

CHERNOFF: There were no plans. It was just fantasy.

IGNATOV: You were distraught that your father had abandoned you.

CHERNOFF: I merely wanted to know what happened to him after he was arrested.

IGNATOV: Your Honor, there is no record of any Chernoff in State Security files. He was never arrested. He simply abandoned his family.

CHERNOFF: I'd like to offer evidence.

JUDGE KOVALESKY: We've already ruled on your petitions.

CHERNOFF: I was not aware of that.

JUDGE KOVALESKY: Had you had proper legal counsel as we advised, you would be aware of everything.

CHERNOFF: Then I want to call my witnesses.

JUDGE KOVALESKY: We have considered your lists of witnesses and already ruled. They have nothing to add to these proceedings. My dear Collette Petrovna, I can see that you are a passionate young person. I can see that you have been led astray by foreign ideas and false impressions. I myself have a daughter your age. I urge you to stop this farce and save yourself. Admit what you have done, accept the preliminary investigative report. It's not too late. Our justice is firm but fair. Embrace it; see the error you have made.

CHERNOFF: Your Excellency, I hope your daughter is here in court today to see what becomes of people who follow their consciences.

The next witness was KGB colonel Vasin. He testified that Charles Spaulding was a CIA agent well known to the security forces. He also stated that Chernoff was often in the company of at least two other known CIA agents whom he could not name because they were still under surveillance. Chernoff was not allowed to cross-examine "for security reasons."

Following Vasin were a series of witnesses, including two Jews who declared that Zionism was anti-Soviet, several people who had confronted Chernoff in front of KGB headquarters, and a neighbor, Plotkina, who had kept notes on the activities she witnessed in Chernoff's hallway.

CHERNOFF: Did you see me do anything illegal?
PLOTKINA: Undoubtedly.
CHERNOFF: What specifically?
PLOTKINA: It's all in my statement.
CHERNOFF: If the judge would instruct her to answer.
JUDGE KOVALESKY: The witness has already been very clear. But let me ask her anyway: Comrade Plotkina, did you record the defendant doing anything illegal?
PLOTKINA: Yes.
JUDGE KOVALESKY: Then we can accept the written statement as fact. The witness is excused.

The final witness was the architect Roman Guttman.

PROCURATOR IGNATOV: Comrade Guttman, you are not yourself a so-called refusenik.
GUTTMAN: No.

IGNATOV: Nevertheless, you were intimate with the defendant.

GUTTMAN: I am her friend.

IGNATOV: You were witness to the many times the defendant met with the CIA agent Spaulding.

GUTTMAN: I knew Charlie Spaulding.

IGNATOV: You don't deny you saw her pass letters and documents to him.

GUTTMAN: I don't say one way or the other.

IGNATOV: So you don't deny it.

GUTTMAN: No. I have no idea what passed between them.

IGNATOV: You were present at the apartment of Feldman, at the apartment of Tsipkina, and also at the so-called Moscow Hebrew University.

GUTTMAN: Yes. But the past is irrelevant. It is the future I care about.

IGNATOV: The future is completely in her own hands, comrade. As to these meetings, Chernoff was there with you.

GUTTMAN: Ask her these questions.

IGNATOV: She's already admitted it.

GUTTMAN: Then why ask me?

JUDGE KOVALESKY: You must answer the question.

GUTTMAN: If she says she was there, she was there. The past does not concern me.

IGNATOV: You took automobile drives with Spaulding and the defendant Chernoff into the countryside in order to evade the authorities and to exchange secret documents and instructions from Israel and America. Is this not correct?

GUTTMAN: I don't know anything about secret documents. I did take several rides with Spaulding, but that is the extent of it.

JUDGE KOVALESKY: Comrade Guttman, I must ask you again to truthfully reply to the questions.

GUTTMAN: But I am being truthful.

IGNATOV: These are the letters we found in Chernoff's apartment. Do you recognize them?

GUTTMAN: Yes. I recognize the handwriting. But I will repeat a third time; I have no interest in the past, only the future.

IGNATOV: This letter in particular.

GUTTMAN: Yes, yes. This letter.

IGNATOV (*striding over to Collette Chernoff's table and waving the document in front of her face*): Let the record show witness Guttman has identified the treasonous documents as being in the possession of defendant Chernoff.

Chernoff was allowed to cross-examine. She rose from her seat, studied the witness carefully, and then, suddenly and decisively and without asking a single question, sat down again. Guttman was excused, but for some reason he hesitated. The guards were forced to escort him from the room.

From the first moment I saw her I realized that her health had been broken. Her skin, which had always glistened like untracked snow, was hollowed out and gray, as lifeless as tin foil. Her lush, rounded body, which I had found so irresistible, had melted away, leaving only branches and thorns; and the fantasy of black hair that once fell about her shoulders like fresh milk had been chopped into a crown of nettle, her ears sticking out like two dried figs. Her nose had become hawklike and her lips thin, white, cracked, and tight, as if clamped shut by door springs. Illness had closed its wings upon her and let out a sour, metallic smell that stung me as I passed the prisoner's dock. She sat there, behind the barrier, calmly watching me. Only her eyes had any strength left, two fierce jewels hard as steel, guarded behind two iron lids. I latched on to these and did not let go until I was led from the room at the end of my miserable performance.

Some weeks before, the police had come for me at Tishinskaya. I had spent the days after Collette's arrest pacing my apartment and, after Mother went to sleep, drinking myself into a stupor. Now they finally arrived and my mother wept in terror, but I went willingly, even happily—whatever might happen, I would finally learn something about Collette.

I entered the office of the chief investigator and handed the duty officer my papers. He commanded me to sit on the bench along the far wall. From my perch I could hear the bright quack of typewriters and a stream of meaningless conversation rising over the partitions. People came and went, some in uniform, some not, some with briefcases, some with tins of cookies, some with armloads of manila files, some with shopping bags. No one so much as glanced at me. I then understood to what extent I did not exist for them. I would exist when they decided it was time for me to exist, and then I would exist for the purposes they intended and nothing else. But there was also a strange, unsettling familiarity about the scene, as if I had been here before. The bench beneath me contained the penned carvings of names and phone numbers—ILYA, VALODYA, KOSTYA—and I had the sense that I knew them—and the wide face and cropped hair of the young duty officer reminded me so much of the boys I had come across in the countryside on my hikes and summer service—and the scent of floor wax was exactly the same as it had been in my grammar school—and the voices beyond the partitions the same as those in my own office: endless complaints dotted with explosions of laughter. I had been here before because every place in Russia was the same as every other place. And also, as always, I had the sense I did not belong in any of them, and that the inch or so of air around my skin was the only thing I truly owned.

At long last, my name was called—not that there was anyone else waiting—and I was escorted past a series of small offices and secretarial pools to a narrow, cheerful room that contained a large desk outfitted with red bunting, several luxurious leather chairs, a carpet decorated with Soviet emblems entwined with sheaves of wheat and sunflowers, and on the wall, beside the photographs of Andropov and Fedorchuk, what looked to be a real oil painting in the Critical Realist style of the last century, something halfway between *The Barge Haulers on the Volga* and *Tsar Mikhail and His Boyars,* clearly done by someone in his or her art-school days, maybe the chief investigator's wife.

A hidden door in the rear of the office opened and in came an officer wearing a full-dress jacket with braided epaulets and countless medals and ribbons. His trousers were the color of gathering clouds; they were perfectly pressed with a deep, sharp crease, and I could not help but notice how the fine gabardine fell from his knee in soft, elegant streams. These were no ordinary police trousers. I thought immediately of my uncle Max, and I wondered which Jewish tailor had taken up his needle in hope of moving his family into some present-day Veshnaya. The officer introduced himself as "Vasin, Vasily Nikolayevich," and asked me if I would like a cup of tea or perhaps a Fanta. A strong and disconcerting aroma of damp wool filled the room when he removed his jacket, and though he hung it carefully in his closet and closed the door, I sensed that, beneath the pressed creases, a more fundamental slovenliness ruled his life. He smiled at me, pressed a button on his desk, and called for the tea. From his shirt pocket, he offered me a cigarette. My hand autonomically reached out. Maybe it thought a cigarette would make me look more confident. But I refused the tea, for there could be nothing more revealing than a teacup rattling in its saucer.

Vasily Nikolayevich Vasin was a colonel. Of course, there were colonels on every street corner in Moscow. My own cousin Danka was a colonel. No one paid any attention to them. Here, though, in this magnificent office with its three telephones and innumerable intercom buttons, prancing about in his beautiful trousers and polished shoes, this Vasily Vasin seemed quite formidable, the more so for his easygoing and relaxed disposition.

"Need a light?" he said.

Vasily Vasin sat down. There was a large file on the desk in front of him. He pushed it aside as if someone had placed it there by mistake.

"So the matter in question is your friend Collette Chernova," he began. "I know you are aware of everything, you are a person of intelligence and conscience, so I won't play games with you. I'll just come to the point. We don't need your testimony. The evidence is all there. She could easily get the death penalty. All her meetings with the spy Charles Spaulding. All her dealings with agents of the CIA posing as representatives of the press. All her writings and antics intended to slander and humiliate the Soviet people. We have dates; we have transcripts; we have phone calls. Are you sure you don't want a Fanta or a Pepsi? Nescafé? So, comrade, we don't need you. We also have all those letters. She had a huge collection. Piles of them. Seditious letters."

"Perhaps they were love letters," I said.

"So you know the letters?" he murmured. "But no. My understanding is that they were seditious. In fact, they are the most serious evidence we have against her. That, of course, and the planned hijacking."

"It's ridiculous," I snapped. "They were just stupid love letters."

"Why don't you tell me your side of it then?"

"She was in love with a man and she wrote to him. What's wrong with that?"

"Nothing. If they were just love letters. To whom were they written?"

"You know all this. Why ask me?"

"Well, all right. Perhaps the problem is they were written in French. Perhaps we don't understand them correctly. Who is this fellow"—he perused one of the letters he now extracted from the file—"Pascal? Who is he, anyway?"

"A friend of her aunt and uncle."

"Yes, the aunt and uncle. You know, they were counterrevolutionaries who defected to France."

"That's a lie. They were in France before the revolution. Collette's grandfather was a great Bolshevik. Read your history."

He lazily drew some smoke through his nostrils. "You're an intellectual," he said. "I'm sure you have lots of books. You know all about the French, French literature, French culture. What its appeal is, I can't fathom. Perhaps you can enlighten me? You see, this Pascal—he seems to have a very elaborate surname. I'm guessing he is one of the so-called aristocracy. France! It calls itself a democracy! Perhaps you can explain to me how a democracy can still have these privileged classes, these parasites who inherit their status as if their blood were sweeter than anyone else's? Oh, well, the arrow will always fall where it is aimed. Each society must advance at its own pace. But why do you suppose all these code words? These so-called refuseniks! They think with all these codes they are fooling us! Do you imagine that by jamming a pencil in a telephone you can stop us from listening to you? If we want to listen, it's not through the telephone. You can tell your friends that, if you want. These letters of this Pascal, whatever his surname is, here, look, I'll just read it to you, *We delivered the baby clothes and are just waiting to hear if they fit.* Baby clothes! Do they think we're children? That we can't decipher such a primitive code? Chernova was smuggling a document to the West, some vital information, perhaps from her place of work, or some slanderous material she wanted printed in the New York newspapers. We already know specifically what the information was in this case, so it doesn't matter. But you see, we understand how you people think. You imagine it is cat and mouse and you are scurrying about under our noses where we can't see you. It's very romantic for you. But no one is fooling anyone. We don't stop you because we don't want to. Why should we? It's a free country. It's only when you go too far, when you break the rules of common decency, when your games become dangerous and treasonous and cause harm to the government and the state, to the organs of the proletariat. And this, unfortunately, is the fate of poor Collette Petrovna."

"I don't know anything about codes," I said.

"I'm not accusing you of anything. I'm just trying to better understand these letters. You are not denying that these are her letters? I can see that you recognize them. This pile she received from France, and these, admittedly few, are the copies she made of the letters she wrote herself and sent through the CIA courier to this Monsieur Pascal and, by the way, to many others as well. Apparently she had a lot of lovers."

"What do you want from me?"

"I just want you to look at this particular letter. This is her handwriting, isn't it?"

"How would I know? It could be a forgery."

"Do you think she hasn't already admitted this is her handwriting?"

"Again, how would I know?"

"Don't you think Collette Petrovna is an honest person?"

"Of course she is."

"I can show you her statement where she admits these are her letters. So what good does it do you to deny it? It will only turn us against you."

"I don't deny anything."

"Comrade. I am not here to hurt you. I am only asking you one thing. Look at this letter. This one in particular."

The way he held it out to me, the odd tone of urgency in his voice . . . I snatched it from him and glanced down at it.

"Now," he said.

"I told you," I stammered, "I . . . I don't know."

"But you do know."

"How could I know?"

"Because you've already read them."

"Not this one."

"No. Not this one, but clearly you have read the others. It would be unwise to lie about this. Do you think we haven't double-checked every detail? Do you believe you didn't leave fingerprints? I can show you the test results if you like. I imagine these are your tears on them as well, because I know it was hard for you. How could that have been easy? Even today, she doesn't deny her love for this Frenchman. Let's talk about the times you drove out with the spy Charles Spaulding—you called him Charlie, yes? Did you think because you drove out to the forest we couldn't trace you? It was illegal in the first place for him to leave the city limits, except on a train to Leningrad or Kiev or on a tour bus. You knew this, yet you abetted his illegal behavior. That alone could land you three years. Normally, quite honestly, you would have nothing to worry about. Because if that was all it was—an American tourist out for a lark—but we know he's a spy, and you knew he was a spy, and you were with him, and you went into illegal areas to avoid being detected and to speak of illegal things and pass information and receive instructions. All right! All right! Perhaps you were unaware of this. We know they walked alone for the most part. They left you in the car or perhaps you went out to hunt mushrooms! To be honest, I am willing to believe you are the innocent party here, just a victim of the American Zionists. I am even willing to believe Chernova was also a dupe of the Americans. I frankly would be willing to recommend a very light sentence for her, maybe even a parole, or at worst we could just send her to Gorky with the Sakharovs. That's not so bad, is it? I'm sure they would get along very well. But I can't do anything for her unless I understand more completely what you were doing in the woods. And you were also present at other meetings, Zionist provocations, public displays, all of it illegal. Suddenly I am worried, because when you add up all these infractions they become very serious, in aggregate very damaging, and though I completely accept that you could be innocent, and I am fairly convinced that you are a loyal citizen—after all, how many times do you have to prove it?—still, this can look very bad to anyone who doesn't have a firm grasp of your character and where you really stand on the issues. I mean, if you were to be put on trial, it could go very badly for you. It could be even worse for poor Collette Petrovna, because now we must add conspiracy, and that makes it unlikely there can be any clemency at all. So I just ask you to think about it. What would be best for everyone involved? We're not asking you to tell us anything we don't already know. Collette Petrovna has already confessed everything. And what really has she done, after all? She is just a misguided young woman. Did she kill anyone? No. Did she hijack an airplane? She never got that far. In any case, how could she have managed it? It was a pipe dream. Did she expose nuclear secrets? Of course not. She didn't even publish a derisive book in the West. Still, it is a very serious case, or at least many of my colleagues think so. But I am trying my very best to find some shred of evidence that might exonerate her. Well, let's be honest, she can't get off scot-free, she broke the law, but if I just had some little kernel to help her. Soviet law requires we investigate every lead. Perhaps you have information that could help her. We just want you to clarify things, and naturally this would also confirm that we are right about you, that you are a loyal citizen. Otherwise, you know . . . well, it could be painful for you, and especially for your mother. To be left alone at her age. Possibly to lose her apartment. And you. I don't know what I could do for you. I know it may not seem this way, but, honestly, I have nothing against you. On the contrary, I want to protect you, because the consequences for everyone could be very serious."

He paused to take the dead cigarette from my fingers and place it in his crystal ashtray.

"You see what I mean?" he said.

"Yes," I said.

"All right, Roman Leopoldovich, let's begin again. So I will ask you: you often stayed with her in her apartment?"

I looked up at Vasily Vasin. There was no enmity in his eyes, no cruelty. They seemed hopeful, even kind. "So, you stayed with her?" he repeated.

"Yes," I finally said.

"And naturally you noticed that she received letters?"

"Everyone receives letters," I said.

"Exactly. And you saw the very letters I'm holding in my hand."

I tried not to look at them.

"You already said as much," he reminded me.

"Yes, all right, I guess so."

"Well, that's all you need to say."

"I can go?"

He smiled at me again. "I can understand why you fell in love with her. She is a very beautiful Jewess, very elegant, very striking. . . . "

"Yes, she is," I found myself saying.

"I wonder, though, did she sew?"

"Sew?"

"She wore such beautiful clothes! I admire beautiful clothing. I can see that you noticed my uniform. You have an eye for such things. Where did she get her clothes?"

"I don't know," I answered.

"You see, that's why I'm asking if she sewed them."

"Really, I don't know."

"Did you ever see her sewing?"

"No. I don't know."

"Very well then, she must have purchased them. But I just have to wonder, where, on her salary, could she purchase such clothes in Moscow?"

"I don't know," I said.

"Perhaps they came from Paris?"

"Clothes come from Paris only in our dreams," I said.

"We don't dream in this office, Comrade Guttman. Here we are honest with one another. So please, think about your answer."

"I don't know. Maybe she inherited them."

"That's possible! Thank you! Because you and I are thinking alike. We're both thinking that obviously either they were given to her, or she bought them with money someone paid her! But not inherited. After all, she never smelled like mothballs, did she?" He laughed.

Vasily Vasin poured himself more tea in the English manner, directly from the teapot into the cup. The happy scent of bergamot circled obliviously around us.

"She received payment, that's clear," he continued. "If it were just clothing, we wouldn't care. It's a typical Zionist activity. Everyone does it. We're aware of this. We don't care about it at all. For instance, the jacket you are wearing. Have you ever seen anyone in Moscow wear corduroy? One of those Jewish groups in New York sent it—if not to you, then to one of your friends, who gave it to you."

I said nothing.

"But you all receive things from abroad. Collette doesn't deny it. I already asked her." He took a sip of tea. "You Jews are always complaining about everything; I suppose that entitles you to dress

better than the rest of us. But as I said, it's not of much importance, so don't worry about it. But in her case—you never saw her
actually receive clothes did you?"

"No."

"So it must have been money."

He leaned back in his chair, smiling.

"Very well, let's summarize. You acknowledge that you lived
with Collette Chernova, and her clothing was extravagant and
was undoubtedly purchased with hard currency. You saw the letters that passed back and forth from the capitalist countries in the
hands of the CIA agent Charles Spaulding, and you have intimate
knowledge of their contents, including all the coded passages and
instructions having to do with foreign lovers, seditious documents,
fabricated invitations etc. etc. She mentions, in code of course, her
intention to hijack a small plane from Tallinn airport and have
it flown to Stockholm. By the way, I am assuming that Comrade
Chernova was unaware you had read her letters, is that correct?"

"Yes."

Vasin sighed. "Even then, you understood she was not completely trustworthy. It's too bad."

He stood up and strode toward the curtains. "Why don't we
get some light?" He fiddled with the cord, then changed his mind
and swung around to face me. "I want to ask you something, man
to man. In all this time you were with the Chernova woman, did it
not occur to you that she was merely using you?"

"Yes," I said, "it occurred to me."

"But you didn't care?"

"No. I guess I didn't."

"Perhaps, Guttman, your father never taught you the meaning
of honor."

"Perhaps not, Comrade Investigator," I answered, "but he did
teach me the meaning of love."

"Ah," he said, deciding not to open the curtains after all, "so
this is love."

In the end, we came to an agreement about my testimony.
On the stand, I would be allowed to utter as few words as neces-

sary, but whatever I said was to adhere strictly to a script he and I invented, and no one, except perhaps Collette herself, would be surprised by any of it.

Less than twenty minutes after my testimony ended, Collette was sentenced to eleven years, three in prison and eight in "rehabilitative labor." As a gesture of belief in our Soviet process of rehabilitation, her property was not to be confiscated.

Chapter Twenty-one

Dear You,

Miriam finally arrived about fifteen minutes ago! She was perfectly happy to be here, so I don't know what Shlomo was going on about, and we went for a little walk in a garden just beyond the gates of this building (you would never know how beautiful it is outside, sitting in this stinky cellar where all you breathe is dust). First, of course, she talked to Yohanan and me together, and then to Yohanan alone, who just sat there very calmly, his eyes still in his book, nodding, and then Miriam came over to me and said, Hey, let's go outside. It was hot, of course, but I didn't mind. Actually, I like hot. Sometimes I don't even want to come to Jerusalem in the winter because it's too cold and wet, not that it's not wet at home, but there's something about Jerusalem in the winter that makes you sad. Maybe it's the rain dripping off all those black hats. Anyway, she opened the door for me, and we stepped out into a yard that seemed totally abandoned, strewn with old tires and broken boilers. I hadn't really noticed it on the way in, but now I took a moment to take it all in. There were coils of rusted barbed wire heaped in a pile, old traffic signs stacked against a wall, some wooden crates filled with unusable machine parts swimming in crud. Resting under a messy old pepper tree was a skinny gray cat licking its paws and mewing to itself. And then I had this sudden flash! Was it déjà vu? Had I been here before? But that was impossible. And then I realized it wasn't even my own memory I was remembering! Because it wasn't me who had been here, but Pop.

This was exactly the way his old courtyard looked in the house he grew up in, the one he always told me about, the one he called Veshnaya.

All these memories came flooding over me, all the fairy tales he told me, and I had to take a deep breath and let it out, and I swear I almost cried, even though I don't know why. But then it was over, and we made our way out of the yard and down the narrow streets of Geula. Dressed as I am in my killer short-short skirt, I knew I could be yelled at or worse by the local black hats, but that is precisely why I put on the leggings, so no one could say I am immodest, and though I am wearing my fabulous sleeveless camisole with the lacy bit along the neckline, I was wise enough to stow a white, long-sleeved linen blouse inside my backpack, which I am now wearing over the camisole, unbuttoned, yes, but tied at the waist, so my arms are covered for modesty, yet I am gorgeous at the same time. And OK (as I mentioned before), there is a teensy bit of skin showing between my tights and my polka-dot socks, but it's so little and so perfectly nowhere (not the ankle, not the thigh) that even the Satmar rabbi couldn't find it offensive. I would say the buzzword for me today is *demure*. Of course that didn't stop some guy from calling me a harlot and spitting on the ground, but Miriam told me to ignore it. He's an asshole, she said. I love Miriam.

So we stayed off the main drags, you know, Yehezkel, Malchai Yisrael, Kikar Shabbat, and just wandered the lanes and alleys. Those blocks were mostly Belzer and Dushinsky Chasidim. They can be crazy. But everyone left us alone.

At some point Miriam asked me, Are you afraid? I told her, No, not at all, why should I be? Maybe because you're the youngest here, she suggested. No, I said. Then what is it? she asked me. I don't know, I said. (Sometimes I think that's all I say—"I don't know." But there comes a time when you have to know something, doesn't there? When you say, I KNOW that. I know that *absolutely*.) And that's when I blurted out all the stuff about my doubts and about my father and about the voices in the mud and just *everything*! She listened very carefully, of course, because that's what she always does. And then she told me her thoughts, which I am going to put down here as best as I can remember:

"As I listen to you, I think, what a wonderful girl. How lucky your parents are, your grandparents, your teachers, and your friends. You are so young, yet a person of character, of judgment, of sensitivity."

I had to interrupt her. "Miriam, you said 'parents.' You know I don't have a mother."

"Yes," she said. "Of course I know that. Still, when I said 'parents,' I don't think it was a mistake, because God leads our tongues to speak truths we may not be aware of ourselves. You have many parents, Anna. God is your parent, too. Nature is your parent. Life is your parent."

"Maybe even you. A little bit," I said.

She smiled at me and said, "And you know what, Anna? I believe you have listened to all your parents and learned from them all. God is in your blood no less than your biological father. I think you sense that. Do you sense that?"

I said I didn't know.

"But look at the world, at the state it is in. You know the joke, when there is a cease-fire with the Palestinians, we cease, they fire. Isn't that true? No more intifada, that's what they said. And then what happens to your father? You know how many people died that day? Eight people. Twenty-seven were wounded. One girl is in a coma. She's not much older than you. Another woman is burned so badly she will look like a monster for the rest of her life. But it's not just that. Look at the world. Everywhere you look people are dying, fighting, starving. Why do you think that is? Do you think for one minute it has to be this way? Are we doomed forever to kill each other, to die of disease and drought and cruelty? Shouldn't there be enough food to feed everyone? I don't think it has to be this way. I don't think we have to just go on the way we have always gone on. I think the world can change. I think we can change it. You can change it, Anna. All we have to do is act. We only have to do what God wants us to do. What do you think is holding us back? What do you think is making the world such a terrible place?"

Her voice was so beautiful and tender that even the leaves of the trees were still, and the lady moving toward us with her baby carriage made not a sound, and the little boy at her side sucking his thumb had no footsteps, and the three scholars across the street argued their Torah without any words coming out of their mouths. I noticed their long stockings were striped like mine, only in chestnut and black, and their slippers were purple, the color of night, and I liked that. If I could describe it, I'd say Miriam's voice was like a sweet, soft trumpet or maybe a flute or violin, weaving its way around my insides the way sometimes Mozart does or maybe R.E.M. or Ehud Banai does, like the call of the shofar from far, far away that told the tribes of Israel it was time to gather, time to march, time to come home. But I better write down the rest of what she said, so that it is never forgotten.

"What is missing in this world?" she asked me. "There is only one thing. Messiah. Why is there no Messiah? He has no place to call his own. No house from which to send out his armies of angels. The very center of the universe is broken. No wonder people fight each other over nothing! No wonder you get mad about things that don't matter. Everything is upside down, and the thing that really matters most is far from us. But you see, we can change that. It's easy to do. No one has to tell you how. We have to build God a house. A Third Temple. The last, final, and eternal Temple of Jerusalem. We cannot build it ourselves, of course, only Messiah can do that. But what can he do without us? He's crying for us. He's lonely. And so he is unwilling. We must clear the way. We must lay the ground. You and I will knock down the pillars and high places of the Canaanites. You and I will go to the very center of the universe, where God revealed his covenant to Abraham our father, where God commanded David the king and Solomon the king, and we will reopen the doors to redemption. It's not a hard task. But it cannot be done without us. No one is saying to you, you have to do this. We are only asking, do you want to do this?"

So she asked me, "Anna, do you really want to do this?" And I said, "Yes."

I couldn't stand it another minute. I threw my arms around her and squeezed as tight as I could. My head was on her chest, and I don't know what happened, but tears came out of my eyes, and then I don't know why, I started blubbering, and I just couldn't stop, and then she put her arms around me, too, and held me for a long, long time, and I could hear that she was humming her little tune, the one she hums, and she began swaying back and forth and back and forth, until for some reason, all of a sudden, I felt so much better, so much better, almost as if she had lifted me off the ground and held me up in the palm of her hand, so that I was floating above the sidewalk and above the grass and above the trees and above the rooftops, and when I looked down on everything, on all the houses and all the people and all the shops and all the cars and all the stoplights and the kids playing football in the street, I wasn't afraid. I was just me.

And then we came inside and Miriam said, I have to go now, will you be all right? And I said, Sure, and so here I am.

And then another guy came; he wore a fat red beard and a large knit kippah with long, beautiful red sidecurls braided all the way down to his shoulders like two lit candles. He was young and I think he must have been handsome, too, but in all honesty I never saw his face, because he stood just inside the door with his nose down the whole time and Shlomo was right in front of him totally blocking my view. He was carrying an Uzi slung over his shoulder, so he was in the military, on leave, I guess. Or maybe he was Shabak and he was taking a busload of kids on a field trip. Anyway, he gave Shlomo a couple of plastic grocery bags and then he was gone.

Shlomo said, "This is what you are taking up to the mount." He handed me two books, but they were *so* heavy, and a little Kodak camera.

"These books are really heavy," I told him.

"If your pack is too heavy, leave some of your real books here, and I'll get them to you tomorrow," he said.

"Why are they so heavy?" I asked.

"They're special books," he said.

Obviously he thought I was stupid.

"Now, put your camera around your neck," he said. "When you go though security, just open your rucksack as always, let them look. They won't really look anyway. The waqf guards will also look at you but will not touch you. Believe me, you're not in any danger. When you arrive at your destination, you will leave the books in the place I told you. That's all. Nothing more. But first, you will spend time wandering around, taking pictures, enjoying the sites. Talk to tourists, if you like. Then, when you are ready, as you approach the steps to the Dome of the Rock, you will turn right into the area that looks like a park, going down some steps. It is the direction of the eastern gate, the Golden Gate, but you will not go to the Golden Gate. You continue straight on the path between two groves—why they allow the groves I don't know, since the law strictly prohibits planting trees on the Temple Mount—but anyway, you will come to the next path. Turn left. Which is north. Just as I showed you on the map. Walk a few steps more, to the place where I showed you, where there is a good-sized rock with the little black mark on the base of it, you'll have to look carefully to see it, and suddenly you will become too hot, too tired, and you will lift yourself upon the retaining wall of the grove, and you will sit in the shade of a tree. You will fan yourself. If someone comes by and asks you, you will tell them you just need a rest. If someone wants to talk to you, talk to them, no problem. Be yourself. But when you are all alone and no one is bothering you, take the books out of your backpack and also another book, one of your own, and read for a while. As you do this, you will slip the two books I gave you behind the retaining wall, and place them between the wall and the rock, just as I showed you, and cover it with brush and dirt. We have practiced this, so you know how to do it so quickly and smoothly no one will ever see you. Then you just put your own book back in your pack and continue your walk. Head up to the dome through the eastern qanatir, take a few more snapshots or just look around, whatever you feel like, and then simply leave the mount like everyone else through the Chain Gate."

"Shlomo, I know all this," I told him.

But this wasn't enough for him, so he repeated the whole thing again. And while he was speaking I guess I just sort of tuned out and remembered what Miriam had said to me when we were alone: "Anna, don't you realize the time of the Third Temple is upon us? This little, seemingly simple thing you do is a link in the chain of Messiah. When you go there today, you will look like an ordinary, secular Israeli girl. No one will imagine the true nature of your soul and the blessings you carry with you. No one will guess that you, my Anna, my darling, my precious Anna, are a true soldier in his army, a noble Daughter of Israel, a Deborah, a Yael."

"A Miriam!" I said.

She laughed, and her whole face turned into gold. "Anna!" she said to me. "The beauty of your soul shines from your eyes, for I believe that the Shekhinah has blessed you and touched you."

"Me?"

"Oh yes, Anna! You! Are you ready to do her work?"

I told her, yes, I was.

When Shlomo told it, I felt a little funny in my stomach, but when she told it, I knew everything was right.

Chapter Twenty-two

✡

THREE DAYS AFTER THE TRIAL THEY CALLED me in. It was the same Vasily Vasin.

"You lived up to your side, now I will live up to mine," he said. "You see, we're not so bad. You have the wrong idea of us altogether. We both are men of belief."

"I don't see myself as a man of belief," I told him.

"Well, in any case, you are here for your reward, and you shall have it. There's no reason to make a big show of anything. It's always best to avoid a scandal. All the papers are in order."

He handed me a thick envelope.

"I want something else," I said.

"Really? What is that?"

"I want to speak to Collette."

"I don't think that will be possible. You can write to her. She can write to you. In some time, of course, you may be able to visit her, but not until she is settled and shows her willingness to be rehabilitated."

"Anything is possible," I said, "but not that."

"Too bad," he said.

"Vasili Nikolayevich, I only want five minutes."

"She's already on her way east. What can I do?"

"I'm sure there's something you can do."

He twirled his fountain pen between his fingers.

"Well," he said, "I suppose there is always the telephone. No one, not even in Magadan, is very far from a phone."

"Magadan," I gasped.

"The very end of the earth," he nodded. "I tried to warn her."

"How can she survive Magadan?"

"We have the very best doctors. Don't you worry. You know, though, it's possible she's still in Butyrka, awaiting transfer. So perhaps she's even closer!" He smiled at me in a friendly way. He did not call anyone to check.

"She's in Moscow," I cried.

"Quite possibly!"

"For pity's sake, Vasin, let me see her."

He sighed. "I've already gone so far out of my way for you. We all have. Oh, Guttman, cheer up. You have your whole future in front of you."

"Vasin, what do you want?"

"There will be no news conferences. No interviews. No scandal. You talk to no one, even out of the country."

"Fine."

"Well," he mused, "perhaps I still have some power around here to do something." He gave me the agreement to sign. It was already completely prepared. "If you break your word, it is only poor Collette Petrovna who will suffer."

"When can I see her?" I asked.

"Go sit in the reception room. We'll call you."

I sat on my bench for many hours, watching the day officer lazily type on his machine. I had a ballpoint pen with me, and I did not hide the fact I was carving initials into the bench. I wrote my own, and then next to that I spelled out the name COLLETTE CHERNOFF in Roman letters. I spent a great deal of time on it, blowing away the sawdust and filling the carved-out spaces with deep blue ink.

At last a lieutenant came in through the hallway door and signaled me to follow him. He walked briskly, and I had to run to keep up with him. We entered a tiny elevator that still used a handle to operate. He shut the grate and we descended into a large garage. I followed him to a waiting Volga sedan; he opened the door for me and stood there stiffly as I got in. He sat down beside me and pulled the curtains on all the windows, tapped the driver, and off we went. Moving north through the city, I sensed the life outside the car: the sunshine still bright in the early afternoon, new snow sparkling on the sidewalks, young people like myself laughing and smoking as they walked, packs of teenagers up to no good on their way home from school, girls in long braids holding hands and telling secrets, shoppers emerging from milk markets and meat stalls, the kiosks doing their brisk business of cigarettes and candies, boys in their red bandanas gobbling down glazed chocolate syrki. I thought to myself, it has its beauty, even if it is also cruel; it has its passions, and they are not skin deep. But in a moment that Moscow was behind me, and the gates of Butyrka were opening before me.

They confiscated the food I had brought but let me keep my copy of Yehudah Amichai. Then they led me through a series of hallways and past several gated enclosures. No one spoke to me. All the doors on either side of the hall were shut tight; nevertheless the guard rattled his keys as we walked to warn anyone who might inadvertently come into the hall. I put my hand on my stomach. I suddenly worried I would need a toilet—I had to urinate but was afraid to ask. I understood I had to control not only my emotions but my body as well. At last there was a single open door. I entered, sat at the table as I was instructed, and watched as the guard stepped behind me, standing more or less at attention.

The room was very clean. The floors had been mopped and the walls freshly painted. I sat down on a chair that was bolted to the floor. The table was bolted as well. The room was well lit with two rows of fluorescents. A one-way mirror was obvious on the back wall, giving observers a suitable view of both seats in profile. Mounted near the ceiling were two video cameras, one pointed at me and one pointed at the chair opposite. There was no attempt to camouflage them. In about fifteen minutes the door opened again, and standing in it were another guard and Collette. She wore the clothes of a prisoner, a rough, black muslin dress, worker's shoes and socks, a knit sweater, and a woolen scarf tied around her neck. Beneath this sweater and scarf she seemed a kind of midget, with only the needles of her shorn hair popping out like shoots of angelica. Though she was not restrained in any way, she moved slowly, and with great effort. She sat down across from me and folded her hands upon the table. Her guard took up his place behind her. We sat there for what seemed a long time, but it may only have been seconds. I'm sure she was aware, as was I, that we were allowed but a few minutes together.

She was the first to speak.

"How are you?" Her voice was so much the same—but coming out of this strange body, this almost unrecognizable face.

"How are you?" I replied.

"I want to tell you what's happened to me in these months, but you already know the most important thing."

"I do."

"Is this a book for me?"

"It is. It's in English. I hope that's all right."

She thumbed through the pages.

"They interrogated me every day for six months," she began. "But they never let me see anyone. I never knew if anything was real, what they were telling me. But I could understand certain things from their questions and demands. I understood very quickly no one else was arrested. That meant they didn't really believe the charge of hijacking. When I saw that the trial was open enough for Lonya to be present, I knew they would not give me the harshest sentence. I was so relieved, I wept. The real case, the real issue, was always my father. But I don't know why. I still can't figure it out. It was so long ago. If he was a victim of Stalin, so what? They would tell me, and that would be that. If the records were really lost, they would just make them up. So what's the big secret? But maybe it was really just against the Americans. Charlie. They wanted to make an example of him. They're worried because no one is afraid to be with Americans anymore. That's the problem."

She rested her chin upon her palms the way she often did when we were talking across the kitchen table. "You don't look so good, Romka. You needn't worry so much, I'm fine with everything. Tell me about you, about everyone."

From behind her, the guard announced, "No speaking of personalities."

"People are more frightened right now, but that doesn't stop them," I said.

"No speaking of activities," he added.

"Your friends are fine," I went on. "Your family is well. Cousin Lonya all of a sudden wants to see his relatives wherever they happen to live. His parents do, too. Your aunt Lorrette is in good health. I don't know about her young friend. But I wanted to tell you something. About before."

"They already told me. That's why I said nothing during the trial."

"Something else."

"No, it doesn't matter. Roma, I want to explain myself to you."

"You don't have to do that," I said.

"This will be the only time. I kept it from you, I don't know why. The last time I saw you I tried to tell you, but then I just couldn't. By the time I was arrested there was nothing I could do about it."

"You were going to do something about it?"

"Yes, I think so. But then I didn't, and then it was too late. And then I simply wouldn't. Because I wanted her."

I briefly looked up at the guard. His eyes were half focused upon the wall opposite him; he seemed bored, but I knew he wasn't. This was a big day for him, a break from the usual tedium. My own guard was breathing quite easily and naturally, but I felt his presence like a finger jabbing me in the back. Collette was also calm. She ran her fingers through her hair in the way she always did, but not finding the long, loose strands to push back over her ears, she awkwardly folded her hands back on the table.

"I was arrested on the twenty-third of August," she began again. "Roma, I was already four months pregnant. But back when I first learned of it, all I could think of was that I had to get out of the country. And then somehow I decided on an abortion. What kept me from it, I don't know. I was still too busy writing letters and making demonstrations. It was foolish of me, I guess. And then they took me. I must have been expecting it, because we all are, but who really expects it? It was 1982. Not '52. Or maybe my calendar was wrong."

She laughed. She was light as air, in fact, as if nothing held her to the earth. Perhaps that is why the chair was bolted to the floor.

"I didn't tell them. I just thought I was being detained. I'd already been detained, right? But at my first interrogation I knew they were creating a serious case against me. They had a confession all ready for me to sign, on that first day! I actually laughed at them. So they threw me in my cell, all alone with a bucket and not even a mattress. Nothing to read, no paper or pencil. They gave me a cup and a spoon, a wooden spoon, maybe so I wouldn't dig through the stone floor and make my escape! The windows have slats, Roman, tilted upward so all you can see are little slivers of sky. Never the yard or the street or, God forbid, a person. That was the main rule. No persons. No talking. No way to know there was anyone in the world left alive, except for you and your team—your guards, your interrogator. When the other prisoners were let out to clean the halls or carry the tubs of tea or kasha, my door was always closed and the trap always shut. They were not allowed to speak in my hallway. But I knew they were there. You can't hide the sound of scrubbing and grunting or the guard clapping his baton on the wall as warning. Still, I understood I was not a regular prisoner, and I was not going to be here for a short time. And then there was the food. A few grams of fat, a few grams of dried fish, a little kasha and soup if you were lucky. I didn't think it would bother me so quickly, but almost immediately I became weak. Then the diarrhea. Just the smell of the steel bars, the painted concrete, and of course the bucket. I became violently ill. Then it dawned on me—oh Roma, I'm a terrible mother!—it had to be the baby inside me. They want to kill me, I said to myself, but I won't let them kill my baby. The next time they called me, I told Vasin the truth. He went crazy. He ordered tests. More tests. I said to him, 'You could have just believed me. I always tell the truth.' He apologized: 'Collette Petrovna, I never intended to insult you.' I laughed at this. He's a very earnest person. A complicated person. I don't hate him at all. Isn't that funny? I like him in many ways. Of course immediately he used this against me. If only I will confess, all will be well. I can go home with my unborn child, no problem. Roman, I thought about it. I thought hard about it. To have a child in this place—disgusting! Revolting!" She sighed, and ran her sleeve under her nose. "Do you have a cigarette?"

"They took them from me in the guard room."

"I have some mahorka. I'll smoke that." She took from the pocket of her simple dress a kind of cigarette that she had constructed from a tightly wrapped strip of *Pravda* filled with tobacco stems that had been ground into sawdust. She raised the cigarette to her lips, arched her neck toward her guard, and received from him a lit match. The newsprint wrapper flared, and she inhaled the rancid smoke. The room quickly filled with the scent of hot tar.

"But I couldn't do even that for her," she continued sadly. "I couldn't confess to something I hadn't done. And they wanted names, as always. And I knew, once I confessed, I would have to give them names. You give them one thing, they take it all. They said as much. But even if they didn't at first, they would later say, What kind of confession is this? Is it just lies? Just for your convenience? We need names! We need names! I knew this already from the first version of the confession. I did this with so-and-so. I did that with so-and-so. At so-and-so's house this happened. I wasn't there, but so-and-so and so-and-so said this. So I ask you, how could I confess, even for her?"

"You couldn't have," I said.

"No, I couldn't have. And so time went on. My food improved a little, in fact—first, when they thought I would do anything to get out, and then later when they became frightened. They gave me milk every day, and a small portion of some sort of meat. I got the milk no matter where I was being held, in the cell or in the ward, but the meat only when I was in the cell. They gave me vitamins, but for a long time I wouldn't take them because I didn't know what was in them. Should I have taken them?"

"You did the right thing," I said.

"I think I did."

"Yes, you did."

"But they got angry at me, of course. I think they were more afraid than angry. I am not an ordinary prisoner. The whole world is watching. I could not know this for certain, but I believed it to be so. And it was so, wasn't it?"

"Yes. The courthouse was surrounded by the press. You were in all the international papers, on the radio. You had a message from Sakharov and Bonner, President Reagan spoke about you on Voice of America. Everyone."

"I felt this," she said.

"I warn you again, no personalities," snapped the guard.

She tapped some ash into her palm. "I don't know," she said, "it's like a dream. And yet I'm wide awake. Never have I been so wide awake. He said to me, 'Collette Petrovna! Do you think we can't take this child from you? We can rip it out of you anytime we like!' When he said things like that I felt sorry for him. He was under enormous pressure. He understood whatever he did to me would ultimately come to light, and the best he could do was try to frighten me. When he was desperate in this way, I only pitied him. But he also began to see that this baby was the one thing that mattered to me. He said to me, 'You understand that after the child is born she will be placed in an orphanage? This is standard practice in all the prisons of the Soviet Union. You may give birth to your baby in the prison hospital, but then . . . Well!' I told him, 'The child has a father. The father must have the child.' And he said, 'What father? Are you married? Because you name this one or that one, why should we believe you?' I said, 'Guttman!' and he almost spit on the floor. 'Guttman! Why not the Frenchman? He came to visit you again, didn't he? He spent the night in your house. Well, we saw him slithering out at three in the morning. Why not the American spy? You were lovers. You cannot deny it. Please, don't insult my intelligence.' I no longer cared what he said, but I knew he was finally on some sort of solid ground. How could I prove anything? And the policy was the policy. The child born in prison goes to the orphanage. He had me. He had the baby. I obsessed about this day and night.

"Did you know they shaved my pubic hair when I arrived? It had nothing to do with pregnancy. They do that to everyone. The hair on your head, the hair between your legs. They assume you will be deeply humiliated by all this shaving of hair. I found it just curious, that's all. I studied myself for many days, and found that it simply made me wish I could be a hairless child again, with my grandfather, in our apartment in the Arbat, waiting for Father to finally come home. Goga, I need a place to crush my cigarette," she announced to the guard. He lifted the cigarette from her fingers, crushed it on the sole of his boot, and handed it back to her. She stowed what was left of it in her pocket. "Then, at last, they gave me paper and pen. They suggested I write my thoughts about the case, or even my questions for them. I did not do this. I wrote what I wanted to write. Often, they took what I wrote away from me, even though that is illegal. They said, 'You want more paper, don't you? You're only allowed so much paper in your cell at one time.' Then they gave me more paper. I took it. I didn't care. My need to write was overwhelming. I mostly wrote letters. I think some of the letters they claimed against me were written then. I wrote to you, Roman, more than once, knowing it would never be mailed and that the only person to read it would be Vasin. But somehow I knew that you would be receiving them in your own way, as you always did, my sweet, with a complete heart and half a brain."

She reached out to touch my face, but the guard would not allow it. The tips of her fingers had come so close to my skin that there remained but a single layer of molecules between us. Even so, no distance could have been greater, no space more impenetrable. She went on unperturbed. "In my letters, I confessed to you everything about the child. I described how it looked, how it cried, what it liked to eat, even though it wasn't even born yet. I drew little pictures of it, I told you about the crib I would buy for it, and the dresses and the toys. I said dresses, but I had no idea if it would be a girl or a boy. I named it Lisa, after my grandmother, but then I changed it to Anna. You know why? Because of Akhmatova! I remembered these lines: *No, not under the vault of alien skies, / And not under the shelter of alien wings— / I was with my people then, / There, where my people, unfortunately, were.* And all her words came flooding inside me, as if the walls of my uterus had been breached. I was filled with Akhmatova as much as with the baby. So I named her Anna. I hope to God I did not curse her with poetry.

"But you know, all the milk and the meat and the pills, none of it really helped. My belly expanded, but everything else in me withered up. My feet seemed to become so big, and my face! It fell backward from this nose of mine which has become as big as a house—you see what I mean?"

"Not at all," I said.

"I'm not beautiful, I know."

"You are beautiful."

Her lips unfolded into a small, lucent, even pretty smile. "Whatever happened before doesn't matter, does it? All of that, who cares? What we did out there—it's all in the past. You said it at the trial, and I listened: 'The past is irrelevant. It's the future I care about.' That's what you said."

"That's exactly what I said."

"That's when I knew they would keep their bargain with me."

"Yes, they're keeping the bargain."

"They needed you to confirm the letters. To betray me publicly. That was your part."

"Yes."

"I also did as I was asked. I said nothing about her and waited for you to give your testimony."

"Yes."

"And now they're keeping their word."

"Even they have their ethics."

She let out a long sigh of relief and allowed her head to rest on the table.

"Head up," the guard said.

"Months passed. Months and months. But this baby refused to be born. It knew, didn't it? The kind of world that was waiting for it. I loved that it refused. My baby was a brazen ball of refusal!

"One day he called me into his office. The trial, I guessed, was almost upon us.

"'Collette Petrovna, it is my great sadness that it has come to this. You know very well there would not be a trial if the evidence against you wasn't conclusive. I've showed you document after document proving your guilt. I only ask that you engage me in a discussion of the facts, as two rational people in search of the truth, but you spurn every offer. And now I have to tell you it will not go easy for you. Even if we don't execute you, you will get ten years, or if you are very lucky six, at severe regime, and you know what that means. And what that means for the child you are carrying. But it can still go otherwise. You can still save yourself.'

"There was a woman, Ladovska, maybe related to the great architect, who knows? She also came to interrogate me many times. She was at the trial, sitting behind the procurator; she was the one with the large chin. She used to say to me, 'Don't worry, we'll give your child to a good Russian family.' She did this to infuriate me. 'Why do we give this prisoner extra rations? The baby will be stillborn anyway.' Then, as always, she would say, 'Think it over, Collette Petrovna, think it over.' When they finally presented me with the charges—The Charges in Their Final Form, they called it—I was already nine months pregnant and could do nothing but lie in my bed. I was sick, I was terrified for my baby, I was skin and bones when a woman should be fat and round. They refused to take me to the infirmary because pregnancy is not considered an illness. 'You think this will have a good end,' Ladovska said to me, 'but it won't. Reconsider before it is too late for you.' She was the one I hated. She took pleasure in her cruelty. On the other hand, without her, I don't know if I would ever have been so strong.

"But you know they were afraid of me, too, and I'll tell you why. If there was to be a trial, they knew I would scream my head off from the first second about my baby. It would break open the whole trial. Everyone knows the charges are trumped up; they make no bones about it—but to have a baby involved. Even they knew this was too much. And of course they knew I understood this. They were desperate to keep me silent, but they also had to have the trial proceed. It was Vasin who first broached the idea. But I'm getting ahead of myself. I didn't tell you how Anna was born. Would you like to know?"

"Yes, I would."

"They had called me in to go over my petitions and witness list, which I knew they would not accept in the first place. Instead, they wanted to introduce me to my lawyer. I told them I didn't want their lawyer and reminded them I'd presented them with my list of possible attorneys. 'These are foreigners. You cannot have a foreign lawyer. Even in America you can't have a foreign lawyer.' I said to them, 'Then let Roman Guttman find me a lawyer. I entrust my case to him.' 'We already spoke to Guttman,' Vasin told me, 'and he won't do it.' But I knew this was a lie, because I had the protocols of all the interrogations in my case file and you weren't among them. 'But we got you a Jewish lawyer!' he said. And there, seated in the corner with her hands folded on her lap and looking like a beaten child, was the lawyer, I can't even remember her name anymore."

"Fishman."

"That's it. Fishman. Poor thing. But it didn't matter, that's exactly when I went into labor. Ladovska jumped up. 'You're faking! Everyone can see that.' 'So what is that all over the floor? Orange juice?' You know, they are so ludicrous. Whatever they make up, that's what they believe. Now Vasin leaps into action, but not in such a way as to get his uniform dirty. He dials the phone! Poor Fishman, stuck in the corner, is glued to her chair. Ladovska has her hands on her hips, deciding if I am a great actor or just a woman having a baby. In come the guards, but they don't know what to do either, so I say, 'May I please go to the infirmary?' But it all was happening too fast, probably because I was so undernourished. I was having contractions all the way down the corridors. Can you imagine, we'd take a few steps, a guard on either side of me, and I'd collapse to the floor. They were very sweet, really. They'd wait patiently for me to stop writhing and then lead me farther into the depths of the prison. When we got to the infirmary, no one had bothered to tell them anything, and the questions started all over again. 'Well, we'll have to find her a mattress. The doctor isn't here till tonight. Sit over there and wait.' But in the end they took pity on me. That's often the way it is in here. It was only three hours later Anya was born. And this was when everyone started to panic. The child could not stay in the prison. But what to do with it? What to do with me, if they forcefully took away my child?

"They didn't wait very long. The next day Vasin came to see me. It was the first time he'd come to me and not the other way around. My breasts had no milk, and they had had to rush out to a party dispensary to find formula for her. He asked if he could feed her. I said to him, 'Oh, Vasin, you are too kind!' But he remained cheerful, pulled up a chair, sat very near to me. Never had he been so physically close. Before the baby, everything had smelled more disgusting than I can even describe. I couldn't get used to it the way everyone else seemed to. Vasin himself had an oily smell, like oysters. But now I realized it was actually some sort of cologne. 'Collette,' he said to me, the first time he had ever uttered my name in that way, 'I want you to listen with an open mind, just this once. On the occasion of this wonderful miracle. Can you do that? When I see this beautiful child, I also do not want it to end up in an orphanage. You might as well be sending it to a labor camp. She'll end up a thief or worse, because they all do. That's what they learn there. I know by now you are not going to sign a confession, you are not going to see reason and allow yourself to be rehabilitated. You are determined to continue this Zionist insanity and undermine everything that is good in the Soviet Union. I accept this. I am sorry for you, but I accept it. The trial is going to be happening soon, I am allowed to tell you that much, and there is no avoiding it. You can count on a severe sentence, and there is no avoiding that at this point either, unless you change your mind. But there is no reason the child has to suffer. I have a suggestion,

I offer a solution. What if the child were to go with Guttman? He is the father, after all, isn't that what you said? What harm could it be if he took the child? Wouldn't that be the best for everyone?' He looked at me lying there with the baby asleep in my arms, for they had let me keep her after feeding her her bottle, and then he added, 'After the trial, of course.' I knew what he wanted now. My silence for her freedom. 'Till then, we'll keep her in a nursery, but you will be able to see her every day.' And for the first time since I had been in Lefortovo, I felt I could breathe.

"Our time will soon be up, my darling Roman. You have a question for me."

"No."

"You want to know . . ."

"No."

"Who is the father."

"Collette," I said, "I am the father."

That was the last time I saw Collette. She disappeared into the camps, and then, according to the report of the medical examiner, she died of "natural causes" one year later. But I was already in a far-off land, beginning a new life, with a new child.

Chapter Twenty-three

✡

THE DOOR OPENED AND CLOSED, open and closed, as if Abdul-
Latif thought I might have evaporated into the bedsheets. Each
time he peeked in, he made that clucking noise that Arabs often
make, and then he would quickly disappear behind the locked
door.

Finally he stepped into the room and stood with his hands on
his hips, appraising me. "You are not getting better," he said. "You
are not drinking my water. My water is not poison for you." He
strode up to the bedside and grabbed the glass that had been sitting untouched on the night table. "Look!" he cried, and drank
half of it himself. "Now you!" He pressed the glass into my hand,
but my fingers could not find a way to hold it. He lifted the glass
to my lips, but I turned my head away and the water dripped down
my chin. He cursed in his own language and slammed the glass
down. He began pacing in front of the bed.

"You know, Mr. Guttman, my daughter Hanadi is seventeen.
She is the youngest one. She will be married before Marya, I assure
you. Marya cannot find anyone she likes, and I won't force her into
anything. Her mother would, but not me. Those ideas are over for
me. But Hanadi has had a thousand offers, and she likes too many
of them, if you ask me, so she will choose. I want her to be married
as soon as possible. It's the only way to save her. You know what
Hanadi has told me? She thinks we should throw you to the crowd.
She thinks it's the right thing to do. We should throw you to the
crowd, and then she can go out with her friends dancing. Can you
hear them? Of course you can. They get louder and louder. Very

angry. Upset. It's all the men of the town, and the boys, too. Probably my wife is with them. They want to cut off your head and throw your body at the foot of that Israeli settlement up on our hill. Kfar Tikva. It's only been there a few years, but they already have beautiful houses, a school, a grocery, a library. At first the soldiers came to push them out, but they returned and rebuilt. Now we have to look at them every day." He walked over to the window as if to peruse the Jewish village, but the window was too high to look out of, except to see a bit of sky. He came back to me and sat down. "Come in here, Hanadi!" he called out.

The door slowly opened, and Hanadi shyly stepped in. She was very slender and petite, with large, dark eyes, and a smooth bright complexion. Her cheeks were the plump cheeks of a schoolgirl, but her lips were a woman's. She had tied a green bandana over her forehead and a black checked kaffiah around her neck.

"You see?" he said. "Brigade of Al-Qassam. Woman's Auxiliary."

He said something to her in Arabic, and she nodded.

"*Young* Woman's Auxiliary. But if I tell her to bring you something sweet to eat, she will do that, too. She's a good girl." He said something else to her in Arabic, and she left the room.

"You're thinking, why do they want to harm me? What have I done to them? You can't in all honesty say you are a civilian, can you? So they are within their rights. Legally, I mean. Being in reserves means you are still a soldier." He looked me up and down, at the split, dry lips and sunken bloodshot eyes, the wounds still not fully healed and the skin cracking open between my fingers, and he sighed. "I don't know why I saved you. So much trouble on my own head."

Hanadi again shyly opened the door. She carried a small plate with some cookies on it. "*Mammoul*," she said. It was the first time she had spoken in my presence, and her voice was lovely—untinged with the cynicism of Jewish teenagers, just the voice of a young girl on the brink of life—but the little plate shook in her hands; she didn't know what she was supposed to do with it. Abdul-Latif reached out his hand and grabbed a cookie. "Mmmm," he said, biting into it. "Not bad. Nadja, my wife, used to make them so beautifully. These are from the bakery. They're not bad. Just not the same." He said something again in Arabic, and Hanadi laid the plate on the table beside me. "If you eat our *mammoul,* you'll be very thirsty, and then you will have to drink," he said. "It's an Arab trick." And he laughed.

There was suddenly an urgent knocking on the exterior door.

Abdul-Latif called out in Hebrew so I would understand, "Marya, Marya! See who is at the door." And then he added to me, "Marya is my other one. I better see what they want."

Abdul-Latif stood up to go.

"My friend," he said, "if you think this is just another dream of yours, if you think you are still talking to birds, you are very wrong."

And with that, he motioned to Hanadi, and they went together though the door. Again the key turned in the lock.

Chapter Twenty-four

☪

IN THE DAYS LEADING TO MY SHAHADAH, I was immersed in prayer. I bathed my feet and hands in the waters of el-Kas, the well of al-Aqsa, which they told us rises up from the rivers of Eden, and I entered the great mosque and stayed there for hours on end, meditating. Then I would take the bus back to Jabal, to Walid's place, where we would talk and study late into the night. Only then would I sleep a few hours, lying between Walid and Fayez on the hard floor. In the morning we would wash, pray, and prepare a little hummus and tea. He always had dates and figs, sliced apples, and sweets of various kinds, and at night there was usually maqluba. We were never hungry, even though we fasted on Tuesdays and Thursdays. Walid had found us a small room where no one knew us, but this room made Walid despair. He often talked about his real house, which he had never seen. It had been in the village of Umm Kalkha near al-Ramleh. He wore the key around his neck. His father had given it to him, his father who also had never seen this house. Yet Walid could describe it in the most vivid detail, and I, too, felt as if I once had a life within those walls. "Umm Kalkha was abandoned before the war," he said bitterly. "They were so full of fear, they left it all behind. They thought nothing of it. The idea that they could fight for it never even crossed their minds. They left their fates to the cowardly Nasserites and Hashemites, may Allah have mercy on them, and this is all that is left for me." He spit on his key and polished it between his fingers. I said to him, "And my father, what will he say to me?" And Walid said to me, "This jihad is fard al-ain. The slave may rebel from his master, the son from his father. Your father does not have the power to stop you, for your power comes from Allah, praise be to the All Merciful." Every day I spent many hours alone with Yusuf al-Faruk, my sheikh, who organized the operation, for I had been taken into the Battalions of Qassam. Yusuf al-Faruk trained me day and night, and I, like a falcon on the path of All-Knowing Allah, swooped up his leavings. These were my happiest days. These were my days of light. "For the call!" I repeated after him. "For the Muslim Brotherhood!" I wanted to care only for Islam and for the purity of my soul at the end of days. Paradise was always before my eyes, for the life of this world was worth nothing, and I yearned to yearn for death, saying, as Yusuf al-Faruk instructed me, "Truly there is only one death, so let it be on the path of Allah."

And so I prepared for my martyrdom, and I did not go home for a very long time.

Oh. A stab into my heart that can no longer feel! A vision through these eyes that have no right to see!

I am standing before the blank wall, with Walid and Sheikh al-Faruk and Ra'id Mashriki and also Hassan Bahar, and we are all pinning up the posters, FROM THE RIVER TO THE SEA! ISLAM IS THE ANSWER! THE BATTALIONS OF THE MARTYR IZZ AD-DIN AL-QASSAM, THE GUARDIAN OF AL-AQSA! I am wearing a suit, yes, a gray suit and a tie, a blue tie, a white shirt, but around my head is a white headband, and on it the words GOD IS GREAT, and around my waist is a holster and in it a pistol, and in my arms is an AK-47, and in a scabbard tied around my left bicep is a khanjar, thirsty for blood. And look! My beard, the one I grew after I was reborn, is gone. I look at myself in my suit and my nice oxford shoes, and I almost feel like laughing. I'm practically the old me. Hassan Bahar steps behind the camera and waves at us, and Walid and Yusuf al-Faruk and Ra'id Mashriki step away, and there I am, alone in front of our artful backdrop of flags and slogans, and I glance down at my necktie and my oxfords, and I rear up to the camera and cry, "I am ready for business!" And I hear Sheikh Yusuf's voice, "If

Allah wills it!" And I answer him, "If Allah wills it!" And Sheikh Yusuf asks, "And what business are you ready for? For the business of Allah, Lord of the Worlds?" "Yes! For the business of Allah, Most Merciful and Magnificent!" And he says, "Tell us, O Shahid, what are your plans?" And I answer, "God willing, it will not be Jerusalem, it will not be Tel Aviv, but where they believe they can hide from the justice of Allah, Lord of the Worlds, in their suburbs and their enclaves and their safest places." "Tell us then," he urges. And I tell him, "Tomorrow, if Allah wills it, I will destroy the Jews on bus line forty-seven, and, Allah permitting, my soul will go to Paradise where I will meet the Prophet and his Companions, peace be upon them, and the souls of the infidels will burn on earth and also in Hell."

"You will kill many offspring of pigs and monkeys!"

"The Messenger of Allah, peace be upon him, said, You will indeed fight against the Jews and you will kill them to the point where the rock and the tree will say: O *Muslim! O Abdullah! There is a Jew hiding behind me. Come and kill him.*"

And the voice, which of course is Sheikh Yusuf's, cries, "Ever since the first hour, the Jews hated the Muslims and their Prophet. In fact, our Prophet, Muhammad, may he find favor always, was never safe from these Jews. They tried to kill him three times. One time, they tried to kill him by putting a heavy rock on his head. Another time was when they placed poison in the forearm of a goat for him to eat. And a third case was when the Jewish boy, Lubaid bin al-A'asam, may Allah's curse be upon him, put a magic spell on him."

And now another voice, this time Walid's, "Wasn't it the Jews who set fire to our precious al-Aqsa?"

And then Hassan Bahar from behind the camera, "Weren't they the ones who killed our Muslim brothers while they prayed in the holy month of Ramadan in Masjid al-Khaleel?"

I answer, "Yes! They cut open the stomachs of pregnant women and murdered our Muslim babies, they tore down our houses and uprooted our olive trees, they burned our villages and slaughtered our young men!"

And now Ra'id Mashriki calls to me, "Wasn't it the Jews who transformed the mosques of Palestine into bars for alcohol and gambling? Did they not turn them into compounds for animals and garbage dumps?"

"Allahu Akhbar!" we all cry as one. "Allahu Akhbar!"

And Sheikh Yusuf al-Faruk says, "Show us then, how you plan to execute your mission!"

Now, finally, I can tear open my shirt and show them! But I must be extremely careful not to pull off any buttons or rip the material in any way, or even wrinkle it too much, and this takes quite a long time to accomplish, so it does not make quite the impression I had hoped, but at last my shirt is open and I can fully display the neatly packed tubes of explosives wrapped around my waist in the explosive belt that had been so cleverly hidden beneath the three-piece suit I am wearing.

In the camera you can probably see Sheikh Yusuf's hand, because he gets so excited he forgets to stay out of the picture. "Such a blessing from Allah, magnificent in his mercy! Such a weapon, who has seen such a weapon before?"

"And I will have other weapons as well," I tell him, "a great quantity of weapons. This pistol, this knife, and these grenades. I ask Allah, Eternal and All Knowing, only for this, to bestow martyrdom upon me and victory also, not one or the other, but victory in martyrdom!"

"Yet we rely not on weapons but on Allah, Lord of the Worlds."

"My living and my dying belong to Allah!"

"And what do you say, O Shahid, to the Cubs of Hamas?"

"Oh, young boys and girls! Remember, soldiering is not the way for all, but if, Allah permitting, you are called, you must answer with all the blood in your veins. Do not spare a drop! Mujahideen of Palestine! Tomorrow the storm of revenge will rain down on the occupiers of your land!"

"How sweet is death for the homeland! May the prayers of Allah be upon you!"

"The blood of the martyrs is calling me."

And then very calmly, Sheikh Yusuf asks, "O Shahid, tell us, is there someone you would like to greet?"

And I answer him, "Yes! This is my greeting: Peace upon you, Fadi bin-Rashid al Husseini al-Hijaz! I say to you, my friend, my brother Fadi, with whom I share but one heart, one heart in Islam, to you, Fadi, I say, today is the day of your happiness!"

"And where is Fadi al-Hijaz?"

"In Paradise, drinking from streams of purple wine."

"Fadi al-Hijaz, martyr of Jabal! He killed two soldiers with one stone! And what else do you have to say to Fadi al-Hijaz?"

"That this operation is under the banner IN HONOR OF FADI AL-HIJAZ, for whenever I think of Fadi, whenever I see his image on his martyr card or on his poster, I always say, *O Allah, Most Magnanimous, make me like him!*"

"God willing, you will depart for Paradise tomorrow! A bridegroom going to his wedding! Full of love! Full of hope! And what is your name, O Shahid?"

I hold up my Kalashnikov in my left hand and my Qur'an in my right hand, and I say, "My name is abu-Fadi! For truly now, I am father to him who delivered me here."

From behind the camera I hear Hassan Bahar say, "I think that's enough." But I say, "I want to say something to my mother." And he turns the camera back on.

I take from my pocket a piece of paper and unfold it. I am seated now on the cushion, and the belt is pressing into me a little painfully. I read.

"Mother, Father, though you have not seen me for several months because I am among the hunted, know that you are in my thoughts, indeed are always in my thoughts. Do not weep for me. In fact, have a party, the wedding party you always wished for me. I am married only to Islam and to the cause of my Muslim Brotherhood and the people of Palestine. Do not cry for me. I will be in Paradise and will be married there to my seventy hur al-ain, they are my brides. Often, in the hovels of the camps and destitution of our village, I have held before my eyes the unbearable beauty of these maidens. Their skin is like fine silk, through which you can see into another world, a better world, the world to come. Often in the stench and filth of this existence, I have breathed in their ethereal perfume and listened to their heavenly song. Do not cry for me one single tear, but eat sweets and dance. And of the one whose name cannot be mentioned, tell her there is no better end to the bitterness of oppression than this. For her, revenge! For you, the blessing of jihad!"

And then I hear them all shouting with joy, "Allahu Akhbar! Allahu Akhbar!"

Was I happy then? I must have been, because I was smiling the whole time, and the smile never left my face. But as I fly from this scene, and the whole of it melts into the shoreless sea of God's mind and becomes for me but the faintest afterglow of a long-exploded star, and I see myself standing at the bus stop in my excellent three-piece suit, my Samsonite briefcase in my left hand, and my right hand clutching the Mercedes-Benz key in my pocket, I have to wonder to myself, what, after all, did I truly believe? Where, in the end, was my happiness? Why did I press the unlock button before I boarded that bus? It was the eyes of that young and beautiful girl. Eyes I recognize, for I have seen them through their closed lids. They belong to Dasha Cohen.

Could I have seen in those eyes my seventy brides calling me, not from Paradise, but from here in the land of the Jews? Or was it merely that I had never trusted in them in the first place and that, underneath it all, I hated Yusuf al-Faruk and Walid Bannoura?

Then what, O Allah, my Protector, was that smile on my face?

☯

Dear You,

For a long time, I was in my *Fushigi Yûgi* stage, which is what I always explained to Pop when he rolled his eyes at me and told me

I better read Pushkin or Lermontov instead, because otherwise I'd end up as just another Israeli ignoramus. It's a stage, Pop! I'd tell him. But now I see this was basically true. *Fushigi Yûgi* was merely a step in the direction I was going anyway, and I had to take that step in order to arrive where I am, which presently is a grassy area just above the Damascus Gate. I'm sitting here enjoying the shade for a minute because Yohanan needed to use the restroom. He was getting a little panicky because we didn't know where one was. We'd already passed the hotels and the police station when it hit him. I remembered there's a tourist place for Christians called the Garden Tomb where some of them think Jesus was buried, and it's just off the Nablus Road. We saw a sign to it, and Yohanan said, I gotta go, so I told him, go ahead I'll meet you down here. He hesitated to leave me because he was worried something might happen to me, I'd get hassled by some guys or something—Yohanan is very chivalrous. But what could he do? So off he went to Jesus's tomb, and I came down here to wait. My pack is very heavy anyway, and it felt good to take it off, plus now I was schlepping his, too, because he didn't want to go through security with the Christians. So the packs are sitting at my feet right now. (My red high-tops do make my feet look happy!) There are a few trees up here and some old stones sticking up from the ground where people can sit. Some French tourists have taken the one bench that rests against the city wall, and, as for me, I'm sitting on a piece of cardboard an Arab guy gave me when he saw I was looking for a place to put myself. It was so sweet of him. I said, *Shukran!* which is thank you in Arabic, and he was very excited and said, *Tikalimi aravit?* But I had to say, No, I only know a few words, and I had to say this in Hebrew, which was really embarrassing because I've been trying to learn Arabic for *years,* or I guess actually I've been talking about learning Arabic for years because I never really did anything about it. Anyway, he looked disappointed and walked away, and that made me sad. And this is exactly the kind of thing that would have set off a *Fushigi Yûgi* adventure—finding a stranger, the stranger being kind, but because Miaka comes from another time and place there is a misunderstanding, and then, well, you know, it gets complicated, and then you have a . . . well . . . a *plot*.

The emperor Hotohori says, "Just when the empire is on the brink of destruction, a girl appears to open the portals to another world and acquire the divine powers of Suzaku." That's exactly how I feel today. Not that I'm really like Miaka who becomes Suzaku No Miko. But I'm also definitely not just good old Anna Guttman anymore. Rabbi Keren and Miriam made it so clear for me. God is only waiting for me. He has always been waiting for me. I don't mean I'm special. It could have been any other "me," anyone, like Shana or even Nirit, with whom I do not get along at all, but it just so happens that today it is me.

I'm not saying that God actually spoke to me, because so far he hasn't said one word to me. But as Miriam says, God works in a veil of silence.

And guess what? The sign I got was when all the noise stopped. You would think I would feel alone and scared. No bugs and tree bark to speak to. But now I know that silence is truth. And boy, is that a load off my shoulders.

Oh, here comes Yohanan, looking MUCH RELIEVED! He has his bounce back, for sure. Though he is not smiling, but that is because he almost never does.

~~~~~~~~~~

And now here I am alone. We went down through the Damascus Gate and onto El Wad Road, and, just as we were told, Yohanan went down toward Bab al-Qattanin, the Cotton Merchants' Gate, and I walked on toward the Western Wall. I had wanted so much to share with him the vision of the space around the Damascus Gate, but by the time he arrived it was already getting late and he said we had to hurry. But when we got through the souk and were standing not too far from Bab al-Qattanin (by the way, its real name is Sha'ar HaKutna), Yohanan took my hand one more time. For those of you living in the twilight zone, really religious boys don't touch girls, ever. They're all shomer negia, as they call it, at least in public and a lot of them in private, too, so now this is *two* hand holdings in one day. And both with me! Anyway, he took both my hands in his, and he stopped us from walking, and we faced each other and looked right into each other's eyes, and we just stood there looking at each other for a very long time. It wasn't awkward, like you might think. We were two sphinxes impervious to the sands of time. Then he said, We have different things to do today. I know, I told him. And I just want to make sure you're OK with your part, he said. I know what I'm supposed to do, I said. I've practiced it before and I've been over it a gazillion times. So no sweat. You can stop right now, he said. Why? I said. I'm just saying, he said. Are *you* going to stop? I said. No, he said. Me neither, I said. Anyusha, he said (he's the only one of my Israeli friends who ever calls me that), you're an amazing girl—to the eyebrows—and I don't even know why you would want to be my friend. And then *I* smiled at him because he's such a doofus. Because I like you, I had to tell him. Then *he* smiled at me. And then, finally (!!), he let go of my hands and went off in the direction of his gate. I watched him for a minute, then went my way, too. This is the happiest day of my life.

Now I'm standing at the top of HaKotel Street, which is the walkway above the plaza of the Western Wall, and I'm scanning the scene and thinking about things. I noticed, by the way, in a little nook where HaKotel ends and the road goes up a steep flight of stairs toward Misgav Ladach, two yeshiva students in their long rekelekh and bowler hats sneaking a joint—I swear to God. They're passing it back and forth beneath their coats. Below me, the square is full of people of every variety. Closest to the wall, the Haredi and knit-caps daven. They even set up arks with Torahs inside and hold services. Each little group has its own little tabernacle, so to speak. What they don't realize is that they are all praying with the same voice. But there are also tourists without a tallit or even a kippah. They fold up prayers and shove them between the stones of the wall. Frankly, I don't think that's going to work. On the other side of the mehitza all the women have their chance. It's a big mishmash there. A lot of patio chairs are set up, and mostly the women are yakking it up. But you see here's the problem, and it's never been more obvious than when you look at this scene. They're praying to a retaining wall built by Herod, and it has nothing to do with the Temple. They're praying so fervently to nothing at all because they want so desperately for it to be the thing they seek. It's like praying to a shadow on a cave wall. That's Plato. But the sun is actually right behind you, outside the cave. All you have to do is turn around and you'll see it. Of course that's not so easy. The sun is so bright it burns your eyes. But in time you can get used to the light, and once you do, you realize that everything you thought was real just isn't. This is called philosophy. So I ask you, why are they praying to a wall? God isn't there! And why isn't God there? Because he's in his house. Where is his house? Who knows? But he's also supposed to have a house here. It says so in Exodus. Solomon didn't build a *retaining wall* for God to dwell in! He built a Temple! So when I look at these idiots praying to a stupid wall, I know God has led me here today.

But I want everyone, and especially Pop, to understand. I don't hate anybody, and I especially don't hate or even dislike Arabs and Muslims. Like that guy with the cardboard. He was really nice. And I don't hate or dislike Germans or Russians either. Maybe Hitler, but even Hitler had his good points. For instance, he enjoyed dogs and was a vegetarian and designed the Volkswagen. So what I mean is, I am not *against* anyone. I'm just *for* something. Something that really doesn't have anything to do with this world, but a whole new world. Everybody I know hates Arabs right now, but even when they bomb us or blow up buses or shoot at us and throw stones at us, I know it is not completely their fault. I think of Nuriko who does bad things to Miaka but only out of love for Hotohori and because she has it all wrong in the first place. I think of Tasuki who is always making dumb mistakes and getting himself in trouble, but inside he has a good heart.

But I also see now that *The Book of the Four Gods of Earth and Sky* is not my book. I realize that the Four Gods are not the real God, and that no matter how beautiful that world is, it's not my world. In *Fushigi Yûgi* there are gods of fire, water, earth, and wood. But in our world, the real world, there is only one God, and he is the Creator of all things and speaks with only one voice. I was crazy to think that things could talk to me.

OK, then. I've said my piece. Maybe not everything, but as much as I can get down on paper. I'm going to go down the stairs and through the security and into the square and up the ramp, and there I'll be. My destination.

So everybody, I love you! Especially you, Shana!

And Babushka, don't worry!

And Pop, dear Pop, please, please feel better soon! I know you will! The world will change for you. It will change today and every day from now on. You just have to believe it will.

Chapter Twenty-five

✡

IT SEEMED THE HEAT OF THE DAY HAD PASSED, and a cool breeze passed through that small window that I imagined looked out into a modest enclosed court. The window could be reached only by standing upon a chair, but I decided that in spite of its small size, I might be able to climb through it and escape through the back of the house or perhaps crawl across the rooftops without being spotted. Though how I would get out of town, I didn't know. And if I did make it out of town, how would I find my way back to the army checkpoint? I decided I had to get up. When at last I managed to throw my legs over the edge of the bed, I felt a wild dizziness overtake me, and my arms did not have the strength to push me up. I fell back against the pillow to catch my breath. My tongue was swollen and my body ached, but for some reason my eyesight had become extremely acute and I was able to see every detail of that room; every crack in the plaster was like a map of the country over which we struggled. The whole land was laid out for me, the geography of our suffering. Oh, my country was a beautiful country, my land a land of brilliance. Each road and each river, each wadi and each deer path, led to cities and settlements, villages and farms. In the Negev, at Shizafon, I could see the flag of my army unit flapping in the afternoon breeze. Just beyond, the young American workers of Kibbutz Yahel and the scrapes and holes of the excavations at Rosh Horsha, the tourist shops at Mitzpe Ramon and the guesthouses of Keturah, the date groves of Kibbutz Samar and the camels riding out from Shaharut, the ancient walls of Mishor HaRuhot and the wild happy children of Ezuz running around half naked through the miracle gardens their parents had scratched from the sand. To the north was Tzfat of ancient miracles, and Sasa and Kfar Nahum with its neat rows of houses and gilded olive groves, the forests of Meron and the smooth calm of Kinneret whose fruitful waters receded more and more each year as a dire warning, and all the way to Kiryat Shmona in the Hula Valley, the land of the tribes of Naphtali and Dan; and in the west the beauty of the golden city Haifa and its sister Akko, and Hadera, Herzliya, and Hulda, one more precious than the other, to me, at least, to me.

I wondered where my strength had gone. Maybe that bastard had poisoned me. I'm glad I didn't drink his fucking water, I said to myself.

I wondered about that little Palestine sunbird, because I would have liked to talk to him again. I should not have gotten so angry at him. Why is everyone so angry? I asked myself. For instance, my beautiful little Anyusha. From the beginning, she refused to talk about her mother. I supposed she thought it would be disloyal to me, but I always suspected something deeper. That somehow she was angry with Collette for doing what she did, for knowing she was pregnant and still going forward with her obstinate ideology, for not putting her baby first, and for simply giving her away. That's how Anyusha saw it. She said, "You know that money Aunt Lorrette left me? I don't want it. Give it to the starving children in Ethiopia." But as far as I could see, there was no logic to this, or any other, anger. Like all things imaginary, it connects things that in life are not connected. Sometimes with imagination you get great works of art or science. Airplanes, for instance, or *Don Giovanni*. Other times you get monsters and griffins, half lion–half bird, half woman–half fish, bridges to nowhere, storm troopers, terrorists. With anger and love, who can say what the outcome will be, only that once you enter the space of the imaginary, there are no keys to let you out. There are only passages that lead to dreams and nightmares, and no mother at the end to wake you up and pack you off to school.

I've only been truly angry once in my life, and that was the great disaster for all of us. I was so young, I always told myself, just a boy, really, just twenty-five years old. What does a boy know of his own feelings? What can he understand about consequences?

I had just discovered Collette's cache of letters. I remember quite clearly how I had entered the apartment with my stolen key, strode into the bedroom, tore open the lovely box she had hidden under the bed, and scoured the letters like a grave robber stripping the corpse of its gold and jewels.

My mouth is still upon you (he wrote). *Your mouth is still upon me. And more than that. I have fucked you in every way imaginable, and in every place—at the office, in the park, at the club, on the beach—wherever I am, that is where I have fucked you. I come thinking of you. I wake up in the morning hard and wet, dreaming of you. Never forget this, my love. No matter where you are or whom you are with, you are with me.*

I knew these words would never leave me, not for one second for the rest of my sad existence. I hated Pascal. But I hated Collette more.

With the exquisite care of the practiced criminal, I replaced the grim letters in their pretty container and slid it back under the bed, exactly as I had found it. I could not help but notice the pleasure I took in this, in making sure nothing was out of place, that my existence in this moment had been obliterated.

T T. That's how his letters were signed. I puzzled over this for a long time.

T T.

Ah! Of course! What an idiot! *Toujours pour Toujours. Always Forever. Always Forever.* This was their secret bond. He signed his thus, and surely she signed hers. Always and forever, the door was closed to me. Collette and Pascal were warmed within the four walls of their love, while I was exiled into icy space, into the chaos of my injured pride, where everything else was, except for love.

I stood up and, with great difficulty, put on my jacket. I stumbled into the hall. As always, even in daylight, it was dim and impregnated with the smell of cookery and cheap perfume. I had the key in my hand. I'd have to replace it on the hook another time, because she would know everything if she came back and the door was unlocked. I pressed the key into the keyhole, but it wouldn't turn—the lock was jammed. Suddenly the door at the end of the hall burst open. It was Plotkina, taking her dog out for a walk.

"Roman Leopoldovich!" she cried happily.

"Nina Yurevna, hello."

"It's nice to see you. Are you all right? You look upset."

"No, I'm fine," I said.

"The key is stuck?"

"It's fine, I just have to jiggle it."

"But Roman Leopoldovich, are you sure? If there's any way I can help you?"

"I don't think so . . . ," I said.

"Why don't you come in and have some tea. Vova can wait a few minutes for his walk."

"No, honestly, it's all right."

"Here," she said. She took the key from my hand, yanked the door hard against the jamb, and instantly the tumblers fell into place.

"No, you're not all right," she said. "Come on in. Just to take the chill off. You don't have to tell me anything. I could use some company."

Plotkina smiled pleasantly. As always, her eyes sparkled with kindness and cheerfulness. And yet, looking at them, I felt nothing but the coldness of death.

She very gently shushed Vova when he pulled on the leash.

"You know," I said to her, "I think I will come in."

And then I unburdened my grief upon her, down to the last detail.

Oh, I wanted to sleep! I lay back on the pillow and stretched out my arms. But the bed upon which I lay was like a rock, a stone, that would not accept my body. It cut into me as if it were unable to bear the weight of my bones. I understood its message to me: I, and not the twenty-three-year-old waitress Aviva Oren or the young father named Itamar Ben-Magid, should have been among those blown to pieces; my organs, not theirs, transubstantiated into goo and ammoniated gas. My existence could no longer be tolerated on this earth, and the bed was trying to cast me off.

But then I realized it was actually something in my back pocket pushing me up, pressing into my skin, something sharp and hard. I dug into the pocket and found, of all things, a book.

It had a lovely felt cover the color of wet hay. I didn't remember ever having this book, or ever putting it in my pocket, but there it was. It had the seductive aroma of horses and school glue, and in my hands it was as supple as cashmere. I ran my fingers across the cover, as one might the skin of a new-shorn sheep, wondering at it. I held it to my cheek. I brought it to my lips. I touched it to my forehead.

Then I opened it. Flowers and birds and leaves and stars and hearts came rushing out at me, dancing before my eyes in a brilliant rainbow of crayon and pencil, watercolor and pen, a whole botanical garden blooming in my hands.

My Thoughts on Coming Face-to-Face with Death
by Roman Guttman
Spring 1996

And below that, near the very bottom of the right-hand corner, in letters festooned with roses, pansies, and carnations:

Created by (The One and Only!)
Anna Romanovna Guttman
xxxxxooooo!!!!!!

I caressed each letter with my fingertips, and for the first time since I was a child in Moscow, tears welled up in my eyes. And yet they would not shed. I put my hand to my face. It felt foreign to me, like burnt paper. My God, I said to myself, I have to drink water. Water.

It was then the door opened, and Abdul-Latif entered. In his hand was his knife, the curve of which shone bright like the sun.

☪

Oh, my father, act! The great dawn of revenge is upon us.

But I am not to witness it! For in the book Anyusha made, I have seen my own fate! The letters of her name, she drew in the colors of Paradise, and therein I divine the message for which I have been waiting, spelled out in a language I cannot read. Anyusha! It is not your father I am meant to guard but al-Haram al-Qudsi al-Sharif, our beloved al-Aqsa! That is my task! At last!

Father, Father, I must fly. May Allah reward you with good. I can do nothing for you. And as for the Jew, Roman Guttman, it is too late. He cries for water but has not the strength to walk, not even the strength to crawl, and though the water is but a hair's length from his lips, he shall not drink it.

Farewell! I fly to my reward!

Chapter Twenty-six

✡

"THIS IS MY SON'S KNIFE," he said to me. "Do you think I don't know who you are?"

"His knife?" I managed to say.

"We call it a jambiya. I don't know where he got such a thing. They gave it to him. Then they gave it to me. This is what I have left of him."

"Please," I said. Or tried to say.

Suddenly he thrust the knife in my face. I wanted to turn away, but with his other hand he grabbed my head and pressed the blade just beneath my eye. A rivulet of blood fled down my cheek. "Why did you come here?" he howled. "Did you think you would be welcome here? Outside, they don't know who you are. They don't care. They see only that you are a Jew. But I know who you are. Do you think I do not know the names of every single one of you? Why did you come? Tell me!" The knife twisted between his fingers and deeper into my skin.

I wanted to tell him why, but nothing came out but dry spit.

"Speak!" he said.

"Dasha Cohen" is what I finally muttered.

"What?"

I didn't have the energy to repeat it, so I closed my eyes and told him with my thoughts. Because suddenly, in the gloom of this house, in the bed of the killer, in the hands of my murderer, it was quite clear to me.

It was the day I had first seen Colonel Vasin.

He showed me a pile of her letters. So what? I thought. I cavalierly flipped open the first one. I even smiled at him. But this was not one of the letters I had read in Collette's apartment. It must have been written in Lefortovo. Overflowing with desperation and grief, it exploded in my hands. She was pregnant. That is what Vasin wanted me to see. She was pregnant, and it could not possibly be mine. Yet the letter was addressed to me.

"Perhaps," he said, "this will change your attitude."

When he was done with me, I fled his office and ran through the streets I had known since childhood as through a labyrinth, blindly slamming into corners and dead ends. Finally, I simply stopped running. To my amazement, I was standing in front of the little café on Dzerzhinsky Square where we all used to meet and where I had first set eyes upon Collette. Unlike on that frigid day now so long ago, the windows were not steamed up, and the door was propped open to let in a little cool fresh air. I ordered a coffee and sat at the table near the window to look out onto the square as we used to do.

The coffee was mere sludge, but I kept sucking at it until my mouth was full of bitterness. I grabbed a cigarette and held it between my teeth unlit and stared out the window.

Why me? What did I have to do with a child?

There was a small commotion a few tables away. A woman, blond and pink-skinned and slightly pudgy in that sensual Russian way, was scolding a little girl who had refused to eat her sturgeon sandwich. This was no apparatchik's wife with painted nails and smuggled blue jeans—just an ordinary woman, a clerk or a cashier. Her daughter wore the usual pigtails with white bows, the white apron and heavy brown shoes, but her socks were bright red and so were her shoelaces. She was only three or four, but already I could see she was one to be reckoned with. Her mother desperately tried to keep her voice down, but the idea of such a waste of money finally overwhelmed her and she cried out, "Dasha! Who do you think you are, the tsarevna? Eat your fish!" But little Dasha crossed her arms in front of her and turned up her nose in a gesture of utter contempt. I was certain her mother would wallop her then and there, but instead she began to laugh. The pose her daughter had struck—so grievously insulted, so regally above it all—was just too much. She laughed a mother's laugh and suffused that miserable café with a kind of holy music: the pleasure she took in her daughter's willfulness, the joy she experienced in the flight of that little bird, her child. At last she managed to say, "Very well, Dasha, what about a napoleon?" Dasha's eyes lit up in anticipation of the custard and the chocolate and the layers of pastry, and I saw something I had forgotten existed in the world: delight, pure and simple. Delight in this place, in this time, in the banquet that was set before us.

Dasha ate her napoleon very slowly, exulting in every bite. When she was done, her mother—who had wrapped the spurned slice of sturgeon and white bread within a sheet of newspaper and stowed it in her purse—gathered up her things and said, "Come, my starling, let's go home." The little one rose, licked her fork one last time, and took her mother's hand.

I couldn't help myself—I called out to her, "Dasha! Tell me, was the napoleon *that* good?"

But by then they were out the door and instantly carried along by the stream of pedestrians flowing along the great thoroughfare. I looked at her empty plate, at the fork licked clean, at the crumpled paper napkin smeared with chocolate, and I knew, knew in the deepest part of me, that I wanted that, too—and I wanted it with all my heart.

I'd forgotten that episode in the café, forgotten all about it—until the day in the hospital when I saw that girl on the news and they announced her name.

Of course it wasn't the same girl! I knew that absolutely. And yet—and yet. I could not help believing, and believe to this day, that the child who had shed so much light in the darkest of my days had finally been punished for my sins.

I opened my eyes again, and Abdul-Latif was crying.

"I don't understand why you are here, if only to torment me. Why torment me? My son is dead. You think there is glory in his death? Only idiots think there is glory. For me there is only sorrow. Only sorrow. You come here to increase my pain? You cannot increase."

"No, no," I said. "No more pain." And now I did call upon every fiber of strength within me, and I pushed myself up on my elbows, and took the point of his blade in my hand and pushed it down toward the floor and said to him, "I, too, have a child. I want to go home to her."

Without another word, he slipped his arms around me and lifted me up and helped me, step by step, to the back door and into my own car, which was waiting there.

When the crowd heard the car start, they came running, their screams filling the air around them, but Abdul-Latif waved the knife in the air and cried, "I am the father of the shahid! This is his holy jambiya! Make way for my will!" And the men parted before him.

We drove along at breakneck speed through the little village and out onto the rough highway. All the while I held Anyusha's book in my hands. All those pages she had left blank now seemed filled in. I'd had no idea she'd made that journal for me, but we were always on the same page, Anyusha and I, always walking in the same direction. And now my only desire was to return to her, to tell her the truth of her life, and set her free.

Chapter Twenty-seven

☪

I SEE HER THERE, with her blasphemous red sneakers! Look, her leggings are pink-and-white stripes! The tiny skirt she is wearing is fringed like a cowboy's vest. She is wearing cheap plastic bracelets of colors so bright they remind me of the fancy cocktails I used to drink. And look, her fingers are deluged with rings, just like an Arab woman's—but her face is as white as salt, and the mop of stuff she calls hair, as black and shapeless as a moonless night, is like a spider coming to rest on the top of her head.

She is so small! Her arms are two delicate anemone, and her walk is awkward, like a giraffe's, for her feet are too large for her body. She can barely lug her backpack and stops every few steps, but not because she is tired. She just likes to look at the people on the plaza below, to study the face of some little child, as if looking at an angel, or to listen to the bitter drone of the Jewish rabbis echoing off their famous Wailing Wall. Now she stops again, this time merely to examine the cracks in the stone pavement, then she stops again to add a little lipstick to her lips, pink and glittery, almost as if she had dusted her mouth with diamonds, and now she stops again, just to look up at the sky.

Little Anyusha, where is this cruelty coming from? Do you not understand the Muslims will never abandon al-Aqsa? Never relinquish it? You will shed the blood of every single believer in Jerusalem, and more will come to take their places. You will explode the Dome of the Rock, or burn the pillars of al-Aqsa from within, reduce them to rubble and trash, but Caliph Umar will return from the grave to clear the rubble and trash with his own hands, for this is the Mosque of David that the Prophet visited on his Night Journey, this, the farthest mosque, where your people were condemned and ours elevated. It has been given to us by our God, and you, little Anyusha, cannot take it back.

Can't you hear me? I am coming at you, buzzing you like a fly, stinging you like a wasp. Take no more steps! Throw down your backpack! Return to your anonymity in the suburbs of Tel Aviv where the trees grow thick as grass, and the Indian almond scents the air, and the nightingale sings you to sleep, and the pitango and shahor ripen into thick sour fruits—think of them and go back! Can you not see me? My blood drips from the sinew of my neck, and my lips are coated in melted asphalt, and my eyes have hardened into bone—do I not frighten you?

She is going down each step, slowly marking her way with song. What is she singing? *My love, watch how the day fades like a dream, and if you feel that I am far away, don't be afraid* . . . It's that Ehud Banai. The debased rock-and-roll of Israel. Why is she not singing a prayer or a psalm or reciting a verse of her Bible or her Talmud, but a silly love song for starstruck teenagers that in any case is yesterday's garbage? Her socks go up only to her ankles, and the pink-striped leggings only down to the middle of her calf, so that a narrow ribbon of flesh is visible, burnished with threadlets of fine hair that sparkle in the sun. This little sliver of skin—what is it?

She approaches the guard post now, with its bulletproof windows and lazy Magav officers. They take one look at her and wave her through, glancing absently into her backpack as it rolls through the X-ray. She stops to chat with them, I don't know what she's saying, but they laugh, all three of them, and then she is on her way down to the plaza.

Now I assail her, like a bee, like a jet plane, swooping around her head, but she does not even notice me. Allah, All Merciful and Compassionate, I fall upon my face, which is all that I have left, and beg of you—how can I stop her? I lay this very head in front of her feet to trip her and cause her to fall down onto the pavement, but she steps over me as if I am not there. I fling myself like a sharpened arrow at her heart, but she smiles. She stops and takes a drink of Mei Eden water from a plastic bottle. She walks on, almost skipping but for the burden of her pack, and she looks like any schoolgirl loaded down with textbooks, shoulders hunched forward, lumbering yet weightless.

She now approaches the Mughrabi Ascent. Perhaps I should fly up to the gate, warn the waqf guards, but I cannot seem to move. I hover above the young Anyusha Guttman, just as I did above her slumbering father. What wrong have I committed? I have testified there is no God but Allah, and Muhammad is His Prophet, I have said salah each day in its time, I have paid zakat as much as I could and even more. I have done jihad. I have been a shahid. My name is on a poster. Look, I can see it now: Amir Hamid, fine looking, thin-featured, boyish even at twenty-one, brand-new suit, holding a Kalashnikov in one hand and a grenade in the other. I'm standing guard atop al-Aqsa itself, holding my grenade in one hand and my AK-47 in the other. I straddle the whole of al-Aqsa, I'm even larger than the mosque I intend to protect! Well then? Why am I not allowed to protect it?

She is already in the line of tourists, making her way up the ramp. Up, up she goes. She hears nothing but the voice of her purpose. I know that voice well. If I could only make her hear something else. If only she could hear how the pigeons are squawking and the feet are shuffling and the stones are creaking and the trees are whistling. But her ears are shut tight with the wax of her one God.

Anyusha! Listen! Listen to me! You who heard the voice of the scarab and the lizard, the voice of the bicycle and the cardboard box, the voice of the doorknob and the flower pot—why can't you hear my voice?

She approaches the gate now. The waqf guards sitting on their plastic chairs, eyeing the tourists. They're not afraid of bombs—why should they be? They're on the lookout for Christians, to confiscate their Bibles, to catch them moving their lips in prayer so they can evict them. That's their job! Bombs? The efficient and terrifying Israeli border police have already checked for bombs. And for guns, for knives, too, because in their hearts the waqf know that all police are the same, wanting nothing but a nice day and no upsetting incidents, and so they go about their business watching for someone muttering the Lord's Prayer.

Anyusha! Can't you hear the colored tiles of Qubbat as-Sakhrah complaining about the weather? Can't you hear the butterflies discuss their hurt feelings? Can't you hear the carpets in the entryway of the mosque moaning softly? Can't you hear the doors of the Golden Gate yearning to be opened? Surely you can hear the kaffiah on that old man coo in the breeze and declare how much it is enjoying the afternoon sun?

Oh these voices! Far below the Dome of the Rock, the dead are rising already, preparing to say their salahs. The soldiers' rifles are uncomfortable in the heat, and say so, but the peach that the old woman is eating is laughing out loud, and, Anyusha, your backpack is weeping, can you not hear it?

But I hear it. I hear it. I hear the voices on the bus that just pulled up to the stop at which I am standing, my hand on my detonator, and I hear all their conversations at once, each one distinct as a note on a piano, and I even hear the words speaking their own words to one another, and I hear the tires on the bus fretting under the weight, and I hear the mirrors on the bus bemoaning what has just passed from sight, and I hear all around me the anxiety of the traffic lights, and the cleverness of the motor scooters, and the contemplation of the cups and saucers at the café across the street, and the laughing of the sherut as it passes the bus, and the resignation of the stuffed bear in the little boy's bag, and the pride of the milk in the baby bottle and the bewilderment of the finches in the poinciana tree, and the window of the office behind me, tall and stately, bragging about itself to its neighbors, and the rhapsody in the mind of the Arab gardeners, and the priggish vanity of the kadaif in the bakery window, and from the apartments nearby the chatter of stuffed peppers and schnitzels, and from the sky the happiness of the airplanes and the confusion of a pair of dragonflies, and from the new building going up the vaunting of the girders and the loneliness of the Thai workers, and from the young women sashaying down the avenue the song of their earrings, and from the ground below my feet the earth itself laughing, laughing, laughing.

And now my finger cannot press the unlock button on the ignition key of the Mercedes-Benz, and my belt of C-4, which has been loudly cursing me all day, suddenly falls silent, and I step back from the curb, and I sit on the bench, and I hear my own heart ululating. It all goes backward, and none of it ever happened, and I am still just a boy in my father's garage, and Fadi is alive and smoking Time cigarettes, and Dasha Cohen is just arriving from Odessa holding her mother's hand, and Nadirah is teasing me in the garden of my uncle's house.

O Allah, You have blessed me with a great blessing! O Allah, I am free of You!

But I look up, and where is Anyusha? Wait! She has stopped! She is a frozen thing, a pillar of salt holding her knapsack, looking at her feet as if they were made of jewels. Suddenly she retreats down the slope, clutching her evil bag, and runs back to the Wailing Wall where the Jews in their black throngs are keening. See her! Little golden Anyusha pushes her way into the crowd of men. This one looks at her, that one, then another, but she does not seem to care. They call out after her, "You! Little girl! Stop!" And in English, "Stop, you girl, stop now!" But she doesn't stop, she begins to run, runs up to the wall where only the men are praying. And they run after her, screaming, "Stop! Stop!"

And now, at the very wall, she at last turns to face them. She smiles, always she smiles, and her teeth are just like milk teeth, a little space of good luck between the front two, and her gums are the color of tea roses. She lets down her backpack and sets it before her. They in their black hats and white prayer shawls ring about her, seething and cursing. Now someone grabs her, some Jew.

But from above, the Arabs are beginning to shout, too: "They are trying to take al-Aqsa! They are murdering us! They are desecrating our holy places! They are building a synagogue right under our feet!"

And you can hear the Israeli police crying, "Quiet down! Quiet down!" And the Arabs are now coming together in larger numbers, and the waqf guard is going crazy, and all of the voices I heard just a moment ago are blotted out and all there is is shouting, shouting, shouting, "The Jews are murdering us!"

And from the mount, the rocks stream down, and little Anyusha, her lips sparkling like cut diamonds, looks up to where her heaven should be—but only stones, stones flinging themselves like wolves upon ewes, meet her gaze. For the muezzin is bleating on the loudspeaker, "Muslims! Brothers! Muslims! Brothers! Defend al-Aqsa to the last drop of blood!"

Oh, little Anyusha—please, Anyusha, listen to my voice: *Now you must run! Now you must run!*

But the stones of the faithful rain down upon her, till shots ring out above. And then all is silence.

Chapter Twenty-eight

✡

WHEN I OPENED MY EYES I REALIZED I was in an ambulance. The shriek of the siren was unmistakable, and beside me holding my hand, a medic.

"Moishe!"

"Shhhh, shhhh," he said. "My name is David."

"Am I alive?"

"That fucking Arab should have taken you to the hospital right away. These people are so stupid. You've been missing three days. You're on TV and the newspapers."

"Three days?" I said.

How I wanted him to be Moishe. I wanted to tell him, I wanted to say to him, Moishe, I see you really are an angel after all, and I get it—you saved me for a reason. You saved me so that I might realize that the truth I withheld from my darling Anyusha is the thing that will set her free, free from the prison of my past.

There was salvation in the air, in the smell of antiseptic and motor oil, and in the bright lights of the ambulance, and in music coming from the driver's radio. And I rejoiced.

When we pulled up to the emergency entrance of Hadassah Hospital, I was surprised that so many people were waiting for me. There were cameras flashing, cordons of police and Shabak, for some reason Sepha Katsir, but no Mother, no Lonya, no Daphne, no Anyusha.

At first I was very confused. They were asking me questions to which I had no answers. *Tell us in detail what you were doing in Beit Ibrahim. And what precisely was the nature of your visit to Darya Cohen? What are these blueprints we found in the back of your car? And now, what can you tell us about your daughter, Anna? Who are her associates? Please think. We'd like names.*

"Why do you want to know about Anna?" I said.

It was four days before they would let me see her. Her face was bruised, but little else showed how deeply she had been injured. They'd propped her up so she could sit and watch TV, and when I came in, she tried to jump up—but the most she could do was lift her arms to embrace me. I held her for a long time, breathed in the honeyed scent of her skin and felt the breath of her rise beneath my chest—her life, so powerful, so precious, so frail. When I finally let her go, she gave me a little wink. We sat for a long time, saying nothing. I was careful not to stare at her, not to make her think I was worried. But I was watching her from the corner of my eye all the time, until at last she seemed to be ready to talk.

"Hey Pop," she said.

"Hey."

"Something happened to me I can't explain."

"You were hit with a rock."

"No. Before."

"Before?"

"Yeah. I was somewhere. I guess near the wall. No. On the Mughrabi Ascent. Going up to the mount. I was going up there."

"Yes."

"I was going to do what they wanted. It was just to put some stuff there, for others."

"I see."

"All of a sudden there was a kind of racket in my brain—not exactly a million voices, but a voice I hadn't heard before."

"Voice? You hear voices?"

"I never told you about them. Stuff just seems to talk to me. It's not like psycho voices. It's just—I don't know."

"It's all right. I have something like that, too. I guess we're two peas in a pod."

"Yeah," she said. "But this was a sad voice I could just barely make out, a kind of nagging voice, a whiney voice—and I realized it was my own voice I was hearing, and it wasn't happy with me."

"No?"

"It wasn't only not happy, it was scared. It felt something was wrong, really wrong. And my feet stopped me right there."

"As if your feet knew more than you did."

"Yeah. Then—I know you're not going to believe me—I heard Mom's voice. Mom! I mean, I never heard her voice in real life, so how could I even know it was hers? But I *did* know it was hers. It was definitely Mom, and she was saying, It's okay, it's okay, go ahead and do it, do it. It was her voice, for sure—and she said, It's the *right* thing to do, and you should always do the right thing, to stand up to all of them and be courageous and do what is right!"

"Yes, sounds like her."

"But this other voice was kind of yelling at me, too, and it kept stopping my feet from moving. Mom was saying, Be strong! Go on! But the other voice, if it was a voice, was just sort of shaking and asking me, Are you sure? Are you sure? Because my feet just wouldn't move!"

"Honey, sometimes our bodies—"

"So I had no choice but to just stand there and think! And I thought about Mom, and I tried to picture her, to see her, though all I could see was that photograph you have. You know the one, with the hat. But even though I really couldn't see her, I could feel what she was saying to me, you know what I mean? And I got it, you know? How what she did when I was born—how important it was. How big it was. And it was just the same as what I was doing now—I mean, what I was about to do—it was just as big, just as important—so I could really get inside what she went through and how she made her decisions—and I just, I just, honestly—Pop—*I . . . couldn't understand it.* I don't get it! I don't. Not that I ever knew exactly what she did, only that—in the end, are you supposed to hurt people? Are you supposed to hurt people to help them? Because look at us. Look at you, look at me. What good did she do us?"

"She gave us life, Anyusha."

"That's when I said to myself, *No*. No. I don't want to be her. I don't want to be like her at all. I won't hurt other people just to be good. I'd rather be bad. I'd rather be weak. I'd rather be a great big nothing and never do anything at all."

"No, sweetheart, don't cry, don't cry."

"And then I couldn't. I just started running, I don't even know where. And I let everyone down."

"No."

"And that's why God punished me."

"No, no, my sweet."

"Yes, he did. He did. He did."

And she cried in a way I had never seen her cry before. Not as a baby, and not yet as a woman, but as a young soul who already was broken in two.

Chapter Twenty-nine

☪

I WOULD CRY FOR MERCY, BUT THERE is none. I have not ascended, nor found peace. I seek death. He taunts me with life.

Yet Allah, Shaper of Beauty, has not rejected me. No, no. He waits for me. He waits for the hour in which I finally find a voice that can be heard amongst the living.

But do not pity me. Save that for yourselves, you who live—who still have hope!

Anyusha, Roman Guttman, farewell! Live on this land as if it were your own. But every so often look up and see: it is I and not the moon that illuminates your night.

Allahu Akhbar! For the peace that never comes!

Chapter Thirty

✡ ☾ ☯

ONLY LATER, I read the stories in the papers.

The one that sticks out most in my mind is this:

Investigators rounded up seven members of the ultra-rightist Temple Army of the Institute for Redemption who employed at least five children, none older than fifteen, to help carry out their mission to destroy the Dome of the Rock as a first step toward building the "third" Temple in Jerusalem. The incident caused a deadly riot on the mount that resulted in two Palestinians being shot, one fatally, and several Israelis wounded by thrown stones. Police eventually found their way to the Blessings of Israel Yeshiva led by Rabbi Gershom Keren. Keren, born in America, and a follower of former Jewish Defense League and Kach founder Meir Kahane, who was assassinated in 1990, said in a press conference Wednesday, "It was never my intention for any children under my care to be involved in any violent activity whatsoever. I deeply regret that these events happened. The restoration of the Temple is possible only through the coming of the Messiah, and though we must prepare for him, and be constantly vigilant, it is through God's will and God's will alone that this miracle will be accomplished. In the end, the dome and the mosque will surely come down, but only by God's hand, and on that day, blessed be the Name, all people shall worship the one true God in his one true sanctuary. We all only wish for peace." Of the children involved in the plot, four were apprehended on the mount, and one, Anna Guttman, daughter of the noted architect Roman Guttman, was severely injured when incensed Arabs began flinging stones down from the mount onto Jewish worshippers at the Wall below. Her presence there at first appeared unrelated, but later testimony indicated she had been part of the plot. Explosives found hidden within books in a backpack proved to belong to her. Accused Temple Army member Miriam Levy denies there was ever any intention to bomb the Western Wall and suggests that young Guttman had simply "stopped to pray." Guttman's mother was the refusenik Collette Chernoff, who died in a Soviet prison after being convicted of treason for her Jewish activities in 1983. Anna Guttman is thirteen years old. Doctors at Ichilov Hospital in Tel Aviv are uncertain if she will ever walk again.

Over the next months, Lonya came to visit often. By this time he was already with Daphne, and I could see that even with all his concern and anguish over Anyusha, he was happy and so was she. My mother did her best, too, but her best was always so very little. Katya called from America and flew over for a few weeks. She brought her kids, but not Oleg, who, she said, was sick. She stayed with Mother. We saw them when we could, which was not often.

Anyusha went through therapy, first in Tel Aviv, then at Lowenstein in Ra'anana, and finally at home. As far as I know, she never saw her friend Yohanan again.

One day I saw her sitting in the garden watching a pair of finches feed in the birdhouse. We had been circling around each other for weeks, months—I don't know how long. Her hair had grown long again, and she had taken to blue jeans and sweaters. She did her homework in the privacy of her room and took her meals as if eating were a kind of punishment.

"Two little siskins," I said, "male and female. It's nice to see the birds are back."

"Yeah," she said.

I plopped down beside her on the patio stoop. Her hands were gathered around her knees, probably because her legs hurt so much. Without fully realizing it, I did the same. The birds fluttered and pecked, and then flew off.

"Oh, well," I said.

Anyusha grabbed for her crutches and began the arduous work of standing up. I remember wishing with all my heart that she would just stay with me awhile. And then, for some reason, she let go of the crutches and sat back down.

"Pop?" she said.

"Yes, honey?"

"Pop, I need to ask you—"

"What?"

"About—"

"What?"

"Mom, I guess."

"What about Mom?"

"About Mom and me. About why she—I don't know."

"Why she left you?"

"Yeah."

"She didn't."

"Yes, she did."

"No, Anyusha. She loved you so much she gave up herself to give you freedom."

"I don't believe you."

"Wait here," I said.

I went into my bedroom and took down the photograph of her mother that had found its place again on the wall and brought it out to the garden. There I pried open the backing from the frame and removed from it the letter I'd kept hidden there—the letter Colonel Vasin had given me that day in his office. It had grown old and yellow, the creases hardened with time; but when I unfolded it, the scent of Moscow in all its beauty and terror seemed to billow forth, and the strong, brittle handwriting of the woman I loved flew off the page and danced through the flowers and bushes of our little Israeli garden. I held the letter up to the sun and read it to my daughter, word for word, omitting nothing.

It was then, for the first time in so many, many months, that she folded herself into my chest and allowed my arms to hold her.

We sat there that way for a long time, until I noticed she had fallen asleep.

And so the years have passed. We've gone through another intifada, dozens of peace initiatives, a war in Lebanon, withdrawal from Gaza, and then we invaded Gaza again. It doesn't seem to matter. I've gone to America many times now to see my father and also Katya. Her kids are grown, and she's grown lonely. Love, however, has also bloomed in places. Daphne and Lonya, I've already mentioned, and though Daphne has breast cancer, her chances of survival are good. My father remarried yet again. And just a few weeks ago, Marik's first wife, Irina, asked me to come back to Moscow to see her. We've been e-mailing and talking on the phone. She has not changed at all, and when I speak with her, I feel I have not changed all that much either. I know this is a lie, but it is the kind of lie that yields results.

Sometimes I still see a head fly by my window, but it no longer seems to be weeping. Sometimes I still drive to the desert but don't stay so long, and I take along water and food. I often visit Dasha Cohen, who is still alive, and still in a coma. She is twenty-five.

Anyusha, unfortunately, never fully recovered from her wounds. She always had a pronounced limp. She called it her Peace Prize. I was grateful for it, because it would keep her out of the army. As a teenager she joined several Israeli-Palestinian youth groups and wrote wonderful stories about imaginary universes. Instead of the army, she volunteered for ambulance duty in the territories. She was killed in Jenin by a sniper. She was nineteen.

I try to visit her every day. It's on my way to work. I made a little bench for myself, and I sit there and tell her I love her. I bring her my drawings, so I can show her where the gazebo is going to go.

ACKNOWLEDGMENTS

I gratefully acknowledge the help given to me by many friends and colleagues. My readers, Jennifer Futernick, Sam Lavigne, Michal Evron Yaniv, and Tamar Yellin, all added immeasurably to this work. In Israel, Roni Hefiz and Tamara Mendelsohn and their children Daniel and Michal gave me guidance, especially relating to young people. Thanks also to Hagit and Yoav Zeff; Aryeh Green of MediaCentral and his family, Michal, Moriya, Yonatan, and Katie; Itamar Marcus of Palestinian Media Watch; Walid Salem of *Palestine Journal*; my Negev guide, Alon Shirizly; Michael Loftus for his help in Jerusalem; Amir Gutfreund for sharing his knowledge and his home; and Orly and Eitan Eldar for their friendship and wisdom. For help with the Russian portions of this book, Sasha and Masha Ortenberg were indispensable (plus they reminded me how to curse authentically); Olya, Seryoga, and Liza Rakitchenkov aided with stories and Russian language; and to all my Russian friends wherever they ended up, the Kriksonovs, the Preismans, the Khazanovs et al., my gratitude. And, finally, a big shout-out to Annie Blackman, age fourteen, for the delightful drawings that illuminate these pages.

But most of all I would like to thank three people without whom this work would never have taken form. To my editor, the gentle poet Deborah Garrison, who said yes and never looked back. To my true friend, agent, and champion Michael Carlisle, who loved it from the first and wouldn't give up no matter what—I owe him more than I can say. And to my beautiful and patient wife, Gayle—first reader, true inspiration, and partner in all things.

Books, publications, and Web sites used in the research for this work of fiction were many. But important among them were Gershom Greenberg's *The End of Days* (Oxford), *Gulag* by Anne Appelbaum (Anchor), *Occupied Voices* by Wendy Pearlman (Nation), *Drinking at the Sea of Gaza* by Amira Hass (Owl),

Natan Sharanksy's seminal *Fear No Evil* (Public Affairs), the less-well-known but equally poignant *From Leningrad to Jerusalem* by Hillel Butman (Ben Mir), and Helene Celmina's remarkable *Women in Soviet Prisons*, found online at vip.latnet.lv/LPRA/celmina. I am especially grateful to Paul Steinberg for allowing me to use the interviews and martyr videos he and Anne Marie Olivier transcribed in *Road to Martyr's Square* (Oxford) as templates for some of my martyr dialogue. I would also like to thank the University of Colorado Soviet Jewry Archives for generously opening their uncataloged collection to me. The Akhmatova poem is taken from *The Complete Poems of Anna Akhmatova*, translated by Judith Hemschemeyer (Zephyr). The epigraph is from *Now and in Other Days*, 1955, translated by Stephen Mitchell in *The Selected Poetry of Yehuda Amichai* (University of California). *Fushigi Yûgi* is a real series of graphic novels: *Fushigi Yûgi: The Mysterious Play* by Yuu Watase, translated by Yuji Oniki and Kaori Kawakubo Inoue (VIZ Media). Translations of the Qur'an are by Thomas Cleary; Qur'an and other texts also translated by H. M. Shakir on the University of Michigan Web site, A. Yusuf Ali at sacred-texts.com, and Marmaduke Mohammad Picktall at USC-MSA. Hadith from various sources, including *Sahih Muslim*, translated by Abdul Hamid Siddiqui at iiu.edu.my/deed/hadith/muslim, *Hadith on Torments of the Grave*, translated by Dr. Norlain Dindang Mababaya at wefound.org.; *Hadith* collected by Paul Halsall at fordham.edu; *Shaikh Muhammad as-Saleh Al-'Uthaimin*, translated by Dr. Maneh Al-Johani at al-sunnah.com; and *Du'a* compiled by Mutma'ina at geocities.com/mutmainaa/dua.html. Also of help were Madrassah Inaamiyyah and Muttaqun.com at the Islamic Society of North America, especially for prayers. Peace to you all.

A NOTE ABOUT THE AUTHOR

Michael Lavigne was born in Newark, New Jersey, and educated at Millersville State College and the University of Chicago, where he did graduate work on the Committee on Social Thought. His first novel, *Not Me*, received the Sami Rohr Choice Award for emerging Jewish writers and was an American Library Association Sophie Brody Honor Book and a Book of the Month Club Alternate. It was translated into three languages. He has worked extensively in advertising, for which he has won numerous awards, is a founder of the Tauber Jewish Studies Program, and spent three years living and working in the Soviet Union. He now lives in San Francisco with his wife, Gayle Geary.

A NOTE ON THE TYPE

The text of this book was set in Sabon, a typeface designed by Jan Tschichold (1902–1974), the well-known German typographer. Based loosely on the original designs by Claude Garamond (c. 1480–1561), Sabon is unique in that it was explicitly designed for hot-metal composition on both the Monotype and Linotype machines as well as for film setting. Designed in 1966 in Frankfurt, Sabon was named for the famous Lyons punch cutter Jacques Sabon, who is thought to have brought some of Garamond's matrices to Frankfurt.

Composed by North Market Street Graphics,
Lancaster, Pennsylvania

Printed and bound by Berryville Graphics,
Berryville, Virginia

Book design by Robert C. Olsson